THE ONLY SONG WORTH SINGING

THE ONLY SONG WORTH SINGING

BY RANDEE DAWN

CAEZIK
SF & FANTASY

ARC MANOR
ROCKVILLE, MARYLAND

*

SHAHID MAHMUD
PUBLISHER

www.caeziksf.com

The Big Music
Words and Music by MICHAEL SCOTT
Copyright © 1984 DIZZY HEIGHTS MUSIC PUBLISHING, LTD.
All Rights Administered by WARNER/CHAPPELL MUSIC LTD
All Rights Reserved
Used by Permission of ALFRED MUSIC

Nightingales
Words and Music by Paddy McAloon
Copyright © 1988 EMI Songs Ltd.
All Rights Administered by Sony Music Publishing (US) LLC, 424 Church Street, Suite 1200, Nashville, TN 37219
International Copyright Secured
All Rights Reserved
Reprinted by Permission of Hal Leonard LLC

Cover art by Dany V.

ISBN:978-1-64710-157-2

First Edition. First Printing. April 2025.
1 2 3 4 5 6 7 8 9 10

An imprint of Arc Manor Inc.

www.CaezikSF.com

For the music makers, the dreamers of dreams,
and Sylvan Bernard, who led me here.

Contents

A Dark, Worn-Down Place 1
Forever's a Rather Big Dish 10
Those Who Owe You Back 15
A Tiny Wisp of Loveliness 21
A Braid of Song 29
A Technicolor Film Starring Himself 34
What Is Rare, Is Wonderful 40
Stupid-stitions 45
She'll Learn Ye Fine 53
An Eternal Nowness 57
There Was Light, Once 61
The Weight of No One's Expectations 64
A Radio in His Mind 72
Beyond the Strange, Pale Wonder 75
Another Man of Rhythm 80
That Kind of Luck 83
All That Glitters 87
A Distant Circle of Light 91
Gnawed Through by the Tiniest of Teeth 95
A Musical Equivalent of Escher Drawings 98
All Manner of Facts and Fancies 101
True Eyes Opening 105
You Terrible Fraud 109
Like Listening to Diamonds 114
The Scent of Cranberries and Blood 120
Things of No Account 125

The Only Song Worth Singing...136
Now I Tin Whistle...143
The Imago 148
A Hair on a Flea on the Ear of a Horse 150
A Web of Shards 155
A Hypothetical Sídhe Special Case...160
All Eyes on Me...165
Beautiful Melodic Bees 173
A Very Different Bucket O' Fish 179
Do You Blame the Water?...184
Dance with the Thunder...189
The Main Event 195
Stars Like Souls Encircling My Heart 205
That Terrible Skeletal Smile 202
Songs Call to You...205
Love, of a Kind...212
A Caught-Breath Moment of Wonder 218
Be My Butterfly...223
Beg Your Boon 227
The Center Cannot Hold 233
Music of His Heart 239
Glossary...248
Coda and Acknowledgements...249

A Haon

I have heard
the big music
And I'll never be the same
Something so pure
Has called
My name

—Michael Scott, "The Big Music"

A Dark, Worn-Down Place

1979
Outside Dublin, Ireland

Misty, gray morning arrived with soft padded steps. It crept across the patched, puddled front yard of a cottage as if trying to erase it. The house itself might not have minded: It was a worn-down place, a weary frown in the world.

Here? a voice quieter than the mist asked.

There was no reply.

Someone shrieked inside.

The cottage's battered wooden door clattered open, shattering the quiet. A wild, curly-haired boy called Padraig leaped from the inner gloom, smacking his bare feet into the mud. One grubby hand clutched a heel of bread; the other held a knob of butter that was melting into his frayed jumper sleeve. The six-year-old gave his wrist a quick lick and his cheeks lifted with a devilish grin. He'd made it. He was outside.

Away from Herself.

With a deep breath the boy took in the sharp ammonia of the chicken coop nearby, the earthy scent of the bulls in faraway fields, the tang of the fog slowly vanishing to make way for whatever sunlight might emerge.

A dented pot hurled itself from inside the cottage and clipped the boy on the shoulder. With a cry, he dropped the bread and toppled backward into the dirt. Rubbing his shoulder, he reached for the bread—and froze.

Herself stood in the doorway, glaring. Her gray-threaded braid leaked wiry hairs; her apron was only half-tied on. Not quite forty, she looked twice that age, as if she'd been drained from within. The woman—his *máthair*—knew he'd taken the bread and butter, just as he knew she'd thrown the pot at him. She'd thrown worse, including her fists.

But they both knew something else: He could always outrun her, even if Herself was feeling lively.

"God's comin' for ye, boy," she growled. "Comin' for an *arracht* like you."

The boy picked up the dirtied bread heel and stuffed it into his mouth. It tasted terrible, coated with mud as it was, but he chewed with relish, and then held up his hands to show them empty.

Herself's face knotted. "Stay out there in the mud, then. Best place for ye." She yanked the door shut and the lock clicked.

Padraig stuck his tongue out and clambered to his feet. He'd won today. It was a game they played—she never gave him breakfast, and he always had to steal it. Then Herself could come after him with the hazel cane. When he was fast he could get away before she walloped him on the shoulders, the legs, the back. When he wasn't—well. Those days he spent in the cellar. Either way, it ended with her calling him a freak. A monster. Not even her son.

Today, she'd only gotten him with the pot. He pulled down his jumper to see a bruise emerging. But it was worth it. He could be in the world today, not beneath it.

Now? came the soft voice again.

Too soon, came a deeper-voiced reply.

The fine hairs on Padraig's neck lifted, though he didn't know why. As if to wipe the feeling away, he ran both hands through his thick, dark curls. The oil and crumbs fell away and his grin shifted. Now he'd have to figure out where he wanted to be on this rainy morning. He'd have to be gone until Herself's mood un-soured, so not until dark, most like.

"This here's a *worn-down* place," *Athair* had pronounced the moment they wheeled the family cart onto this desolate little plot several months ago and called it home. No one argued. It was a rough spot enclosed by thin sticks of trees. Grass didn't even grow. The cottage listed on one side of the settlement, while a termite-eaten tool shack seemed to stand by sheer cussedness on the other. The shack's latch often rattled in the breeze, as if someone—some*thing*— was trapped inside.

And it was a *dark* worn-down place, at that. Morning dawn unfolded hesitantly around here, struggling to be born. The night wanted to remain.

"Some places, they're worn *up*," *Athair* had been fond of saying. "Like yer favorite blanket, where the warp and the weft thin. Things—places—get loved right through, so they do. Threadbare, and so. And then sometimes y'can see what's on t'other side."

2

Padraig remembered seeing the other side once. *Athair* had taken him down the stone fence at their old homestead out west, pointing to an impossibly bright light shining deep in a copse of trees. The air had been crisp and cold on that day, but he'd been able to feel heat from that light. Padraig had stared directly into it. The light shot into his brain, making him stumble backward. But a second glance allowed him to see *through* it, to another place. Not the trees. Not the fence. To another world. His heart had raced. His mouth had tasted of lemon and sugar. He'd wanted to crawl into that light, and reached for it.

Athair had jerked his hand back. "Not for you, son," he'd warned. "You'd be dead in minutes."

This new home they had moved to—this bare, foggy *nothing*—was the opposite of what Padraig had seen at the worn-up place. It was overused, but unloved. Nothing shone through at all. On that first day here, Padraig had planted his bare feet on the muddy ground and waited—but the land had neither spoken nor sung to him.

I will not stay, he'd promised himself. This was not his place.

Nowhere seemed to be his place. But he had stayed.

Athair hadn't.

Now, the boy closed his eyes and hummed the English alphabet backward. It soothed him after a run-in with Herself. Back at their old home he might have spent the day at the monastery, where the religious men would have fed him oatmeal or soup. One had even promised him a place in their abbey *scoil* when he was old enough. But then his family had moved. When *Athair* came back this time, Padraig swore he'd ask to be sent to the monks. But who knew when his father would come wandering up the path again? *Athair* frequently vanished for weeks at a go.

Until then, Padraig was on his own with Herself.

Drizzle tickled his cheeks. The sky was going to fall soon, and he'd be soaked *and* hungry. Well. There was nothing for it: Today would be for the old Brady house. The Bradys weren't using it anymore, and it was dry. He kept his treasures there.

Stomach burbling, Padraig shot another look at the cottage, which remained as closed as a vault. Squaring his shoulders, he ran into the mist and the morning swallowed him.

Follow, came the soft voice.

Malachi's entire childhood felt made of rain. When it wasn't raining it was promising to, with sunny days blinking past like dreams of light. When you lived near Dublin, that's just how things were. But when the sun did visit, it was as fine and glorious as a well-played tune.

On this particular Saturday morning, the forecast was Not Yet Raining, with a 100 percent Chance of Chaos. He could credit Ciaran with that. Mal's friend from down the road had arrived shortly after breakfast, and the pair of them were fidgeting at the kitchen table, sweet milky tea and buttered toast cooling in front of them as Mam put away the dishes. She kept peppering their guest with questions about school and his family and Ciaran grunted his answers. He was more interested in swinging his legs under the chairs restlessly, aiming for Mal's shins. Mal darted his own feet aside, cracking his knee on the underside of the table.

"Ow," he groaned.

Ciaran chuckled.

"More jam?" Mam turned at the sound.

"No, ma'am," said Ciaran.

Mal hissed, "*Go raibh maith agat.*" He was forever correcting Ciaran, who had eight other brothers and sisters and sometimes acted as if he'd been raised by wolves. Visiting his home was like stepping into a whirlwind for Mal, whose only other sibling—a much-older sister—lived down in Dalkey.

Ciaran clasped his hands in front of him as if he'd just entered church. "No, *thank you,*" he enunciated. Then he grinned through a mouthful of crumbs.

They couldn't have been more different. Mal was an indoor boy—quiet, solitary and bookish ... except when he sat at the piano. The moment his practiced hands danced across those keys he came alive: high color in his milk-white face, lightning forming in his watery blue eyes. He'd whip his wispy blond hair around as if possessed. The moment he stepped away from the music, he was once again his usual polite, obedient self, an adult in an eight-year-old's body. Most of the neighborhood children despised him. More than once he'd ended up headfirst in a rubbish bin on his way home from *bunscoil*.

Ciaran was different. Tall and sturdy, with flopped black hair and even darker eyes, he had a direct gaze and intensity about him that could be charming or terrifying, depending on his mood. Most folks feared him, the way you'd fear anything you couldn't control. Four months and eight days Mal's senior, he took the lead in regularly instigating adventures among the two of them.

It made him very handy to have over on a Saturday.

Now he reached over and stuck a finger into the remnants of Mal's tea. "Cold," he declared. "Yer done." He scraped back his chair and flashed a conspiratorial glance at Mal. "C'mon, so. I want to check somethin' out."

"It's raining," Mal complained.

"'Tis *always* raining!" Ciaran laughed. "Y'can't live inside all yer days!"

The boys tumbled from the house laughing, racing through the streets like savages. Long hair flying, they tore through back gardens, kicked at fences, and scared cats. Mal would never do those things on his own—but with Ciaran, he let the wild things inside run free. They whooped and hollered as if banishing demons and then struck out across the fields. Bigger and faster, Ciaran held the lead for most of their long, aimless flight—until he skidded on a patch of mud, arms windmilling. Mal shot past him with a laugh. This was how things often happened between them—Ciaran would start an escapade, then Mal would latch on, eventually taking over. They left their neighborhood behind, whisking beyond the edges of their known world—and kept going.

At last, Mal felt a burning in his side and came to a slow stop. Ciaran joined him a moment later, and they stood gaping at where they'd arrived, chests heaving. They were surrounded by shacks and cottages of peeling whitewash, roofed with heavy, crumbling turf. It smelled bad here, like someone had left the toilet unflushed. Chickens bobbed at their ankles. In the distance, cows lowed in rich, bass tones.

Mal felt he'd run backward in time.

"Check out this feckin' place." Ciaran led them around the quiet clutch of houses.

Mist closed in, settling on their hair and shoulders like a caul. Soft whispered sounds, almost like voices, made Mal whip around, but he couldn't see anyone else. "We should—" he began, just as rain bucketed down.

"Bollocks!" Ciaran darted toward a rough-looking house with a gaped-open door. They ducked inside. The place smelled of mildew and dust and absence, and the dark was so total Mal felt caught by it. He toggled a light switch, but the blackness held.

"Feck." Ciaran strode to a wall and yanked aside a torn curtain. Pale gray light filtered through the exposed window, revealing scruffy, dusty furniture, a few stools and a rusting cast-iron stove. A scent of mildew pervaded the house. They rooted around in the kitchen's drawers until Ciaran turned up several partly-melted candles and Mal discovered a box of matches. Soon, glowing flames flickered atop the stove.

"Well, ain't this something." Ciaran scuffed his foot on the ground, kicking aside some clothing. He booted a child's toy into a corner. "Whole house and nobody even in it."

Mal shivered. The adventure had soured. Mam would expect them home and they were nowhere near. They shouldn't have cut across the fields. Now they were stuck, and his stomach knotted. "Why'd you bring us *here*?" he whined, voice spiraling.

Ciaran made a face. "Didn't *bring* us nowhere. Don't get all soppy. Yer the smart one, you figure out how we get home."

Mal clasped his hands around his shoulders. Frightened and cold, he hated how weak he'd just sounded. He turned his shaking leg into a rhythmic tap on the floor and instinctively curled his hands into soft arcs. A piano would be just the thing now. Music drove away the darkness. Mal didn't like many things about himself—he didn't make friends easily, he was shy, he disappeared into his own head—but he loved that he could play the piano. Music lived in his bones. He knew he was good at it in the same way he knew he had blue eyes. When he played, he was *himself*. No one else mattered.

5

A tune surfaced, sliding from his mind into his mouth. He hummed it softly, then louder, then louder still over the patter of the rain on the roof. It was a song from his father—or maybe his uncles—an old folk tune about the rising of the moon and a mud-walled cabin. The music bubbled up and out, intensifying as the words filled in and he began to sing. The song wrapped around his shoulders, gripping him like Dadai's big arm.

Ciaran listened, his heavy brow furrowed with interest. He was used to this; Mal knew he didn't have to hold back when the music came to him if Ciaran was around. After a moment, Ciaran found a place for himself in the song and slid in with a tin whistle he always carried in his jacket pocket—one he'd undoubtedly lifted from music class. The high clear notes of the whistle dipped into the tune while Mal clapped here and there, shaping the rhythm. They disappeared into the song, pushing aside the dark and the wet, forgetting where they were or how they'd arrived.

The half-opened doorway filled with shadow.

Padraig hesitated outside the Brady cottage. He was drenched. He wanted in—but the empty house was full of music. *Athair* had told him stories of what happened if you left an empty place to stand open—anything might move in. Maybe *daoine sídhe. Sídhe. Aes sídhe.* The Folk. People of the mounds. Descendants of Tuatha Dé Danann. Exactly why the powerful, potentially magical creatures would abandon their kingdom for a rickety old cottage with a two-month-old eviction notice tacked to the half-open front door wasn't important. The point was music. Padraig had heard the *sídhe* could be mean and churlish and full of pranks—but also that music was their favorite food.

He craned forward. Human ears weren't meant for *sídhe* music. It drove them mad. Padraig didn't much feel like going mad this afternoon, but he was trembling from the chilly wet and had no place else to dry off.

Well, if I start feeling a bit mad, I'll run away.

But then came voices—not so deep, not so high—and a whistle and a clap and a stomp, and without realizing it he'd moved into the doorway.

Not *sídhe.* Just boys like himself, faces shadowed and lit by flickering candles. Older than he was by a few years, and bigger. But everyone was forever bigger than Padraig.

He stepped into the candlelight and the music died.

"Holy Mother o' God," said the tall, dark boy. "Y'frightened the life outta us, y'feckin' moron." He took a step toward Padraig. "Jaysus, it's just a *leanbh*, Mal."

The smaller boy didn't have every word of English in him yet, but he had no restraints on Irish. And he was no baby. His hands balled into fists and he shouted: "Not!"

The others flinched. "Got a pair of lungs in him," muttered the lighter-haired one, who was seated on a stool. "Hey, this isn't … your house, is it?"

Padraig paused. He recognized these boys now. Over the past weeks, he'd watched them and the other village children through colored panes of glass in the church as they lapped up crackers from the priest on Sunday, or when they ran around like wild things in the *bunscoil* yard. They hadn't seen him, he was sure. He was just one of many rural urchins who crowded the edges of their lives—not homeless, though not entirely homed, either. But now they were in his part of the world, a long way from their neat, close houses with indoor bogs and sinks with hot water taps—homes with *two* parents who made tea and probably didn't own hazel canes.

"Bradys," he pointed at a hanging picture of the family. He'd been friends with Michael Brady briefly, but then the family had picked up and moved out one day—not even a word of goodbye. "Gone."

"Culchies, I reckon," said Ciaran, chucking his chin at the eviction notice. "Didn't pay their bills."

The blond boy examined the photo on the wall with a candle, then turned to Padraig. "Well. We're just hiding out until the rain quits. That fine by you?"

The dark one pocketed a tin whistle and made a soft noise. "Jaysus, Mal, we don't need his *permission*." He hovered over Padraig, who still hadn't taken more than two steps inside, and put his fists on his hips. "So yer not a *leanbh*. What are you, then?"

Padraig told them his name.

That got the dark one laughing. He leaned up on the door and wiped an eye. "Why—funny?"

"Ah, it's just—" he caught his breath. "That's the oldest old man's name I ever heard—'cept mine." He tapped his chest. "Ciaran. That one's Malachi but we call him Mal so he sounds like a normal defective."

Mal tossed a sock from the floor at Ciaran's head.

English. Padraig's heart stirred as he drank in the sound. Herself and *Athair* spoke only the old language at home. What English he did have was thanks to the monks, who'd told him he had to learn the true tongue—that the Irish words were the wrong ones to know. Padraig could understand most of what these boys were saying ... but only just.

"You sing," he said. "Sing more?"

"That shite?" Ciaran waved at him. "Just pissin' the time away."

Padraig set his jaw. He didn't care why they'd played, only that they had been playing. Music was in the air, it was lovely, and it soothed him. But he knew from *Athair* that musicians didn't always make music just for the fun of it. Sometimes, you had to trade to get the sounds. He darted around Ciaran and yanked open the cast-iron stove in the corner. Reaching inside, his fingers scraped around until he found what he wanted. He pulled out his arm—now streaked with old cooking grease, and held out a coffee tin. Prying open the top, he offered its contents to the boys.

7

"Here," he said proudly. "Then—more music?"

"Hey!" Ciaran grabbed the tin first. "He's got biscuits!" He waggled the packet.

Mal had his chin in his palm, fingers lightly brushing his mouth, watching the scene. Padraig wasn't sure he liked being looked at like this. It felt like an adult was making a decision—gazing into him and seeing something wrong.

"I'm desperate for eats," said Ciaran, tugging at the plastic with his teeth. "Y'want some biccies, too?"

"Pick something else," said Mal.

"Yer jokin'."

"I'm not." Mal frowned at Ciaran. "Look at him."

There was nothing wrong with Padraig's hearing. "O-kay," he imitated a word he'd heard frequently. "More at home. Lots."

Ciaran made a face, then returned the packet to the tin. "Eh, just coddin' ya."

Mal peered in next, sifting through broken bits and coins. He fished out one of several smooth oval pebbles and held it in the flat of his hand.

Padraig considered. It was a strange white stone he'd discovered in the stream near their old house. Stones were useful: A person could suck on them when there were no snacks around. They made you feel like you were eating if you kept at them. It was a good trade.

Mal held the whitish pebble in the pale gray window light, then made it disappear into his pocket.

"Brilliant," Ciaran sulked.

Padraig dragged a broken chair toward the boys and took a seat in anticipation.

"I think we just got our first professional gig." Mal nodded at Ciaran. "Ready?"

Ciaran grinned. "G key, eh?"

Mal sighed. "Yes, *key of G*. Where we left off."

"Listen to this, boyo," Ciaran winked at Padraig and counted off: "*A haon, dó, trí.*"

Padraig clapped his hands together. Irish was different music than English.

The boys began to play. They formed sounds from the air, from memory, from their bodies—throats singing, hands batting a table, air pushed through a cheap school whistle. Strange warmth stole over Padraig as he listened and hummed along. There was a rightness to being here with Ciaran and Mal, like a key fitting in a lock. Like having *Athair* around again. Lightness stole into his heart.

At last, gasped a soft voice.

This time, not only did the hairs on his neck lift, Padraig thought he could almost hear a voice. A low murmur that seemed to come from the walls around him. He jerked his hair around but saw nothing in the darkness.

The music never stopped; the others didn't seem to hear what he could. With a shrug, Padraig released himself to the tune. Joy bloomed in him and for a second he could have sworn he saw colors shooting from the boys' heads. He took in a deep breath, preparing to join in.

Bring them to me, came another soft noise, a whisper like a skittering across the roof.

It ain't safe, came the second, deeper one. *You know what'll happen. You told* me.

I will make it safe.

A long silence. *I wish that were true.*

Padraig jerked his head around—but saw nothing in the darkness. The music never stopped; the others apparently hadn't heard anything. With a shrug, Padraig let himself get caught up in the tune again. Then he lifted his voice into the song.

And when that happened, they were heard.

Forever's a Rather Big Dish

1996
Boston, USA

"Call it," said Gac, sending a shiny quarter into the air.

"Heads." Ciaran grinned at the roadie.

The strange American coin flipped end over end and landed in Gac's waiting palm. "You lose, boyo."

"Feck." Having lost, Ciaran would have to jog over to the convenience store to pick up supplies. On the one hand, he was starving—the last things he remembered eating were questionable deli tray scraps in the dressing room before the show—but he was warm and cozy in the hotel bar now. He could tell Gac—or Gac's lookalike fellow roadie Jack—to do the supply run anyway; that's what hired hands were for. But fair was fair. He slipped his arms from behind the two girls flanking him on the couch and flashed a bright smile. "Two outta three, then."

"G'wan with ya." Jack poked at him. "Bread. Beer. Corn nuts. Twinkies. The bus and van are empty as a pocket."

"We'll come with you!" chimed the girls: Kay and Katie. Another matched set.

Ciaran flashed them a sly look. Aye, and they would indeed later on, something he was anticipating mightily. But he feigned indifference with a shrug. "More's the same to me."

The night air outside the Boston hotel caressed him with cool hands. It was gone two in the morning and the quiet streets shone silver from a recent drizzle. Ciaran stretched long, smoothly-muscled arms over his head and twisted his

10

frame, getting a satisfying click from the spine. Across Kenmore Square, he spotted the beacon of light and processed food known as Store 24 and started across the street without even glancing for oncoming cars.

A yawn seized him and he ignored the old superstition about covering his mouth. Nobody really believed that shite about your soul flying out and the devil flying in. Ciaran didn't know where his soul actually resided, but he doubted it lurked in his *throat*, itching to vacate given half a chance.

Fact was, he was hard pressed to decide what he wanted more right now—food, sex, or a good night's sleep. He toyed with the idea of telling the ladies to take the night off so he could get some real rest—then chuckled, dark hair flopping from side to side. Sleep was a waste of time. Much better to squeeze every drop of joy out of his waking hours, making random wagers with the help, snuggling with the pretty hangers-on, or knocking back drinks with funny-sounding names like jackhammers. He'd pounded a few of those earlier in the evening and his skull was still gently thumping.

This was the life, wasn't it? The one he'd anticipated for years, from the moment he, Mal and Patch got serious about the band. *Wine, women and song* he'd been promised, though as one journo had suggested, in America it was *beer, broads and bombast*. Ciaran just called it rock and roll, and he loved how it felt—onstage and off. What the others got out of it was a little less clear—they never indulged like he did, and surely it wasn't *all* about making music. Yes, music was a very fine thing, but it had its place. It had never been the whole thing for Ciaran.

He paused mid-square and gazed around, hearing the heels of the two groupies clicking on the tarmac in the distance. Three weeks in, less than that 'til home. It had been an excellent first tour abroad, and he'd tumbled for America. The expanse of the place grabbed hold of his imagination, the land and skies shifting as their bus crisscrossed the continent. He never got bored staring out those windows, headphones pumping tunes through his Walkman. This country without end was familiar yet foreign, and he was an explorer.

With a devilish grin, Ciaran leapt onto the sidewalk and up a wide set of steps that led to a shuttered Pizzeria Uno. Facing the square, he envisioned it full of fans and spread his arms wide to embrace them all. He was the sole focus of a stage spotlight, guitar dangling from a shoulder, still alive with the last chord of a tune. Adulation rolled in like waves, enveloping him in love.

Magic.

Now, Ciaran knew that he'd never have made it this far without the others: Mal was brilliant on the keys, Patch precisely the sort of enigmatic, low-key bass man they needed. They'd made do with rotating drummers. But Ciaran's gifts stretched beyond the guitar. He had a way with people—could plug into a new person and feel around their psyche as easily as he might tune an instrument. He could play them like a song, in time. In this business, that could be more valuable than being able to write a melody like Mal or craft a lyric like Patrick.

If he chose, Ciaran was certain all of it could be his—and his alone.

Arcing his arms around, he made an air windmill Pete Townshend would have approved of, then bowed deeply. Chuckling at his own absurdity, he wiped the hair out of his eyes and heard a noise out in the quiet of the square.

A single pair of hands was exaggeratedly applauding.

Clap. Clap. Clap.

Chastened, he glared into the blue-black of the night. Nothing stirred. He couldn't even see Kay or Katie. The clapping ended as quickly as it had begun. He slouched warily to the street and backed away toward Store 24. Nothing else was open at this hour—bars shut down in this town at the ludicrous hour of two a.m., and to everyone's dismay, so had the Pizza Pad down the street. The convenience store was their only hope: Without proper supplies, the *craic*—the fun—would not commence half so fine.

Voices filtered through the night mist, and he glanced over a shoulder. The girls were here again, trailing him several yards back like fetches, bumping shoulders and whispering. No doubt one of them had been behind the clapping. He hunched his shoulders and picked up his pace. They'd popped up at the band's first gig in Los Angeles three weeks earlier and had hung around after each ensuing show until Mal caved and gave them VIP laminates. They were harmless, they were game, and familiar faces in a country of strangers were always welcome. Still, their persistent presence puzzled Ciaran. The band was good but didn't warrant such attention, not yet. They'd amassed a bit of a reputation back home thanks to a well-received first album and a brief mention on the radio by a true music legend, but were almost invisible on this side of the pond. Yet somehow, they'd acquired groupies.

On that first meeting in LA, Ciaran had found them terrifying and kept his distance. But somewhere around Chicago, after Kay and Katie made it clear they were in it for more than a backstage pass—clarity being achieved by their undressed appearance in his hotel bed after a gig—he got over it. He wanted, in a way, to be like them: Their confident, wholly *American* way of walking right up to a person to declare their intentions was a lesson he intended to learn.

He ducked into the harsh fluorescent brightness of the store, snatching up a carton of milk and a clutch of day-old croissants, tossing them into a basket. He swore at the lack of beer. Pre-made tuna sandwiches and rolling greasy hot dogs made his hollow stomach turn over and growl at the same time. He'd just picked up a box of something called Pop-Tarts when a warm wave of dizziness engulfed him and brightness pierced his brain. He was floating. He was soaring.

Jaysus, didn't think I was that kind of hungry—and his legs buckled. The basket clattered to the floor as he reached for a shelf. A second wave crested in

12

his head, then rolled over him. His knees hit the floor as the wave receded. He blinked away yellow spots.

"Goodness." A purring, feminine voice snaked out to him and he glanced up to find a small hand with impossibly slender fingers extended. "Are you entirely … well?"

A moment earlier, she hadn't been there. The store had been empty except for Ciaran and a bored attendant behind the register, who'd been wiping his nose on his sleeve. And yet. Here she was: Not Kay, not Katie—not even close. She appeared untouched by the night mist, with thick ebony hair that shone with health and framed a delicate, angular face. Her large moss-colored eyes sparked with mischief, her thin-lipped mouth lifting to one side as if she was enjoying an inside joke. He hauled himself to his feet and realized she barely reached his chest. She was the most fragile, petite being he'd ever seen. He pictured wrapping his hands entirely around her waist. He could put her in his pocket.

That was, once he convinced her to return to the hotel with him.

"*Táim togha*—I mean, yes, I'm fine." He flushed. Stupid Irish, always rose up on him in times of stress. They'd pounded it into his head at the hedge school,and over here it was *completely* useless. What he wanted right now was fluency in French. That would suit this … gamine with the knowing smile before him.

"Now, Ciaran." She tilted her head. Her voice held the hint of a lilt, an improbable whiff of home. "You can do better than that. How *are* you?"

The shop could have been burning down around them and he would not have noticed. His head throbbed but his heart beat faster. "Starvin'. I could eat forever."

"Forever's a rather big dish." She tapped a finger on the box he still held. "Tarts aren't what you need. I can offer something more … substantial." Her green gaze roamed his face, and he felt hundreds of fingers tapping on his skin, as if looking for access.

I can see that you hunger, came a voice in his mind, echoing of home. *Let me in.*

But she wasn't talking. No one was talking. His mind was wrecked and this *voice* was inside. Ciaran shook his head, trying to clear it. *Get hold of yourself, eejit. She's just some girl.* Swallowing, he loomed over her. His confidence returned. "And just how might ye go about doing that?"

She set the flat of her hand on his bristly cheek. A burning heat coursed through his body, like whiskey felt going down. Without a word he bent to her, their lips meeting in a fierce, searing connection that awakened every cell in his body. The raw contact was overwhelming, and he felt his knees soften again as they shared that long, aching kiss. Her hands slid into his hair and grabbed hold, pulling hard on the roots. The pain was beautiful, clean, everything he desired.

When she released him, he had to lean against the shelves. "Jesus Christ," he whispered, touching his mouth. A taste of ashes and peat lingered on his tongue.

The woman laughed, a high tinkling like silver bracelets clanking together.

13

"Not quite. I'm Sheerie. We'll meet again … soon." She backed away and that piercing light slid like a needle out of his mind. He couldn't move, just watched her slip out of the store with a tiny wave. The moment the door shut he raced to the exit, shoving past Kay and Katie, who'd been waiting outside. Launching himself into the light rain he scanned the square for her.

And found nothing.

Those Who Owe You Back

Leaning against a concrete barrier outside the hotel, Patrick drank in the early morning air. The Charles River sent out whiffs of tidal dankness that reminded him of the Liffey back home.

He ached for a walk. Sure, it was past two in the morning and he barely knew this city—but those facts wouldn't stop him from roaming. When Patrick walked, he could be nameless. A nobody. Not Padraig nor Patrick nor Patch. He was himself—whoever that was.

The ache turned into a tug, an invisible cord pulling against his wrist with a whisper of delights. *If you go*, he thought, *last night might happen again*. The girl in the jacket. The hospital. The light. Anticipation flickered inside him. But another part cringed, cowering. *Ah, I'll just run off again.*

Because last night had been terrifying.

The night before, he'd slipped from the venue after the show and disappeared into Boston alone. He'd chosen dark side streets, twisting and turning but never feeling lost. The ground had sparkled with a sheen of wet that made him feel he was walking on water. The quiet had been godlike, as if he'd been left in sole custody of an emptied world. He'd walked with unhurried care, relishing the idea that no other human knew exactly where he was.

But then had come this sensation of being followed. His nerves jangled, and he'd picked up his pace. Darting around a corner to escape, he'd come upon a hospital, ablaze with light and movement and chaotic intent. Halting, he'd stared at the sudden burst of life.

" 'Tis something of a … worn-up place," a voice had said.

Patrick had whirled. A woman in a denim jacket leaned on a nearby tree—not a doctor or a nurse about to report for duty across the street. Then her words had sunk in. He'd backed away a step.

Worn-up place. There it was, *Athair's* voice shaping the phrase. Bullshit, of course. A made-up story to entertain a boy. All of it was stories aimed at children and the simpleminded. Patrick was a grown man now and understood how the world worked.

"No fear, Padraig." The woman had lifted her heart-shaped face and stepped over to him, slipping her hand into his. Her touch was like sunshine, her curled hair waves of the ocean. "There. Look." She'd raised their joined hands and gestured toward the side of the building. A small pulsing circle of what ought to have been brick glinted. The whispers returned. They called to him. He wanted to crawl into that light.

"Now you see," she said. "So. Will you come along?"

If he'd drawn closer and stared into that light Patrick knew what he would have seen: The Other Place. But no—that couldn't be. *Does not exist.* The monks had drummed all that nonsense out of him. They'd saved him. They knew best. He'd tried to read the woman's face, but the light was poor. And yet—there'd been a sense of home about her, like a fragrance or an aura. It was as if she were the light itself.

Stories. Superstitions. We have the true Word, the true Stories. Lay down your old ways. The monks had fed him, clothed him, taught him. They promised he was no longer a broken, abandoned thing. A boy with a future.

Then he'd heard some strange combination of his father's voice—and the monks': *Run.*

Patrick had released that sunshine touch like it burned and fled down the street. The light had faded and the hospital buzz dropped away until the only sound had been his footfalls slapping against slick streets. When reason returned he was a block from the hotel, unsure how he'd arrived.

That had been last night. He'd escaped.

So why did he want it to happen again?

Which was why he stood here now, procrastinating. Patrick couldn't bear his cramped hotel room or the packed, stifling atmosphere of the lobby where Ciaran held court. All of this—the music, the road, the travel—was so easy for Ciaran. It fit him like a tailored suit. Mal, as usual, rose above it all, an observer in the corner scribbling in spiral-bound notebooks and occasionally deigning to talk to someone he felt worthy. Most days, Patrick didn't know how to feel. The music—that was everything; onstage, he didn't think, he just *did.* But for the twenty-two-odd other hours of a day, when they no longer needed to be a band, he barely had a grip on who he was.

For now, he could pretend he was just waiting for Ciaran to return with supplies.

Then he would decide if he could brave the walk.

The soft slap-slap of sandaled footsteps on concrete made him turn, offering a lazy grin at Mal as he wound his way through the parking lot with a dazed expression on his scruffy face. "C'mon inside there, Patch." He gestured. "You aren't going to leave me with *all* the women, are you?"

"As if that's a dire situation for you. I'm fine here."

Mal blinked at the skies. "In case you hadn't noticed, it's raining."

"I don't melt."

"Then at least hunker in the garage," he pressed. "You'll catch something and we'll be after canceling shows."

Patrick folded his arms. "Look, *mam*, I'm all right with myself out here. You know I never get sick. It's always you and C damaging yourselves."

"Well, at least give me some comic relief up there. I'm tired. They won't let me leave."

Patrick rubbed his forefinger and thumb together in a "world's smallest violin" imitation. Mal loved lording it over his followers too much to refuse an audience. "Yer a big boy, Malachi. Wave goodnight and leave. Or pick a likely candidate and wave goodnight and leave together. Who cares what they think?"

Mal glanced off to the side, and Patrick realized that he actually did care. Quite a lot.

So they ignored each other's advice and leaned against the wall in a companionable silence, raindrops nestling in their hair like gems.

Mal cast a glance in Patrick's direction. Beads of rain had gathered in his curls and now dripped softly against his cheeks like tears before falling away.

It was all so familiar.

When the boy called Padraig had stepped into that falling-down house all those years ago, interrupting Mal and Ciaran's impromptu jam session, Mal initially thought their music had summoned one of the fair folk. The boy had been so *small*, so thin, made of breath and rowdy hair.

They don't feed him enough, Mam had whispered once he convinced Padraig to come over. The boy had scarfed down several sandwiches and enough tea to require a second pot, and Mal had caught him stuffing his pockets with biscuits when he thought no one was looking. *A child needs fuel to grow.*

Astonished at the idea of not having *enough*, Mal had begun a campaign to improve things for Padraig. He brought him his hand-me-downs and extra rasher sandwiches when they met at the cottage again, and spent hours reading books aloud while Patch followed over his shoulder. He was *Patch* almost immediately to them, just like Malachi became Mal and Ciaran just C. Mal liked playing *múinteoir*, happy to have a place to share his smarts. Anytime he thought he could be doing something else with his time, he'd palm the small white stone in his pocket that Padraig had given him in exchange for making music. Clarity returned every time.

Now Padraig was Patrick, and he'd grown taller with full cheeks and expressive emerald eyes that crinkled with delight. Mal still saw the boy inside, that strange little one who lived left of center, someone he knew well—and also not at all. The boy who stepped inside and stayed, at least for a time.

A shuffling of paper and shushing of cloth down the sidewalk roused Mal from the memory. A person of indeterminate gender was rolling their way, pushing an overstuffed grocery cart packed with tied-down belongings. It was springtime and the weather had been warm that day, but this person was bundled for an Arctic winter beneath layers of clothing, string, multiple hats, gloves, and even a scarf. Two gaunt wrists jutted from the overstuffed sleeves, eclipsed by a pair of fingerless gloves. He—or she—seemed to have formed from the night itself, insubstantial and yet far too present.

Patrick craned forward, hand on his back pocket. Mal exhaled irritably; the man had no willpower. He'd never seen Patch pass an open cup or outstretched hand without giving something away—quite a feat, considering the grubby, yearning faces they'd grown up seeing back home on O'Connell Bridge.

Makes for a land o' beggars, he could hear Dadai's voice saying. *My hard-earned punts to no good end*. In Mal's house, no one gave to those who demanded alms. A man handed out what he liked to the deserving, not to beggars. Patch had never asked. He was all right. Mal's fists closed instinctively and he drew in a breath to express disapproval.

"Hsst," Patrick told him. "I'm full aware of where you stand, Mal. You only give to those who'll owe you back later."

Mal's eyes widened and he bit his tongue.

The cart-pusher ground to a halt before them, face highlighted by streetlamp glow. But Mal couldn't make out specifics—just a bit of sharp cheekbones and angled jaw. Much stronger was the miasmic odor that wafted their way—a scent of swamp, rotten things, and an unexpected fruitiness. Mal held his breath. Patrick opened his wallet but froze before taking anything from it.

The person stared at them a long time, breath coming in short, smoky gasps, dark eyes boring into Mal. Then out came the expected gloved hand. "Spare somethin'?"

Mal turned away, wishing it was over, arms folded. His breaths were shallow, but his eyes still watered from the stench. He could just *leave*, but he wanted to fire back at Patrick. Wanted an argument. How dare he, after all Mal had done. "*Ná bac leis. Imeoidh sé*," he whispered. *Ignore him. He'll go away.*

Patrick rolled his eyes, pulling out a few bills. "Mal, you always know how to bring out the holier-than-thou in me."

The need to be away from the man—Mal had decided this must be a man deep within all those layers—made him fidget. This was not safe, what was happening. They should have gone into the hotel. He grabbed Patrick's hand. "He's just gonna buy something to drink with it."

Patrick shrugged him off, sparking with anger. "So will *I*," he growled. "What's gotten into you?"

Mal shrunk back against the barrier wall.

"Down to my last ones." Patrick held out two bills. "But—here."

A clawed hand scratched the money from Patrick's palm—then latched on, holding his hand fast. "I know of ye," he said, then whispered something Mal couldn't make out.

"Hey!" Mal straightened as Patrick tried to pull back. "Let him—" but the clawed fingers had already retracted.

Abruptly the man's aspect changed. He stood taller and his dry, cracked lips peeled back to reveal tombstone-gray teeth. He smiled at Mal. "And for ye," he said, tearing a bright red woolen cap from the stack on his head, moving with such agility and speed Mal did not even see him step from behind the cart, "a prezzie." He slid the hat over Mal's hair and face until the wool engulfed him.

Mal raked at the fabric, yanking it back off again—only to find the man returned to the cart as if nothing had happened. "I'll get the police."

The man made a dismissive cluck, eyes shifting between the two of them, finally landing on Patrick. "*Fear gorta*, sent on a *mission*," he said in a low, dark tone, eyebrows waggling. "To test. To *see*. She's comin'." He glanced at Mal and his face transformed into a grimace of delight. "As fer ye. New mission now, I decide. Such interestin' times ahead for thee. Ye will never see the *fear dearg* comin', so you won't. But I'll be 'round."

With that, he whirled his cart around and raced off down the street, faster and faster, at impossible speeds—and then—vanished with a flash of light and a *pop*.

Patrick and Mal goggled at each other. Mal wasn't even pissed at him anymore. "What the holy hell was *that*?" Mal asked.

"Crazy woman," said Patrick, his voice light and insubstantial. "I give her money, you get a hat."

"Her?" Mal chuckled nervously.

"Well. Clearly it was a woman."

"You need yer eyes examined."

"And you need your head looked into." Patrick's eyes softened. "So. Sorry I said that a minute ago. Yer a good man, Mal."

And all was right between them.

Mal turned the hat over a few times. It was ugly as sin and yet … he had a compulsion to put it on. He slid the red wool over his long locks and down to his ears. "Is it me?"

"Abso-feckin'-lutely," said Patrick. "Star quality. Needs a wash, though."

Mal supposed it was true, but the moment he thought of removing the hat a melancholy settled over him. It fit so well, why bother taking it off? Who cared that it had come from a homeless androgyne who spoke Irish? Clearly, he was more tired or drunk than he imagined. He was about to suggest that they head inside when someone started shouting.

Ciaran was barreling at them from across Kenmore Square, glancing over his shoulder every few seconds as though he was being followed.

Mal gestured showily. "Can't miss us here, C. Big as life."

"And wearin' a hat," Patrick tossed in.

Ciaran skidded to a stop like a steam engine halting on the tracks. He swiped a thatch of hair from his slick forehead. "Either of you head cases spot someone come out of the store back there?"

"Just the VIP girls." Mal shrugged. "We were kind of—distracted. Wait until you hear this—"

"*No,*" Ciaran barked. "Not *them*. A girl. Alone."

Mal bit down on a laugh. Ciaran's seriousness was so *funny* all at once. The man rarely got this worked up about anything other than a good whiskey or making music.

"Patch?" Ciaran barked again.

Patrick had been staring down the street and jerked to attention. "Huh?"

"Can ye stop bein' off with the fairies again? This's *important.*"

Patrick ground his teeth together. "No, Ciaran. The only woman we saw got my last two dollars and raced away with a grocery cart. Satisfied?"

"*Geall dom nach bhfuil tú ag insint bréag?*" Ciaran slid into the Irish, insisting Patrick swear he wasn't lying.

"*Geallaim duit nach bhfuil mé ag insint bréag,*" Patrick promised. "What'd we miss?"

Ciaran waved a hand. "Never mind. Too tired to get into it with you now." He blinked, as if seeing them both for the first time. "You two're like drowned kittens out here. And what the hells is on your *head*, Mal?"

Mal couldn't hold it in anymore. It was all so very *funny*. He couldn't even say why, but it was as if a snake inside him had uncoiled and his shoulders began to heave. His laughter pealed across the square, rising upward until he could barely breathe. The others started with bemused smiles, but they couldn't resist the sound—and in a few seconds they were leaning on each other's shoulders, laughs coming from deep within. It was if something they'd been holding on to for weeks had burst. Mal's face began to hurt.

When they came down from the high, he wiped a tear from his eye and gave the hat a tug. "Greatest gift I ever got."

And they were off again for one more round, leaning against the parking lot wall in the rain, not caring if anyone saw or heard.

A Tiny Wisp of Loveliness

"Patrick. A moment of your valuable time?"

Irritation bloomed in Rich's voice, an early warning sign of an explosion to come. Their manager was a big man with a thick head of prematurely graying hair and a face that always looked freshly scalded.

Patrick snapped to. "Sorry sorry," he muttered. Could he help it that no matter how many times he ascended in a lift—*elevator* they insisted on over here—he had a hard time concentrating? He hadn't even seen one before his fifteenth birthday, and the giddy sensation of gentle flight always stole his attention.

"*Again*," Rich intoned, and began reminding them of the imminent radio station performance. "This is important, men. All the info was in your tour packets, which I'm sure you read thoroughly." He stared at Ciaran.

"Word for word," Ciaran promised. "For example, I know this's the place that can't pronounce my name right."

"Not the whole radio station." Rich sighed. "Just the one DJ."

Last week, they'd all phoned into this station, and the DJ had spent about half of the remote chat gibbering about Ciaran's "most unusual" name. He'd also used the soft C again and again.

"Just introduce me as 'Ed' today," Ciaran advised. "Nice little Anglo name. One vowel. One consonant."

To their surprise, names had become tripwires during the tour, and the Boston DJ was far from the first one to stumble. Firsts had generally not been an issue, but Ciaran's name was where things began to slide off the cliff. By the time Americans hit their surnames it was like they were managing a mouthful of marbles. Boston might claim Celtic origins, but apparently *Malachi O'Riogh-bhardan*, *Ciaran O'Conaill* and *Padraig Dubhghaill* had them all but choking. Early on they'd suggested conceding to being introduced as plain old Riordan, O'Connell and Doyle, forget the Irish spellings and sounds, but Rich had quashed the idea as likely to baffle the already confused.

Patrick hadn't cared. He'd gone by so many names in his life he put no stock in the latest iteration. Speaking a person's name had little to no bearing on knowing who he actually was.

Ciaran felt differently. "It's politeness, innit?" he'd said. "Call a man by his true name or don't call him at all."

In any case, they trusted Rich. They owed him most everything they had today. Three years earlier, a certain audio cassette of them playing songs on the street had wound its way to his offices, and Richard Guthrie had taken them on with a gruff, "Might be somethin' there." In the ensuing years he'd become the grown-up of their outfit, herding them this way and that, tracking down opportunities, organizing promotional schedules, explaining the finer points of their contracts, and ensuring they fulfilled their obligations. He also was responsible for reminding them to shower with soap at least once a week.

Hell, it was easy to forget.

To save money, Rich had come on the tour to serve as road manager, but that might have abruptly changed. In the car on the way over to Newbury Sound Studios for this performance, he'd explained about questionable financials being discovered on the books and how he had to fly back home to look into things this afternoon—but Patrick had drifted from that lecture, too. The events of the past two nights were occupying a lot of real estate in his head, leaving little room for mundane details, like how they were about to be more or less on their own for the remainder of the tour.

Now, they exited the elevator and paused in front of a door at the end of a hallway. Rich rang the buzzer, then cleared his throat. "Off to the airport now. I'll listen to you lot in the car. Show's a half hour at best, and the station has the best signal in the city, so it behooves you to play nice."

"Hey, Ed, you're behooved," Mal elbowed Ciaran and laughed. Patrick frowned; Mal had always had a good sense of humor, but since last night he seemed to find everything hilarious. Patrick eyed the red wool cap on his head, wondering how a manky thing like that could seem to softly glow.

The station door opened to reveal a lanky man with a shock of red hair and the appearance of someone who'd been stretched on a taffy pull. Robin was their part-time drummer for hire, and had as of this morning been promoted to a second job: substitute tour manager. He ran a hand through his ginger ruff and pushed his glasses higher on his nose. "Well. So. Good. All set up."

"Drinks!" Ciaran announced. Robin gestured at a small red refrigerator at the back of the space. "Grand. Time to get something wet."

They strode into the room, which was large enough to set up their full kit, including soundman, plus a small table with microphones hovering on retractable arms. The trio peeled off to their respective corners—Ciaran to the cooler, Patrick to his bass, and Mal to the electric piano.

Robin shadowed Mal anxiously, muttering, "Lemme show you something weird …"

Keeping a wedge of his attention on them, Patrick slung his instrument over a shoulder and plucked at the strings. He walked out a few lines, nodded, then knelt to the instrument that truly had his heart: his mandolin. Cradling it like a beloved pet, he strummed the strings and felt an inner trill at the happy twang.

"Patch," called Mal. He wasn't laughing now. "Hey, Patch."

Patrick stepped over to the piano, which had the keyboard covering lowered. Mal looked like the world didn't make sense.

"Eye something for me." His voice was thin and tight. "Need to make sure I haven't gone out of my head."

Robin looked as if he might burst into tears, and Patrick gave him a pat on the back. He'd always been important to the tour—first and foremost, as head roadie in charge of the gear. Then, they'd learned he was a fill-in drummer and recruited him for that, too. Back home on the streets, the trio's combination of rock mixed with folk and traditional tunes meant a bodhran or handheld could generally compensate for the lack of a drummer, but on a tour in front of a thousand or more people every night, they'd needed some muscle. Robin had volunteered for *both* positions on the condition he didn't have to do any promotional events. Now as road manager he was taking on a *third* job, making him utterly indispensable. They couldn't afford to have him burn out. Eventually, they'd need a fourth permanent member in the group. But for now, Robin was perfect human spackle.

Among all of those jobs, Robin's No. 1 priority was Mal's personal digital piano, which they'd spent the earth to have shipped overseas. Mal had been firm: No tour if he couldn't play the instrument he had a connection to. Robin treated it like a foster child. If something had gone awry, Patrick feared Robin would be suggesting seppuku before the day was out.

"Nobody's been at it all night," Robin said, knotting his hands so hard they'd gone red. "I packed her myself and she's been in lockdown in the van since the gig."

"Good, fine," said Patrick. "You're in the clear. What's got you ditherin', then?"

"This." Mal flipped the keyboard lid up with a flourish.

Patrick's arms slackened and he nearly dropped the mandolin. "That's hilarious."

"No joke."

Every one of the piano's keys was black. A whole keyboard of all flats and sharps, with no naturals at all. But it wasn't just a color change. Darkness radiated from the entire instrument, and Patrick felt he was standing next to an abyss.

Thou shalt not fuck with the instruments, he thought.

Mal dipped his head under the piano casing. The first thing he'd done after paying it off some six years back was to etch his initials on the underside with a cheap tool. He ran his fingers across those letters now like reading Braille. His head popped up, long strands of hair falling into his eyes, and he tugged at the cap on his head, as if it could give him answers.

"Mal?" Robin queried.

Curling his fingers, Mal pressed down on the keys. The chord came through clear and precise—but Mal yelped, flinging his hands back. He winced, his fingers curling tight as a crone's. Face tight, eyes bright, he brought them down again on the keys and held them there. The sound was perfect, but Mal's face twisted. He ran his fingers over a chord, then a second, and the start of one of their songs— then jumped back, sending the stool clattering against a wall. He flapped his hands before him as if they were on fire and cursed beneath his breath.

The room fell silent; all eyes on Mal. "Ah, we've seen that one," Ciaran called over, a bottle of beer halfway to his mouth. "It's a radio show, Mal, they can't see you bein' all drama queeny."

A soft chuckle ran through everyone else, and conversation resumed naturally.

Patrick leaned in as Robin danced around the piano. Mal held out his hands; each fingertip had been seared an ugly red. "Jaysus," Patrick muttered.

Dark keys were one thing. Mal could play the piano with his eyes closed; he'd had to, since their shows often began in darkness. But *hot keys*? What could do such a thing? The piano was plugged in ... maybe it was a misfiring circuit?

Still, that wasn't the worst of it. Mal's expression wasn't so much of pain as confusion. Betrayal, even. Music wasn't about pain; it was about the greatest pleasure. It was as if the universe had gone askew.

With a glance, Patrick asked, *Ceart go leor?*

But the small shake of Mal's head and the doubt in his eyes made Patrick nervous. No, things were definitely not *all right*.

Ciaran finished off the first of what he expected would be several beers that day when Patrick joined him at the makeshift bar, bass slung across his back like a quiver of arrows.

"Mal's piano," he said. "Seen it lately?"

"Why, what's it gonna do?" Ciaran wagged bushy eyebrows, smile thin. He'd felt itchy and distracted since they'd walked into the studio.

"It's all black keys."

"So?" Ciaran chuckled. "Got somethin' against black keys?"

"They burned him. Playing it."

Ciaran made a braying sound, topped off the bottle and set it aside. "Good one. I'll sort this out." He aimed himself toward the makeshift soundstage where Mal was gingerly rubbing cream onto his hands—but midway there his chest constricted and his head lit up with a fiery buzzing. For a moment, he wondered if he was having a heart attack and grabbed at his shirt, stopping hard.

Patrick slammed into his back. "Hey."

Ciaran glanced to one side, and the moment he did so the pain vanished, as if it had been designed to simply get his attention.

Here.

And there she was, the gamine from Store 24, leaning against a wall on a far side of the room. She had her hands tucked behind her back as if hiding something, and her gaze fell on him like a physical blow. He was instantly wrapped in a powerful, urgent desire. Ciaran's lips burned faintly, a searing sensation that dropped lower and lower. He altered course and blazed toward the woman—Sheerie, she'd said—as if a cord had been yanked. He wondered if he'd be able to stop moving once he reached her, or if he might just go clean through the wall. But his feet knew when he'd arrived, and he locked in place before her.

"You." His voice was a raspy whisper.

Gradually she lifted those eyes to him, a slow smile revealing perfect, rounded teeth. She was exactly as he'd dreamed of the night before, a tiny wisp of loveliness he couldn't have ignored if he'd been dying. Next to her, he was nothing but a hairy lump.

" 'Tis me," she said in a teasing, lilting tone. "Now, you aren't going to faint again, are you?"

The beer in his gut solidified. "Never did." He took a breath. "You—vanished."

"That happens, from time to time." She slid her eyes to one side as if giving the matter consideration. "But I always come back."

The room felt too small. The ceiling was resting on his head. Ciaran's clothes were leaden and his temperature had risen ten degrees. The buzzing between his ears had turned into a dull roar like the one he carried off the stage after a show. Images of what he wanted to do with her filled his imagination; images of what she would do with him felt even more potent. They were so strong he was willing to make them real in front of God and everyone else in this room.

"I've been watching you," she drawled. "You interest me."

Patrick arrived with a sweep of cool air, and the room expanded again. "Wrong direction," he said with a forced brightness. "Who's your friend?"

Sheerie's head cocked to one side as she examined Patrick. "Have we met? We have, haven't we?"

"I—I don't think so," Patrick stammered.

Ciaran wanted to shove him across the room. This wasn't Patch's thing; she wasn't supposed to be looking at *him*. Heat rose in his face and his hands began to twitch.

"Gonna introduce us?" Patrick asked Ciaran.

"No." He tore his gaze from the woman to glare at his friend, who had broken out in a light sweat. "Feck off."

Patrick's face reddened, and he stepped back. "Well—ah—when you're done with him can we—er—have him back?" he spluttered at Sheerie. "There's this *show* to do, y'see." He seemed to consider adding more, then trotted away.

"He's sweet." She smiled.

"Sweet gives ya cavities. Holes in yer head."

Sheerie rose up on the tips of her toes and ran a hand down Ciaran's jaw, fingers tickling his stubble. He caught a scent of earth and trees and had to check himself. She whispered, "I might like you better."

"Might? If *what?*" Until now, her interest hadn't seemed conditional.

"Show me what you're made of," she purred. "Prove you're not just some *páiste* playing air guitar to an empty street."

Surprise gripped his throat. Of course she'd been the one applauding in Kenmore Square. Now here she was, calling him a child in Irish. A tiny voice piped up in his heart: *Who—or* what—*is she?*

A piercing whistle cut through the room and he turned. Patrick lowered his fingers from his mouth and gestured at Ciaran to come over. It was time to begin.

"You don't go *anywhere,*" Ciaran ordered her.

She chuckled. "I go where I like."

He backed up, not wanting to take his eyes from her, but had no choice as he approached the small carpeted area set aside for the show. Once there, he grabbed his guitar and slung it on roughly, then stared up at the ceiling as everything washed through him. He was riled. He'd been teased. He was *desperate.*

And then he made a soft, amused sound. He felt like a teenager. Recognizing it made him feel less like a *páiste* and more of a man. He cast Sheerie a wicked smile from across the room. She was his, if he was up to the challenge. Instantly he knew that he was and that once they were alone they were going to have a very, very good time together. All he had to do was ditch these irritating people around him.

Removing the guitar pick from his teeth, Ciaran glanced at the others. Ten minutes in this room and they were a mess. Mal looked glazed and exhausted—and now had on a pair of ridiculous white cotton gloves—while Patrick stood stiff and tight-lipped, refusing to meet anyone's eyes. Ciaran didn't give a shit. He relished the chance to see where Sheerie's challenge would lead. He was so consumed with thoughts of her mouth on his that he didn't even blink when the DJ butchered their names while introducing them live on air.

"Let's get this feckin' thing started already," he growled.

Patrick hissed, "If you'd had your mind on the music and not on your *adharc* we'd've started ten minutes ago."

26

Ciaran smiled pleasantly and made an obscene gesture. Then he counted off: "*A haon, dó, trí.*"

They played.

Or rather, they tried to play.

For Mal, it all went to hell within the first few seconds. His swirling piano melodies and crashing accompaniments came with a jolt of pain—whether from the fresh burns on the pads of his fingers or *new* burns being applied with each contact he couldn't tell—and for the first time ever he felt fearful while sitting in front of his instrument. His chords were disjointed, his rolls hesitant and unclear, and he stumbled and tripped like a novice.

On top of that he had to constantly push aside the logical voice in his head, the smart one that had always earned him high marks in class, which sent out incessant warning flashes: *This is wrong, this isn't how a piano works, this isn't how the real world works, keys don't just* change color *and* burn *you, stop now before it gets worse.*

Yet *how* could it be worse? If the one thing he knew was true and real in his life—his music—had turned on him, who was he?

So Mal doubled down, putting more concentration into playing than he ever had before, feeling the dark keys draw him in. It was like being consumed, teeth grinding at his fingers, his wrists, his arms. No pain there—just a louder, more insistent voice, telling him, *you've lost it, you'll never play properly again, you're a fraud and a failure just like Dadai always suspected.*

And he knew the answer to the question of who he was. Without music, he would be just like everyone else. *That* was the worst thing he could imagine.

Tension wrung sweat from him as if he were running for his life, and after just a few songs he was drenched despite the air-conditioned studio. Drained, he signaled for a break and sang an a capella *sean-nós* so he could turn away from that hungry, bottomless keyboard for a moment.

When they resumed he had his emotions in check and resolved to do the best he could. He played mechanically, without his usual frenetic freedom. Get the job done, make it just a job, survive, and cope later with the disaster of his keys, his hands, his talent, his career, his *life*.

Only after he had his mind right did Mal hear how Ciaran and Patrick were failing to pick up the slack. They were drowning him out with dueling guitar and bass, each one trying to out-volume the other. At one point Patrick traded his bass for the mandolin and tried to overshadow Ciaran's enormous Rickenbacker, which had everyone in the room snickering behind their hands. Between the musical attacks they shot daggers at one another and exchanged not a moment of patter.

Ciaran, though—he was the worst. During several instrumental breaks he appeared to forget he was even in a band, ripping into heavy-metal jam mode, shredding and soaring as if possessed by Eddie Van Halen. During the *sean-nós*, where he was not needed, he leaned down and spitefully drank every cup of water in the studio.

At last, they reached the end of the set list and the room fell silent. There was faint applause, largely from Robin in the far back. Mal brought his head to rest on the piano with a soft thud, then winced at the feedback whine. The DJ was talking to his radio audience, botching their names once more, wrapping things up.

Patrick didn't wait to be excused. He all but threw the bass at Robin, snatched up his mandolin and stormed out.

Mal stared at his hands. The gloves were intact, but his skin throbbed under the cloth. He turned his head to Ciaran. "What's wrong with himself?"

Ciaran shrugged. He was busy scanning the room and not finding what he sought. He swore in two languages. Then a third.

"Right, then what's wrong with *you*?"

"Nothin'." Ciaran scuffed his boot toe on the rug.

"Well, since everything's brilliant, how about a note of congratulations to me, then?"

Ciaran gave him an oversized grin and two thumbs-up.

"You are a funny, funny man." Mal straightened and gestured at the keys. "Look at this cacked-up piano."

His friend peered over. "Unusual. Hadn't noticed."

"Right. Because you two were re-enacting the Jimi Hendrix revival."

Ciaran rubbed his hands together with glee. "Believe I won that."

"And what's your prize?"

He made a *fft* sound.

Peeling off the gloves, his hands aching, Mal scraped at the keys with a fingernail. They were cool to the touch now. And this—it wasn't paint. The black went straight through. Someone had gone to an enormous amount of trouble to fuck with him and his instrument, and he would find out who. Shuddering, Mal pulled the red hat down more firmly. It was like a second skin; he'd even slept in it the night before. Immediately, he felt better by a degree or two.

Ciaran was still scanning the room.

"Lose something?"

Startled, Ciaran turned around. "She said she always comes back."

A Braid of Song

Patrick's fingers leapt across the mandolin strings with practiced ease, the lilting melody calming and centering him. With one waggling movement he made the notes trill; the next, his fingers slid up and down the short neck to let the tune soar. Patchy green grass crunched beneath his feet as a soft buzz of voices rose and fell like the wind, as if he had an invisible audience. He all but ignored the wide park he was crossing, head deep in the tune—not even a song, just a little nothing he invented as he strolled along.

Crafting the tune let him shut out the mess they'd made of the radio show. They'd never had a collapse like that, an utter inability to connect through the notes. Sure, Ciaran always liked to show off, and Mal could disappear in his head during a show—he would say he was *going to the Green Place*—making it hard to wind down an instrumental jam from time to time, but they always found a way back to one another. To the core of the music, the song itself.

But the problem had started before they'd ever hit a note today. Mal's insane piano switch. The way it had *singed* his skin. Strange as that was, though, what kept poking at Patrick was that woman with Ciaran. She'd been … wrong. He didn't know how a person was *wrong*, but that's the word that kept coming to mind. Then she'd acted as if she knew Patrick—and he sensed that she was right. But they hadn't met before. He'd have remembered her. She was out of place.

That wrongness stuck in his head like an out-of-tune instrument. His fingers dragged on the fret board.

Shite.

He stopped walking, stopped strumming. Breathing deeply, Patrick took in the sloping parkland around him, then stared up at a gold-domed building atop a nearby hill. All around him staunch trees stood like sentinels at their posts, watching, guarding. He located one that was so burled at its base it appeared to be bubbling out of the ground, and he slumped in its half-shade, resting his head on the bark.

Running his hands over the instrument, Patrick waited for it to speak to him again. He tried recapturing the melody, but idle gazes of passersby poked holes in his concentration. After a few moments, he tossed his cap in front of his crossed legs. Busking. Everyone understood that, wherever in the world you went. No one would look askance now.

"A haon, dó ..."

Properly summoned, the tune returned and he dove into it, exploring every curve and sinew.

His body was on Boston Common, back protected by a sentinel, but in his mind Patrick returned to Grafton Street. The three of them had made music there nearly every day for years, honing their craft while tucked behind a guitar case thrown wide to accept alms. They stood in the sun for tourists and the rain for locals and were one instrument, one person, a braid of song that went on and on. Spinning out hoary old folk tunes, an obligatory chart song, and then finally some originals, they were impossible to separate. When they did this thing together the noises became music and they became *other*.

And Patrick knew where he belonged.

When he was still Padraig he had not understood how the music could be his the way it was for his friends. Mal and Ciaran made music so casually that when they'd let him join in with his halting, cautious voice or hesitant tapped beat on a tin can, he was always waiting for the moment they would send him away.

Mal had gone beyond just helping Padraig learn music, though. During the months of their regular meetings at the Brady cottage he began hauling in bags of old clothes. Padraig refused charity, but then Mal would leave them behind all the same. Herself might've asked where her son was getting hand-me-downs, but that would have required acknowledging his existence.

Eventually, Padraig became a regular fixture at the supper tables of Mal's and Ciaran's homes. Mal's mam in particular took an interest; long after the dishes were clear she'd quiz him, as if trying to get to the bottom of something important. Eventually Mal would pull Padraig into the piano room, where they'd share a bench and Mal would instruct his friend. When they were playing music, the questions stopped.

One day Padraig came home from hanging out at the Brady cottage with the guys just as a car—a *car!*—pulled out of their muddy front yard. Herself watched it bump onto the main road tarmac, and as soon as it was out of sight she had him by the ear and out came the hazel stick. *Government! Gardai!* she'd shouted over and over. Someone had reported her for neglect and they were coming back to get him. They would take him far, far away and put him in a stranger's house. Was that what he wanted?

If the stranger's house had been like Mal's, Padraig might not have minded. But it wouldn't be. Padraig panicked. Government was not trusted in his household; they came and wrecked things with rules and regulations. Unable to think clearly, he stole a tenner from Herself's stash under the mattress, put on three layers of Mal's best clothes, and boarded a train west. Then a second train north. He disembarked a few miles from the monastery and walked the rest of the way. If far, far away was his only option, he would choose his destination—not the government. It broke him to leave Mal and Ciaran behind, though.

At least the monks took him in.

And for the next ten years, he was a mostly-good Catholic, English-speaking *Patrick*. Named after *the* saint, after all. He was wiry and smaller than the others and learned to read and write in English and Latin. And he had a taste for the guitar. The moment he graduated from the abbey *scoil* he took two trains again back to Dublin. He tracked Mal and Ciaran to Grafton where they were making music, finding them bigger, scruffy and still breathtakingly *present* in a way he'd never felt himself to be. The pair of them were so practiced, so bright and personable and endlessly inventive with their audience that Patrick had hung back, unnecessary. Cast out.

But then they brought him back in—for the second time—and in exchange he swore to be every bit as wondrous as they were. He spent hours playing with them on the street, then went home and practiced until his fingernails broke and bled. He soothed his raw throat with pots of honeyed tea. He lost his night job and didn't care. He was always there, on time, for their public sessions. The change they earned was pint money for the two of them and rent money for him, but that made him work all the harder.

Came the day when they were running late. Patrick had been left alone at their usual gathering spot, improvising for an hour. He'd started out slowly on the acoustic guitar, building some momentum with ballads and a little Van Morrison, but no one paid him much attention. Then he'd had an idea. Picturing Mal's bright grin and the twinkle in Ciaran's eye, he took both into himself. Straightening, he caught the eyes of several tourists, who smiled back and snapped his photo. The fitted-on smile felt right. The music followed, as did the money. His chest swelled.

After a long bout of coins being tossed, his hands grew sore and his smile faded. So he took a break, bending for a drink of water—and caught Mal and Ciaran watching from across the road. They had big-brother grins and were applauding.

That day he understood that the music was his, too.

Grafton faded and Boston Common returned.

Patrick's hands had been moving the entire time, but now he had the through line of the song. It was more than just notes; it had shape and imagery. He willed the song to come closer, repeating the same phrases over and over in the hopes they would catch alight.

Then a second melody wafted in like a delicate breeze. His mandy was no longer alone; a friend had come to join it, but he pushed aside the need to know more and dove deeper into the music, letting it carry him along.

How long the twined threads lasted he couldn't be sure. The sun burned off the dull morning haze and warmed his back and head. Soft gusts tickled at his ears and neck. He hit no off notes, just the right ones. It was a rare, remarkable moment, and he wanted to make it stretch into forever.

There was another noise amid the two now, the familiar jangle of coins at his knees. A swish—a deliberate placement—of paper money. He detached a bit from the music, realizing a semi-circle of onlookers had stopped and stayed, watching at a respectful distance. Another conscious thread slipped from the song and he heard his own accompaniment, a tin whistle like the one Ciaran had used that first day in the cottage, dancing high on his notes and filling in the spaces. Whatever direction he took the tune, the player followed expertly.

Patrick caught a glimpse of wavy, russet-colored hair partly obscuring a pale face and closed eyelids, hair that tumbled over the shoulders of a young woman's denim jacket.

A denim jacket.

Surely, there were too many in the world for it to be the same woman with the same jacket he'd seen outside the hospital.

Patrick peered closer. The top half of her body bounced and wove with the beat they were creating. One eye cracked open, revealing an otherworldly cerulean. Her mouth lifted from the edges of a small whistle as she deliberately nodded at him—a signal he interpreted without thought. They followed the line, then another—and he exited the tune, bringing his fingers down on the strings in one last tremolo.

The applause came in soft, enthusiastic waves, his head still humming with the intensity of playing. He felt as if he'd left this world and was only now coming back in pieces. But he remembered his Grafton Street smile and sent it out to the crowd with genuine delight. The applause grew even stronger. A few children were pointing at him, or just above his head, though he couldn't understand why. Patrick gestured at his musical partner, but she had shifted to one side. Her tin whistle—a cheap-looking thing with a bitten-up plastic green top—poked from her denim jacket pocket like a pet.

His hat was overflowing with coins and paper. A stray dollar escaped in a brisk breeze, butterflying across the grass until it caught flat against a tree. One older child raced after it, peeling the money from the bark. She brought it back, shyly placing it with care in the hat.

"Thanks," he said, genuinely moved by everything.

"The colors," the girl whispered at him. "How'd you do the colors?"

Patrick tilted his head. "Colors?" Maybe the girl had synesthesia. He'd heard of people who saw music, tasted color. "That was just for you," he whispered back and her cheeks pinked.

His redheaded partner was crooking a finger at the girl, who bounced over to her. She whispered something into the girl's ear, and the child made a squealing noise, clapping her hands over her mouth. Then she darted back into the crowd, picking up an older woman's hand.

Without music to hold them, the crowd was starting to disperse, and Patrick knew he should say something to the whistler. They'd been good together. No—they'd been *extraordinary*. She was looking at him now, a half-smile shifting a gentle spray of freckles across her nose. Her heart-shaped face was turned to one side as if she could hear frequencies he could not, and she raised a hand in salute.

"What'd you—say to her?" The question came out haltingly; that it came out at all was the real surprise. Patrick was not a person who randomly struck up conversations with strangers.

"Magic," said the woman. "That you an' me were from *Tír na nÓg* and that's what we do."

There was a teasing tone in her voice and—was he making that up, the sound of the West Country in there? Could she really be from home? "Cute," he said. "Load o'shite, but cute."

She raised an eyebrow. "Is it, now?" There was a long, awkward pause—and then she laughed. He thought of bells. Something in his chest resonated and loosened. "Call me Caitlin." She said it as they might at home—*Cat-leen*.

"Gimme a few more words and I'll know *exactly* where you're from," he said. "And it won't be the *sídhe*."

Caitlin hopped up with a light, graceful movement, her red waves flowing. *Like the ocean*. "You know best," she said, turning away.

"Wait—" The thought of her vanishing as quickly as she'd arrived made him heartsick. He had to know where those sounds had come from. How a fellow musician from home had simply landed next to him in a random part of the world. And how soon she would let him touch that incredible mane of hers. "Don't go."

"I won't be leaving you," she said, holding out a hand. "But you will need to follow, Padraig."

33

A Technicolor Film Starring Himself

"All this money looks the same," Patrick told Caitlin, stacking the bills by denomination on the lacquered mahogany table. It was easier to pay attention to the money they'd earned than look her directly in the face. "It's all green. All the same size."

As he toyed with the money a shaft of light crawled over the edge of the table, then faded away. They had a glorious view of the park from a private corner table—perhaps the best in the whole restaurant, if Patrick guessed right—and it spread the city below them like a mural. Outside the sun notched up every color's hue, as if he'd walked into a Technicolor film starring himself.

None of this made sense. They'd entered this upscale tavern steps from the gold-domed state house dirt-smeared and windblown, shabby of clothes and clearly not the usual clientele. A sea of businesspeople filled the tables for lunch, and one woman visibly wrinkled her nose as they stepped inside. He'd anticipated an immediate dismissal from the premises, and wouldn't have argued.

Instead, the hostess had offered a bright smile, hugging menus close to her crisp white shirt. "Can I help?"

"We're not expected," Caitlin had said. "But there is room, isn't there?"

The hostess's smile had hitched briefly, like a skip on a record. She'd run her finger down a list of reservations. "Good news. We've just had a cancelation."

Patrick had been too surprised to comment when they'd been given their fine seats, and instead took to counting their earnings.

"The final tally?" she asked now.

"Sixty-two dollars and twenty-seven pence. Pennies. Cents." He dared a glance at her and a tickle ran down his neck as he concentrated on that small freckled nose. Her eyes were still off-limits; she unsettled him with her gaze. Instead, he ran his mind over what he did know of her: Caitlin. Blue eyes. West country accent. Marvelous improviser on the tin whistle. Someone who spoke his language.

And knew his name before he'd given it. His Irish name.

"Tell me something." She settled a hand over his fingers, which had been tap, tap, tapping on the wooden table.

He stilled. "Anything in particular?"

"Anything's a start."

"I don't know how to talk to you." The words were out before he a had chance to call them back.

"Speak how you like. Tell me about the music, if that's easiest."

It was. He spoke of his band. Of Mal and Ciaran. Of the tour. Words and words and words. Lunch arrived—whiskey and oysters. Steak with a tremendous dollop of creamy mashed potatoes and a pile of glazed carrots. A colorful salad for her. He went on and on between forkfuls, as if she'd unplugged a dam, eating and talking and never feeling either empty or full. The meat was hearty, the potatoes cheesy, the oysters briny, the whiskey not as good as home but— still, a nice tang that stoked the fire in his belly. Caitlin never lifted a fork, and when he finished, she pushed her salad at him. He tucked into that as well.

Then, silence.

"Done?"

He glanced around. There was nothing left on the table to eat, unless he planned on pouring sugar packets down his throat. He'd run out of words, too.

"You play beautifully," she stated. "Music's something you're made of, much as skin and bones and blood."

His head buzzed from the drink and his stomach was as taut as a drum. It was the clearest truth he'd ever heard.

"How can you know that?"

"I know things you don't, Padraig. I *see* things. Things you don't even realize yourself." She leaned back in her chair. "We were good, weren't we?"

Patrick felt fogged. "What happened out there on the Common?"

"It was splendid." She smiled. "But you know what it was. You've felt it before."

He had, but never with such intensity and certainly not with a stranger. He, Mal and Ciaran aimed for it every time they took the stage, and with luck and a good audience they might stumble into that fluidity after an hour's warm-up, lost in an extended jam that layered and folded and created something brilliant and new out of one of their little tunes. In those moments you didn't care if you'd become a hot ball of sweat, that your shoulders and lower back ached, that your feet were on fire, or that there was a dull, appreciative roar just a few inches from the lip of the stage. That was when you were in the music and part of it, but it happened rarely enough that it was possible to forget how it might transform a place, a night, a person.

To have felt it with Caitlin was beyond imagining.

"The mandolin's not your usual instrument, though."

"Bass. Guitar if we need it. But—I like the mandy. It sounds like … water."

Caitlin grinned. "Ever try playing water?"

He laughed softly. "Suppose not."

"I'll show you one of these days."

He didn't know how to take that. Certainly not seriously. Just a bit of banter. "I had a good teacher," he said instead. "An' taught myself a bit." He straightened, eyes wide. "You should hear Mal and Ciaran. They're so much better than me. They're the true thing."

"Truer than a man of the mounds?" She spoke the English this time, instead of saying *sídhe*.

He waved that off. "Y'can drop the airy-fairy shite," he said. "Kids've all gone home."

Caitlin shrugged.

"Come tonight," he urged. "We've got one night left in town. We're leavin' in the morning."

The waiter slid the bill face-down on the table. "When you're ready," he said, and stepped away.

Patrick turned it over, remembering that he'd given his last money away the night before and left the radio show this morning before Robin could hand over their per diem. He was skint. Well, skint except for the busking earnings. He'd never even thought about the cost of two whiskeys, a steak platter, oysters and a salad. "Er," he began, then spotted the total. It came to forty-nine dollars and eighty one cents, which seemed an absurdly low sum. And if a person added a 20 percent tip—

Sixty-two dollars and twenty-seven cents.

"Quite a bit of luck you're having lately," she grinned.

Patrick eyed Caitlin. She must have had something to do with all this. But what? "Ah, you know the owner. Nice trick."

"Never been here before in my life." She pushed her chair back. "C'mon, then. Don't you have a gig to get to?"

Without a spare penny, pence, or cent on him, there was no choice: Patrick had to get back to the venue on foot. He'd be late for soundcheck, and the others would be pissed at him, but they'd lingered over lunch too long.

"Still coming?" he asked as they headed down Commonwealth Avenue.

"Wouldn't miss it." She slipped a hand into the crook of his arm. He liked it there. It felt right.

They walked in silence for a time. Patrick had mixed feelings about the show ahead. On the one hand, the itch to get onstage and play was crawling in him again—and with a friendly face in the audience the show couldn't miss. But he had no idea what state he'd find Mal or Ciaran in once he arrived. Maybe Mal would have gotten used to the new configuration of his keyboard. Maybe Ciaran got laid that afternoon.

But Patrick doubted either of those things had happened. He braced for possible encounters with a distracted zombie and a horny bear at the venue.

Caitlin piped up. "I'd say 'penny for your thoughts,' but I don't have one."

"Thinkin'," he said. "Me and Ciaran—we had a row today." And then he was talking again, telling her that the nice boys he'd introduced her to in his stories were not, perhaps, in their best grown-up moods. He explained about Rich's quick exit, the radio show that morning, the strange woman who'd soured everything. He didn't stop until they'd reached Kenmore Square.

"Jaysus, that's got to be me word limit for today," he said. "Or the week."

"That woman you met at the show. Do you know her?"

He shook his head. "Why?"

"Because just now—you sounded … jealous of her."

Patrick waved her off. "F'Christ's sake, I've had my share of time with C. And I never want him looking at me the way he looked at her."

"She must be something."

"Yes. But." He bit down on the rest of that thought. Patrick had never known someone to stick in his head so firmly before, someone he barely knew. The woman had been alluring, but it wasn't attraction he'd felt. She made him think of a warning light, flashing. "Not my type. Got a frost on her, the way she looks through you."

Caitlin's face tightened, then relaxed. "Well. Not my business. Guess your friend'll have to take care of himself."

"Always does."

"Still," she began. "An apology never hurts."

"Owes me that, being such an eejit."

"No. You should apologize to him."

He let her hand slip from his elbow. "Like fun. That was not *my* doin', what happened back there."

"Not the point. Just—" she hesitated. "You ought to be the bigger man here. Maybe he'll need help soon. And you won't want this between you."

"Help?" Her ambiguity needled him; what had seemed playful earlier now sounded smug. "You know somethin' I should hear?" They rounded a corner onto Lansdowne Street, with the purple wall of the venue looming less than a block away. He turned her toward him. "Really. I don't know a thing about *you*. You've let me blather on all afternoon. Where're you from? What were you just doing wandering around with a whistle in your pocket? Do you even *have* a last name?"

Caitlin folded her arms, deep blue eyes dancing. Evening was nearing, and twilight was coming down slowly. The whole sky was full of purples and blues and greens. "Make you a bet," she said. "If I can't get into the club without your assistance, I'll answer any question you ask."

Funny, he thought. *This seems to* mean *something to her.* "And if you do get in?"

"Then you—" she tapped his chest with a finger, "apologize to your friend."

"Aw, you know someone at the door." It was the same kind of excuse he'd leveled at the restaurant.

"Swear I don't." She sauntered toward the backstage entrance while Patrick loitered several paces behind. From what he'd witnessed the night before, the venue—Citi—was impregnable, even to a pretty face. You needed a backstage VIP pass or a ticket to get in, and the place wasn't yet open to the public for the night. He reached around to feel for his own pass—but it was gone. He looked up in surprise just in time to see Caitlin disappear inside.

Patrick raced over and pounded on the purple door. An enormous bouncer peered out. "Em, I need to get in."

"Got a pass?"

"Lost it."

"Gots to have a pass."

"But I'm with the band."

He'd already shut the door. Patrick knocked again.

"*What.*"

"I am the band."

Behind the bouncer, Caitlin's laughter trilled again, bells in the darkness. "He's right. He is the band."

The guard glared at him suspiciously but held the door wide. Patrick slipped under his arm and jogged over to Caitlin. "Full of tricks, you are."

"Tricks and treats. And a little bit o' truth, when the time comes." She handed back his pass, a laminated card clipped to a lanyard. "Fell out of your jacket at the restaurant, and I happened to find it. Lucky thing."

"I'm thinking to call foul on a technicality." Patrick slid it back into his pocket as they approached the stage. Ciaran loomed up there, thunder in his face, watching him.

"I win," she whispered and he was charmed all over again. "So—do it."

"Do what?"

But Caitlin had disappeared into the shadows.

Ciaran jumped from the stage, standing a little too close to Patrick. "Forget something?"

Patrick took a deep breath. "Soundcheck. I know. Sorry. So, look, C—"

"Glad to see your brain still functions," Ciaran growled. "Mal was wondering if you were gonna bother showing up for the *gig*."

"No, I wasn't!" Mal called from the far side of the stage.

"Lost track of time." Patrick swallowed. "Also, sorry about this afternoon. Walking out and all. Was what a kid would do."

Poised for a fight, Ciaran hesitated. There was nothing to battle with. A slow, familiar smile parted the light beard around his mouth. "Ah, forget it. Doors're in a half hour. We should get somethin' in. Where the hells you been?"

"Ah, it was *grand*. I played in the park and there was this woman—" He turned to introduce Caitlin, but she'd gone. His stomach dropped. Ciaran returned to the stage and hoisted Patrick up. "She was just here. Named Caitlin. Has a tin whistle. From … home."

Ciaran grunted and glanced up from adjusting his guitar's foot pedal. "Y'know, if ya'd had yer mind on the music and not on your *adharc* we'd've started about a half hour ago."

Patrick's hands curled into fists, but Ciaran had a wide grin on him now. "Ah, feck off," he said, heading to his bass.

Mal shouted out the key and the tune, and they fell to their instruments and music just like always. As if nothing had changed.

And it hadn't. At least, not yet.

What Is Rare, Is Wonderful

Most nights, Ciaran would do anything to delay a show's end. That final encore was the best, and the worst, moment of the evening. A firefly blink of light and perfection, final notes spiraling from speakers, hovering over the audience, seeping into their ears and back out through raised fingertips.

Those last minutes were sweeter than whiskey, savored amid the pounding of his heart and the ache in his back. A show that went well was a perfect balance of desire and fulfillment, ecstasy and a little death all rolled into one. He was addicted. But this night, their last in Boston, chimed differently. This time, as the notes swirled away into the skies, a different sound echoed in his head. An urgent summons.

Come.

And the moment that final note hit, he was out of there. He dropped his guitar and was backstage before Mal and Patrick even finished with their bows. High feedback whine from the abandoned instrument chased him down the corridor to their dressing room.

Once inside, he flung his soaked shirt away. It caught on the edge of a chair, steaming from the immense heat his body put out. That had truly been a barn-burner of a show, over two hours long, and he should be ready to collapse—but adrenaline sang in his head, his ears, his blood.

God, but it had been beautiful out there. The opposite of that morning's radio gig. Mal's keyboard worked just fine—none of this shite about all black keys or his fingers hurting or whatever'd been making him boo-hoo earlier. Ciaran figured he'd just had a brief case of the prima donnas at the radio show, then got over it. The man had leapt on that piano like a long-lost lover, golden hair flying

40

as he'd nodded and swayed to the songs. He'd played the *hell* out of that thing, kicking over his stool with a flourish and letting loose a throaty growl that sent those songs into the rafters to fill every inch of the room.

And Patch had stopped trying to be the big man onstage, coming back from wherever he'd buggered off to that day with a gleam in his eye and a presence Ciaran hadn't ever sensed in him. Said he'd met a girl or something. Well, every city had its Monto district; a horny bastard could always find someone willing. Ciaran and Patch had sawed back and forth with their guitars in a dance, passing the spotlight between them. All three of them—with Robin on the drums—had locked together, cogs and wheels in a well-oiled machine.

As for his own performance, Ciaran felt positively elevated. All he'd had to do was *think* about that girl Sheerie and it was as if the instrument began playing itself. He threw himself around the stage, possessed by the unexpected sensation that all eyes were on him for once, with his bandmates mere shades of gray in contrast. The chance to show off and be admired for it—well, that was what a man lived for, wasn't it?

Cold water brimmed in the sink basin and he shoved his face in, making ecstatic bubbles. Firm slaps of appreciation landed on his bare shoulders, but whatever Mal and Patrick might be saying behind him was muffled by the water and the music still filling his ears. He rose up from the sink with a gasp and sprayed drops around like a dog.

Come. Time.

The words were ice picks driving through his skull. He staggered backward, toppling into the sofa. Ciaran slammed the heel of a hand into one eye and clutched an armrest. This wasn't a migraine. It was a voice in the front of his brain, a summoning-like feedback whine that ripped through him. Two words, and he was paralyzed.

Come. Time. Now.

Taking a deep breath he steadied himself and thought back: *Wait.*

No. Now.

It was the girl. The woman. The—Sheerie. Funny name, that. Of course she was here, mere feet outside the dressing room door, waiting for him. A pleasing enough fact, even if the piercing call in his head was not. During the show he'd caught sight of her in the crowd, her stillness making her stand out amid the hundreds of throbbing, dancing fans. Bright and shiny, it was as if she'd come with her own spotlight. Their third meeting would be unlike the others, and it made him tremble with anticipation.

But Ciaran did not care to be ordered about. It didn't matter that leaving the room and following that voice was the only thing he could think clearly about. There was something … uncanny about that woman, something that pulled him to her and blotted out all other sense, and that was a bit terrifying. Exciting, but terrifying. As so many things in life were.

41

"Y'alright there, C?" Mal leaned toward him, holding out a towel.

Ciaran waved him off. "Headache." He dried his face and patted under his arms, then turned back to the sink mirror. He'd never thought of himself as a magnet for the ladies, even if pulling them had never been a problem. He had the square, sturdy face of his father and deep-set eyes of his mother, an unusual combination he'd heard referred to more often as "having character" than "handsome." Yet he'd always made that elemental look work for him, so long as he paired it with a sunny smile or witty remark. Without either, Ciaran knew he could be intimidating; Da had once joked that his son would make a terrific bully if he'd only put his mind to it.

He gave no thought to any of that when he stood in front of Sheerie. When she looked at him, her gaze confirmed that there was no better vista in the world.

That cool, pointed voice came again—gentler this time, but still insistent—and he fought back a bit longer, dragging a comb through his wet hair and yanking on a mostly-fresh blue shirt. *Almost*, he tried to think back at her, tweaked at how she'd gotten into his brain. There was one more thing to be done.

"*Taraigí anseo.*" He beckoned at Mal and Patch to come over, and without question, they folded together as they always did after a show, wrapping arms around each other's shoulders and leaning forward, heads touching, eyes shut. Like a sports team on the field, but with a meditative quality. This was a good, calm place to share after a show; here in this circle he heard nothing but the three of them sharing the same air, the same breaths. He couldn't remember how or when the ritual had started, but by now it was a requirement after each performance. It said: Wherever they might go next, there was always this circle to come back to. Within it, they were unbreakable.

During the long moment of silence, Ciaran felt nothing awry in his head. Then Mal spoke for them all: "*An rud is annamh is iontach.*" *What is rare, is wonderful.* They'd had a rare night, and no one knew when they'd see the like of it again. One more held breath, and the huddle came apart. They glanced at one another, then slipped out into the real world.

But Ciaran could not reach her.

Ten minutes ago he'd spotted Sheerie across the room, where she sat half in shadow at a cocktail table alone. No one acknowledged her, no one came over with a drink or to take an order. It was as if the talking, smoking, drinking well-wishers now crowding the VIP section of the otherwise cleared-out venue didn't even know she existed. But Ciaran saw her, and he knew her patience had to be waning.

He'd been trying to get to her ever since walking out of the dressing room, but the moment he stepped from the riser by the bar he was swarmed by record company reps, journalists, and the occasional fan who'd leaked through. He smiled for them, signed a few CDs, shook hands, and mumbled about being grateful for all the affection. And he *was*, but he had a different idea of affection right now—and it had nothing to do with this lot.

Rich's voice echoed to him: *Surly musicians do not make for happy record company people, and keeping record company people happy is half your job.* So he pasted on a broad smile, pulling it so wide his face hurt, and gave side hugs to the company reps while posing for photos and attempting to keep an eye on that square table in the back.

Frustrated, he turned to one side, hoping to make a break for it. Instead, he encountered Kay and Katie. They stood shoulder-to-shoulder, faces alight. "That was the best show we've ever seen!" Katie cried.

"Yeah!" echoed Kay.

Ciaran wasn't certain he'd ever heard Kay say anything that didn't underscore her friend's words. He liked them, but they were in the way. Everyone, everything was *in the bloody way.* "Yeah," he snapped. "You'll be able to say you fucked me when."

Their faces fell and he nearly felt bad—a person shouldn't kick a puppy just 'cause it gnaws on your boots—but then he glanced at the cocktail table and found it empty.

"Gawd," said Katie. "What'd *we* do?"

"Yeah," sniffed Kay.

Ciaran rubbed his eyes. Sheerie or no he was perhaps ten seconds from making a run for the side doors. The room was closing in on him. His chest tightened. "Mebbe it's time for you girls to get on home," he said in a thin, dark voice that didn't even feel like his own. "Ain't you got lives or something?"

"OhmyGawd," said Katie. "The ego has landed."

A hand snaked forward and brushed Katie's bare shoulder. She yelped and jumped back as if singed. Sheerie slipped through the breach. "You may go," she said in a soft, insinuating voice. "I'm here now."

Gaping, the women stared first at Sheerie, then Ciaran. What happened next appeared to go in stutters, as if a strobe light had been turned on: Katie reached up a hand to take aim at Ciaran's face—he felt the slap coming—but no blow landed. Sheerie caught the girl's hand with one lashing movement and held it in midair.

"What did I say?" Sheerie asked, still using that languid, soft tone. Her fingers tightened. The hand curled inward.

"Ow, ow, you're hurting me." Katie cringed, tears springing to her eyes.

Kay tried to pry Sheerie's fingers away but a searing look made her cower. She shoved Ciaran. "Help her, you asshole."

"Answer me," said Sheerie. "What. Did. I. Say."

"You said, you said—" Katie's voice was garbled.

"Stop," Ciaran ordered. "It's all right."

"Is it?" Sheerie continued to close her fingers. Ciaran thought he heard bones crunching together. "Is it truly?"

43

Katie nodded quickly, beads of tears flying from her cheeks.

"All right, then." Sheerie released her. Katie curled her hand to her chest; it glowed an angry purple-red. "Thank you for your services," she told the girls. "You are discharged. Go away now. Quickly."

The girls scattered like released mercury into the party. The last thing Ciaran heard was a gasping sob and a comment about ice, then a second voice that might have been Mal's. But none of that stuck with him; his eyes were only for Sheerie, and he stared at her with a combination of fear and awe.

"You have a way with folk, you do," he said.

That metallic laugh again. "You do as well."

"Y'don't know me."

"Oh, I know you better than you imagine." Sheerie set a hand on his chest, a fiery touch he'd been thinking about for hours, but he flinched slightly before settling against it. "Now tell me … do you still hunger?"

His heart raced. "Depends what's on the menu."

She clapped her hands together and made a delighted noise, bouncing on tiptoe. "Everything you could ask for, *anamchara*. Everything. In exchange— for everything."

Ciaran wasn't looking for a soulmate, no matter how alluring Sheerie was. But he also was beyond whatever she had to *say*. He wanted to see what she could *do*, and they were done playing around. He took her hand in his—such heat in that touch—and led her to the door. Outside, the bracing night air made him draw her close, his large hands nearly swallowing her head whole as he turned her to him. Her hair brushed against his wrists, curling around like manacles. "Fair trade," he whispered huskily. "Everything. For everything."

A slow smile split her face. "Yes."

"How do we begin, then?"

"Like *this*," she whispered, and swallowed him whole.

44

Stupid-stitions

"And that's the end to *that* story," Patrick told Caitlin with forced lightness as Sheerie and Ciaran slipped away across the room. "True lust finds a way."

They had perched on the edge of the stage as the rest of the after-party swirled around them. Reconnecting with Caitlin had been easy; the moment Patrick emerged from the dressing room with Mal she tapped him on the shoulder. He led her away before anyone else could interfere, and they retreated to a corner of the stage. Once settled, they popped the tops on two bottles of beer, clinking them together with an easy "*sláinte*," then took good long swallows.

"So that's the one." A tight, uneasy concern drifted across her face.

"Reckon he don't even know her name." Patrick took another drink.

She eyed him. "Unquestionably." When he raised an eyebrow, she added, "Well ... most of her sort use pseudonyms, don't they."

Patrick bit down on a smile. Ciaran was in for a surprise if that one asked him to fork over cash at night's end. "And you know that how?"

"Never you mind." Leaning forward, she smiled and he felt his head clear. There was pleasure in just watching her move. "Quite a show tonight. You had good teachers, whoever they were."

"Was Mal who taught me the piano," he said. "Hours of getting those keys to do what I wanted. Showed me how to read music and such."

"Did you ever try ... without someone showing you how first?"

He took another drink, considering. He'd taken his instruments to their next level on his own, in that cheap basement apartment night after night—but he'd always had someone who introduced him. Patrick shook his head. "Never had the chance. Or the talent."

"Shouldn't sell yourself short."

"Better to know yer limitations."

"What if there weren't any?"

"Any what—limitations?" He chuckled. "Y'getting metaphysical on me?"

"Answer the question."

Patrick had a hard time imagining a world without boundary; his life had been made up of limits imposed on him—by Herself, by *Athair*, by the monks. And, he had to admit, he imposed his own limits out of fear. Only with Mal and Ciaran could he ever let loose and ignore the warning signs. But as close as they were, that could be a form of limitation, too. "Wouldn't know what to do with myself," he shrugged. "This's gettin' awful serious. Y'didn't strike me as a serious sort of girl."

"Oh, I'm not." Her eyes twinkled as she slid closer. "I'm the opposite of serious." She set the beer bottle on one finger, then lifted it in the air. It spun on her finger, bubbling within. And then she … lowered her finger. The bottle hovered in place, twirling on its own.

Patrick's jaw dropped. "Yer a magician."

She swiped it from the air and took another gulp. "You might say such." She turned her impossible blue eyes on him once more. "Your teachers. Tell me about them. Tell me … what they did to you."

"They taught me things."

"I gathered that much, Padraig."

"Well—Mal—" He offered a small smile across the room to where his friend stood by a cocktail table, chatting with the VIP girls. One of them was waving her hand around, looking distressed. "He's brilliant at the piano. He says he *goes places* when he plays—"

"I'm not interested in Mal," she interrupted. "Not now. I'm interested in your other *múinteoir*."

Patrick's heart beat faster. Journos might ask questions with that sort of curiosity—*how'd you learn to play*—but not with this intense urgency. He had two-sentence sound bites for them. Caitlin wanted more. He was abruptly desperate to share everything with her.

But this wouldn't be easy. The monks … had different ideas than Herself and *Athair* about what a boy should learn. And they did not countenance talk of magic.

"There's a long answer and a short one," he said.

Padraig only met the monks because he'd spilled the milk.

Or maybe it was because of Cronin's bull.

In any case, he crossed paths with the monks when he was just turned five, starting with the one who changed everything for him. The minute he started telling Caitlin about them, he was there again—back to being a boy. Standing on a stile, overlooking the ragged, rocky pastures of the western county where he'd spent his earliest years, trying to figure out if he could outrun a bull.

He'd been chased out for the day by Herself in what was becoming a routine: With *Athair* missing again—gone for eleven days and counting—she had little patience for the child in her care. When he'd spilled milk from his mug that morning, she whisked him out with a swat on the behind from her hazel stick, then chased him across the muddy yard until he escaped over the fence.

The loss of the milk was one thing. The problem was she would *never* clean it up. Even if the milk soured and hardened and stench filled up the whole tiny house she would not touch it, and wouldn't let him touch it either. And so long as it remained, she'd be equally as hard and sour with *him*.

So there Padraig stood, shoeless, stomach crawling within, trying to figure out which neighbor he could pester for some spare milk. If he came home with a bottle, perhaps Herself would let him back in before dark. But in order to get to the closest neighbor, he'd have to cross Cronin's land—and that meant possibly encountering Cronin's bull. Most days, he could outrun it—but being hungry meant he was tired a lot. So he stood on the stile and dithered.

"And how is the lay of the land?"

Padraig was so startled he wobbled on the stile and tumbled backward—but not into a cow pat. Instead, he landed in someone's arms. Suddenly he was looking upside-down into the face of a reedy man in a coarse brown robe. The man's skull stood bare to the world, except for a ring of hair around the crown. Padraig slapped his hands over his mouth and squirmed mightily. Monks reached into your body and tugged out your soul, Herself said.

Grinning, the monk set him down, picking up a walking stick and burlap bag. "And where're you bound, young man?" When Padraig held his silence, he added, "Don't be afraid. I'm just on my way home." He had a soothing voice that sounded nothing like anyone from the area. He gestured with the walking stick to a stone building beyond Cronin's field—the monastery. Padraig *knew* of the place, but had steered around it the way he avoided Cronin's bull.

"Can you speak?"

At that time, Padraig had just a smattering of English. He touched his chest and risked opening his mouth. "*Mise* Padraig," he said.

Nodding, the monk changed tongues. "My apologies, Padraig. I wondered if you lacked the power of speech. Now I see you simply speak the wrong language. You may call me Brother David. So. Is this your field? You don't seem like one of the Cronins."

Padraig shook his head and the story of the milk came tumbling out. Herself wouldn't clean it up because the *sídhe* had to come and have a drink, and if you denied them the offering they might become vengeful and steal you away or turn everything you owned into ash or … then he'd run out of possible punishments. Herself was the one who knew all the rules, all the stories.

For much of the time he was talking, the monk was biting down on his lips, trying to suppress a smile. "Jesus save us," he said when Padraig finally quieted. "A child chained to *and* completely ignorant of his own history. So much untangling to be done. I don't suppose your mother ever mentioned Tuatha Dé Danann? The Milseans? Even—heaven help us—Mr. Yeats?"

He shook his head. Herself hadn't. "*Athair* did." They were glorious stories, of ancient warriors and bloody battles and conquered people. But it all ended the same, with the defeated going underground, taking their incredible strength and powers with them. Sometimes, they came back: to visit, to bedevil, to reward. One never knew what to expect from *sídhe*.

"You mean to tell me that these great warriors … are now reduced to demanding castoff milk?" The monk raised an eyebrow. "Are you aware of the English word *superstition*, Padraig?"

"Stupid-stition?"

Brother David laughed. "Something like that. Ancient stories that *sound* like truth—which may even *have* some truth in them—get twisted 'round. They turn into reasons to keep your kitchen floor unmopped." He nodded toward the stone building, which glowed in the morning light. "We have much to discuss, I believe. Will you come with me? There's more milk than we can drink at the monastery. You could help by taking some home."

So began Padraig's association with the monks. They were a small group, some of whom rarely spoke and some of whom ventured into the community regularly to help out as needed. They chanted. They raised chickens and cows and tended a garden. And they had a small, single room in the monastery set aside for *scoil*.

"Perhaps one day, you'll join the other local children here," Brother David suggested as he held the door wide and revealed rows of tiny tables and chairs and an expansive slate board covered in white markings. Patrick thought he'd been given the moon; the idea of other children, of books and learning and—if he were honest, a whole day away from Herself—that was more important than gold. He'd've handed over his soul in that moment, to be admitted to school.

Life took a turn for the better after that. Over the next year, whenever Herself shut him out, Padraig ran to the monastery. He picked up English—words for bread, water, earth, sun, sky, prayer, Jesus. He learned his name actually was Patrick. He liked being surrounded by quiet adults who asked so little of him—clean up after himself, carry something from one end of the building to the other, toss some seed to the chickens out back. Brother David also insisted that he take a bath once every three visits, at least. And as time allowed, sometimes he and Brother David would stroll around the monastery grounds together.

Patrick would zoom around for a time, racing through the grasses with energy he'd never used to have, finally returning to the monk's side for a chat about whatever was on his mind.

But his favorite moments came when Brother David took out his guitar. The monk's face would fill with light as he plucked lively sounds from the air and wove them into something that made Patrick's insides turn over. Music filled him in ways bread and lessons couldn't; it got into his body and made his feet do strange things. When there was music in the room, Patrick dreamed of running *to* something for the first time, instead of running away from it. Music gave him hope. Music was magic.

Even if that wasn't how Brother David would have put it.

Then one day, it ended.

Patrick drained his bottle, thirstier than when he'd first come off stage. He'd gone on forever, the noisy party raging in the background, but Caitlin's attention never wandered. He felt electric, jittery, present and alive with her gaze on him. He didn't want that to fade. So he told her more than he'd ever planned to, the longer-than-long version. And he still hadn't told her everything.

"Bit of a *seanchaí*, you are," she said now. "Among all else."

He shrugged, a pleased flush creeping up his neck. "Oh, I'm no storyteller. It's just what happened."

"Well, you can't end there." She swatted at him. "What went wrong?"

Patrick took a deep breath. There was what went wrong, what went right, and what went wrong again. And all he wanted right now was to finally get a chance to run his hands through her thick hair. To see if her skin was as soft as it appeared. He wanted to skip to that part, but didn't know how to do it. He'd never been like Ciaran, who could scoop up a woman's hand and draw her to him with his need.

As if reading his thoughts, Caitlin's fingers brushed against the back of his hand. "We have all the time in the world," she said. "Take it. Tell me."

Just over a year after meeting the monks, Patrick's family fled the county. Everything got piled into a cart in the dark of night, and they escaped to another little cottage on a rough plot of land just outside the capital city. Patrick never did find out why they had to disappear like that—might have been neighbors getting nosy, *Athair*'s debts, maybe Padraig made too much noise when she landed her stick across his back.

But knowing that he would probably never see the monks again made Patrick sob quietly the whole ride across the country.

The next three years had bright spots: He met Ciaran and Mal, and they'd fallen headfirst into making music. He'd had friends for the first time. But *Athair* was absent for even longer stretches, and Herself began withholding food from Padraig in addition to wielding the stick. She began calling him names, insinuating he didn't belong in their house.

She was mad, clearly. But Patrick couldn't see it then. She was his sole anchor to any sort of family life but acted like he was dragging her down. So finally he made good on a vow he'd told himself the moment he set foot on that muddy plot of land: He would not stay. He ran off. Back to the monastery.

Thus ensued several weeks of negotiations. Patrick would not return home. Herself would not admit monks into her cottage. At last, *Athair* returned and arranged for everyone to meet in a pub—though Patrick didn't learn any of this until much later on—where he signed away guardianship of his son to the monastery until Padraig was sixteen. He told Brother David and Prior Gerry that the boy was slow and uncoordinated and needed all the help anyone would give him.

He needs his father, David had gently admonished, but Gerry shushed him.

I've done my best, Athair reportedly said in reply. *Not enough, but my best. The boy is … a wild thing.*

At last, Patrick was part of the monastery. They gave him a small room of his own and he had to keep up with some basic chores, but his main job was to attend the *scoil*. He loved it: He was one of twelve students in the class, and the brothers traded off teaching duties, each with their own specialty. Brother David helped with English lessons—less learning the language than the crafting and writing of it now that Patrick was older—while others came in for a few hours each week to teach sciences, maths, music, history.

Even Prior Gerry took an hour or two each week for his own expertise: religion. They read the Bible aloud starting from Genesis all the way to the very end, and every so often he'd interrupt to explain what was happening and why it was important. He knew every chapter, every verse in the Good Book, and to him those were the most important stories to tell.

To Patrick, all those tales—how the world was formed and populated, families created, instructions on how to live your life—had the ring of the familiar. They made him think of *Athair's* stories—very old, full of battles and babies and ways of looking at the world. Of magic and spells and the random ways the *sídhe* might disrupt a person's life. One day, he said as much during class.

Prior Gerry had not taken kindly to Patrick's comparison. "You are still a child, Patrick," he replied in a cool, dismissive voice. "And so I can understand the appeal of such inventions. But those are myths, and myths are a digestion of true history. They keep your people down, clutching at superstitious, magical pap."

Patrick—who was twelve by then—had learned years earlier how to evade a hazel stick or broom, but he was less adept at dodging an adult's well-phrased, condescending argument. Embarrassed, he stared at his hands and didn't reply.

But Prior Gerry wasn't done. He kept Patrick after dismissal that day. Without glancing up from the papers he graded at his desk, he said, "I have tolerated a certain degree of … eccentricity in allowing you to stay here, Patrick. Your parents refused baptism—we decided to discuss it with you later. You needed a place to live—we found you a room. Brother David says he sees great potential in you, and while he is something of an unusual man himself, I have been willing to follow his lead." The older man raised his head. "But I draw the line at talk of sprites and fey in school. This is no place for the mystical. It is a place of learning and faith in Jesus Christ. I will not permit disruptions of that kind."

"Yes, Brother," Patrick had managed. He knew he was here on sufferance. That everything he thought he'd known was wrong, or a lie. He'd spent the last several years trying to erase the superstitions, the *magical pap*. But it was like being told he had to ignore he had two hands, or a nose. He would have to work harder at unlearning.

"I need your word that if you are to continue with us, there will be no more talk of … magic."

So Patrick promised. He clearly still had a lot to learn.

For the most part, it worked. He talked himself out of it. When he imagined his father telling him those stories, he learned to see them for what they were— tales to help children fall asleep. But in doing that, some of the spark for school left him. His grades became erratic. He put so much effort into learning what he was *supposed* to know, he let everything else fall by the wayside. Only his music lessons mattered. When he and Brother David and some of the other monks gathered, whether to sing or chant or play tunes, that was when Patrick felt his whole heart beat again. He lived for those moments. Not so much school.

A few more years passed, and one afternoon Brother David took him on a walk around the grounds. As Patrick's English had improved, the monk had slipped into a more natural mentor mode with him, but they were often challenged to find the time to stroll as they'd once done when he was a boy.

"I believe you have a birthday coming up," Brother David said. "A milestone, even."

"Sixteen's not so special," said Patrick, but even in saying it the age felt that much closer to adulthood.

"Have you thought about what you'll do next?"

"Next?"

"Well, Patrick, unless you plan to enter service, it's probably time for you to consider what direction the rest of your life will take. We're a small stone building in a remote section of the country. You've been cloistered. But there's an entire world for you to explore."

He hadn't given it any real thought. There wasn't anything he wanted to do, other than read more books and play more guitar. And neither of those things felt like anything the world would *want* from him. He had all kinds of skills— with animals, with farm work, with repairing a sink if it sprang a leak. "I don't know what I want."

"Well." Brother David put a hand on his shoulder. "Give it some thought. Perhaps you'll track your father down again. I imagine he's not done ... telling you things."

Patrick made a dismissive noise. "I'm not a kid anymore."

"No ... but not everything he told you was for children. I imagine he still has much to say."

"Superstitions," Patrick said. "I'm shut of those. Stupid-stitions was exactly right."

Brother David let out a long breath, then glanced over his shoulder. He spoke in a low voice. "It is possible to believe in more than one set of stories, Padraig." His use of Patrick's Irish name landed hard. "Not everyone thinks so—you saw that a few years ago when you riled up Prior Gerry with a little heresy. True, I disapprove of superstition. Superstition allows us to use wishes and hopes to substitute for the concrete things we can create or fix with our hands—our actions. *That* is why they are concepts for children."

"But you want us to pray," Patrick fired back. "How is that different?" A crack in the trees made them turn, but there was no one around. He barreled forward. "Why isn't Jesus just another kind of ... fairy tale?"

Brother David stared at him long and hard. "You ask a complicated question," he said after a long pause. "And after three decades of worship, inquiry and study, I can only say ... I don't know, Patrick."

Patrick was stunned. "Then how—"

The monk held up a hand. "I no longer believe it matters if we know a literal truth here. Billions of people have read the stories in one single book. The book you had to read aloud in class. And billions of people believe those stories. In my heart, I believe as well—even if I have a harder time reconciling it in my head. It doesn't matter, though. It is that belief—and how we take that belief into the world—that makes them *real*. Stories can create reality, if the story-tellers are clever or powerful enough. Why do you suppose I fought so hard to bring you here, to keep you away from your parents? I am just a man. But the stories that support me, that keep this house of stone and light standing—they are what allowed me to bring you here. To give you a chance at life."

A soft clearing of the throat made Patrick look up. He felt dazed. Prior Gerry's assistant, Brother Leon, was watching them intently, arms folded. Had he heard their discussion? "You're wanted," he told Brother David. "And there are chickens to feed," he added to Patrick.

That had been Patrick's last conversation with David.

She'll Learn Ye Fine

"I left the monastery after that," Patrick told Caitlin now. "Went back to the real world, like he'd said I should. Found C and Mal playing music in the street and … here we are."

Caitlin shook her head. "You didn't just *leave*. Not like that. Not buying it."

He'd told her so much—why was this next bit so difficult? "Not selling." But how to explain that a few days later Brother David was gone, sent on a six-month retreat? How during that time Patrick had turned sixteen—and the next day was told by Prior Gerry that he was no longer welcome at the monastery? The abandonment was both acute and familiar.

Patrick stared at his hands.

"Your monk understood quite a lot," she said.

He shrugged. Even all these years later, the memory was raw. There was just something about him that drove people away. Everyone but Ciaran and Mal, that was.

"Your monk was also full of a lot of shite."

Heat rose in his cheeks. "Why'd you say a thing like that?"

"Well, he taught you plenty. But he also un-taught you plenty. Worse with that Gerry fellow. Your own language isn't *wrong*, Padraig. It's yours. Your father's stories weren't wrong. Or superstitions."

"Oh, right, so they're real."

"What do *you* think? Have you ever decided for yourself?"

No one ever wanted to know what Patrick thought. He'd gotten used to that, too. He'd learned to ride in everyone else's slipstream. What did he believe in?

Music. It chimed within him. It spoke all his languages. While inside a song, it was his religion. It was his magic. He was a place where both of those things could exist, so long as there was music being made. With everything else, he had doubts.

"Your parents weren't children," she said. "But they believed."

"They weren't much as parents go," he said, staring at his feet as they swung from the stage. Thinking of Herself and *Athair* was disquieting no matter how many years had passed. If he never saw her again he'd be satisfied, but the absence of his father was an ache he couldn't ignore. "Ignorant. Living inside children's stories."

"But what if they weren't?"

He narrowed his eyes. "What does that mean?"

"What if it wasn't all … nonsense? What if what your father told you—what your mother believed—wasn't simply *stories*?"

Patrick jumped to the floor. "I'm getting more beer." He didn't want to leave her, but that was not a line of thought he cared to pursue. Maybe she was setting him up for some kind of joke. Maybe she was completely off her head, and he was only now seeing it. He snatched up a few more bottles, shook a few fans' hands, and returned to the stage to find Caitlin in conversation with Mal. They were talking about his hat.

"Silly thing," he heard her say.

"Not silly at all," said Mal, pushing some of the red wool back. A lock of hair tumbled out. "A gift should be honored."

"Even if it comes from a *lofa* tinker y'didn't even have a coin for?" Patrick stole behind him and hopped back onstage. He didn't look at Caitlin, afraid of what she might say next.

Mal flushed.

"Always should give to those folk." Caitlin's voice had a dark lilt to it.

"Thieves and layabouts," said Mal, folding his arms. "That's what I was taught."

"You gave to Padraig, didn't you?"

Patrick sat straighter. He'd told her that? He didn't recall.

"He must like you," said Mal. "Getting the whole story in just a day. Anyhow. Patch was different."

"Well, what's done is done and can't be undone," she said. "Though I'd watch yourself. *Fear dearg*'s been spotted 'round these parts."

The red man. Patrick had heard that phrase just last night, from the strange woman pushing the cart. It had rushed right over him as he'd chewed on her other words: about being on a mission, to test … something. Someone. *Yer in good hands, though y'don't know it yet,* she'd whispered to him. *She'll learn ye fine.*

Who was he supposed to be taking lessons from this time?

Patrick caught Caitlin's eye. She winked.

"Honestly, it's like this whole town is secretly Irish or something," Mal's smile was confused and jerky. "Feels like I'm hearing it more here than back at home."

54

"Might be a reason for that," Caitlin told him. "Some folk just … attract the *sídhe*."

He laughed. "Y'got a live one here, Patch."

"C'mon, Padraig," Caitlin elbowed him gently. "Only stories, right?"

"Don't bother him with that, miss," said Mal. "He won't have anything to do with the old stories. Think he developed an allergy as a kid."

"From the monks."

His eyes widened. "You *are* gettin' the whole biography."

Patrick peeled the label from his beer bottle, focusing on not reacting. His gut was churning, and he'd developed a sour taste in his mouth. After being dismissed from the monastery with as little explanation as he'd gotten when his family fled to Dublin, he'd lost interest in all stories, religious or otherwise. *Best to let the dead stay sleeping*, he thought. *No good comes from a backward glance.*

Mal craned his neck; the VIP girls were waving for his attention again. "Ah," he sighed. "My public. They're leaving in the morning, poor things. One of them hurt her hand." He touched his cap and nodded at Caitlin. " 'Til later."

"Mal." Patrick's voice was flat. "Your piano."

"Yes!" Mal continued to back away. "Right as rain. Back to its old diverse self, black an' white keys livin' together in harmony. Damndest thing." And then he was away from them, rejoining the crowd.

Patrick brooded. He wanted to get out of here. Nothing was making sense.

"Have you used up all your words?" Caitlin asked.

He shrugged.

"Well, I have plenty to spare," she continued. "Like, I'd love to know why you're curled up in a big sulk. Thought we were doing quite well for a bit there."

"I'm done talkin' about the monk. And about the … fairy stories. That all right by you?"

"Certainly. You want a conversation to go someplace else, you can take it there." She touched his hand again. "Maybe you have a few questions for me?"

Patrick's face softened. He felt as if he'd swallowed a live bird, a fluttering thing inside him desperate to escape. "Anything? And you'll answer?"

"I promise."

"Why'd you cheat on that bet earlier today?"

Her smile faded. "Of all the things in the universe you could ask me, that's what you most want to hear?" When he didn't answer, she shook her head. "Maybe I had to cheat. Maybe you can't lose. There's a lot of luck floating around you today, wouldn't you say?"

Patrick narrowed his eyes. "I wouldn't say that, no."

She shrugged. "So ask another. But—don't ask what you won't hear the truth about. I don't lie."

"But you hide things."

She waggled her fingers. "Name me someone who doesn't. Not every truth is ready for hearing the moment it's born. Not every person is ready to hear all truths at all times."

"You read that in some fortune cookie?"

She winkled her nose at him. "Go ahead. Satisfy your longings."

Patrick leaned back on his hands, the moment drawing out. He had so many things to ask and didn't know where to begin. Didn't know if he *should* begin. They were strangers; no matter how much he shared with her, that wouldn't change in a day. But he was so intensely drawn to her—not just attracted, but on an instinctual, gut level—that he needed to know why. Until now he'd been open to her otherness. He had his own otherness, and with her around it felt more ... natural. But now part of him wanted to walk out.

No—run.

"Stay," she whispered, reading his thoughts again. "Stay a little longer." She lay flat on the stage. "I'll tell you one true thing: You were gorgeous tonight on that stage. Been a long while since I've seen something so beautiful. I couldn't turn away."

Shifting a bit, Patrick rested his hand on her cheek. She was so warm, a tiny engine pumping away. The bird was his heart now, its movement filling his chest. He didn't want to move.

"Where are you from?" he whispered.

She cupped her hand over his. "Let me show you."

Their fingers laced. Patrick closed his eyes. And—

An Eternal Nowness

They were airborne.

Scooped skyward, Patrick was a kite, he was a plane, he was a bird, pushed along, moving. Like in a lift.

Elevator.

His hand gripped Caitlin's, knuckles white with the effort, afraid to look. Seconds ticked by—*a haon, dó, trí*—but the spaces between them were infinite. And then it was gone, wind, movement, time.

But her hand was still in his.

Tension slid from his body as the world rushed back. He blinked like a newborn into sunlight. As his eyes adjusted more came clear: The sun was enormous, the sky it hovered in, bolder and bluer even than Caitlin's eyes. They lay alongside one another exactly as they had on the Citi stage.

A scent of apples and horseflesh and wine and spice wafted over him, and he bolted up. The world widened and it turned out the stage, the venue—everything—was gone, replaced by a grass so soft and fine it was like a deep-pile silken carpet. Each blade was precisely like the other, stretching in every direction to the horizon, undulating and shimmering in a forever distance.

The *nowness*, the *presence*, the *clarity* was absolute. There was no past, no future, just eternal present.

"Know where you are?" she asked softly.

Patrick reached into the soft grass to touch the earth beneath. Warm and alive, it pulsed against his skin like the body of a great animal. He thought of standing on the ground in his bare feet as a boy, feeling it live beneath him, speaking, growing, being. This was a hundred times more than that. Gently, he tugged out a tuft of the warm ground, dirt crumbling like cake between his fingers. The hole mended itself before his eyes.

He gasped. His teeth chattered. "This is the worn-up place."

"Not exactly." She waited for him to look at her. " 'Tis the other side of the worn-up place."

A tremble came over him and he contracted into a ball, squeezing his eyes shut.

Caitlin lowered her face to his, their noses touching. "This is *your* place, Padraig. It's been waiting for you."

He couldn't hear that. She'd put something in his drink. This was a very fine hallucination. No, it was a horrific one. "Take me home."

"Oh, Padraig. You *are* home."

His throat was closing. The air was choking him. "Then take me back where we were. Now, *bleaist* ya."

A soft puff on his face turned into that lifting wind, and they were skybound again, lifting, elevating. Then it was all fading, replaced by raucous voices and glasses clinking. He could breathe again.

Jerking upright, Patrick scanned the room. Citi. Boston. Not home, but a sane place. He yanked his hand from Caitlin's, scrambling off the stage, stumbling to the ground. Whirling, he scanned the room for someone who'd seen them vanish and reappear. But no one was watching. Mal was still leaning on a table in his fresh white jacket, talking to the girls; waiters and busboys ran around to deliver drinks and collect empty glasses. The world had not changed.

Patrick turned on Caitlin, sitting at the stage's edge. That stillness he'd felt with her a moment—a lifetime—ago was gone. "You *drugged* my beer."

She folded her arms. "You know that's not true."

"Then what did you do to me?"

"Offered a bit of truth. I did try to warn you."

"Y'don't warn someone about something like that." He began backing away. "You just don't feckin' do it in the first place. And what—was that—" He wouldn't put it into words. Words made it real. "Stay there. Leave me be."

Whipping around, he looked for a place to dash away, but the room felt blurry. Not quite real. Stumbling, he collided with a busboy, whose tub of dirty, half-filled glasses and plates flew into the air. Patrick rebounded off him, tumbling hard to the ground and landing on his elbow. A jolting yellow flash of pain screamed through him. He was vaguely aware of everything else happening in slow motion: plates, glasses, bitten-into food, warmed beer and wine, all soaring in the air. But the paralyzing pain in his arm made it impossible to move. At any second, it would all slop down directly on him. Cringing, Patrick raised his good arm over his face and braced for impact.

Everything fell. Everything shattered against the already-sticky floor, a cacophony and riot of sound, a song no one wanted to hear.

He felt nothing.

Silence. He lowered his arm. Broken glass described a shape all around him, like a chalk outline at a murder scene. But he was untouched.

"What the holy hells?" Mal's voice cut through the room, where everything had gone quiet at the moment of the crash. He rested a hand on his forehead. "My *head*, Jaysus—"

Mal had been touched. He was … well, he was very *red*. A great stain spread across his white jacket, viscous crimson liquid coursing through his hair. He looked like an extra from that movie *Carrie*. But … this wasn't blood. Patrick let out a long breath. No, it was too pale. Cranberry juice. Wine. Grenadine. Oddly thick, though.

A lone orange slice slid down Mal's lapel like a runaway boutonniere and slapped on the floor.

Robin leapt into the breach, fluttering with concern. "Aw, what the—your head—what hit ya—"

"Saucer." Mal gasped, then glanced over at Patrick on the floor. His frown turned into a scowl.

A woman tittered.

The moment broke. Mal wheeled on her. "Think it's *funny*, ya—"

Robin shushed him, but Mal wrested away. He had always been sensitive about being perceived as ridiculous. Furious, he glared around the room, nodded once, then stiff-armed his way through the gawkers. He was out the door in a matter of strides.

The busboy, who hadn't even been knocked over, held out a hand to Patrick. "Makes no sense," he was muttering. "We didn't even bring out the cranberry juice tonight." He pulled Patrick to his feet. "Jeez, man, you're a lucky sonofabitch. You coulda ended all sliced and diced." He glanced between where the spill had hit Mal and the glass had avoided Patrick. "That just ain't right."

Patrick picked up a single shard of glass. He should be on his way to the hospital now with dozens of cuts or worse. But it couldn't be luck. That was what Caitlin had been selling, and she was clearly a hypnotist as well as a magician. Or else she'd put something in his drink.

He glared at Caitlin—she'd never budged from her spot on the stage—her blue eyes flashing at him. A strange near-smile played on her lips. Her body vibrated with the faintest twitch. There was something apart about her right now, neither of the past nor the future. Something that contained an eternal *nowness*. Something that lived in an infinity of waving grass and a too-bright sun.

What if they weren't simply stories?

Patrick's first instinct had always been to flee. Brother David had admonished him over and over for taking the easy way out. *The problem with running, Patrick, is wherever you go, there you are.*

And, he realized now, sometimes whatever you were trying so hard to escape … was faster than you.

Ciaran was long gone. Mal had just left. He was the last man standing, even if his legs were wobbly.

He would not run. Not this time.

Lifting a hand to Caitlin, he beckoned. "This time, you follow *me*."

She came along easily, as if she had no substance at all.

There Was Light, Once

"Tell me … what you desire."

Sheerie's voice was in his ear yet faraway, a whisper of leaves on the ground and the rumble of an oncoming train all wrapped up in one. The sharp edges of her fingernails traversed Ciaran's cheek, tickling over the unshaven jaw, down his soft neck and to his chest, tugging on tufts of hair as she went—an eager explorer in fresh territory.

Ciaran shuddered. Every muscle quivered, and he was having a hard time focusing.

Where's the light? he thought for a moment. *There was light, once.*

Given the choice, Ciaran preferred to see every inch of his partners in bed; the all-too-brief moments of skin on skin, hair intertwining, shadows and folds and blemishes and scars. He liked to read his bedmates like maps, tracing imperfections with his fingers, then his tongue. But something about Sheerie had been overwhelming. She'd risen up on her knees atop his hotel room bed, smile sharply darting onto her mouth, hips tucked to one side. That marvelous hair seemed even longer and shinier than before, draped down half the length of her small, thin frame.

And she positively—glowed. Not like radiation. Not like health. Not even like light. But a shine was on her that hurt his eyes even as it pulled him toward her. Ciaran had flipped off the light switch and they'd been bathed in moonglow through the windows. But then the room went chilly and dark. It echoed, like a cave.

Where are we?

But of course they'd never left the room.

And now, a pause. Her fingernails retreated. All of her—retreated. But it was still dark and cold.

"Tell me," she urged again. "What do you want?"

"Anything?" he asked, trying to match her tone but sounding like he was a teenage virgin all over again. A shiver ran through him.

"Be positively honest. Don't hold back."

So now she was a genie, asking for his pleasure. "I want," he said, and stopped. Why was it hard to put that into words? Had he ever been asked before, so earnestly?

What do you want ... for lunch? ... to play? ... to see? He heard those all the time. But Sheerie wasn't asking his favorite color.

"World domination," he said, and chuckled.

"A given," she shot back, and then her mouth was on his. He wrapped his arms around her slender form, and they spun around and around in the sheets, spinning so far for so long surely they must fall out of the bed—but the bed kept going, as big as they needed. The touch of her was even more extraordinary than he ever could have guessed; each kiss had a different taste, each caress from her delicate hands finding new places to make him tremble. It wouldn't be long now.

"But," she continued after a moment. "I want to know what *you* wish. Your most personal desire, Ciaran. Give it to me."

I want something ... of my own, he thought.

"Ahhh." She sighed.

Had he said that aloud? He must have. Ciaran's face flushed. He hadn't known how much he meant it until the desire came out in words. It was as if she'd convinced him to unveil a truth so hidden it had been invisible even to himself. But it was real, and it had been said. Ciaran had felt so plain sometimes, so ordinary. Being in Mal's shadow all these years, knowing he was seen as lesser in comparison. Then when Patrick had returned, all the things Ciaran had gathered for himself that felt unique—silent enigma, clever musician— well, Patrick had those too, along with a funny innocence. Patch walked around as if the world were forever new, forever unknowable. With those two, Ciaran often felt like the hack in the band—easily disposed of if someone had to be tossed overboard.

Sheerie's hand paused in its search for new ways to tantalize, and she settled it against his heart. "I hear you in there," she said. "Blood and muscle and life. You live at full throttle, my love. It's why I chose *you*. Everything else I must do can wait. I will be with you now. You have so much to give."

He said nothing. She was constructing words around him like a poem, creating mysteries from his breath.

"I want," he said again, but didn't follow it up this time.

She set a finger on his lips. "I understand completely. And I will give it to you."

"Give me—what?"

"What I promised before." Her hand returned to its hunt, more quickly finding purchase this time. Her fingers wrapped around him and closed gently, then with more intensity, and he shuddered again. "Everything."

The Weight of No One's Expectations

Mal emerged from the shower, head buzzing. He was having a hard time processing everything that had happened that day. Or—to be honest— everything that had happened since the night before. When they'd met that strange … person on the street.

Ye will never see the fear dearg *comin, so you won't.*

Caitlin had known what that meant. So, he suspected, did Patrick.

The red man.

I was the red man, back there.

Mal reached into the wet strands of hair to feel a knot, big as a coin, rising next to his temple. Burned fingers. A dousing and a thunk right in the sally. And the impossible headfuck of a piano that had changed colors and temperatures twice in a day.

It was too much.

The bizarre incident at Citi—he could have laughed that off. Maybe. After-parties were a kind of performance, too, and he knew how to be his best in front of fans, or journalists, or executives. They always watched the frontman the most carefully. So while he'd much rather have been off to the side chatting up a pretty woman, like Patch, or cutting to the chase by leaving with another, like Ciaran, Mal had stayed put. Played nice. Did his job.

But then someone had cackled.

Cackled *at* him.

That pushed him over the edge. He'd gone from being the star of the evening to the butt of a joke. Didn't matter how incredible the show had been; that was all anyone would remember of the evening. And it had been such a random, strange thing: Mal had been several feet away when Patch went down. The contents of that washtub should have landed on *Patch*. Instead, they'd been repelled from their natural resting place and flung in another direction.

The red man. The fear dearg.

Mal had read hundreds of books in his life. But folklore wasn't his strong suit. His parents hadn't cared for the old stories, so he'd had to dig up whatever he could at the local library. After meeting Padraig, he'd done a fairly deep dive, including coming across a collection of stories culled from around Ireland by W. B. Yeats. That had been a surprise, to discover the hobby of a legendary poet.

But it had been a bigger surprise later to find out how much of that book was probably invented nonsense. Yeats and that Lady Gregory, full of privilege, dilettanted their way around the country, likely getting some whoppers told by the so-called quaint, rural locals. Then Yeats came home and wrote a book of inventions and half-truths that might have stumbled across some actual folklore. Or, at least, that's what Mal's *múinteoir* had insisted.

Mal remembered very little of the book—but those words … *fear dearg* … they echoed. He'd seen them before.

He shook his head, rubbing the long blond locks with a towel. Too late to think about it now. He leaned toward the mirror and parted the strands, eyeing the bump briefly, then covered it up again. If Mal was vain about anything, it was his lion's mane. It deeply pleased him to have grown out his hair; that, along with the curling beard he'd been working on for months gave him a rough, untamed sense of self. He'd always been the good son, the studious child, the musical prodigy who won awards and played for politicians and got punched around by lesser mortals in school.

But when he and Ciaran had first taken to the streets to play their songs, something had shifted inside. He'd stopped going for regular haircuts, donned sandals, and chose loose-fitting garments. He shifted aside the golden boy mantle and felt like himself. The music sounded the same, but suddenly—he was no longer so easily defined. No longer contained. It had been gloriously freeing to carry the weight of no one's expectations but his own.

Satisfied now, he pulled the hair into a ponytail.

Would look even better with a red wool hat on.

The random thought was so startling he glanced around. Was someone else in the room?

Plucking the hat from the shower, where it had gotten the same washing his suit had, Mal was surprised to find it bone dry. And suddenly it was on his head again. A lightness settled through him. Clarity. Joy, even. All of that cranberry juice hitting him really *had* deserved a cackle or two. A person just needed perspective, and a good shower.

And a hat.

65

Silly, Patrick's friend had called it. She'd been a lovely thing, with a face that reminded him of home. Lucky bastard, Patch. Didn't even have to make an effort, and the beauties came running. Sometimes—in a corner of his heart he barely acknowledged—Mal missed the days when Patch had been like a personal project. He'd never had to worry about the little lost boy being better than him at anything. Runty, half-wild, needed instruction on everything. Mal had liked that dynamic.

But then Patrick had upped and vanished, without a word of farewell. Three years of friendship and—*whoosh*. Gone. Mal had wondered if he and Ciaran had invented him. Seven years after *that*, he turned up on Grafton, hunkered in a doorway, watching them play.

Lookit you, fear gan ainm, Ciaran had said once they noticed him. *Back from the dead.*

The nickname had never been kind, but calling Padraig a nameless man had hit the nail so square on the head, and Ciaran had delivered it with such affection that the boy had never objected.

Nor had the man. Padraig had been all grown up but was still smaller than either Mal or Ciaran. Otherwise, he looked the same—wide green eyes, round cheeks, a dusky look about him. *'Tis me,* he'd said. *Same as ever. Only, it's Patrick now.*

No, really, Mal had said. He'd wanted to be polite. But he'd honestly thought he was staring at a ghost. *We thought you were dead.*

A few weeks after Padraig had stopped showing up at the cottage to make music, or at Mal's for Sunday supper, Mal and Ciaran had gone to his house— this falling-down shack in the middle of a mud patch. Ciaran had bravely knocked on the door and they'd asked after him. Padraig's Ma had a face like a fist and eyes like glass marbles as she leaned out and said her son had died. No emotion. Flat tone. Then she'd slammed the door.

Mal had run to the roadside and vomited up his lunch. Of course it was a lie. But a lie of that magnitude coming from an adult was something he'd never experienced before.

Not that you got sick. Not that you'd gone missing. That you'd died, Mal had told Patrick, right there, on Grafton.

Well, they're both gone now. Patrick had appeared unsurprised to learn that he'd been declared wiped off the earth. He told them that his father had vanished after Patrick was accepted in the monastery *scoil,* and his mother moved without providing a forwarding address. Her obituary had been sent to the monastery in an unmarked envelope a few years later, and that was the last he'd thought of her.

That had brought the mood down even lower. They were strange and awkward with one another. Mal half-expected Patrick to give them a wave and move on. Instead, he'd glanced over their shoulders and lifted his chin. *You two got an assistant? 'Cause someone's volunteering to be yer roadie.*

A thief had grabbed their guitar case—which held not just Ciaran's instrument but a full and generous day of wages—and was attempting to take off down the road with it. Without another word, Patrick dashed after him. He was remarkably fleet, barely seeming to touch the ground as he bolted away. Ciaran and Mal had joined in the chase, and the three of them had thundered through the streets like the pack they'd always been.

They'd made the thief very sorry, then gone out for drinks.

From there, they'd mapped out the rest of their lives.

Mal wanted to see him. To talk about the … incident at Citi. About Yeats and invented folklore and … whatever the hell a *fear dearg* was supposed to be.

Dressing quickly, he trotted down the hotel hallway. He slowed at Ciaran's door, biting his lips at the sound of guttural moans and heaving sighs. As it had been more than two hours since Ciaran had last been seen inside the club, Mal had to give him a tap on the hat for sheer endurance. And yet—those noises—they had a faraway quality. More distant than what a person might expect to hear on the other side of a hotel room door, as if they came from the bottom of a deep well.

Move along, he told himself, crossing the hall to Patch's room. A *Do Not Disturb* sign dangled from the handle, just as it had from Ciaran's, so he waited a moment to see if the sounds on the other side matched. But all he heard were heated voices. He knocked—and the door fell open.

"Patch?" he leaned inside. "Only me. We need some words."

"Later," he heard Caitlin whisper. "Not now."

Maybe he was interrupting something. It was bad form on the tour to go calling this late at night, particularly when … visitors were around. He began to back away—but then Patrick was standing in the light. "No, no, Mal. You're definitely wanted. *Needed*, even. You're going to love this."

Inside, the room crackled with tension. Caitlin sat up on the dresser, legs crossed. Her beauty struck Mal afresh, with that angular face, soft pale skin, and thick wavy hair that shifted in its own breeze. One glance at her and Mal imagined running through the grass without his shoes, climbing the tree next to his parents' home, the sun dappling his face through the leaves—

He shook his head. *Where the hells did that come from?*

Only then did he catch the unhappy look on her face and the storm in her eyes. She was turning a tin whistle over and over in her hands, barely glancing up. Patrick sat on the bed across from her, arms folded. His chest rose and fell rapidly, as if he'd been running.

"Wasn't thinkin' you'd have company," said Mal carefully.

"Oh, I've got *so* much more than that."

Caitlin's head shot up and she gripped the whistle.

"G'wan," Patrick prompted in an acid tone Mal had never heard him use. "Please share."

The electricity in the room amped even higher, as if emanating directly from Caitlin. Small hairs on Mal's arms stood on end. But she said nothing, just stared furiously at Patrick for a long moment.

Whatever anger Patrick had in him dissipated, and he finally spoke in a bone-tired tone. "That's what I thought. Lies. A game. A crock of shite. Rich put you up to this? Y'should get a feckin' *award*, you should. Had me fooled all damned day."

"Watch yourself," Caitlin said in a serious, thin voice. "I'm here to help, but I don't have to stay."

"Then don't." Patch was on a roll Mal had never seen before. He was—injured, in a way. Not physically. But inside, somewhere. She'd convinced him to let her in—and something had gone wrong. "I don't feckin' care. I'm not that gullible and you're not that pretty." He pointed at the door. "Y'can leave any time."

"Patch, ease off," said Mal. "What'd she say?"

"C'mon," Patch cozened, as if talking to a recalcitrant puppy. "Or should I share your fairy story?"

Caitlin jumped from the dresser and made no sound as she landed. The whistle slipped from her fingers, rising in the air like a baton, or a wand, and the room burst with music. And not just any music—it was *their* music. The anthemic bombast, the folky twang, the traditional instruments all came from that night's performance, blending into something familiar and also entirely new—but what was playing it? There was no speaker, no device, nothing in this room. Just … the air. Caitlin moved her fingers and the whistle twirled, the sounds speeding up and blending together.

Mal's head throbbed. Another twirl and the music became a crescendoing hurricane. Mal clapped hands over his ears and squeezed his eyes shut. "Stop!" he shouted.

The sounds cut off and the silence echoed. Mal opened his eyes and gazed around the room. Everything … sparked. It was as if embers had been drawn to the outlines of the world. The mundane hotel room with its mass-produced furniture and ordinary corporate bed, the old thick carpet— every inch, detailed in glowing greenish-yellow embers that did not burn. The whistle had returned to her hands.

Astonished, Mal gaped at the sole wall covering, a painting of a sailboat on an anonymous sea, and he would have sworn the canvas rippled in the breeze and tiny waves lapped against the hull.

"Said it before." Patrick's voice was sandpaper. "Yer a trickster."

Mal shook his head. "Patch, this is no trick."

The burning lights faded. The boat stilled in the painting. Caitlin threw open a window sash and the embers revealed themselves for what they always were— fireflies. En masse the glowing insects rose into the room, swooped around the corners—then flew out the window, disappearing into the night. Caitlin turned to Patrick.

68

"There are many things I might be," she said in a low tone that rumbled in Mal's belly. "A liar isn't one. But you have no standing to call me anything when you walk through this world, eyes shut. You asked who I was, and I told you. But who are *you*? Padraig? Patrick? Patch?" She slid a gaze at Mal. "*Fear gan ainm?*"

"Go," Patrick whispered. "Don't make me throw you out."

She tossed her head back and gave a pretty laugh. "Y'couldn't if you tried." She held out her hands and let out a long breath. Mal could have sworn he smelled flowers. "There's a reason for all of this."

"All of what?" But his voice was still flat, and distant.

"Everything. Whatever you've wondered about in your life. Why your parents were … the way they were. Why your friend is having—"

"The worst day of my life." The words came from Mal's mouth, but it was as if she'd plucked them from his mind. He felt light, and unreal. Maybe Yeats hadn't been a full fraud. "But you're not real. You're not supposed to be … real."

She ducked her head and gave Mal a half-smile. "Ah, you always were the brightest penny, Malachi. You've been seen as well, for good and for ill. Still and all, I'm not here for you."

She reached for Patrick's arm. He flinched away. "So there it is." She sighed. "You aren't ready. Suppose I'll have to try another day. You and me, we've all the time in the world. But listen well, Padraig: Your friends do not. So don't wait too long to need me. Don't cling to the wrong set of stories forever."

Mal had thought all his surprise had been used up for the day, but he was wrong.

"Please." The anger had drained from Patrick. He had a slight hitch in his throat. "Please just leave."

"So I will." She turned to go, slipping around the half-open door before tossing a final thought over her shoulder. "One more thing." Her blue eyes flashed. "I *am* the prettiest creature either of you will see in your lives. Don't forget it."

She whisked out the door with the speed of smoke finding a draft. Mal raced after her, but she was already gone. The hallway was empty. When he returned to Patrick's room, his friend was emerging from the bathroom with a towel, wiping water from his face.

Mal sat heavily on the bed. "Well, that was—"

Patrick hurled the towel to the ground, then kicked the wall. His boot cracked into the plaster, leaving a dent. "I *liked* that one, I did."

Mal stared at the broken wall.

"Y'know how hard it is to—to like one of 'em? So fast? So easy?"

Mal nodded. They met dozens of new faces every day. Most of those were easy pickings for a night, if the circumstances worked out. But almost none of them were people you cared to have hanging around in the light of day. Patrick made it even harder, just being his shy, strange self.

"Well, if she liked you we already knew she was a bit odd." Mal tried a smile.

"I just wanted her to be normal. Instead, she's off her head."

"You don't want normal," Mal countered. "Normal is safe. Normal's boring. What you don't want is whatever she told you she is." He paused. "What *did* she tell you?"

Patrick paced the room. "That—woman—listened to me pour my heart out, all day. She got me talkin'. I told her everything. And then she turned it 'round on me. Drugged my drink! I mean, very fine drugs but I was *not* lookin' to hallucinate during the party—"

Mal shook his head. He had no idea what Patch was talking about. He hadn't seemed drugged at Citi and was way too sober now. "Yeah, but what did she say? She told you somethin' you *really* didn't want to hear."

The pacing increased and Patrick rubbed his neck, clenching his fists. "Brace yourself for this. She told me she was a *sídhe*. A feckin' *fairy*. As you do."

Mal gripped at the bed sheets until his fingers trembled. Caitlin had conjured music and light and fireflies from the air. Not just any music, either: *their* music. From that night's show, even. It was impossible on a number of levels: The only recording of any show on any night was made at the soundboard, and Mal would retrieve that cassette from his soundman in the morning. But that had been no recording, anyway. That music sounded exactly as it had while they were on the stage. As if plucked from time itself and relocated. "And you didn't … believe her," he said quietly.

"No!" Patrick nearly shouted. "Do you?"

We've all the time in the world. But your friends do not.

What had she meant by that?

Twenty-four hours ago, Mal would have laughed at the sort of nutter who'd even entertain the idea. Fae in the real world. Following a far-from-essential group of musicians all the way across the pond. And for what? For *fun*? "You know, Patch, nothing's really made sense to me since last night, when we were standing out in the rain. When we met that … tinker. I've been burned by a piano, hit with a flying saucer, dunked in red goo, and seen my own songs burn the air. Caitlin's declaring she's a supernatural being … well, that's practically something I can make sense of."

"We're all tired," said Patrick sourly. "It's gone three."

Mal rubbed his chin. "So she told you she was a …" He waved the words aside, unable to make himself say *fairy*. "So, maybe she's a nutter. But why were you so angry, Patch? I've never seen you like that."

"Because—" Patrick folded his arms. "I thought we were getting somewhere. You need a diagram?"

"Not good enough. Not for how pissed you were." He paused. "Fact was, you believed her."

Patrick leaned against the wall, half-turning away. He tensed up and became the mirror image of the young man who'd shown up in a doorway on Grafton, watching things from afar. He'd been dead and lost and found—all at once. And

70

so he was now, again. "I'm tired," he said. "It's been a long one."

Mal set a hand on his shoulder. Weariness was settling into his bones, too. "So don't answer me now. But this world's full of things we can't explain away. Maybe Caitlin's one of 'em."

A Radio in His Mind

Darkness buried Ciaran. He was surrounded by it, darkness and empti-ness. There were no dreams in this place. A high-pitched *brrring* rose, coming from a distance. Then it swirled around his face. He lashed out, swatting it like a mosquito—and connected.

Something splashed into his face.

Ciaran jerked up in his bed, instantly awake. Faint morning light streamed through the hotel curtains. A beer bottle from his nightstand dribbled the re-mains of warm ale into the carpet. But the sound was still there—a phone with a flashing light, ringing, ringing, *brrring.*

With another mighty shove, he knocked it off the nightstand, too, and the sound went away. The clock insisted it was 8:32, and he fell back against the pillow, exhausted. He wiped the remnants of stale beer from his face.

An hour from now they'd be on the road again. Off to … where? New York City?

Without glancing at the other side of the bed, he knew Sheerie was gone.

Sheerie. What's that short for? he'd asked.

For me to know and you to find out. And why is it taking you so long to disrobe?

Beyond that, he didn't recollect much of their evening together. There had been darkness and coolness and promises. There had been action and movement and nails and scent and exaltation and mouths. Twisting, he spotted red teeth imprints on his shoulder. He wondered what other ways she had marked her territory.

Blinking at the white, cracked hotel ceiling, Ciaran became aware of a throb-bing in his skull. His skin burned. His feet pricked with tiny stabbing jolts. He was all-over sore and smiled like a satisfied cat. Rising up on his elbows, he reached for a cigarette, but they were soaked with beer, too.

He ran his hand over her side of the bed, which was as smooth and empty as if it had never been touched. Of course, it had. If she'd been there right now with that ripe, round arse and small, pointed breasts, eyes boring into him again as if plumbing his soul, he'd be on her in a breath. She'd been very, very good; endlessly inventive and tireless. Between rounds he'd been the one stopping to catch his breath or gulp water. Sheerie never even broke a sweat. At least, so far as he could tell in all that inky blackness.

But there had been light. Just before exhaustion claimed him he'd seen her on a chair, opposite the bed. Not a stitch on, coated in blue moonlight. She'd had his hat tilted jauntily over one eye.

You'll do, she'd said, nipping at her forefinger.

Thinking about her got him going again, though the present sensation between his legs was nothing compared to the anticipation of seeing her later. She'd be in New York, he had no doubt. Ciaran reached under his sheets, figuring he had another couple minutes, might as well make them count—

Music!

A garble of notes and melodies and harmonies and phrases and, holy mother, *entire songs* flooded his head. It was as if a switch had been flipped. He had a radio in his mind, blasting with a set of songs that he knew—instinctively—had never been heard before. Sure, one echoed a tune he'd been fiddling around with for weeks, but the rest—fresh as a newborn. He concentrated on the songs and the notes slowed, spread out, revealed themselves. A complete and perfect song.

His song.

Ciaran vaulted out of the bed humming the main hook, knowing the key, the chords, the arrangement like a photo of his own face. He scrambled for the green spiral-bound notebook buried in his travel sack and yanked it open. Hotel pen in hand he began scribbling. The song—songs!—rolled from him like flames licking the page. Music rushed out so fast he could barely catch hold, but soon his hand was racing across the lined pages, and as each one filled he flipped to another and another, without a break.

After a few pages he tried willing the sounds to hold for just a moment— then backed up, plugging in a lyric here and there, a few words, placeholders to keep things together. Finally he topped everything off with guitar chords— funny how he'd started with piano notes, an instrument he'd never played well—

Like a door slamming shut, the music cut out.

The pen dropped from his limp fingers and he sagged against the chair. His hand felt dead but his arm burned with a fire that crawled up his shoulder. His head was full of air, his cheeks full of blood. Rising, he stumbled awkwardly against the bedsheets, mouth dry.

Someone knocked at the door. "C'mon there, C—time to get a move on."

Robin.

The clock now revealed it was 9:18. He'd been writing for nearly an hour and it had felt like minutes. Ciaran braced the notebook on his chest and ran his fingers over the pages, shaking his head at how finished each song looked. The staffs were orderly, notes round and filled in, words split where they needed to fit the music.

"Five," he croaked at Robin. "Gimme five."

Ciaran had never written a whole song before. Bits and pieces, riffs, maybe a bridge. That was not his territory. Maybe this was how it felt to be Patch—or Mal, especially—when building a tune. Did it come to them the same way? He grinned, covering his mouth, reading through the songs again. They were good—and they were all his. Sheerie had cracked open something inside him, something that had been waiting all this time.

Stretching once more, he threw himself into his clothes and his belongings into a duffle bag, then headed to the hallway. Robin had an ear up against Mal's door.

"Bad form." Ciaran wagged a finger. "Anyhow, you need a glass to get good sound."

Robin pounded on the door. "Mal, this ain't fair. We're gonna hit traffic. We gotta leave." Turning, he thumbed at Ciaran. "He's in there. Give it a go?"

"Aw, and here I thought you'd been promoted or something."

"Aw yerself." Robin frowned. "You got the feckin' key."

They all had keys to one another's rooms. Partly it was safety, part tradition—an "in case" thing. A *Do Not Disturb* sign meant what it said; otherwise, it was knock-and-enter at will. Even knowing that, the keys rarely went used.

Waving Robin off to the elevators, Ciaran clicked his way in. "Piano man," he crooned. "Make yerself decent." He pushed on the door, which swung open just enough to catch on something. Shoving harder, the door gave way—followed by a yelp.

Glancing around, Ciaran found the obstruction: Mal himself. He'd sunk down on his knees in front of the full-length mirror that hung on each room's wall just outside the toilet. He was staring wide-eyed at his own reflection, then half-turned at Ciaran's entrance. His mouth gaped.

Then, so did Ciaran's.

Mal's hair was gone.

Beyond the Strange, Pale Wonder

The front of the bus was quiet as a library. From time to time the driver's CB radio crackled with static, but since pulling away from the hotel in Boston, no one had spoken.

Mal stared out the bus's wide front window, watching the white highway dashes slide beneath them like an indecipherable code. A wheel inside his head felt like it had gone on overdrive and thoughts jumped from Caitlin to Patrick to Ciaran to the inescapable fact that he *no longer had any hair.*

First thing that morning, he'd woken with an odd chill on his head but hadn't given it much thought. The night had been a long and very strange one, and he kept running scenes through his memory. *I met one of the fey,* had been his first thought. The second had been: *The world hates me.* The pads of his fingers no longer felt burned, but when he'd looked at them they were smooth and unlined. He had no fingerprints.

So he'd packed, dressed and headed to the toilet to get cleaned up, passing by the mirror. Peeling off the red wool cap, he hadn't known what he was even seeing at first—it looked like a child had taken safety scissors to his scalp. Not skull-bald, but with clumps of too-short hair clinging amid a wasteland of nothing.

His legs had gone soft and he sank to the floor, unable to move until Ciaran barged in.

Ciaran found it all hilarious. "You musta gotten *ossified*, my man. You let the VIP girls do this to you, or what?"

The words felt like a lone cackle coming from the back of a room. Mal had jumped up and blasted him, letting Ciaran have every ounce of fear and fury he'd bottled up inside since yesterday. But instead of slipping away or yelling back or offering condolences, Ciaran stared out the window until Mal had spent himself.

Then he'd chirped, "Wrote me a song this morning."

"And why should I give a glowing shit about that?" Mal shouted back.

They hadn't spoken since. The moment they'd clambered on the tour bus together—Patrick was already there, always the first in the ride no matter how late the night, as if he feared being left behind—Ciaran had stomped off to the back and shut the dividing door.

Patrick did a double-take straight out of a classic comedy once he spied Mal.

"Not a word," Mal had snapped.

So now no one was talking to anyone.

Music drifted from the back of the bus. It was big and comfortable enough for them to sleep in, with a living space and tiny kitchen up front, a sleeping section in the center of stacked bunks like coffins, and a separate private back area that could be closed off from the rest of the ride. It was more than they needed most of the time—just the three of them rattling around with a driver—but the record company had hired a separate RV for the equipment, roadies, and other hired hands. Now that he was their road manager, Robin could have chosen to join them on the main bus, but he'd gone to the other vehicle. Familiar territory. Besides, who'd want to be riding with a bunch of sullen mummies?

The notes came haltingly from the back, then clearer and smoother, like someone learning a song for the first time. *Wrote me a song this morning*, Ciaran said. Was this it? And by the way, when was the last time Ciaran wrote *anything*?

Mal had been too preoccupied earlier to ask or offer congratulations. He ought to go back there and hear this new creation, tell Ciaran his baby was beautiful. But losing 99 percent of his hair in a matter of hours had taken it out of Mal, and he couldn't summon the energy. The hits kept coming and he didn't know how to dodge them. *The world hates me*, he thought again, continuing to stare at the passing scenery. Nothing changed now that they were out of the city; they were hurtling through tunnels of trees, green metallic signs, and rest stops.

He caught Patrick staring at him in the window reflection and sighed. "Go ahead. Ask."

Patrick leaned forward on his knees. "All right. What'cha do that to yer head for?"

Mal made a soft choking noise. "You think this was *voluntary*?"

He shrugged. "Maybe you wanted to make a point."

The spinning slowed, then sped up again in his mind. "You really think I shaved off all my hair because I want you to believe that we met a supernatural being last night."

Patrick grunted. "Never thought you'd get conned so easy. The lady does tricks. Any good magician can—"

"Play our own show back to us?" Mal tapped his travel sack. "When the only copies are right here with me? And play it with no speakers? No sound system?" He paused, breathless. "Oh, and I almost forgot—make the room rain fireflies at the same time?"

"Illusions. Somethin' in our beers. There's always explanations."

Mal nodded. "There are. Just not the ones you wanna hear."

Patrick sighed. "Stories like hers ruined my family. Made Herself insane, actin' like I was some kind of *creature* instead of her kid. *Athair* didn't help, fillin' my head with his 'stories,' but at least he didn't come after me every damned day with a *stick*."

They'd never talked about this, never gone deep about the rot in Patrick's home. All Mal knew was he'd had a lot of freedom to roam, and ultimately that had led him to a monastery school. Mal and Ciaran had seen firsthand what kind of person his *máthair* was after he'd disappeared—but they'd never heard in detail what went wrong. "I'm sorry, Patch. I didn't know."

"Didn't ask, did ye?" Patrick grabbed a beer from the small refrigerator, taking a deep swig. "Never asked." He paused, staring out the window, face slack. "She asked. She wanted the long version."

Mal watched him sway with the rhythm of the bus. "We play onstage together every night. You know there's something to all that. The way we connect. The way I get caught up. Like we're there, but we're not there. I think there's a whole world—or worlds—we don't know about. That we just barely skate past with each show. I think you know it, too. What's happening to us right now is beyond the strange, pale wonder we see every night—I agree with you there. But … what's so wrong with considering that what she said might have truth in it?"

"You weren't raised by a crazy woman." Patrick's voice was low and angry. "Ain't right to live in a filthy house covered in milk an' food she won't pick up, acting like little invisible people were watchin' every move, thinkin' that …"

"G'wan," Mal said softly.

"That there was some other place y'might go to where things were better." He hesitated. "The monks thought that. They called it Heaven. *Athair* told me that, too. But he showed me … worn-up places." His eyes lit up. "Bright spots that shouldn't be there in the world. But he never took me. Maybe he took himself. But he never took me away. Never made me safe."

Mal's throat constricted. Patrick was like a raw wound this morning. Caitlin had frightened him, sure, but she'd yanked away some kind of emotional scab.

Encountering Padraig all those years ago had been to meet someone outside Mal's experience. His parents worked; he went to schools where Irish was starting to get a toehold again, since it was faddish and a little rebellious—if not very useful. Along the way, he and Ciaran had picked up history and patriotism lessons. But whatever couldn't be found in textbooks or rationalized away had been ignored by Mal's school. Old and crinkled things that lived on the edges of life, breathed by the land since the days of legends—those were children's tales. Enlightened minds were embarrassed by their existence. Over in America they'd put a leprechaun on a sugary cereal box as a mascot. The old ways were a joke.

But Padraig was different. He'd eye a spiraling circle of leaves and debris outside a building and wish it well. It was the *sidhe* dancing, he'd say: "They weren't pleased you didn't bless them. But next time you'll know better."

The first time that had happened, Mal had elbowed Ciaran to keep him from laughing. Mal had liked Padraig's odd touches; it was like getting a glimpse through a portal, beyond which lay shadowed, unknowable things. As they grew older, the stories had faded, though part of Mal wanted to believe those old tales had once been possible. Then Patrick had come back from the monastery as a different person: burning to make music but no longer entertaining fantasies.

"I'm sorry—" Mal began now.

Patrick frowned. "Do *not* pity me."

Mal nodded. "The thing is, I've decided to assume that Caitlin is *not* a lunatic."

Patrick fell back into his seat. "Then we've got nothin' to talk about."

"We have to." Mal suppressed a quaver in his voice. He felt fragile and exhausted. The weird things that had happened were making him timid, and he did not want to give in to fear. He held on to Caitlin's return and thread of an explanation like a lifeline. "Humor me," he said, and it sounded like begging.

Patrick wouldn't look at him. "You wanna act like this has something to do with … that *woman*. And it doesn't. If it did, then why would she bother with me?"

"You felt bothered?"

Patrick didn't answer.

"Look, I don't know how *sidhe* work."

He ground his teeth. "Santa Claus doesn't exist. Neither do fairies."

"Once you thought they did."

"For the last bleeding time, Malachi, *shut it*." Patrick turned to stare out the window.

When Padraig had returned to them as Patrick, he'd come stripped of his sense of wonder. No more bowing or special wishes or rituals. At the time, Mal hadn't cared; they weren't children any longer, and such behavior felt like an oddness too far. But not until this exact moment did Mal have a full sense of what was lost when Padraig became Patrick. Whatever portal there may have been was latched shut—and the only person with a key to open it again now acted as if it had never existed. It left Mal feeling they were vulnerable against forces they did not understand, forces that were invisibly massing around them.

Somewhere in Connecticut, the bus driver pulled into a rest stop for a leg stretch and a coffee. The others joined him for fresh air and—in Ciaran's case—a smoke.

Mal stayed inside. With Ciaran and Patch keeping their distance, he decided to listen to some of their old shows. Pulling out his travel bag, he withdrew a padded case of cassettes. As keeper of their concerts, he had several hundred tapes back home of their shows for both posterity and use as learning tools; since arriving in America he'd collected another twenty or so, all cut directly from the soundboard feed.

Selecting the Boston recording, he popped the cassette into his Walkman and rested the earphones on his head, over the cap. Settling back, he closed his eyes and smiled at the first crackle and snap of the feed being turned on. Next came the white noise of the audience, punctuated by an occasional whistle. But that went on for a strange, long span. Mal strained for his piano introduction. They usually began—and had the night before—in darkness as he ran out the first bars of their opening tune. Nothing. No melody, no keyboard, nothing. Just audience. He boosted the volume—it wasn't muffled, it just wasn't there.

Then Ciaran's guitar blasted the room awake and Mal nearly dropped the Walkman, hurriedly turning down the sound. Patch's bass, Robin's drums all slid in as expected for the first tune. But there was no piano backbone to the song. Just rhythm and guitar, the flesh and the meat. No vocals, either—at least not his own. Patch and Ciaran alternated with backgrounds, which came in clear and focused; Ciaran was even slightly off-key. But Mal—it was as if he'd never come onstage. He was gone from the tune, gone from the band.

Erased, he thought.

He fast-forwarded, but each song was the same. He tried a second show, then another with increasing frenzy. He just wasn't there anymore. This was a band touring with two members and a hired drummer. So he popped a store-bought tape—Prefab Sprout's *From Langley Park to Memphis*—into the player and "Nightingales" started up in his headset. Paddy McAloon's voice came through whispery and true. He shut off the machine, staring at it with a glazed expression.

Mal knew in that moment that if he phoned Dublin and asked someone to check his collection, each one of those saved tapes would be absent a singer and piano player.

Heart thudding, he tried gulping air, driving down a panic attack. Nausea swelled in his gut, and he jumped up, racing to the tiny bus toilet. Leaning on the sink, he stared into the mirror. A shadowy-eyed man with a ravaged head wearing a ridiculous red knit cap stared back at him. Mal yanked off the cap, turned to the ceiling, and let out a howl that went on and on until he had no more breath and his throat felt as if he'd swallowed sandpaper.

"Let me be," he whispered into his closed fists. "Let me *be*."

Nothing happened.

After a time, he used tissue to clean off his face and blow his nose. There was nothing more to be done. He rooted around in his toiletries kit until he came upon his razor. Taking the blade to his scalp he scraped and washed and scraped again until the planes of his skull were as smooth and unblemished as a newborn's.

79

Another Man of Rhythm

New York City

For the next two days, they were ghosts to one another. The bus pulled into New York City and except for required press interactions and soundchecks, they were strangers who didn't speak. Patrick hated it but had no idea how to break ice this thick.

Onstage at the Palladium shows, though—it was a different story. Competitive anger flowed between Mal and Ciaran as they ran through the set list with vigor that was bracing and terrifying at the same time. Ciaran had stepped up his game, shoving aside show protocol with boisterous, almost frantic performances. Their guitarist attacked his instrument with a fervor that literally drove him to his knees—and then he'd leap up again like a panther, a commanding, intense light burning in his eyes. He looked different since coming to New York, as if he were being re-drawn: Those big cheekbones and jaw were more prominent than ever as they pushed through song after song.

Mal struggled to keep up, Patrick noticed. Usually he was the powerful heart of any performance, alternately gabbing with the audience and wringing himself out behind the keys—but Ciaran had grabbed the lead now, and Patrick knew to get out of the way. He stepped back from the shows, keeping the rhythm steady and leaning into Robin at the kit. It was like trying to dance in the midst of a cudgel fight. Easier to watch the night unspool with wonder, his heart bursting with a combination of awe and pride. He might not be a major player for these shows, but Patrick was part of *this* band in *this* moment, and by

80

Christ they had their shit together onstage. Both nights, they crushed their set list and beyond, playing for nearly three hours.

Then the shows ended, and they returned to their corners. Each night, the rapturous applause died away and the audience went home and all they were left with were aching muscles and a blasted, hollowed-out sensation. Patrick hoped they'd kick back post-show with a pint as they'd done so often before, maybe meet some of the locals and turn it all into a good exhaustion—but after their traditional backstage huddle both nights, they fell apart, with little to say.

The second night, Patrick tugged at Mal's sleeve as he headed out of the dressing room door, but Mal jerked away.

"Bear with," he muttered. "Best to keep apart. Bit of an … experiment."

Before Patrick could even answer, Mal slipped into a group of record company executives for a chat. He tried next with Ciaran, who was sitting at a table with the ever-present Sheerie, and tried to kick up a conversation. But Ciaran just stood, gave him a solid slap on the back that jarred his organs, and walked out of the venue with his girl. Sheerie glanced once, briefly, over her shoulder at Patrick—then went back to ignoring him.

Defeated, Patrick was gathering his belongings to head back to the hotel when someone tapped his shoulder. Suzanne, their bright penny of a person from the record label's PR department, hopped over with a tousled-looking man in tow. A bit older than Patrick, more full in the chest than Ciaran, the man wore a tattered black T-shirt and an unshaven face.

He's a muso, Patrick predicted.

"Tom O'Doyle," the newcomer said, giving Patrick a firm handshake. American accent, Irish face and name. "Any chance we're related? My granddad hailed from Mayo."

Patrick hesitated. He was delighted to have been sought out specifically, but why did every American think he'd *know* some random person back home with a similar last name? "Er—"

"Ah, I'm fuckin' with you." Tom grinned. "I mean, he did, but you must get that everyplace you land."

Patrick laughed, and it felt good. He liked Tom immediately.

"Tom's in a local group," Suzanne said. "They've got a residency in midtown. Thought you two might have a few things in common." Having done her duty, she vanished into the crowd.

Tom laughed, a full, rich sound. "Right to the point. We do a little a'this, a little a'that. Mostly I drum. Bodhran if it calls for it. Not half as good as your singer on that one, though. Anyhow. Good to meet another man of rhythm. And that mandolin of yours—nice touch you have on it."

They were quickly off and talking like old friends, something Patrick was thirsty for. Tom had many kind and insightful things to say about Patrick's band, not just the live shows he'd attended, but about the intricacies of their tunes. He spoke with the knowledge of a man who'd parsed their catalog closely.

They ended up at the bar to drink foamy pints of beer, and weights dropped from Patrick's shoulders. It was good to speak with someone again, to focus on tangible pleasures like chord changes and fingering and not to have to think about impossible, ridiculous things. Tom lived in Brooklyn with a cat and a most-of-the-time girlfriend in an undeveloped, unzoned empty warehouse. He and the guys could use the whole floor to rehearse in, if you didn't care about shitty acoustics. He'd been at it about fifteen years and understood the practical facts: At this stage, he was never going to be the next Larry Mullen, and his group was never going to approach U2. He'd always have a day job—music teacher surfing from school to school—and that was all right. He got paid to make music. Most didn't come half so close.

"I even got a groupie, kind of." He laughed. "Marlene—that's my girl—she comes out and whoops it up at every show, right up front. That gets everyone else going. You know what that's like, having somebody in your corner. Makes everything else easier."

Patrick recalled his afternoon on Boston Common, with Caitlin. She hadn't been a groupie; she was a peer. But even that wasn't the right word. She'd been so much *more* than that. Caitlin had reminded him what it was like to be bound to a person in the moments you were making music together. He missed her with an ache that resembled hunger. Their time together had been unnerving and cut short—but it had come with moments of bliss like … well, like fireflies in a hotel room. He'd felt seen with her, right until the moment it became impossible to have her around. Three days on, he wondered if she ever was going to fulfill her promise to return.

Then he wondered at his wondering.

The night slipped into morning, and the venue around them changed into an after-hours dance club. Rippling bass pounded from the speakers as Donna Summer began feeling love, and it became impossible for Patrick and Tom to hear one another. They slipped out a back entrance, and Tom shook Patrick's hand, offering up a business card.

"I know you're all slippin' out of here day after tomorrow," he said. "But if you got a few spare minutes, we soundcheck for Friday's show 'round five. We've even got a mandy, like you call it. It'd be great to have you in even if it's just for shitting around before the place opens up."

Patrick held back a smile; bands with business cards were a marvelous *only in America* moment. Music did that, pulled people to you and pushed you toward others. Happened all the time at home but not so much here in America, not until now. Patrick had never played with any band other than his own, and felt a tingling thrill at giving it a go.

"I'll be there," he told Tom.

That Kind of Luck

*C*iaran was pacing.

Up and down the venue's interior, guitar slung across his back, gnawing on a cuticle. Onstage, Mal was noodling through the piano's keys, absorbed and content. Ciaran was neither.

Sheerie was late. No one knew where she was.

"Sorry, man," said their soundman. "Don't know who you're talkin' about. Only lady I've seen's the one in the coat check—"

"Piss off," Ciaran growled and paced again. He perked up as two busboys approached the bar with fresh glasses. "Hey. You two."

They took a step back as he bore down on them.

"Seen a woman about this high, long black hair—" Their round-eyed stares were so blank he wondered if he'd slipped into the wrong language. "Ah, you feck off, too."

Back to pacing.

Ciaran's life had shrunk to two things over the last few days: Sheerie and music. All else felt washed out and lifeless—food, interviews, even the shows. He had memories of concerts from the past two nights, of taking the stage and working himself into a frenzy, but they seemed to be someone else's experience. Even when he was onstage the only thing he wanted was to be elsewhere—fucking, writing. Both of those things provided a similar sensation—that of warm arms encircling his body, holding him deliciously close. Maybe it was a bit restrictive, but it was an embrace he'd leaned into without question. Giving in was so easy.

Sheerie wasn't the only one who was late.

"Where is the *fear gan ainm*?" he called to Mal. "We were supposed to check twenty minutes ago."

The noodling continued. "Your guess's as good as mine," said Mal, distracted. "He'll be here." He paused in playing. "And by the way, how 'bout droppin' that particular nickname? It's not as cute as you think it is."

"*Bíodh an diabhal agat*," Ciaran swore at him. *Go to hell.*

"Think I'm there a few steps ahead of you," Mal said, picking up the tune again.

Ciaran didn't ask what that meant, didn't want to know.

He'd been so busy since leaving Boston. Writing took up almost every moment of his time; not writing meant the radio in his head kept playing the same tune over and over until he transcribed it. The only times the volume turned down were when he was with Sheerie or playing onstage. He had no time to think clearly and certainly none to attend to daily tasks—Ciaran couldn't recall the last time he'd brushed his teeth, taken a shower, had a meal, or talked with someone other than Sheerie for more than a few moments.

Yet he wasn't hungry. He didn't miss being social. He had *her*. He'd sit at his hotel desk and she'd bring him glasses of water or alcohol or things so foul he would spit them onto the wall and have to shovel water from the bathroom tap directly into his mouth while she rolled with laughter on the bed sheets. He didn't even have time to be angry because the music screamed at him. He'd run out of paper once and began writing on any surface that would take ink. Half a song now decorated his room's wall, another half he'd written out on a wrinkled white shirt. The music *insisted*. He could only obey.

Having music pour out of him was new, frightening, and addictive. Before this, the best he'd ever done was a handful of half-realized tunes the band occasionally knocked around during soundcheck or rehearsal, but they'd never flowered. He'd added lyrics here and there into some of Mal's cannily-constructed songs over the years, but he was no wordsmith, either. Ciaran was full of riffs, phrases, bobs and bits—ingredients, no recipe.

But these days he woke at first light with a fevered brain, jumping to the desk afire with a new melody or chorus or lyrics. He'd write until he fell across his arms into a hard black sleep without dreams. When he woke, it started over again. At times, he could push the music back into a low, persistent thrum—like if he had to be at soundcheck or onstage, but otherwise, it was like trying to drink from a fire hose. The music was an imperative, begging for life.

Was he enjoying himself? No time to consider.

Beneath all of it was a growing, gnawing guilt. Like he was cheating, using Mal's test answers at school again. Like these songs weren't really his after all.

He watched as Mal dutifully walked through his part of the soundcheck. His eyes were closed and he leaned back on his stool, fingers finding their marks with unerring rightness. He'd always been like that. Music came from deep within him, a well that never ran dry.

Ciaran thought about how music was coming to *him*. How he hadn't learned to draw it out in dipperfuls. But he would. Maybe the music wasn't really his right now, but he'd figure it out. He always had.

Or—he'd make Mal show him the way.

Like he had last time.

Music class. Age six.

Ciaran and Mal had been virtual strangers that day they were paired at the school piano to test for skill level. He'd sat with this perfect little blond boy alongside him, a boy who already read books without pictures, who always made the *múinteoir* smile, who had never annoyed anyone in his entire life.

Ciaran had hated him on principle.

What Ciaran could do was sing. Had been doing it since he could talk. Sang at parties, sang at wakes, sang the minute anybody asked. What he hadn't learned was an instrument—Ma and Da liked music off the radio or telly but never made it themselves. It wasn't part of the life of his chaotic house, so they didn't know what to do with a singing boy.

On test day, Ciaran took first turn at the piano and banged out tortured note combinations far too loudly until the *múinteoir* ordered, "Enough."

Mal went next, playing without waiting for a say-so, following none of the notes on the page. He buried himself in a song he was making up as he went along. As Ciaran watched, the perfect blond boy disappeared, his carefully-pomaded hair breaking into strands that fell over his forehead. Mal's notes came furious and fast, establishing a pattern but never completing a tune. Even at that young age, Mal was already the best piano player anyone had seen in the school. Probably in the entire county.

Ciaran had never seen someone who was the best at anything before.

At last, the *múinteoir* came up behind Mal and set a gentle hand on his shoulder. "Thank you," she said with genuine feeling. Ciaran's cheeks burned. "We will have a different spot for you, Malachi," she added, then moved on to another student.

Mal scanned the room as if he didn't quite know where he was.

Showoff, thought Ciaran, and as soon as the teacher's back was turned, he shoved Mal so hard the boy tumbled off the piano bench. He hit the floor with a dull thud, and the other students tittered. Ciaran did not feel better, though. He was still a crap piano player. He was crap on *every* instrument at that point. He was six, for Christ's sake.

He leaned over to where the blond boy was rubbing his knees. To his credit, he wasn't crying out and didn't run for help. Mal looked up at Ciaran with wide, moist eyes.

"Show me how to do that," Ciaran insisted in a low, quiet voice. "You show me how."

He expected the boy to go sob in a corner, but that wasn't Mal. He slid back on the piano bench and curled his hands over the keys. "Start like this." He sniffled once. "Hands go here."

Ciaran had respected that. Mal didn't look like much, but he was tough. He was no *piteog*. Mal made the music dance; even at six, he could bend it to his will. And all these years later, he was still doing it.

The venue's door slammed open and Patrick strode in. He jogged to the stage, taking the steps two at a time, cheeks flushed, humming a tune.

"Well," he told Mal. "What're we waitin' fer?"

"You, I reckon," said Mal as Ciaran pulled himself on the stage.

"It speaks!" Patrick cried.

"Never stopped."

"*Cacamas*," Patrick swore. "You two've been ghosts."

Ciaran checked the tuning on his guitar. He didn't disagree, but he was on a roll. They'd have eight albums of material—more!—before he was done. If that meant he had to disappear for a few days, the others would survive.

"How's the 'experiment' going?" Patrick asked Mal.

"Nearly done. Just one more thing. Tonight's a lottery draw."

Ciaran perked up. "Lottery?"

"It's about luck," said Mal. "I've been on one kind of streak, while Patch here's gone in the other direction. So … I'm testing it tonight."

"You're off your head," said Patrick.

"Nobody's got that kind of luck." Ciaran nodded.

"Well," said Mal, "we're about to find out."

All That Glitters

After soundcheck they located a small television by the Palladium's long bar and sidled up before it, each slurping down a bottle of beer while they waited. A half hour earlier, Patrick had sprinted to a corner store to put his money on a single lottery ticket—Mal was specific, it had to be Patrick's money—and returned with a series of numbers printed on a rectangle of paper that resembled a store receipt.

"That's it, then," said Mal. He pulled a second ticket from his pocket and set it under his beer bottle. "So. I'll explain a bit."

Patrick almost didn't care what the reasoning was; the others were speaking with him again, and that was good enough for now. "G'wan."

"Seems to me you hit a run of good luck around the same time as I hit the skids," said Mal. He pointed to Patch's busking success on Boston Common, the seat at the restaurant, the tab that came to exactly what Patch and Caitlin had earned. "And, of course, meeting the young lady herself. Then—my piano. The drinks that went flying. They should've hit you, Patch. That's how physics works. Instead … anyhow, that sealed it."

But the last few days had been quiet. Mal had kept his distance from Patrick, saying there might be a connection between them, like an invisible beam keeping things in balance. So now they had to experiment.

"It's superstition," said Patrick, hearing *stupid-stition*. "Like footie players who never change their socks."

"No, it's proper science." Mal was resolute. "If I'm right, you'll have just made your fortune, buying that ticket."

"And if you're wrong?" Ciaran tipped his beer bottle back, swallowing.

"I'll need protection from busboys and trays of glasses."

"Or, nothin'll happen and we can go back to whatever looks like normal." Ciaran raised his substantial eyebrows.

"Wouldn't mind a bit of normal." Mal sighed.

"I thought normal was boring," said Patrick. "Safe."

Mal shrugged. "Maybe I'm goin' at this all wrong. But there's an answer here and I'm gonna logic it out if it breaks me."

Patrick turned to the television set, which was airing a game show. He wasn't sure how he felt about all this. He didn't feel very lucky, and what was luck, anyhow? It sure wasn't something a person *was;* it was happenstance. Random. And it didn't show up just because a nutter claiming to be a *fairy* made it happen.

Athair would have felt differently. So would Herself.

Patrick refused to think about them. Instead, he flickered back to the dimly-lit bar called Kennedy's near Grand Central Terminal. Tom O'Doyle's invitation to play had been a lifeline these last few days. Neither Mal nor Ciaran had picked up their phone or answered their door, so between gigs, Patrick had been left to his own devices. At first, he'd taken to wandering the city, losing himself in Central Park or riding the ferry between Manhattan and Staten Island. But then he found Tom's business card in his pocket and realized he knew one person of substance in this city. Patrick began popping into Tom's band's soundcheck for the last two afternoons, and he'd been welcomed easily. Their brief bursts of camaraderie had warmed Patrick's soul—even as guilt threaded through him for playing with musicians who weren't Mal or Ciaran.

Hanging out with Tom's band also meant he could push away the alien awkwardness that had sprouted between him and his actual bandmates. His friends had turned strange, and he worried they were becoming strangers. Patrick felt poised in an uncertain limbo where he was waiting between lightning and thunder.

At least now Mal was speaking with him again. He'd asked for the lottery ticket, and Patrick had jumped to fetch it, surprised at the thrill that had run through him when making the purchase. *What if I win?* he'd wondered. *What if I'm ... lucky?*

Patrick had never wished for anything as random as luck. But in that moment, he'd thought of Caitlin. How she'd made him feel lucky. When she'd been with him, life made sense. The sun had shone brighter, the breeze blew fresh, colors exploded with life. When they'd been together, it was as if he'd stepped into a movie starring himself. Except then she'd gone and spoiled everything. Too much ... *not possible* at once. Now, though, he yearned for that special feeling again, as if the world was there for him and not just in spite of him.

Ciaran lifted his head from a notebook he'd been scribbling in and gestured at the TV word puzzle. "Easy one. 'All that glitters is not gold.'"

"Thanks much," said Mal. "I was still guessing."

"You think there's a chance?" Patrick asked him.

Mal grimaced and took another drink. He was putting a good face on it all, but it was just that—a mask. Patrick could see him clinging to this half-baked idea because he had no other good ones, and didn't know what to say.

Ciaran scraped back his barstool and leapt to his feet, hitching up his trousers. A smile split his face as he jogged to the far end of the bar seconds before Sheerie walked in the room. It was as if he could sense her. They embraced, and Patrick wanted to laugh—he was so tall and she so short—but the sound died in his throat. Her arrival had lowered the temperature in the room ten degrees, and Patrick felt uneasy.

Ciaran led her to the bar. "You three oughta officially meet," he said, wrapping his arms around her protectively.

Patrick doubted that Sheerie needed protection from anyone. Yet as he got a good look at her, he noted how she had changed. She wasn't precisely the same pale, ephemeral woman he'd met in Boston. She somehow was more *here* now, her presence solid as a brick wall. As if she'd been unwell before and now had returned to full health. Ciaran, on the other hand, must have caught whatever she had in Boston—despite his beaming smile, the roses in his cheeks were gone.

"You're late," Ciaran said, dipping his face against her neck.

Most of her kind use pseudonyms, Caitlin had said.

Patrick had heard it one way in Boston. Now it resonated differently. *Her kind?*

"I'm never late," Sheerie purred.

The mention of "lottery" pulled Patrick back to the TV set and they stood in silence as the balls went tumbling. Eight spat out, rolling down a long tube. The hostess read the winning combination aloud.

"I lost," Patrick murmured. "Those aren't the numbers."

Mal sighed, then chuckled in a dark, slow way. "Same here. So, experiment concluded. No luck for you. Guess Caitlin's just another freak you met on the road. I concede. Still, she does do some very pretty tricks, you got to admit. Me, I must be just accident-prone."

Patrick did not feel vindicated. He felt … sad. It was as if a black hole had opened before him, and once again his life was ordinary as ever.

Ciaran cleared his throat. "So like I was saying. This is Sheerie. Sheerie, meet Mal and—"

She offered her hand, but only to Patrick. "Yes, we nearly met once. Padraig, I believe? That is the name you're using?" She set her fingers against his and for a moment he couldn't breathe. He was sinking into that black hole. When she released him, Ciaran was laughing gently.

Patrick gasped.

"Yeah, she has that effect on a person," Ciaran said. "An' it's Patrick these days, darlin'. Though it's cute you know his old one."

Nothing she does is cute, Patrick thought. *It's a good imitation of cute, but she's fake through and through.*

Silence drew out between them, and she did not offer her hand to Mal.

"Anyhow," Ciaran said with a bit too much shine in his voice, "I think you both know she's been with me for the past couple of days, and it's not making any sense for her to have to get from city to city on her own when we have this huge bus."

A moment of silence. Then Mal sat up straight. "No feckin' way."

"I'm looking forward to joining you." Sheerie smiled as if Mal had not spoken.

It was an audacious suggestion. Not even that; it was a declaration. Strangers did not come on the bus. Women did not come on the bus. The bus was an inner sanctum; having an unknown walking around was like inviting them into your bedroom. Roadies and Robin were one thing, but even close friends were not invited up for more than a quick drink, if that.

Patrick could feel Mal steaming up a head of reasons to object, so he leaned over. "It's all right," he said, using Irish so she wouldn't overhear. "Let her come."

Mal coughed. "You're joking."

"Look," he told Mal. "She don't come with us, maybe he ends up in a rental car or something more stupid."

"C'mon, they hardly know each other. He's not gonna throw things over on her account."

They glanced at the couple. Ciaran was gently massaging Sheerie's shoulders. Her head had tipped forward, a curtain of hair obscuring her expression.

"You wanna test that?" Patrick murmured. "I don't know if we come out good if we test him."

"She gives me the shivers," said Mal.

Patrick couldn't say why he was so certain about this. But seeing Sheerie with Ciaran unsettled him. The pair of them were like bruised fruit just before it went rotten. He wanted to keep an eye on her, and by extension, Ciaran. Just for a few days. Then they'd be home again—and surely she wouldn't be coming to Dublin. But there was more to it. The moment his hand had touched Sheerie's, Patrick had felt that dark chasm open in front of him. The next moment, he wished only to be pulled away from it—by Caitlin. She'd said she would return. And if she did, he wanted to make sure *she* would have room on the bus, too. There was some strange shit stirring around them again, and Caitlin might just know a few things.

You aren't ready, she'd said.

He was now.

A Distant Circle of Light

Mal bounded off the stage, euphoric. They'd done it, played three shows in the big American city, each performance more electric than the last. They were, in record company parlance, *red hot*. The after-show gathering was packed with producers, other musicians, and executives all clamoring to offer drinks and give them pats on the shoulder. There was talk of having the band return for *Saturday Night Live* before the tour ended. Offers of shared projects rained on Mal's head until he felt that maybe, actually, they had won the lottery—just not the one they'd bought a ticket for.

During the post-show revelry, Patrick introduced his new pal Tom, and the three of them congregated in a corner with Mal on the pennywhistle, Patrick on the mandy, and Tom beating out a rhythm on a table. But they weren't left alone for long; Suzanne brought over the label president and the impromptu *seisún* ended abruptly with promises to do it properly sometime soon.

By the time Mal finished glad-handing the president—*why'd he wear a tie to a rock concert?*—he was sapped, post-show adrenaline replaced by exhaustion. Three back-to-back shows was not easy, and he was looking forward to a travel day with no performance at the end of it. If nothing else, his throat could use a break.

He ended up in his hotel room at half-two, hoping for a good night's rest. Sleep had been elusive since he'd arrived in New York; he'd been on alert for the next strange, impossible thing coming for him. His few sleeping hours had been populated with scenes Bosch would have appreciated—fiery pits and tortured faces, skewered animals and poisoned landscapes. And himself, bound and gagged and forced to sit in a corner while the world burned around him.

He shuffled into the bathroom and flipped on the light, surprised anew at the person in the mirror. Hard to believe he'd turned into this echo of himself in less than a week. Touching the red wool hat on his head—there now as much for warmth as amusement—he smoothed it down. It was comforting. It made him feel lighter. But he was so far down in the depths of himself it was like peering up from a deep hole at a distant circle of light.

Mal blinked, realizing he'd dozed while standing up.

If only they'd won. The money was one thing; it would have been life-changing, but the fact of winning would have been proof that Caitlin had turned Patrick into some kind of luck charm. That there really had been something to her very odd pronouncements. That it hadn't just been sleight of hand, what she'd done in that Boston hotel room.

Luck charm. A gear turned in his head. Money. They never had enough—but Patrick always had something. And he offered it to whoever came along. *Always should give to those folk*, Caitlin had said.

Those folk.

All at once, he didn't think she was referring to the homeless. She'd meant the red man. The *fear dearg*. Mal called up Patch's room. Four, five rings. He'd be asleep by now, unless he'd found another chance to make music with Tom. Solid fella, that one.

The phone picked up on the sixth ring. "This had better be good," Patrick mumbled.

"You never told me what you knew," said Mal, sitting on the bed.

Silence.

"About the red man. The *fear dearg*."

"Mph." He could hear Patrick sitting up, the sheets shifting. "Why ask me?"

Mal let the question go unanswered.

A long pause, then: "Prankster. Really bad practical jokes. Takes babies. Brings changelings. All sorts of old shite. Wears a lot of …" A pause. "Red."

Silence.

"Any idea how a person …" Mal couldn't believe he was saying this, but at nearly three in the morning all things were possible, "gets rid of one?"

The quiet had a different quality now; he could almost hear Patrick seething on the other end. "I'm not yer feckin' *resource*," he said at last. "I don't believe in any of this."

"Yes, you do," Mal said quietly. "And so do I."

Patrick hung up.

I'd watch yourself, she'd said. *Fear dearg's been spotted 'round these parts.*

Mal was dancing on the edge of something, an answer so big it hurt to think of it. He'd save it for tomorrow. It'd be easier to talk about it in the daylight. He kicked his sandals into a corner and whipped the bed sheets back.

The bed … wobbled. Just a bit. Mal froze, and the bed held still again.

Shouldn't've had that third Guinness.

Or maybe it wasn't about how drunk he was. For a moment, Mal considered peering beneath the bed's legs, looking for a monster in the underneath.

He chuckled at himself. *Soon you're gonna expect kelpies in the bath.*

With a shake of his head and a tug on his red cap, Mal hurled himself into the soft whiteness of the sheets. He was unconscious before he sank all the way into the pillow, wearing a small smile.

Then he fell.

À Đỏ

For he comes, the human child,
To the waters and the wild
With a faery, hand in hand,
from a world more full of weeping than you can understand.

—W. B. Yeats, "The Stolen Child"

Gnawed Through by the Tiniest of Teeth

New York City, Still

The door to Mal's room clicked open and Ciaran pulled back his key card. Pushing the door in, he twitched his nose at the stale, stagnant odor that wafted out.

Mal was alone, propped up on a mattress and box spring that rested on the floor, awake but not quite *present*. His blue eyes stared glassily at a muted soap opera on the television, and a mass of sheets and duvet curled around him like a snow bank. He'd been like this for nearly four days, with no sign of improvement.

The news, when it had been new, had been amusing. Ciaran had snickered: *The bed collapsed? What in hells was he doing ... and with whom?*

Robin had brought the update personally to Ciaran's room four mornings ago, gazing uneasily at his walls and bed linens, pretending not to notice that they were covered in musical notations. Their drummer/road manager had kept on point, ignoring more sheets piled in a corner also covered in ink, and stuck with the news about Mal.

As Robin had explained, when Mal hadn't answered either the phone or his door that morning, he'd gotten a passing cleaning lady to click the room open—and found Mal buried beneath his own mattress and bed, unable to move. The bed's legs lay scattered around the room, gnawed through by the tiniest of teeth. It was both comical and ghastly. Wanting to keep it out of the news, Robin had summoned a private doctor, who couldn't understand it either; Mal was bruised and banged up as if he'd fallen or been tossed from a

95

great height. Such a great height—taller than the ceiling of his room—that when he'd landed on the bed it had collapsed beneath him. Buried him. It was a wonder he hadn't suffocated or had anything worse than some deep bruises and a sore, wrenched back. The doctor left painkillers and a hefty bill, which Robin forwarded to the hotel.

With most of a week gone, Mal might not be hurting anymore, but he'd gone blank. The light in his eyes was cloudy. Nothing anyone did roused him. Ciaran learned that a variety of guests had wandered in and out of the room over the past days—record company employees, Suzanne at least twice a day, that new fella Tom who'd come with a bodhran but left without making more than a few dull thuds. Rich phoned from Dublin, and while Mal had cradled the phone between his shoulder and ear, he'd said nothing, and eventually the phone fell away until Ciaran picked it up.

They had one thing going for them: The hotel management was so mortified at the mystery injury on their premises that they comped the band and their crew room and board as long as was necessary. The hotel's manager was also one of the frequent visitors and happily acquiesced to Mal's sole demand: take the remaining bed frame out of the room. He'd sleep without it from here on out. Now, the headboard remained affixed to the back wall, and Mal looked as if he was sinking into the mattress.

Ciaran visited—not as often as he ought, he knew. But being with Mal distracted him from writing music, and the radio in his head was so hard to beat back. During his visits Ciaran ran through every stimulus he could think of—he'd read to Mal, shouted at him, pleaded with him. Then he'd stalk out again.

And of Patrick? Nothing. Fecked off, as per usual. Not very far—Suzanne reported spotting him in Central Park on her way in. But typical Patch: run away from trouble. Ciaran hadn't seen him in all this time.

This couldn't go on forever. That call from Rich had been about more than just sending get-well wishes from across the pond. Ciaran had picked up the receiver after Mal let it drop and had a lengthy chat about the cackery that was going on back home.

It's bad. Rich's voice had been tight with stress. *You've been stolen from.*

With the record advance money, and on Rich's advice, the three of them had purchased a small recording studio not far from Grafton. They'd hired a man to look after bookings and other expenses—but that man had apparently been playing around with the numbers. *As a business entity, you're skint,* Rich had continued. *There's some money in your personal accounts, but—decisions must be made. You're bleeding out from putting the tour on hold, and the venues won't reschedule forever. So you've either got to come home and take your beating or get back on the road and play. If it's the former, we might get sued at this stage for failure to appear. Either way, you can't stay in New York any longer.*

That had been yesterday.

But today, Ciaran had a final, bright idea. No more stories. No more sitting around yelling at Mal. There was only one thing the man truly wanted to hear. And Ciaran had the perfect thing at hand. So after seeing Sheerie off that morning, he'd willed the radio in his head down to a tolerable level—and headed to Mal's room.

Despite being bullied into it, Mal hadn't seemed to mind teaching Ciaran how to play piano when they were boys. Ciaran might not always have been the most receptive student, but every lesson taught him two things: first, how to think in black and white keys and not vocal scales; and second, what it meant to be both passionate and excellent at something. But maybe there was a third thing. Mal had always gravitated to the keyboard in any room, natural as breath. He settled into it, closed his eyes and … *went places*. It was like a religious experience, an ecstasy that poured out note by note.

That passion had kept Ciaran going, until the day he'd been confident enough to sit his parents down and execute a Beethoven sonata, followed with a rendition of "Down by the Salley Gardens." He'd never seen his parents cry before then. Mal had made it possible, with patience beyond his years and kindness beyond most anyone's comprehension. In return, Ciaran became his champion and protector; any kid daring to dump Mal in a nearby wastebin would have to answer to *him*.

The music's inside you, Mal had told him one day after a particularly difficult session. *It comes out when you're ready.*

These last few days, Ciaran had been very ready. The music had definitely been coming out of him. Now it was his turn to share. He zapped the TV off. Mal turned and held out his hand, demanding the remote. Ciaran tossed it across the room. Mal gazed out the windowed balcony door by his bed, letting the hand fall limp. So Ciaran brought out what he'd been hiding since coming into the room: the three green notebooks he'd filled so far with songs.

I suspect he'll give a glowing shit about this, he thought, but even as he handed them over he had mixed feelings about sharing the work. It was a gift that came from nowhere. Maybe they weren't really his. Or, maybe he was short-shifting himself. He'd spent most of his life being around music. He was no slouch. But the ability to turn what he'd always watched from the sidelines into complex, completed tunes—that *had* come from nowhere, and he worried he might jinx it by sharing.

Mal was worth the risk. He released the notebooks onto his friend's lap.

For a moment, nothing happened. Then Mal ran the tips of his fingers over the spirals thoughtfully.

"Open. Read." Ciaran stood and jerked open the sliding glass door. He stepped onto the balcony and let fresh air fill the room.

A Musical Equivalent of Escher Drawings

Mal hefted the notebooks as if they were Christmas presents and he could determine the contents before opening. Curiosity burned off the dense fog lingering in his head. He watched Ciaran on the balcony, facing Central Park, an early afternoon breeze billowing the clothing around him. For a moment, he was engulfed in ill-fitting fabric.

He opened the first notebook's cover, unsure what he was supposed to be reading. Ciaran's diary? Recipes? Notes from fans and friends wishing him well and to get out of the fecking bed already?

None of that. Few words. Something other than words. Immediately, the lines and dots and curls and swoops translated in Mal's ears, filling his head with music he'd never heard before. Each turn of the page beat back more of the fog, and a light sweat broke out on his forehead as he realized what he was simultaneously reading and hearing. The notes tripped around in him in combinations that were unusual, challenging—a musical equivalent of Escher drawings. But they made *sense*, folding together as beautifully as butterfly wings, deceptively simple songs that made his heart race and his fingers curl involuntarily toward an invisible keyboard. It felt like warm hands were rubbing the strength back into his legs, arms, chest … his soul.

He would give anything to bring these songs to life. They were nothing he could describe, not classical, not lightweight, not peppy, not pulse-pounding. They were *older* than any of those forms, more ancient than Gregorian chants. Older than time itself, like the template for all music that came afterward. Mal had never been fully satisfied with the way the songs in his head turned into songs on the page, or even on the stage. They were close, but imperfect.

These were those songs, captured for all to see. Plucked not from Mal's head but—presumably—from Ciaran's.

His smile slid away. The songs were wonderful. Perfect. A *fait accompli*, brilliant and whole and … written by a man who, so far as Mal knew, had never managed to finish a song in his life. The man out there on the balcony, trying to be humble about them. It was a pose Mal had also struck once or twice. Except—these couldn't be Ciaran's. They were … too good.

Jealous much? he thought, and maybe that was some of it. But no, there was more to it. Mal would have been overjoyed if Ciaran suddenly could write this well. If *anyone* could. These songs were pure emotion, turned into pen scratches on lined notebook paper. But that was the problem: They were note-perfect. Not just how they sounded in his head, but how they appeared on the page. There was not a stray mark or mistake anywhere. If Ciaran had been truly composing songs, his changes would be evident. Early pages would show the developing work, later ones correcting the mistakes, altering sections. But these notebooks went on and on and on with no practice pages, no drafts, no hesitation marks. Pulling songs like these flawlessly from the brain onto paper couldn't be done.

Final drafts? Mal thought. *Maybe he's got six notebooks back in his room of rough mess?* Unlikely.

Of course he wrote them, he reasoned. *Some people are … late bloomers.* Ciaran had clearly found his muse, that elusive creature others spent their lives chasing down. Mal went back over each song, lingering, delaying having to tell Ciaran what he thought.

His mind itched. His fingers twitched. He flexed his hands and stretched.

Ciaran turned, gripping the balcony railing in anticipation.

"Brilliant." Mal's tone was hushed. "They're the most beautiful things I've ever seen. How—when did you do all this?"

Ciaran shrugged and visibly relaxed. "Came to me. Woke up one morning and they were in my noggin. Y'know how it happens. Music shows up when you're ready to hear it an' all?"

He listened to me. Mal was oddly flattered. "We have to play them."

"Lookit you." Ciaran laughed. "Like death when I walked in here. Now you're ready for another gig?"

Mal stilled. He'd been so frightened since the accident. The monster actually had been under his bed, a monster called the *fear dearg* with his endless mean-spirited pranks, which meant nothing was safe. He'd gotten rid of the bed and kept the mattress, insisting on keeping one of the bitten-through legs to remind him of what he was dealing with. He stared blankly at the TV for hours, trying to reason with the idea that a mythical creature out of his grandparents' childhoods, whom no one believed in anymore, existed. Not knowing what to do or where to turn, Mal had been seized by a terrible lethargy, and it had been unsettlingly easy to withdraw, to not see people around him, to not stir from his bed for more than a quick piss. He'd been aware of visitors—a long stream of faces came to him now, some familiar, some less so, right there in the room with him. Ciaran. Patrick—though he'd just stood by the bed and stared without speaking for a long while. The others were blurs.

One came in more clearly, though. A woman. Not Suzanne. Not Caitlin. Dark hair, a doll with a tiny waist. She'd come to him and settled on a corner of his mattress, not even disturbing the sheets. Mal hadn't moved—but he had been drawn to her, drawn the way the piano pulled on him. He'd wanted to *play* her. She shifted closer until she was hovering over his face, then ran her hands over his cheeks with a touch as gentle as dragon's breath.

Your time will come, Malachi, Sheerie had promised him in that waking dream. *There is time enough for all of you.*

Her lips had brushed his and it was a bloodless touch, devoid of life—yet it set off something inside him heated and dark like the inside of a flame. When she'd withdrawn, he'd crawled after her, yearning for that touch again.

"Yes," he told Ciaran now. "Let's play. Where's Patch?"

Ciaran waved a hand. "*Him.* Like a *leanbh* sometimes still. Not a sign for days."

"But he was here. More than once." Mal sighed. "I don't blame him. I think he knows a little too much to stay with me for long."

"What's that supposed to mean?"

Mal tapped the notebook. "Haven't you noticed how odd things have gotten lately?"

"Like yer bed? Sure. That's the strangest thing ever."

Mal shook his head. Ciaran wasn't stupid. He just suffered from a lack of imagination sometimes. And Mal knew if he started in on Caitlin and *sídhe* and *fear dearg* they'd lose the day. The music would go unplayed. Right now, that was the only thing worth doing.

"Not important." He waved everything aside. "Caitlin understands."

"Who's Caitlin?"

Mal shook his head. "Forget it. Find Patrick and find the guitars. We need to try your songs—right now."

Ciaran grinned. "There's a piano in the bar downstairs. Management owes us a couple favors. Bet we can use the space—they don't even open until half-four."

"My back—I don't think—it's still a bit sore—"

"Yer fine." Ciaran grinned. "It's a bar. Last I checked, a little *uisce beatha* cures most anything, don't it?"

All Manner of Facts and Fancies

Patrick burst into the hotel bar, mandolin in hand, bits of grass stuck in his curls.

"At long feckin' last," Ciaran growled. "Get in."

Mal had taken nearly an hour to get downstairs. His legs were weak from disuse, but Ciaran had walked him around the room until he felt ready to tackle the trip to the bar. He parked him at the baby grand's stool, framed by windows that overlooked Central Park, then departed briefly to clear things with the hotel manager. On Ciaran's return, Mal wore a blissful look, hands on keys, eyes closed.

Meanwhile, Robin had been dispatched to find Patrick. As usual, he was not far but not near, playing his mandy in Central Park.

"I thought something'd gone wrong," Patch wheezed.

"Opposite. Something's going very right." Mal gestured at a whiskey bottle stationed on the bar. "First, though, start drinking."

Ciaran felt twitchy. He'd been waiting a long time to attack the songs in the notebook, trying to hold off until Patrick got with the program. They had the instruments, the will—and now the players in place. It was time to get started.

"I'm all right." Patrick ignored Mal's offer. "What's all this, then?"

"Meet Sergej." Ciaran waved at the bartender, who'd been dispatched by the hotel to give them whatever they wanted. "I told the manager he'd get us out of here faster if he let us get drunk and play songs, so here we are. But we're not supposed to pour for ourselves."

Sergej offered a three-fingered salute to the forehead, then started cleaning some glasses.

"And if yer not drinkin'," Ciaran continued, shifting one of the notebooks toward Patrick, "get to playing. Key of C-sharp minor."

Patrick squinted at him, glanced at the notebook and nodded. They dove into the tune, just as they always had. No matter how complicated the arrangement, or how fresh to their eyes and ears, they initially fell to the notes like miners searching for gold, hacking away. Finesse could come later.

It went wrong almost immediately. Ciaran didn't understand it; after just a minute or two they were stumbling out of the music—not finishing, not striking wrong chords—just falling out of it. They came to a bumbling halt and stared at one another. Ciaran's chest was tight and the inside of his head felt like someone had gonged it. The radio inside was muted, and now there was just echo. Mal looked as if something had trampled him.

Without a word, Mal stood and grabbed the whiskey bottle, setting it on the piano top. "We're not pourin' if we're not using glasses," he told Sergej, and took a big swig. They all took long draughts and picked up where they'd left off.

"Again," said Ciaran. "*A haon, dó, trí.*"

That did it. Each song exploded into being with the light and heat of a supernova, reflecting off the windows, doubling back, slamming into Ciaran with a blast of heat, then chill. With the drink in them, they could stop thinking so hard about putting the notes together and let the music filter through them like water. What came out was untouched and pure. The burning urgency inside him to get these songs played surged with each tune, as if the music insisted on being heard.

Mal's eyes were bright. Patch's cheeks bloomed with roses. They were sweating, despite the air conditioning. The songs kept coming—and quickly Ciaran realized it wasn't just a good idea to have that slug of drink with each new tune. It was *necessary*. You couldn't look directly at the sun without protection. You couldn't hear this music without guarding your heart. Everything became inexpressibly, unbearably gorgeous. Tears squeezed from his eyes and went flying with each muscular strum on the guitar. The walls seemed to blend, and melt, and pixilate, then restore themselves the moment he looked directly at them. He blessed the whiskey; without it as a buffer, these tunes might draw blood.

Then the bottle was empty and the music came to a halt. Ciaran scanned the bar, but Sergej was nowhere to be found. Over where he'd been cleaning glasses sat a pile of paper napkins spotted with scarlet, but the bar itself was empty. Ciaran ran into the lobby—which was also vacant of patrons or workers—calling out until the manager emerged from a back office. He seemed twitchy, wiping his glasses with a cloth, and explained that Sergej had been taken ill with a sudden nosebleed.

"Can the three of you"—the manager said hesitantly, voice quivery—"can you serve yourselves on the honor system and ... try not to break anything?"

Ciaran raised an eyebrow. Part of him wondered at the empty lobby and the manager's odd behavior—but most of his attention was still on the music.

He waved the strangeness away and returned to the others, closing the door behind him.

"Open bar!" he called out, and everyone sent up a cheer.

Ciaran grabbed a bottle of Bushmills Three Wood from the top shelves. Tossing the cap behind him, he took a gulp and leaped over the bar to set it alongside the dead soldier on the piano.

"Now," he said. "Where were we?"

Hours passed.

The strange, uncanny music filled the empty bar and crept through the closed doorjamb into the lobby. Inside the bar, three drunken players raged, seduced by the sounds and prepared to rock on as long as they could remain standing. Though, as Patrick realized blurrily, pretty soon the standing was going to be very much in doubt.

It was a glorious chaos, but three bottles in, they were falling apart slowly, sinking against barstools, flopped by drink and effort. Mal began resting his head on top of the piano between bouts of music; Ciaran would point and laugh at him, sliding down his barstool until he touched the ground.

For Patrick, it was different. He heard a message in the songs, an urgency told in a language he'd never heard and couldn't pronounce. Looking at Ciaran's notebook was like seeing into a bright golden light, a portal to elsewhere.

'Tis a worn-up thing he's written. The thought came fleeting and then vanished. He was too out of his mind to understand what it might mean. Instead, as they faltered between songs, he forced himself to a shaky upright position and cried out, "One more, Mal! One more!"

Each time, Mal gamely resurrected himself for another go.

The sun began to fade, and that made reading the music more difficult, but no one wanted to break to find a light switch. Time was precious now—Patrick was certain the restaurant attached to the bar they'd been occupying would need to open soon—so they kept plowing forward, waiting to be told to stop, trying to tackle every song Ciaran had written. Part of him wished time would stand still so they might continue doing this forever.

Stop the clocks. This is perfection. Nothing else ever needs to happen.

They spiraled out of a song, and Ciaran passed around the latest bottle. Patrick opened his mouth to rally for "one more," then bit down on the words. There was someone else in the bar with them now. An unfocused someone. Not Sergei—he'd gone home, Ciaran had said. Not another barman; a barman would be behind the bar, not sitting next to it. A woman. A woman who would not stop swaying from side to side.

Patrick clamped a hand on Ciaran's shoulder. "That is the most beautiful woman in this bar."

Ciaran squinted and laughed. "Patch, that is the *only* woman in this bar."

Mal's head struck the piano keys with a mushy musical thud, and Patrick gulped air deeply, trying to clear his mind. *Many, too many drinks.* A warm knot formed in his stomach. He was going to be sick. Soon. Before that, though, he was going to figure out who was watching them. A wave of nausea passed and his sight cleared briefly.

"Ceetlahin," he exclaimed. Swallowed. Tried again. "Caitlin!"

Mal lifted his head from the ivory pillow, smiling contentedly. "And so."

Slipping from her barstool, Caitlin strolled over, hands clasped behind her back. "Impressive," she said to no one in particular. "You should be in a band."

Patrick toppled toward her, and she braced him with her hands. He lurched against her shoulder. "We missed you."

"I know." She cut a glance at Ciaran. "Nice music."

"The *best* music," garbled Patrick.

"Where'd it come from?" She was still staring hard at Ciaran.

Mal flapped a hand. "His notebooks! We're just borrowing 'em."

Ciaran returned Caitlin's stare. "Say what you mean."

She shifted Patrick from her shoulder to a chair and he pushed his hair from his face. Everything felt rubbery. The room was askew. "Those aren't yours," she told Ciaran. "They're not for you. You know that, right?"

"*Cacamas,*" Ciaran swore. "I wrote every word, every note."

"Hm."

"Want to prove I didn't? I'm no thief."

"Put whatever name you want on it, Ciaran O'Conaill. Just understand what it means to have them."

He crossed his arms. "Oh? What's that, then?"

She thumbed at the crimson-streaked napkins on the bar. "Think about it." She stepped toward him, and he flinched back. She tapped his forehead once. "Try using *that* instead of *that*." She gestured at his crotch.

The tension between them cut through even Patrick's ossified state, and he stepped between them. "Hey, hey," he said. "Just friendly talk. Don't think I can take much more." He pulled on her hand and she followed. "Don't leave again. Promise?"

"Had enough, have you?"

"I'm feeling like the underside of a *boot* now." He paused. "Two boots."

"No surprise." She glanced at Mal, who'd blacked out on the piano. "Let's get the both of you upstairs and sober. Then we can talk about all manner of facts and fancies."

"And what about *me*, then?" Ciaran's face was blotchy, his eyes narrowed.

Caitlin arched an eyebrow. "Well. You have Sheerie, don't you?"

True Eyes Opening

The Green Place

Hardly original but perfectly descriptive. Patrick had only spent a few moments in that strange world of grass and sky, whisked there by Caitlin directly from a Boston stage, but it had lingered in his memory ever since. And as the days had passed without her, the call to return had felt louder each day.

And now—he was back.

Though Patrick knew he'd fallen into a hard, drunken blackout in his New York City hotel room bed, he awoke on a carpet of identical blades of grass, pointed as knives yet soft as silk, waving beneath an enormous white sun and a sky the color of Caitlin's eyes.

"You took me back." His voice sounded odd in his ears: half-accusatory, half-grateful.

"You took yourself back." Caitlin sat in the grass next to him. "Though maybe I assisted. A bit."

"But I'm still in a hotel room."

"Are you?"

He sat up. No drunkenness. No headache. In fact—he took a deep breath and inhaled fresh bread and chocolate—he'd never felt more together. More … himself. He wasn't shaking this time. The place no longer frightened him. "So— where are you? Here and there?"

"Padraig, stop asking *me* questions and go find your answers."

105

Scolded, he got to his feet, moving with a light, unfamiliar ease. The ground held no resistance, as if gravity meant less. He blinked, trying to adjust to the brightness, and hunted around the landscape for something, anything other than grass and horizon.

Trees. This place needs trees and shade. He thought of a tree near where he'd grown up, before they'd moved to Dublin. A spreading arc of a creation, the tree had low, thick branches and deep, fluttering leaves. Had it been an oak? A birch? A willow? A hazel?

He turned to one side—and there it was. The spot had been empty moments earlier, but—now it had a tree. The grandest of trees, bigger even than the one in Boston he and Caitlin had played beneath. The white-barked trunk's base spread across a vast swath of the ground, ridged roots popping from the earth like veins, supporting an umbrella-shaped canopy of tiny leaves and catkins that rustled with a sound like applause.

What kind of tree is this, even? he wondered as he started toward it, then answered his own question. *It's a BirchWillow OakHazel. Just what I didn't know to ask for.*

The tree waved at him, calling in a soughing whisper. As he neared, he spied a man sitting on a wide, flat root that bumped out of the ground like a bench. There was nothing special about the man, who was dressed in a threadbare work shirt and faded jeans, a cap tilted back on his head and a mustache beneath his nose like a snoozing caterpillar. He was peeling skin from a green apple with a paring knife.

But Patrick knew him.

A son always knows his *athair*.

He halted at the base of the root, a roaring cyclone of emotions swirling in him.

"*Fáilte*, son." His father took a bite of the peel. "Was wonderin' when you might find me. We'll need to talk, so we will."

I can't, thought Patrick—and the Green Place vanished.

Patrick spasmed once in the bed, trying to open his eyes, but they were so encrusted by sleep he had to force his fists against them and rub. He was dry all over, the inside of his mouth a parched fetid desert, his throat cracked and aching. His head was enormous, a lead balloon sinking into the pillow. His palms scraped against thick stubble on his cheeks.

He forced his eyes open and winced at the too-bright room. Caitlin nestled in a chair next to the bed, knees pulled to her chest, watching him.

"Back already?"

Her voice was a clamor of bells in his head.

"Where—" His voice creaked and she gestured at a mug on the side table. It steamed gently, and he pulled himself to a seated position, propping a pillow behind his back, shuddering at every movement. "Where was I—just now?"

"You tell me."

"I think you know." He flashed on the green, the tree, on an apple being peeled, on *Athair*. His father, who wanted to talk—and whom Patrick had wished away.

"You saw him, didn't you."

Patrick shook his head. "Me head's done in."

Again, she waved her hand at the mug. "It won't drink itself."

Patrick patted the space next to him on the bed and she hopped over, alighting without even disturbing the sheets. He eyed the steaming mug with caution; the thick, milky liquid inside was a swirling, shifting mix of purple and brown. "What the hells is this?"

She didn't answer.

Patrick took a cautious sip, the hot liquid like cinnamon, butter, and a third unidentifiable taste that lingered on the tip of his tongue. It wasn't really even a flavor—more like drinking a memory. His gut called for more, and soon he was upending the mug to get the dregs, licking his lips like a child. "All right, so what was—" but before he could complete the thought, his eyes shot open. The balloon of his head had shrunk. He saw clearly. He was no longer thirsty. "Jaysus."

The other double bed in the room shifted. Mal was in it, asleep, faintly smiling. He hugged his pillow, then stilled.

"How long've we been here?"

She shrugged. "Day? More?" She counted on her fingers. "I'm not good with hours. Or minutes. Or years."

Patrick almost couldn't believe it, but when he glanced outside it seemed like early afternoon. Had he lost a full day in bed, sleeping it off? His stomach made gurgling noises, and he thought of the stubble. At least a day. Likely longer. He'd never slept so; never been allowed to. A boy sleeping was seen as wasteful, a fact just as true with Herself as at the monastery.

He remembered making music at the bar. None of the notes or tunes had stayed true in his mind, but he recalled how they made him feel sharp. Aware. There had been drinking, and vomiting once he'd reached the hotel room. He should feel exhausted; instead, he was good, right ... *ready*.

"Tell me what was in the cup."

"Something you don't believe in," she said. "Don't let it trouble you."

Sharp anger flared—it was as if she'd never left. The rage he'd felt back in Boston, the discovery that she wasn't just some musical soulmate but rather a crazy person had been wrenching. But in the ensuing week the hard edges of that anger had faded—and all he could think of was having her back. She was still so *other*, but her otherness echoed his own. It was an unsettling discovery.

Don't trust her too much. You've no reason to.

Such a reasonable inner voice, one that sounded like the monks at the monastery. So sure of themselves and their truths. Believe in us, they'd told Patrick, and he had. Their notion of family—of belonging—was predicated on understanding that their superstitions were real, while yours were made-up silliness from a backward people. Once Patrick had accepted that, everything had been easier.

Caitlin flipped everything around. Almost.

"We bet on the lottery while you were gone." He let that settle on her. Purchasing that lottery ticket had shifted things in him. Not about winning money, but his ability to accept the impossible. Mal had already gotten there; Patrick had to catch up. Mal had been wrong. They'd lost. But in joining in, Patrick discovered that he'd stepped over a line he hadn't even known was there.

It was like that saying from *The X-Files*. He wanted to believe.

"And?" Caitlin asked him now. "Didn't win, I assume. What did you expect?" He waited.

"Well, it's not that simple. I don't have some box of tricks to show you whatever you think you're supposed to see. I'm not a wizard. Or an illusionist. We've a way of doing things that make sense to us, and it's not required that you see things our way. I'm only here to—" She hesitated. "To wake you up a little."

"Why? Why—me?" He flashed back to his dream. *Athair* in the Green Place. Had he been there, truly, or had it been something else? "I'm tired of always being in the dark."

She held his hand tight and he thought—*we're goin' back to the Green Place, we are*—and though they didn't move, his heart raced and he breathed faster. He *needed* to go back in the way he'd *needed* to play Ciaran's songs. That wasn't half-believing. That was all the way. The world contained more layers, dimensions, and possibilities than he'd ever considered. Music should have taught him that long ago; music had always been a window to another place. Music was *always* worn-up, and it took him places every time he lifted an instrument or opened his mouth to sing.

Caitlin regarded him with her clear blue gaze and set a hand on his heart. "I can feel it, your true eyes opening." She made a tiny, delighted noise. "Like seeing a flower blossom. But—more."

"Don't leave." His voice was husky, and he rested his hand over hers. "You can't. If things go on like they have we'll all be insane. Mal's gonna go first but me right behind. No matter what happens—promise not to leave."

"Don't intend to," she said. "No reason to. But—do you plan on listening this time?"

Her warm touch spread inside him. Made the hairs on his arms stand on end. The extraordinary was going on here, something beyond his comprehension. But he trusted Caitlin. She was like Brother David had once been—leading him over a different stile, across a different field, and past a whole other kind of terror. And when they came out on the other side, everything was going to be different.

"Besides," she said in a lighter voice, "I came to hear more of your stories."

"So you'll tell me tales if I tell you some?"

She nodded.

"Mine are true," he challenged.

"Ah, Padraig! So are mine."

You Terrible Fraud

Those aren't yours. They're not for you. You know that, right?

Ciaran, deep asleep, was back in the bar with the boys. On their third bottle. Drunk as all hells but making some of the greatest music ever played.

Then that woman in the denim jacket had turned up again.

In his dream, he knew exactly how to respond to her. "That's the way out." He pointed. "You're not needed."

But instead of leaving, she took up his hand and dragged him through the doors, out into the vacant lobby, into a scene Dalí might have appreciated. The paintings had all melted. The wall coverings were peeling. The wooden check-in desk had cracked open. A vase of flowers at the center of the space had exploded, sending petals everywhere. The carpet was actively unraveling as they walked across it, threads coiling up his legs.

"This is your fault," the woman said.

The hotel manager raced across the lobby, clapping a hand over one eye. He looked like a man telling a terrible pirate joke. Ciaran reached out and arrested him. "What happened to you?"

The man lowered his hand and his eye bobbled in the socket, then began to tumble out. "Sergei can't smell anything anymore," he announced calmly. "And I'm half-blind."

Then he began to scream.

"See what you've done?" The woman gripped Ciaran's hand more tightly. "You terrible fraud."

Ciaran twisted and turned, feeling like he was drowning, water engulfing him—
And woke, spluttering.

Shaking his soaked head, Ciaran gasped. Sheerie loomed over him, holding an emptied ice bucket. The last drops of water rained on him.

"Arise, my love!" she cried. "I'm *starving*."

For a moment, Ciaran wasn't certain he'd emerged from the nightmare. He glanced at his trembling hands. The reality of Sheerie took a moment to overtake the vivid image of the peeling wallpaper, the raw wood of the counter—the manager's eye dangling on its optic nerve.

None of that happened, he reminded himself, though truthfully he didn't remember getting out of the bar and up to his room. He didn't remember much after Caitlin had arrived and screwed everything up.

His head was pounding, a sledgehammer beating within his skull. Next to the bed sat a steaming cup of what seemed like coffee but smelled more like buttered bread.

Sheerie dropped to the bed beside him and tossed the bucket away. "Drink it," she ordered.

Ciaran was used to accepting whatever she brought him. The one time he'd said he wasn't interested in the odd greenish glop she set on the desk she'd yanked his chair to one side and straddled him, holding the cup against his lips. She was immensely strong for a woman of her size and could pin him in place with her body. "Drink." Her voice had been sweetly menacing. "Don't make this hard." Then she'd slid a hand into his trousers and smiled. "That's quite hard enough already."

Later that night, long after they'd finished with one another, he'd been violently sick. Bent over the toilet, he heaved out whatever he'd managed to eat earlier in the day, tears dripping from the corners of his eyes. His head had screamed with music that demanded to be loosed. But this was his life now. Sheerie wanted, so Sheerie got. Ciaran's body was not wholly his own anymore.

Now, he eyed this new drink she offered. Down the hatch it went. This time it was marvelously sweet and with just a hint of hot spices, and as it slid into his gut, it evicted the whiskey sledgehammer pounding in his head. He collapsed against the pillow, which squelched.

"Better now?" Her nose brushed his cheek.

"Jaysus." The dream was fading. All except Caitlin's editorial commentary: *Fraud*.

Ciaran tried to focus on something not about music. Not about Sheerie. Robin. Where was he? They needed a sit-down. Were they flying home? Were they going back on the road now that Mal had come back to life? He needed—

Sheerie tore the wet pillow from behind him and swapped it with a dry one before his head even hit the mattress. Her other hand fluttered against his shirt,

110

unbuttoning it with practiced alacrity. He took her wrist. "Wait," he said. "I'm drenched. An' I'm feckin' *exhausted*."

"Neither of these things is an issue." She slipped easily from his grip, peeling back his shirt as if flaying a corpse. Then her hands were at his belt and trousers—apparently he hadn't changed before passing out—and things accelerated quickly.

A short time later, Ciaran came around enough to realize he was still half-swimming in his own bed. He heard music, but not from his head radio. Something softer. He forced himself to sit up.

Sheerie was absently strumming his guitar on a corner of the bed. The sound was gentle but the chords—they hardly seemed possible. A person would need six fingers to hit every string the way she was. After a moment he recognized the tune: one of Mal's, arranged into a more countrified version.

"You're full of surprises."

She smiled up at him. "Aren't I just. Are you fully rested now?"

No. But he didn't say the word. He felt bruised and tired. Stretching, he slid off the mattress and found something reasonably clean to dress in. "Look, I've got some things to do. Y'can stay if you like, but I'm stepping out for a bit."

"They're busy." She continued strumming, never looking at her fingers.

"Who?"

"Your friends. They won't see you right now."

Ciaran frowned and kicked his feet into his boots. That was pretty presumptuous of her. "I'll see about that." He stormed out the door only to realize he wasn't sure where either Mal or Patrick was, then realized it was likely one of two places. Shrugging, he strode to Patrick's room and knocked.

No one answered.

He knocked harder.

After a moment, Caitlin opened the door. Her eyes were blue steel and she did not let him in. "Mal's asleep. Padraig's showering." She started to close the door, and Ciaran stuck his boot into the gap—but couldn't widen it.

"It's afternoon," he growled. "Time to be up."

Caitlin refused to move and he couldn't get a better purchase. In fact, the space was slowly beginning to close, trapping his foot. "Haven't you got anything better to do?" She tilted her head. "Like stealing some more songs?"

He gasped, picturing her dragging him through the lobby. Calling him *fraud*.

"I'm not here to help you, Ciaran," she said, though her tone was softer.

"Didn't ask for help."

Her long lashes lowered and she took a deep breath. "You would, if you knew how."

"I'm here to see my pals."

"Well, they're not to see you now. We have things to speak of."

"And so do I. Who the hells do you think you are?"

"I'm the one holding this door. Don't force me to break your foot."

With that, his toe slipped from the remaining gap and the door clicked closed. He tried his passkey—but it no longer worked. Ciaran sulked back to his own room. He was twice her size. They were *his* friends.

But she scared him.

Ciaran paused outside his own door, listening as Sheerie's gentle guitar playing streamed through. At least he had her on his side. Always had Sheerie. In the past week or so he'd had her any number of ways and places and times, just as she'd had him. The hotel and the city had been full of endlessly inventive places to have one another, whenever the mood struck. And it had been the strangest, most earth-shifting *having* he'd ever done. But though it seemed impossible to imagine, he began to think he'd had about enough of her.

"My love?" Sheerie called through the door. "Have you lost your key?"

Sighing, he returned to her. "Time to put my guitar away."

"For whatever reason?" Her voice was like honey. "You're always playing when I'm around."

"It's my job."

"You're just irritated because I'm so good."

"Not the point." Ciaran tried to remember what it was about her that triggered him and came up blank. She was still the same small woman with the waspish waist and absurdly shiny, soft hair, but for the first time he felt nothing. It was as if a light had turned off. Even the radio in his head was silenced.

"Well, I am," she continued. "I'm much better than you are. You need to work harder onstage, my love. Otherwise, someone could come along and take your place!"

He snorted. "You're not welcome up there."

She snorted back. "Who says I have to be asked?"

In a flash he imagined wresting the guitar from her hands and smashing it over her head—but held still. Ciaran was enjoying the silence and calm from having the music muted, alongside a lack of yearning for her. He could see her clearly now: She was a nobody, a nothing. She'd wormed her way into his world and was playing *his* guitar on *his* bed as if she'd owned both her entire life.

The strumming ceased. Sheerie stared at him.

No, he decided, she would not come on the bus with them. She was too much of a distraction. Things should taper off. He would live just fine without her—he'd done so for the last couple of decades. "We ought to talk. I've been thinking."

"So have I." She set the guitar on the ground. "It's a very good thing you told them about bringing me on the bus. They weren't going to let you at first."

Ciaran froze. She had this … way of knowing what was going on in his head. He wouldn't miss that. But—what was she saying? "Who wasn't going to let me what?"

"Mal. Padraig. They weren't going to let you take me on."

He chuckled. "They didn't have a choice. It's my bus, too."

"Of course. I knew you'd stand up for me if they tried to keep me away."

"Suppose I would have."

"You'd always stand up for me."

All the wind left him. She wasn't wrong.

"Do you know *why* they let you?"

"They didn't *let* me anything. I told them and they agreed." He was starting to get worked up again, and the music in his head was returning.

"Because they're going to bring that other woman on the bus, too."

He shook his head. He had no idea how Sheerie knew about Caitlin, but that hardly mattered.

"See if I'm wrong. They won't even give you the courtesy of asking, either. She'll just *be* there." Sheerie nodded. "Got them under a spell."

"Actually, I'd been thinking it was a good idea not to invite *anyone* on the bus."

"Even me?" She turned a kittenish look on him and got on all fours, crawling across the bed. Her face was level with his waist, and she rested both hands on the snap of his trousers. Rising up on her knees, she pressed her lips against his neck, then his cheek, then his mouth. And just as it had that first time, her touch obliterated all rational thought. Everything he'd been considering was gone. No melting or fading—or peeling—away. Just—gone. Any emptiness inside now filled with the image of Sheerie and all the things they could do to one another.

The light was on again. The switch had been flipped.

Even the music was back.

"No, wait—" Ciaran tried. Not even sure what he was negating. Why would anyone say no to *this*? Yet he wanted to push back. Wanted to have control of his senses, of his self—of his life—again. But then a curtain drew across his vision and he was crawling on top of her, pressing down, enveloping her, which was exactly what Sheerie had wanted all along.

Like Listening to Diamonds

"Tell me about Padraig's father," Caitlin asked Mal as they entered Central Park.

Startled, Mal rubbed his woolen cap. That was not how he expected their conversation to begin. The last time he'd seen Caitlin, she'd made promises: *There's a reason for all of this.* She knew why things had gone so pear-shaped, and he was determined to get answers. But he'd sensed that if Patrick was around, his own troubles would be mere afterthoughts to her.

So while Patrick took his time cleaning up, Mal bounded awake, cleared his head with Caitlin's marvelous concoction, hurried into a change of clothes and raced to meet her in the lobby. Five minutes of her direct attention, that's all he needed. Instead, she only seemed interested in Patch.

Mal sighed. "Dunno. Never met the man. Wasn't ever around. Gone for days, a week or more. Mam and Dadai would say he was 'off with the … fairies.'" He cleared his throat.

They wound around an asphalt path, ducked beneath budding trees, and passed rolling hills. It was a pretty spring afternoon, but he could hardly enjoy it. The need to get answers was chewing at him.

"And how did Padraig … handle that?" she asked.

"Look, Caitlin—I—" He paused. "I've got a few questions of my own here—"

"Soon." She set a hand on his arm and a soothing warmth calmed him. "Trust me."

He had to. There was no one else offering. He cast his memory back, trying to recall Padraig again as a boy, what it was like to hang out with him. "Was the way of his world," said Mal after a pause. "Never complained about not seeing his da. His mam was a different story. She barely tolerated him. Kicked him out of that house every damned day."

He'd never forget it, that one encounter with the woman Patrick only referred to as *Herself.*

Tá mo bhuachaill marbh, she'd said. *My boy is dead.* A bold as brass lied to two kids who couldn't argue.

"He was an only," Mal continued almost to himself, putting things together as he never had as a boy. "And that was funny, 'cause nearly anybody we knew had three, four—five. They just had the one, and they were always either chasin' him away or ignoring him entire."

They came to a tall, ragged rock formation that bulged over the tailored green lawn. Caitlin scrambled up it, nimble as a goat, and Mal followed behind, less surefooted. Taking a seat next to her, he admired the spot, which offered a terrific view of the path they'd just come from and, through a parting in the trees, the hotel. Caitlin leaned back on her hands and studied him. "You're sure he was an only?"

Of course, he nearly said, but slowly words he'd overheard long ago crept in. "Rumors. Never something we talked about. What'd he tell you?"

The blue of her eyes swirled. "Rumors?"

He let his mind go, searching. Pictured Padraig in Mal's childhood kitchen. Visiting for dinner. First visit, maybe second. The boy had shown up without shoes so Mal had left his off in solidarity, and at the dinner table they curled their feet around the chair legs like monkeys. After eating, Mal took Padraig in to see the piano and they picked out notes and songs for a while. Sometime later, Mal left Padraig to ask if his friend could stay the night. It would have been a Friday, most like.

Mam and Dadai were in the kitchen still, talking in careful adult voices— but Mal's hearing was excellent, and he lingered just outside the door.

All culchies and muckers over that way, Dadai was saying. *That boy wants watching. Make sure all your rings are in the box when he goes.*

Ah, he's a sweet one, Ma had said. *We could give him some of Mal's castoffs. Poor boy, he's no sibs over there.*

Dadai had made a snorting noise. *Always more to the story.*

Mam had held her tongue.

After a moment, Dadai had gone on: *So, our Jim does work on those shanty roofs time to time, you know, thatching leaks something fierce. Real blight, those old homes, but. Anyway, Jim reports the family keeps to itself. Father off with the fairies, drinkin', gone.*

Pub talk, then. I see.

His father had ignored the comment. *Jim says his cousin's got a turf farm out West, where the boy's family's from. Says they lost a child six, seven years back. Was barely a year gone. Sad story. But. No funeral. Gardai investigate, but it takes two weeks 'cause who gives a shit about—*

Anrai. Mam could use his Dadai's name like it was the worst word in the world.

Well. So. Tragedy strikes. But—wait, no. The fam has this other boy now. Authorities show up and there's this other child. No records of the first, 'cause—like I say, culchies. But this new one's not a year old. Less than. Still, the boy's father vouches and that's the end of it. A long pause. An' that's the boy who's playing with our son in our very own sitting room.

Twins, Mam had wondered in a faraway voice.

That had shut him down a moment. *Maybe. Maybe he got swapped. Like I say, father's off with the fairies already ...*

Mal had overheard Mam swatting him with a dishtowel and imagined her face was not playful. *I cannot believe what I'm hearing out of you tonight, Anrai. Maybe you should think on these things before you start spreading tales like an old biddy.*

Much of what they'd said went over Mal's head, though hearing his father speak of *culchies* had been a bit of a thrill, along with the swear word. The conversation had burned bright, then been buried over the years.

It all came back now.

"Gossip," he told Caitlin. "Just pub blether. He told you all this?"

Caitlin's gaze had shifted far down the path. Patrick was heading in their direction. He looked freshly-woken: unshaven, hair a mass of untamed black curls still damp from the shower, a yellow and white shirt hanging half-outside his jeans. But his smile reached all the way to his eyes.

Patrick. The formerly small boy for whom names had always been slippery, as if they didn't quite belong to him. As if they were only hats he wore to be polite. Patch, who was once so sure *sídhe* existed that he would bless the dust. Until that was taken from him.

"No," said Caitlin, watching him intently. "He doesn't know."

Central Park felt like home to Patrick.

How strange to think such a thing about a green place with squared-off corners, surrounded by concrete and height and noise, a place that seldom let visitors forget it was anything other than a park. But over the past week Patrick had spent hours wandering its perimeter and interior, time he'd never expected to have in New York. It was like a theme park of an actual park—many highlights, no chance of being lost. And Patrick, a little lost himself ever since Caitlin had taken him to her own odd Green Place, was fine with that. His soul opened to have this much space to safely roam, with the comfort of knowing he could always find his way back.

Dangling his legs over the rocks where Caitlin and Mal sat, he prepared himself—though for what, he couldn't be sure. In his heart he knew she was more than the sum of her parts, that Caitlin was someone with a foot in two worlds—but the fact of her still collided in his head with what must be true. Now, faced with the end to delays, he felt nervous and shy. They had a strange intimacy between them, and it made his body tingle.

"So here we are." She rested her arms on bent knees. "Quite a show you all put on the other day. Not much audience, but quite a show."

"Savage." Mal brightened. "Just savage."

They'd been taken up so easily by the songs—almost blended into them. Yes, they'd needed help from the whiskey but still, it had been a high point in Patrick's life. He'd never felt the music so strongly. "I'm glad you were there to hear it," he said.

She nodded. "I'm one of the few who could hear it properly."

They both frowned at her.

"It hurt a little bit, didn't it?" Caitlin kept her eyes on the distance. "Playing those songs. Started off easy, but then got … uncomfortable."

"Suppose," Patrick allowed. "But it takes time to learn new tunes; it's never that easy—"

"*No*," she rumbled "That is not what I mean."

A few leaves fell from a nearby tree.

"You're right." Mal watched them fall. "Without all that drink in me I don't know—it was like my insides were getting undone and tied back the wrong way. My head was splitting."

Patrick nodded. He hadn't recalled pain, just that drinking made the songs easier to … hear. To make. To digest.

"That's unusual, though, isn't it?" She held up a hand. "Don't answer yet. While you were passed out yesterday I learned from your manager that we weren't the only ones listening. Music has a way of … getting out of locked rooms. There was a bartender, wasn't there? Not from around here, I believe. Boy of the Wild Fields, near the Black Sea. In this country eight months. He was there. He heard. And then he disappeared, didn't he?"

Mal and Patrick shared a glance.

"Nosebleed." She gestured. "Blood everywhere. A migraine so sharp it was like a dagger directly between his eyes. He stumbled down to the kitchen and they got him help. He'll come back in a few days, probably. But that nice Ukrainian boy won't ever be able to taste anything again. Burned out of him. The rest of the staff in the lobby—well, they're mostly all right—some vision issues, some ringing in the ears—"

"You're jokin'," said Patrick, horrified. "That's—"

"You said you would listen," she said. "Go ask the manager. Well, you can after he gets back from his operation."

"Operation?" Mal's voice was a hushed whisper.

"His retina detached that afternoon. Right after he spoke with Ciaran. He'll see all right again, mostly." She paused. "Still want to argue?"

Patrick shook his head.

"No one is crazy here," she said. "No one is playing a game or trying to trick or con you. This will be so much *easier* if you don't fight it so hard. This is real. All of it is happening. And it doesn't require your belief or agreement to go on being real and to go on happening."

"But that's crazy talk," said Patrick. "Music doesn't *do* that."

"It can," said Mal. "Pitched high or low enough. But we—"

"Where'd those songs come from?" she interrupted.

Patrick leaned forward. He'd gotten so banjaxed he couldn't recall.

"Ciaran had a notebook of'em," Mal said. "That's why I came downstairs. He said they came to him in a rush—he's been scribbling in his room all this time."

Patrick made a soft, astonished noise. "He never. In *a week* he wrote all that? Not in a lifetime." The park around them seemed to have hushed; the birdsong and chatter from other visitors was gone. He couldn't even hear the cars a few yards away.

Mal's mouth was pressed tight. "Well. I didn't think to ask."

"They were *gorgeous*." Patrick sighed. "Like listening to diamonds."

Caitlin smiled and brushed some hair from his shoulder. "Mal, I watched you the other day. I saw you up on that stage. You close your eyes and you … go someplace. Where?"

Mal waited a long time before answering. "How do you mean—where do I go? I'm right there on the bench."

"Mal. It's all right. Just—say it."

Another long silence. "It's only a quiet place. In me head."

"Be true with it."

He made a small jerking motion, as if pricked. "It's a tremendous … field. A … going-on-forever place." Patrick was gaping at him, but he let the words flow. "Sometimes there's a cottage and sometimes there's a tree and sometimes there's a great white horse. But most of the time it's green from one horizon to the next, soft, waving grasses and everything is so much *more* there than any-where else."

"And it smells like life itself," Patrick murmured. "The Green Place."

Mal's face shone like a sunflower. "Patch—you know it? Ah, Jaysus. Of course you would. Except—I can't stay. Eventually I have to stop playing and open my eyes. The song only goes on so long. And each time, it breaks me a little."

"But you still go," said Caitlin. "You still play."

"Worth it." He sighed. "Every minute."

Patrick leaned away from her. "That's—that's what you showed me. Where you *took* me." *Where I went in my dream.* "I saw it again. While I was sleeping."

"And?"

"There was a tree. And *Athair.*"

Mal tilted his head. "You dreamed you saw your father?"

Patrick met Caitlin's eyes and swallowed. "Wasn't a dream, was it."

She suppressed a smile. "What do you think?"

"I think I'd do anything to go back." His voice was small, but full of yearning. It was true. He'd even believe in the impossible.

Caitlin scooped up their hands in hers. "No time like the present."

The Scent of Cranberries and Blood

Mal had never believed his field was real. It was always a well-imagined waking dream, a self-induced synesthesia. Much as he loved playing piano, the sensation of being watched while doing it was enough to throw him off, so he began closing his eyes when he was small. He didn't have to see the keyboard to make it work.

Early on, the gesture only sent him into darkness—and music was about bursting light and endless color and rapacious energy. So he began focusing on a way to see somewhere *else* when he dove deep into a song. He wanted to turn the dark into something better. And then, one day he'd begun playing, closed his eyes—and saw light. A glaring whiteness that gave way to green, which yielded to blue and a breeze and—in time, sound and smell. He could still hear the tune he coaxed out of the piano and the words he was singing and the crowd he did not want to see roaring, but he was in another place simultaneously. He returned again and again whenever he sat at a keyboard but could rarely stay more than four or five minutes—the length of a song. When the band jammed, he needed to be alert enough to play the changes, so he couldn't go then, but any other chance he got—he took.

Yet when he set his hand into Caitlin's while Patrick took her other, he still thought she was speaking in metaphors, like a therapist might. *Sure, it's real*, he thought. *It's real to me.* That kind of tripe.

But then—

They were there.

Here. The field. His green, imagined place with the impossible blue sky and a scent on the breeze that made him think of freshly-laundered sheets and

120

lavender, of a leather jacket he'd once owned and, improbably, the tang of lime. Patrick and Caitlin sat across from him, buffeted by a gentle wind. He hadn't played a single note, but he was here.

Dumbstruck, Mal leaped up. The breeze stilled. He took a step, stumbling and nearly falling. He was lighter here, somehow. He'd arrived without music, without will. He'd been *brought.*

After a moment, his legs felt firmer and he reached into the smooth, waving grass. It touched him back, more real than any he'd ever felt. Mal kicked off his sandals and wandered, slack-jawed. He felt drunk. Tipping his head back he tried absorbing every sensation that came at him—then on a whim began running, the soft blades whispering between his toes, caressing his skin. He ran on and on, never tiring, never reaching a border or marker or tripping on a hole. However far he went he could always see the others in the distance, and when he rounded to return it took just a few steps to arrive at his destination.

Winded, he collapsed next to Caitlin and Patrick, who lay alongside one another in the long grass. She was chewing on a blade; Patrick had split one down the center and made a whistle with it. They looked like people of a kind, people who had known one another all their lives.

He doesn't know.

But what didn't Patrick know?

"Real," said Mal.

"I never lie." Caitlin sat up.

"Tell me everything," Mal insisted.

Patrick nodded.

"First things first," she said. "Let's begin with Mal. You haven't had much fun lately, have you."

Amid the blur of everything he'd just seen, of the music of a day before, Mal had to remember feeling that the world was arrayed against him. His hair. The piano. The bed. "This is not bad at all." He held out his hands at the Green Place. "But otherwise—yes. That's an understatement."

"You'd like things to be … normal again, yes?"

"Normal-ish would work," he allowed.

"When I left, things changed for Padraig, didn't they."

Patrick rolled over, listening. "Can't you just tell us, Caitlin? Why's everything a puzzle?"

"Reasons," she said. "And—rules. There are rules here. And consequences."

"Who makes up *rules* in a perfect world?" Mal groused.

"Far from perfect." But Caitlin looked pleased. "Very far. But—not me. I'm just a … messenger. What I can say is this: Think of someone or some*thing* that came into your life just before things changed. If you can think of what it is, you have to make it leave you."

121

Patrick pulled himself up. "That's why the lottery failed," he said. "I had a funny kind of *luck* when you were around. And it went when you did."

Mal stared at his hands, breaths coming in low and slow. "I'm one step ahead of you there. The tinker. That was—one of 'em. One of *you*." He flushed. "That tinker tested me and found me wanting." He blinked and turned to Patrick. "He whispered something to you that night. What'd he say?"

"*She*," Patrick insisted. "She whispered to me that I was in good hands, though I didn't know it yet. She said—'she'll learn ye fine. But stay low and quiet all's the same.'" He blinked. "She also mentioned the *fear gorta*."

Mal held up his hands. "The hungry man? Shows up in the famine, brings … ah, feck."

"Brings good luck," said Patrick.

Caitlin beamed. "Not always a 'man,' though. Nice to meet you both." She waited as their gazes settled on her in a fresh way. "See, the things you don't believe in—believe in you. For years this has been so. And we've never been too far away."

"Now, hold it," said Mal, trying to remember the books he'd picked up as a child. "I read about you, years ago. Except—it's a load of shite, what he wrote."

"What *who* wrote?" Patrick asked.

Mal felt his cheeks pink a bit. "Look, Patch, when you first started showing up and blessing the wind and all of that—I went and did some reading. I never met anybody like you. It was like you came out of a storybook."

Patrick's face hardened.

"What can I say, I was a kid meself. Anyhow, there was this one book, came with a great pedigree: W. B. Yeats wrote it. He'd gone out around the country a hundred years ago and scooped up the local stories and wrote a catalog of it all. Hell, he even put in a musical transcription of the *bean sí* call. I ate it up. Believed every word. Least, until I met some actual scholars. Turns out the man couldn't even speak Irish. He made up whole parts. And today, a lot of folks think it's gospel direct from the *sídhe* themselves. Nobody knows truth from story anymore."

Patrick sat up poker-straight, eyes moist. "Doesn't matter. They believe it. So—it's true."

Caitlin smiled.

"Stories create reality if the storytellers are clever or powerful enough," Patrick continued. "Brother David told me that. He meant … different stories. But if he's right—"

"He's most correct," said Caitlin. "For better or worse, that misguided little tome your poet wrote buoys us. What had been fading now sits lively in the imagination. And imagination is sustenance. Without it, we are lost—again. Buried even deeper underground."

"Extraordinary," Mal breathed. "But I was warned about a different fey. The red man."

"Indeed. So. Now that you've named your tormentor, it's time to get down to business. Think about what I just told you. What could you ... leave behind?"

Mal stared into the grass. There had been the tinker, but he—she—it—was back in Boston. There was money. The messages the tinker gave them. And all the rain that night. Then he knew. In one fast movement, he yanked off the red woolen cap and flung it to the side. His stubbled, bald head felt instantly cool—and strangely lonely. "Done."

Caitlin shook her head. "'Tis a bit more complicated than that."

Mal glanced at where he'd thrown the hat. His head warmed again—it had boomeranged back in place.

"Aw, feck," he said.

What Mal needed to accomplish could not be done in the Green Place, so Caitlin brought them back to their rock in Central Park. "I can't assist," she said. "I am heartily sorry. But this is not my doing, and so I can't be its undoing."

"Let's burn this feckin' thing," said Mal, gripping the hat in one hand.

"I like it," Patrick agreed. He ran to a nearby restaurant, returning with a small box of matches. Mal discovered a fissure in the rocks out of the way of observant policemen, and pulled out a small bottle of whiskey he'd taken from the minibar in the hotel. They soaked the red wool with it before pressing the hat into the crevice.

That was the easy part.

"So I just light it and that's an end?" Mal asked Caitlin, heart revving as if he'd been running at top speed.

Caitlin didn't respond.

"At least come closer?"

She shook her head.

Patrick lit the first match, but Mal blew it out. "Lemme. I got this feeling this has to be something I do alone."

Box in hand, Mal crouched over the fissure and dragged the head of the second match against the sandpaper side. It caught beautifully, the flame perfectly shaped and ready. All he had to do was toss it into the fissure. But in that moment, his legs liquefied. The match fell away.

"Mal!" Patrick cried, but Mal held up a hand.

Grabbing a third match, Mal struck it—and hesitated. A melancholy so deep and terrifying crashed over him like an enormous wave. *Don't do it*, the voice in his head said. *This is the worst choice you will ever make. You will never play piano again.*

Mal pushed it away and tried to get a grip. He held the match so long it burned into his fingers and he flung it to the side.

Things went on like this again and again. Each time, he was seized with horrors strong enough to be premonitions: He would lose his hands. His family would die. He had no talent. He would lose his senses. Ciaran and Patrick would be killed horribly. He would be blocked from returning home. Each time, that voice was in his mind, playing just the right chords to steer him from the plan.

"Mal," said Patrick after a long while. It felt as though hours had passed. "It'll be all right. I'm here."

"I can't do this."

Patrick waited until Mal looked him in the face. "You took yourself to the Green Place, Malachi. You can do anything. If it's belief you need to make it real, then—have all of mine. I believe you can. Also, you can't *not* do it."

Mal struck the second-to-last match in the box with a renewed strength. Patch was right. None of those imagined horrific futures meant a damn if he couldn't rid himself of the hat—because Mal was certain he would not survive a lifetime of what he'd been through the past few days. He'd kill himself first.

He dropped the match.

At first, it was just a pile of wool burning. But then the flame turned inward, went soot-dark and almost solid. It leapt, this solid flickering thing, several feet in the air. A cry bayed out, followed by hissing. Not human, not animal. But as if some kind of creature was being incinerated alive.

Save me save me

Came the call. Mal cupped his hands over his ears, cringing.

Save me save me only you can save me

He almost reached for the burning cap. Then the black column collapsed. The voice cut out. And it burned just as any other fabric might.

Mal broke into a cold sweat, shivering. Patrick set a hand on his shoulder.

The hat took a very long time to burn, but they all sat in silence until it was done. The sun drew westward. It was both ridiculous and dead serious, watching a wool cap burn. But they couldn't take their eyes from it. And when the flames finally died, the three of them were left wrapped in twilight on a cold rock, the scent of cranberries and blood in their noses.

Mal felt like singing.

Things of No Account

"We came all this way to go to another *amadán* pub?" Ciaran thumbed at the exterior of Kennedy's. "What makes this place so special?"

Sheerie looped one hand through the crook of his arm. "The hotel is nice," she purred. "I like it there."

So did Ciaran. He glanced over his shoulder, back the way they'd come.

"Oh, no you don't." Mal yanked on Ciaran's sleeve. The fabric slipped loosely and engulfed Ciaran's left hand. "Only one of us who needs more fresh air than me—is you."

That was true. In all their extended time in the city, Ciaran couldn't recall visiting so much as Times Square. All through Mal's … incident and mattress-on-the-floor recovery, he hadn't left the hotel. He was running out of wall space for all the music that kept pouring out of him, and Sheerie had to massage his hand a couple of times a day to get the cramping out of it. He'd begun to notice a persistent pain in his lower back that wasn't going away.

Ciaran shrugged off Mal and tugged his sleeve back into place.

"Besides, there's fine *craic* inside." Patrick bounded in front of him. That red-haired woman—Caitlin—hovered in the background, making his stomach turn. Why couldn't it just be the three of them again? Why had they become a permanent *five* all at once?

But he couldn't say anything. To object to Caitlin was to get them started on Sheerie. And as Ciaran knew by now, she wasn't going anywhere. Nor did he really want her to. So he'd allowed them to talk him into coming out into the city. Into the world. To this … caricature of a pub from home.

125

"There'd better be," he growled. "I got things to do."

But he was curious. This was their last night in New York before hitting the road again, and he didn't like missing out on everything. Patch had been the one to suggest they check out Tom's band, at this pub where the group played of a Friday. Maybe this generic, eejit version of an actual pub was more promising on the inside than the outside.

He ignored an unreadable look that passed between Mal and Patrick.

"Aw, give it a chance." A light above Mal reflected on his bare head, and Ciaran wondered where that stupid red hat had gone. His smooth bare skull was so jarring, it was hard to believe it really was Mal. But … at least they'd gotten him up and moving. He was practically his old self again. And with Mal up, they could finally leave the city. Continue the tour. Maybe fix whatever that rotten financial hole was back at home. The deal was this, as Rich had conveyed on a conference call that afternoon: Not appearing at the next scheduled gig risked them getting hit with litigation. Americans loved to take people to court, Rich had said. Being broke at home wasn't the worst thing ever—they'd lived without more than they'd ever lived with. But being sued in America with no money in the bank threatened to pry open an abyss from which they'd never emerge.

Back to the road again, then. Likely tomorrow's show would be terrible—in a week, they'd only had the one drunken afternoon of practice, if that's what you could call what they'd done in the hotel bar. But the contract only stipulated that they show up and play. It didn't say they had to play *well*.

Mal yanked open the pub door and out flew music, the band inside cranking out a storm of chewy rock sounds. Sheerie visibly perked up, wrinkling her nose as if smelling something delicious. She squeezed Ciaran's arm. "All right. We can stay a bit."

Everyone filed inside, with Ciaran last to step up. A sleepy-eyed woman on a barstool stopped him and held out a hand. "ID."

Sheerie blew a kiss at Ciaran and slipped inside without being questioned.

"C'mon, darlin'. I know I don't look less than twenty-one." Ciaran offered a pants-dropping smile that had worked on women for years. Then he gave a raspy cough.

The woman was no longer sleepy-eyed. Her face went pale and stiff with caution and her barstool rocked as she drew back. That was not the reaction the pants-dropping smile usually elicited. The woman covered her mouth with a tattooed hand.

"Didn't think so." Ciaran humphed and pushed inside, wondering what had gotten in her dentures.

Music engulfed him like a hot bath. The pub was spacious, packed with early weekend revelers drinking and listening to the band, drinking and shouting over the band, or playing pool and ignoring the band. At the bar, Sheerie gestured at a thick, ice-cold Guinness that had just begun to settle.

"On the house," Patrick shouted. "And served right."

Nice piece of luck, he thought. "Gorgeous."

The others toasted with their glasses and pushed closer to the stage, finding a spot off to one side. The band was tight, making good, honest noise, and Ciaran settled in to be entertained for once, rather than having to do the entertaining. They were a standard four-piece, with Patch's pal Tom flailing on drums in the back. Ciaran kept his eye on the razor-thin, pale guitarist, eyeing his finger technique. Mal and Patrick flanked Caitlin next to him, bobbing their heads to the beat.

One song, then another, a glass of Guinness, then another, and there he was—enjoying himself like everyone else in the room, head swaying, hand on Sheerie's arse and all was right with the world. He shot Patch a grin of approval. That disquiet from earlier was gone; the three of them were a unit once again. Another song, another Guinness—and the band launched into Them's "Gloria." As one, they raised their glasses, shouting the chorus with the rest of the drunken bastards in the room. Ciaran touched his drink with Mal's, and they fell against one another, laughing their *amadán* heads off.

Jaysus, I missed this.

At the break, Patrick introduced Tom around. He was a hard man not to like; had that immediate big dog friendliness Ciaran admired in most Americans he'd come across. After a moment, he headed back to the bar to find Sheerie perched on a stool, happily chatting with the stick-slender guitarist. Ciaran strode over, planning to make three an uncomfortable crowd, but the guitarist beckoned at him cheerily and held out a hand.

"Jody," he said. "Big fans of your gang."

Disarmed, Ciaran gripped the hand back. "Good of ye to say so. You're not so bad yourself."

"Swear I met your girl once." Jody gestured at Sheerie. "Looks just like a lady m'friend dated about six, seven years back."

"Tom?" Ciaran asked.

Jody shook his head. "Fella named Paul. Dead now, not even twenty-one, God rest him." He sighed. "Anyhow, not moving in on your space. Just got to thinking about him and that girl." He raised his glass to her. "You're lovelier than she was, of course."

Sheerie beamed at all the attention but slipped her hand into Ciaran's.

It was all music talk after that—preferred instruments, working in the studio—but Ciaran was partly on auto-pilot. Jody was good enough for a jaw, but the man's appearance was distracting. He had a wasted, wan look with gray rings around too-bright eyes and long greasy hair dangling in thick strands from beneath his tweed cap. Ciaran knew the story: You didn't get this way from too many sleepless nights or not eating right. Jody was a destination reached by just one road, with detours often taken intravenously.

Realizing he was staring, Ciaran glanced elsewhere and discovered the others had planted themselves at the pool tables. Patrick was bent over the green cloth, practically kissing the felt, about to sink an easy shot. He missed.

Eventually, Jody realized he wasn't speaking to anyone who was listening and nodded at the game. "I wouldn't recommend going up against Tom over there—he'll steal you blind. We play here so much he's picked up something of a *habit*. We all have, if you catch my drift."

Ciaran turned back and their eyes met.

"Second set's coming," said Jody, setting his drink on the bar. "See you after."

Ciaran lifted his glass with a small nod.

Jody made a clicking sound with his mouth. "Find me then. Got a little something you might be interested in." He headed back to the stage.

An unpleasant heat swept through Ciaran, and Sheerie squeezed his hand. She was still glowing, a little firecracker set to go off.

Post-show, Patrick sat in a far corner of Kennedy's back room, Caitlin nestled close, a beer warming in his hand. He couldn't recall the last time he was this *himself*. Making music in the hotel bar, maybe. But that had been a crazed afternoon. This was normal. Perfect, and normal. Everything was around him and everyone was where they were supposed to be and he was at peace in the world.

Tom's band had wrapped twenty minutes earlier, and after the customary grace period, their dressing room opened for visitors. They'd joined a group of well-wishers and family members in the small space, which held just a few chairs and a bench lining the wall and appeared to double as Kennedy's stockroom. Tom and his bandmates were high on the success of the evening, and so was Patrick—he'd been invited to jump in on the last two numbers using their mandolin.

Over the next half hour the initial crowd of visitors waned, making the space roomier and easier to hear in. Jody pulled out his acoustic, Tom fetched the bodhran, Ciaran offered the tin whistle he always carried—and they started up a *seisún*, sliding from reels right into "Moondance" and then back out into "Carrickfergus."

"You skipped verses!" Mal cried out at the end of one song, but it was a hearty, delighted critique.

Patrick and Caitlin sang along, and her high, clear voice was like nothing that had ever graced his ears. She almost vibrated with the music, surrounded by electric energy that buzzed against his body. During a lull between songs they caught one another's eye and the moment drew out like a long-held note. The butterfly in his chest awakened again. He thought about raising his arm and wrapping it around her, but held back.

Instead, he asked, "What's next, then?" Back in Central Park, they'd put all their efforts into freeing Mal of his demon—but they'd left without getting

Patrick any answers. He worried now what she would have to tell, or show him. He both longed for answers and was terrified of having them. But they couldn't sit on this fence—or stand on this stile—forever.

Her mouth quirked up, and she held out a hand. "Come." Leading him from the storage room, she pulled the door closed behind on the music, which drifted out through the cracks and the keyhole. The bar was largely empty—they were near closing time—and it was quiet. They stood beneath a bare light bulb and she studied him. Patrick forced himself to meet that steady gaze, and study her right back. In the blue of her eyes, he saw his own reflection and made a soft, inward gasp. Whatever she planned to say next wasn't about herself.

"There." She nodded. "Was waiting for that."

"For what?"

"For you to put your monk away. To *see* me. To see yourself. To see all of us."

"*Us.*"

"I want you to know this: You've never been alone. Not really. We've—kept eyes on you."

Well, that's not creepy at all, he started to think—but as if reading his mind, Caitlin frowned and shook her head.

"It was for your own good, Padraig. You'll understand eventually. The thing is … then you were taken from us. From your first home. Brought to this world."

"That's right, Caitlin. People travel. An' the only folks I care about are the ones I came over here with. So whatever this leavin' means … I didn't leave anyone who matters."

"So you're not … curious about what—who—was left behind?"

Part of him burned to know now that she'd asked. But he couldn't form the words. The idea of his *athair* with a lover. The idea of a second *máthair*, when one had been more than enough. Of his monk, wagging a finger. Of stupid-stitions. He shook his head gently.

She touched his hand and the rustling in his heart stilled. "Well, all right. But when you left, a decision had to be made." Her fingers closed over his. "Time to open your eyes all the way."

His head swam. "How can something that makes no sense scare the life out of me?"

"Try not to fear." The touch of her hand was comforting. "I want you to go to what you think of as the Green Place now. Without my help."

She might as well have asked him to fly to the moon. "Yer jokin'."

Crooking a finger, Caitlin crouched to the old-fashioned keyhole on the back room door. "See this?" she said, gesturing. "Your *athair* told you about worn-up places. His words, but they do fine. A worn-up place is like a keyhole—you can see straight through to the other side. Each time someone walks through, they grow a little wider, a little more fragile. Emotions make them bigger, too—and it's hard to shrink them back. They stop being keyholes and become gateways.

So we try to disguise them. But only certain … *individuals* can pass through to the other side by will alone."

"Mal does."

"Mal's a special human. He made his worn-up place with music. But as you know, he doesn't fully *go*. He visits, briefly, and the moment his music stops—so does the visit." She paused. "You, on the other hand, have the skeleton key. You can go whenever you choose."

"All of me."

"All of you."

He shook his head. "But I'm not like Mal. He's born with that music in him. Comes out of him like breathing."

"Oh, no. He works so hard to get there—it just doesn't look like work, because it's joy. But it's in you, even if you never play another note. And the more you believe in it, the stronger it becomes. That's how we work, Padraig. We exist on a cloud of belief. Like your monk told you, belief creates the real. And *I* believe that *you* now believe enough to take yourself there. So—go. Let it happen, don't fight it. And when you're there—speak with your *athair*."

This was his moment. His lit match, hovering over everything he feared. All he had to do was let go. Mal had done it. So could he.

Patrick closed his eyes and let a calm settle over him, a blankness that needed filling. With answers. With anything. He felt a breeze tickle his neck as he visualized the waving grasses, the vast emptiness, and a tree. Above him, the light went out—and Patrick tumbled.

Into brightness—into sunshine—into blue the color of Caitlin's eyes—into—

Baking bread. Rosemary and sea salt. The scent drifted over Patrick's shoulder and he inhaled deeply. He was back, standing on that green waving expanse. A charge flowed through him, a current that spread his fingers and toes and tickled him all the way through.

He was *here*. He'd come. All on his own—and alone. It had been like slipping into a cloak sewn just for his body.

The great tree loomed before him. He was in the sun, one step from the canopy. He strode toward the tree trunk, just as he had before, and there was *Athair*. Da. Just thinking the name made his eyes well. He was still sitting on that same bumped-up root, hands curled around a half-eaten apple. His hat was askew, mustache bushy and dominating.

Herself had been actively dismissive and cruel. *Athair*—Da—hadn't been a bundle of warmth either, and rarely called Padraig by name. Just said *an buachaill* and sometimes added *beag* on the end—*boy* or *little boy*—and brought him places. To town on an errand. To his workshop where he repaired household appliances or shoes or whatever needed fixing. Da had a knack for that and had been much in demand. Once they'd gone to a game of footie. Once, a movie. Da never said much to Padraig except when teaching him how to use his hands and repair the plastic and metal things of the world. But the attention had been gold and Padraig was a hoarder.

None of that happened, of course, when Da vanished. He'd be gone for random periods, then return in the same clothes he'd had on when he left. People assumed he was off getting blasted with drink and had fallen in a ditch. Or maybe he had another family someplace. On his return, he and Herself would shout at each other so savagely that Padraig knew better than to ask to come inside.

After being admitted to the monastery, Padraig never saw them again. Da went missing and never returned to the falling-down shack. Herself died, according to the obituary mailed to the monastery. Padraig didn't even know where she was buried. He couldn't recall if he'd ever cried over the loss of them—but he'd been no one's *buachaill beag* since.

Here in the Green Place, under the tree, it was different. This place was all now—no forward, no backward. And Da was here. He hadn't moved since the last time Patrick saw him, in the maybe-dream. And he looked the same as when Patrick had been a boy—not a thread of gray on his head or in that mustache, as if the years hadn't touched him. Patrick stared for a long while, the warm bready breeze giving the branches a gentle shake. Leaves fluttered downward like wings. It was Da and no mistake.

This is where he went.

The revelation hit hard. Da had come to the Green Place, every time. More surprising, really, was that he'd ever left it. Given the choice of a dirty, drafty cottage with a harridan wife who couldn't stand the sight of him and a strange son he didn't know how to talk to—Patrick immediately understood his absences. He wasn't sure if he could forgive them, though. Da had always had access to a beautiful, safe place. And he'd left his son behind. Patrick's gut roiled and he clenched his teeth. That was the part he didn't think he could forgive.

"Sit," his father said, touching the side of the root. "Come closer."

Patrick folded his arms and remained standing.

"Suit y'self," said Da. "But do have a bit o' apple."

Patrick didn't move.

Athair sighed. "As ye will. 'Tis good you're here, son."

Son. "Am I, though?"

"Mine? 'Course ye are. Never doubt."

Patrick wasn't sure if he felt relief. "And ... Herself. She's not my *máthair*."

Da chuckled darkly. Patrick was struck at how young and healthy, how *together* he looked. "Well, now. That is where things get interesting."

His jovial manner irritated Patrick, who felt cold despite the bright sun. His fists itched and he pressed them beneath his arms, making his body a wall. "Having a good time, are you?"

The older man shook his head. "So. We come to it. G'wan, do yer yellin' at me. Get it all out, I deserve every bit. Then we can get to the good stuff."

Patrick imagined he was a lion, opening his jaw to enormous size and letting out a roar that would wilt the world around them. But everything was happening so fast—Caitlin telling him he could will himself here. The sensory overload of the Green Place. Finding *Athair* just casually eating an apple, like it was any other day instead of the most important one of Patrick's life. He clenched his fists. He wanted to hit something. His head swirled. His legs felt soft and he stumbled forward.

Da leaped from the branch, letting the rest of the apple tumble to the ground. He caught Patrick mid-collapse, guiding him onto the thick branch. Da began to back off, but Patrick gasped: "Don't." He let his arms loose, scrabbling at his father's elbow. "Don't—"

"Don't what, son?" Da wasn't laughing now.

"Don't—don't let go," Patrick whispered. His eyes burned and his heart felt like it might break out of his body.

Da gasped in surprise, then rested his forehead against Patrick's. He pulled him closer. "No, son. 'Course not. Never again. After all, we're home now."

Patrick sobbed softly into his work shirt. Da said nothing for a long while, as the crisp cinnamon breeze swirled and the sun warmed both of their heads. In time, Patrick's tears slowed and his heart began to beat more normally. He pulled back a hair.

Da produced a new, green apple. "All right, then," he said. "Now, will ye share with me?"

Patrick wiped his face with a sleeve. He was exhausted, but this time he accepted the slice. Holding it to his nose, he nearly fell backward. The scent was bigger, fuller than any fruit he'd ever come across. He brought the flesh to his lips and nearly swooned; it was like eating the ur-apple, the one from which all others had been made. He shivered with delight. Da handed him a second, and a third.

They stared at one another. Patrick had never had a chance to do that before, just openly stare at his father. It wasn't the same as looking in a mirror, but more like the echo of one. Da was too young-looking to have a son Patrick's age; they nearly looked like peers. He hadn't aged over here.

"No," said *Athair*, answering his question from what felt like months ago. "She is not your *máthair*. An'—that's my fault, entire."

"Then who is?"

Da considered him for a long time. "Let's start elsewhens. Let's begin at the beginning."

"And ... that's not it?"

He shook his head, the mustache twitching. "The beginning, Padraig, is who *you* are."

Ciaran was slumped against a wall, wearing his drunk face. Sheerie had left, but he couldn't summon the energy to care where she was. He was vaguely aware that Patrick and that strange girl of his had left the room some time ago and that Mal and Tom had started talking pool, then wandered out to the tables. Most of the remaining partygoers had trailed after them, anticipating a match.

His mind reeled from drink and music and a sudden, draining weariness. A line of poetry repeated in his head: *We and all the Muses are things of no account.*

Ciaran murmured the line again and again, emphasizing each word in its turn, working through what Yeats might have meant. *I've got a muse*, he thought. *We're both no-accounts.*

Sheerie was gone. That made him uneasy.

"Things of *no* account," he muttered, trying to sit up. He started to topple forward—and was arrested by a firm grip.

"You reek of an alehouse." Jody chuckled.

"Your mother," blurred Ciaran, then laughed. An unbearable fullness in his gut made him realize he needed to change location. With a few deep breaths, he oriented himself. The room was dimmer than before. Beyond the open door came muted voices and a crack of pool balls.

"C'mon." Jody offered a hand. "Let's look at something."

Ciaran was grateful for the assistance. "I should use the toilet."

"Precisely my destination."

The bare light bulb in the back room's tiny toilet made him squint, but he stumbled to the filthy urinal to take care of business. Behind him, Jody rustled by the sink counter. It took a long time to evacuate everything down to that first Guinness hours earlier, but when he was done, Ciaran turned to the sink and its room-wide mirror. A scarecrow looked back at him. He shook his head, running hands beneath the water, and peeled back his drunken layers until everything came into focus.

Now there were two scarecrows.

Stumbling back, then lurching forward, he squinted at the reflection but both images remained. He touched the mirror and one reflection touched back. The other was Jody. Ciaran ran a hand up and down his slack white shirt, then hiked it up. His throat constricted as he counted: two, four, six ribs. Clearly defined. He released the fabric.

That's not me. That can't be me.

"Yeah, man, I been there," Jody chuckled and pulled out a metal Altoids case from his jacket pocket. Prying open the lid, he spoke to Ciaran's reflection. "No fear. A little a'this and you'll be right as rain."

The box was half-full with what looked like powdered sugar. Jody set it on the counter, slipped off his laminated backstage pass and cut four raised lines out. They resembled bloodless welts.

Ciaran had suspected the man was on heroin earlier, but based on his look there were so many vehicles to put you on that one desperate road. "*Sneachta.*" Snow.

133

Jody laughed. "Here we call it orange whip!" He held out a hand. "Guests first."

Ciaran glanced between himself and the other scarecrow in the mirror. Anger bubbled in his empty gut. Jody took *him*—not Mal, not Patrick—for a comrade-in-noses. Sure, he looked a little worn down. Probably could use an extra meal or two. But no way was he some strung-out, wasted, half-gone druggie.

Or am I?

He shoved the voice aside.

Am I ill?

But it didn't go away so easily.

Another voice plucked at his heart, one he knew well. *Come home, my love. I need you now.* Sheerie must be back at the hotel. The radio in his head had lowered its demanding roar all evening, but her voice was replacing it. The sound was like a ring clamped to his insides, tugging.

What the hell is going on with me?

Jody was watching him.

"What happened to Paul?" Ciaran asked in a thin voice, trying to swallow his fear. His rage. "Your friend."

Jody's mouth twisted a bit, eyes dulled. "Told you. Died."

"How."

Tell me it's a car crash or he had too much orange whip or something.

"Back off, man." Jody stepped away from the sink. "That ain't your business. Tryin' to do you a favor and—"

Ciaran's fist shot out and connected with Jody's mouth. The guitarist bounced awkwardly off the sink, his head hitting the mirror, which cracked, and he sank to the ground. The room filled with scattered powder from the small tin.

My love! Sheerie called, but it wasn't a summoning. It was delight. *More, please.*

Reaching down, Ciaran hauled Jody up by his shirt collar. Woozy, the man's head snapped back, then forward. He swore, spitting blood. "What the *fuck*, man—"

Ciaran rattled him. "How did your friend *die*?"

"Heart attack, asshole." Jody squirmed, flailing at Ciaran's arm. *Not even twenty-one*, Jody had said earlier.

Ciaran gripped tighter, twisting the shirt fabric across his neck. His face went from red to purple. "What happened to his girl?"

Jody gagged, and Ciaran loosened his fist. "Disappeared. Bitch didn't even come to the funeral."

The doorway filled with shadow. "Jesus Christ, let him *go*." Tom leaped into the room and heaved himself against Ciaran, who released his victim. Jody tumbled to the floor, gasping. Tom shoved Ciaran's chest with both hands. "What the fuck is going on in here?"

"Disagreement," said Ciaran, all the anger leaching from him. But not the fear. "Your junkie guitarist's a little too free with his dealing."

134

Jody gaped and spat into the sink. "That's a fuckin' lie. I'm not selling. I was *giving*." He took a step forward, eyes burning at Ciaran. "And I'm not done *giving* yet."

Tom held them apart and turned to Jody. "Looks like we're gonna have to have another talk about this."

Mal slid into view, still holding a pool stick, and took in the scene. "What exploded?"

"Your friend did." Tom tilted his head at Ciaran. "Think we'd better call it a night."

Ciaran's fist was on fire from the punch, and he stared at the raw, red knuckles. Sheerie's voice had been so *happy* when he'd connected with Jody's face, and it had felt good to have her cheer him on. Made him want to do more of it. Didn't matter that hearing her at this distance was four different kinds of impossible.

Maybe I am ill. Maybe I'm losin' my mind.

Holding his hands up in surrender, Ciaran let Mal lead him from the toilet. He brushed past Jody on the way out. A sharp copper whiff came from the man's mashed face, and he turned around. "One more thing," Ciaran said.

"Fuck you," said Jody.

"How long were they—together?"

A long pause, in which both men finally understood one another. Jody's crimson-stained mouth peeled open to reveal gray teeth, and Ciaran couldn't tell if it was a grimace or a smile. "Six months," he spat. "I'm hopin' you get *less*."

The Only Song Worth Singing

Patrick returned to a night so late that it was early, the darkened sky beginning to fade from thick inky blackness to faint morning blue. The streets
were empty, the sidewalks vacant. New York City might never sleep, but clearly
it dreamed.

He was outside. Not in Kennedy's. Patrick glanced up: 45th and 5th. He
had traveled.

Poking at his eyes, he began heading uptown, taking long, deep swallows
of air.

You're part mine, Da had said. *And you're part of this place as well. I've made a
blunder of it, though I couldn't say where I'd've changed much.*

The music—that should have tipped him. Patrick been forcefully blind. So
much easier to pretend that the world was full of impossible tricks and lies, that
there was only one true way to see its shape. Or that music was merely sound
echoing in the ear, not something as vital to the body as blood or tears or bone.
Mal and Ciaran would never understand this. No one could.

Well—one person could.

His shadow doubled on the sidewalk as steps fell in beside his own. Caitlin
said nothing, and he couldn't acknowledge her yet. Back in Boston, she might
have told him everything as they sat there on the Common. That first day. He'd
been so open to her, so in thrall—he'd have believed.

But no, that was a lie he told himself. Patrick had fled the Green Place the
first time she'd taken him there, then thrown her out of the hotel when she'd
been flat-out honest. He'd been afraid. He'd wasted so much time.

Da hadn't fled the Green Place when he was first brought there. His own *athair* had taken him over when he was sixteen and a bit. *The family business*, Da had told Patrick. The *sídhe* were marvelous at so many things, but the clock-works of the world bedeviled them. *Can't even teach 'em, poor beggars*, he'd said. Fey loved wheels that turned and ticking timepieces—not time itself, which was irrelevant to them—and small, beautifully-crafted machines. Things that broke down and needed rebuilding. Things that needed skilled human hands.

So Da came back again and again. Years passed.

An' then I fell in love, he'd said, reading Patrick's stricken look. *Not w'the one you're calling Caitlin. Not her a'tall. But I loved. I love still. How can you spend time here and not fall?*

Now, Caitlin and Patrick arrived at a crossroads: wide, straight 6th Avenue and a smaller, darker street in the high 40s. Lights blinked yellow warnings in all directions. Patrick strode to the center of the intersection and stopped, held by the sight of perfectly straight, empty roads stretching in four directions.

What better place to stand in this hour of knowledge?

He held out his arms. "Neither fish nor fowl. Rain nor shine. Man nor beast. That's me. Both and neither."

Caitlin circled around him. "So you've spoken with him."

"You know I did." He glanced around. The streets remained empty. Something heavy was pressing against his chest and he stumbled, trying not to collapse. He felt made of soft, malleable material. Inconsequential. Everything Da had said was starting to crush him. He didn't know how much longer he could hold things together. Facing her, he choked out, "Why did you do this to me?"

She came to a halt. "Oh, Padraig. I didn't do a thing. Showed you the water and let you drink." She paused. "It was a long journey we took, but you're here now. Tell me things don't make more sense."

"You might've warned me."

Caitlin's laugh was a jangling melody. "And what do you think I've been doing since we met in Boston?"

A lone car headed their way down the avenue. Patrick fought an urge to get out of its way, then thought of Mal and his lottery ticket. Of their vague notions of luck. "What happens if I stand here? What happens if I wait for that car to mow me down?"

She wrapped her hands around his arm. "Good idea! Let's find out."

Da had done most of the talking in the Green Place. He told Patrick about how, as he'd grown up and his own *athair* died, he was considered heir apparent by the *sídhe* and given a place of his own and a title over there. Patrick had nearly collapsed with the absurdity: *So, what—you're Lord Spiral Spring over here?*

His father had not returned the laugh. Hmph. *You couldn't pronounce it even if I told you*, he'd said, offended. A few minutes later he explained how the *sídhe* would come and fetch him whenever they liked, often at inconvenient times.

But he never turned down a summons. He'd go for a few hours, make a few easy repairs, tighten a few screws, maybe go work on his grand project—a clock that could keep time in both places at once. He made friends. He made more than friends.

But you were gone for days, Patrick had argued. *Weeks.*

Over here, time measures different. It goes slower. In the time you've already sat with me, likely an hour or more's passed.

But there's nothing here. Just green grass. And a tree. Certainly, the Green Place held delicious scents and melodic sounds and everything he touched had a sensual quality—but there was an emptiness that surprised him.

Da had given him a gentle cuff on the head. *Daftie. This world contains multitudes. You'll never see the end of it. Longer you stay, it takes you in. More things appear. What you need, it comes. But take it slow. Don't pop yer fuse.* He explained that he'd spent moments and minutes in the Green Place that took up weeks and months of him in the real world—but never minded. At least, until his marriage soured and his absences made holding a proper job impossible. And then—his son had died. His firstborn.

Did ye know of your half-brother?

Patrick supposed he had, on some old and buried level. Herself had photos of a baby that was not Patrick, and out in the shed behind their home near the monastery he'd come across a handmade wooden cradle that had never been his own.

How'd he die? Patrick had asked.

Nothin' to do with over here. Da's voice had taken on a thickness. *Just one day the babe didn't wake. Call it cot death.*

After that, Da had asked the *sídhe* to let him stay for good. The real world was too hard and held too little for him. But then he'd learned the boy who died wasn't his only offspring. He'd sired a second child in the Green Place—but this second son had a different mother. And this second son was just about the same age as the child who had died.

Never learned of you until the day I'd wanted to stay forever, Da said. *She—my love—told me she could no longer shelter our babe—you. Y'see, you're not meant to have happened. Fey are not … friendly toward what they consider mistaken births. Where half of you is from one world, the other half from their world.*

He didn't have to say it. Patrick knew what the real word for his existence was. He'd heard it all his life, from Herself: *arracht.*

But Da learned he could spirit the child, who'd been in hiding, to the other side. Put him under his protection. So that's what he did. Herself was never won over. She got worse and worse. Considered Padraig a changeling.

Which, Patrick realized, he actually was.

Still, Da had said. *You lived. You wouldn't have, over here.*

Patrick had listened with a stiff back, gripping at the bark of the root so hard his hands began to hurt. The enormous truths came at him one after the other like slaps in the face—and he felt nothing inside. Just sat there and nodded as the leaves continued to whisper at him. He thought about how all his life he'd felt like there were eyes on him, but not until Boston had it felt unrelenting. Close.

Now, the car was bearing down. No honking. No goggle-eyed driver reacting to two nutters in the middle of a New York City street.

Patrick's feet itched. Every instinct told him to move. The vehicle was close enough that he could read the license plate. He held fast, and Caitlin held on to him. Then—at the last possible moment, it gently swerved around them. The cuffs of Patrick's jacket quivered in its wake.

"He *saw* us," Patrick shook.

"He *unsaw* us," said Caitlin.

He stared at her.

"Being unseen is an important skill to have. You're learning."

"No, I'm not. I don't understand any of this." Patrick stared at the car's retreating red lights.

Back in the Green Place with Da, time passed. The scent on the air shifted to cloves, coffee and truffles. *Why tell me at all?* Patrick had asked at last. *Why not just ... leave me alone? You were so good at that.*

He didn't get an answer. Everything had begun to fade, as if his question had broken their connection. Caitlin had shown him how to arrive in the Green Place, but not how to leave. And then he was back in New York. On the street. In the pre-dawn.

Safe from all passing vehicles—of which there were nearly none—Patrick and Caitlin strolled through the canyons of the city, passing darkened windows and shuttered shops. Slowly, the city opened its eyes, waking up. Workers arrived to bake bread, power-wash the sidewalks, and unlock shuttered doors. They paused outside the Gothic cathedral that bore Patrick's name. It was a towering, impressive structure, and it reminded him of the tree he'd sat under with Da. Both had undeniable presence.

Hesitating, he forced himself to take careful steps toward the church's oversized wooden doors, Brother David echoing in his ears. The doors were locked for the night, so he set a cautious hand against the wood grain and waited for something to happen.

Nothing did.

He turned to Caitlin. "No lightning. No brimstone."

"You're as welcome inside as ever."

"Then I'm not damned."

"No more or less than any of us are. Consider that idea ... another stupid-stition."

They moved on north, arriving at an entrance to Central Park. The exhaustion he'd felt after meeting Da in the Green Place returned. The hotel was close, but he wanted to rest before getting there, slumping against the low brick wall that divided sidewalk from grass. After a moment, Caitlin joined him.

Soft music drifted their way, a radio in an open window.

He turned. "Da said a lot of things, but he didn't tell me why *now*. Why you'd come for me." His tone was flat and empty. "Tell me why I needed to know all this."

"Because … you left. Home. You came thousands of miles across the water and—it was time to … see."

"To see what?"

"Who you were. Whether you might … have a place after all. With us."

"Grand. Good to know you're not just here to kill me off."

"Padraig, if it was preferred that you be dead, you'd be gone by now." Her tone was cool and he shivered. "You're a … curiosity. There are so few like you who find ways to live."

"What makes me so sp—" the word stuck in his throat and he changed it, "fortunate?"

She closed her eyes and raised her fingers a few inches. The distant music grew louder and clearer; he could make out a sinewy saxophone drifting toward them like smoke. Like fragrance. "This."

Listening, the music flowed into him like water or air. And he understood. He was a maker. He created the currency they valued. He was … useful. Like *Athair*.

"And the verdict?"

"Decision pending."

"Who's doing this deciding?"

"Not me. I was curious. I wasn't the only one sent over, you know. I just got to you first."

"There are *others* like you? Here?"

She blinked. "Not others exactly like me. But Malachi was being tormented—what do you think was doing that? And have you not given Ciaran, and what's happening to him, a bit of thought?"

"Wait—Ciaran, too?" he grabbed at his hair. "Jaysus. I can't do this. I want to go back. I don't want to know."

"Really? It's better not to have those answers?"

"I've never had my whole life turned inside out, Caitlin. There's nothing that's the same."

"Wrong. You are still you. You are still a music maker. Where I come from—where *you* come from—that's the highest calling there is." She rested a hand on his shoulder. "You don't need me anymore. It's all yours now—as much of it as you want."

"What if I don't want any?"

"Tell me so, and I'll call you a liar."

He stared down the long, perfectly straight road they'd traveled. "Don't tell the others. Don't tell anyone."

"I reckon Mal already has some idea."

"Just—don't. I don't want them looking at me different."

"Then you're still happy being their *fear gan ainm*? When you have a true name you were born with, one no one has ever used for you?"

"A—true name?" He held up a hand. "No. Whatever that name is, I don't know it. I don't own it. I don't want to. I want to be Patrick with them. Patch. That's all."

In the half-morning light her eyes had never been more deeply blue. "The name by which you are known is the only song worth singing," she said. "It is the only tune that rings in your heart. To know it—is to know why you are."

"What is mine, then?"

She shook her head. "Only those who gave you life can share it."

He blinked at her, oddly moved. "Then tell me yours."

For the first time since he'd known her, he sensed—if not fear, then apprehension. His chest clenched; she'd never been more real to him than in this moment. Bringing his fingers to her chin, he gently turned her head. Their eyes locked and he regretted nothing. Blamed no one.

"Trust me, this time." His voice was soft, insistent. He ran a thumb over her cheek. "Sing yours to me."

Caitlin bent to his ear and made music in it. Yet—only partly music. It was a mouth sound of no language he'd ever heard. It was made of light and air and flowing things, sweet scent and sharp edges, a gentle breeze puffing over every inch of his body at once. His skin prickled with delight.

"Again. Please."

She repeated it with a smile, and this time he thought he had a grip. An electric tingle swept through him as she sang it. He hummed it to himself, trying to repeat it back—but she set a finger on his lips. "Don't," she said. "I'll be Caitlin here and that's the end of it. That name—your name, any of our names—the true names we're born with are doors."

"I don't understand."

"Think about what doors do. Speak a name and it opens worlds. For us, it allows you one great request—just one. You speak the name and ask the thing and then it is done."

"Like a wish."

She rolled her eyes. "No. With this, you may not get exactly what you want, but you have the right to ask."

"And if you get turned down?"

She twitched. "We lose our name."

He shrugged. "That's so bad?"

She paled. "There's so much you don't know. You lose your name, you're *nothing*. You don't exist."

"Like death."

She stared at him. "Perhaps. It is one of the few ways we cease to exist."

141

Patrick leaned against the stone wall, thinking of touching that church door. He'd half-expected the monk to pop out and box him on the ears for believing all this nonsense. But he hadn't. And apparently the church had no response to the touch of an *arracht*. It was all stories, so it was, and what you believed could be made real. He was beginning to believe something new.

A weight sagged, then fell from his shoulders. Realization set in. He no longer had to fear anything, from anyone. Da—Caitlin—had given this to him and there was no taking it back. He'd never again be the same man who'd woken up with an obliterating headache in the bed next to Mal's the previous morning. He was a new thing, a new being. There was a twirl of excitement in his gut, a yearning for discovery. The caged butterfly in his chest had found the way out, and she was soaring.

He turned to Caitlin, her freckles barely visible in the coming dawn, but he knew they were there. He believed in them the way he believed in her now. He stroked the bridge of her nose, trailing a finger across the small imperfect dots as if charting a course.

He brought his mouth to hers.

It was like going to the Green Place without disappearing. They entangled arms, pressing against one another—and as they kissed it was as if she spoke her name again and again. Each time, it echoed within him as if he'd known it all his life.

Now I Tin Whistle

Philadelphia

Patrick set his bass into its stand and switched off the amp. He was tuned and ready to check as soon as Mal wrapped his interview with a reporter over by the bar. Knowing how Mal could jaw on, there was at least ten minutes to go.

The venue's ceiling pulsed, the rigging and lights shifting and undulating like a living thing, as if the structure itself had a heartbeat. It had been like that from the moment Patrick had struck a chord on his instrument.

This is going to take some getting used to.

Ever since this morning—well, maybe ever since last night, when *believing* turned out to be his gateway to the Green Place and more information about himself than he could possibly digest yet—the world looked different. That was no metaphor: Every object Patrick laid eyes on seemed layered, as if multiple coats of paint had been slapped on inexpertly. He could tell the dead places from the living corners, the worn-up areas from the worn-down gaps. Floors, walls, tables, chairs—all of it had new tunings. Some objects were heightened; others appeared to be fading. He saw surfaces and beneath the surfaces simultaneously, the effect dissipating the longer he looked at something.

If he didn't know better, he'd have thought Caitlin had been slipping him psychedelics.

And if an object had a connection to music? Well, that stepped things up exponentially. Patrick *knew* things about instruments now just by looking at them—Mal's piano radiated … discomfort, which he traced to a problem with one of the lower-octave keys. Ciaran's guitar, slung across his back as he spoke with Sheerie on the other side of the room, gave off a weary scent of old rubber—and somehow Patrick knew that meant the third string would break soon. Glowing fingerprints lingered where Patrick had touched his bass or mandolin, fading away like reverse Polaroids. Now unplugged, the instruments were giving off a persistent needy hum, yearning for attention.

Then there was the venue itself, coated with years of music. Exposed pipes, wires, spotlights vibrated with the streaky colors of remembered sounds, and he understood the dead spots were the places that held no color or movement at all. Mostly, the Theater of the Living Arts was a sturdy, happy place—if pompously named—with plenty of room for sounds to bounce around. Behind the soundboard was an oddly worn-down, dead place, though that shouldn't matter for the show.

Then there were people.

Ah, *people.*

Ciaran and Mal appeared fuller, sharper, of a greater dimension, as if Patrick now wore a pair of high-powered glasses. Caitlin nearly hurt his brain the first time he'd looked at her straight on in the full light of day; she was the brightest creature in the room, a Technicolor dazzling showcase of movement and hues.

But so was Sheerie, in a different way. Where Caitlin flickered and jumped and pulsed with every rainbow color, Sheerie glided in and out of dimensions, a smooth transition of rich, royal shades. Like the woman herself, the contrasts were simultaneously alluring and threatening. She was a small supernova now, hand on Ciaran's arm. Where she made contact with him he dulled slightly, a reflected shadow. Patrick met Caitlin's gaze and she nodded once.

He wondered what he was expected to figure out next.

"What's it like?" Caitlin had wandered over to the stage and accepted Patrick's hand to help her up. They dangled their legs over the edge. She gestured at the empty space before them. "You know, now that you're seeing everything the true way?"

Patrick set his hand on hers, thinking of how they'd sat just like this in Boston. The pair of them, right on the edge of something huge, talking like old friends. They'd had an instant familiarity, like responding to like, even when she threw out riddles and mysteries. Getting a clear answer from her had always been like shadow-boxing. But from the moment they'd taken a seat on that Boston stage, he'd been in love with her. He just hadn't known it at the time.

"You said it once. Like when a flower blossoms." He was surprised by the thickness in his voice. "There's so much more inside. And you—you're at the center. All the colors are on you at once."

Her smile burst with the full spectrum, though her eyes remained pale blue. "I hadn't thought this would be *fun.* And *new.* And *different.*"

"I didn't think the world would change."

"The more you believe, the more it comes. You're over the hurdle. You'll see things change faster now."

"I'm not sure I want that."

She gave his wrist a gentle squeeze. "Don't worry so much. Let it come. There are limits, of course. Rules. You'll learn those in time. For now … just enjoy it, Padraig."

Rules. Of course there would be rules. There must be some kind of … hierarchy out there. On the other side. The Green Place. *Just call it what it is: Tír na nÓg,* he thought. *Land of the young.* There were a dozen other names, but that one had come from Herself and Da. He had a vague memory of hearing about royal courts. "One of those rules—it says you can't warn us?"

She shook her head. "If I'd sat down with you in that Boston park and announced who I was and who you were, you'd've left me in dust before I finished. *That's* why I had to let you see it for yourself. But—Mal. I wanted to help. I did what I could. We're just not meant to … interfere in each other's … activities."

Herself had all kinds of stories about the *sídhe*. What stuck most clearly for Patrick was their capricious nature. A person could sleep on the wrong hillock or speak the wrong set of words or cut down the wrong tree and their whole life could be upended in an instant. If a fey took offense, you were theirs until they chose to release you. Sometimes, even if they didn't take offense—if they just wanted to mess around with you—you were also theirs.

"Why not, though? If you see someone in trouble, can't you help?"

She tilted her head. "You're confusing us with superheroes. We're not. *You're* not. Interference could lead to war. You don't want to be in the middle of that. It could also lead to exile. To be only on this side of things, all the time. Most of us in exile don't survive; we're not made for this world over the long haul. People are fun to play around with—but too hard to understand."

"You seem to do all right."

"Well." Her cheeks flooded magenta. "Maybe I'm not the only teacher here."

He was absurdly delighted. "You helped Mal. Didn't that count?"

"I talked around it. Not smart, but—" She paused. "I don't like telling you 'no,' Padraig. I did it less for him than for you. But not everyone would see it that way. That particular fey—the one you saw incinerate in the hat—he'll want retribution, eventually."

"He's not dead?"

"We're hard to kill. The same's true for you. At least, I think so."

Patrick wasn't ready to examine that yet. He leaned forward and their foreheads touched. He kissed her cheek. "That's from Mal," he said. "This one's from me." He pressed his lips on hers and it was like drinking a sunrise.

When they parted, she reached into her denim jacket, revealing the pennywhistle with the well-gnawed nub. "I had a wooden whistle, but it wouldn't whistle." She grinned.

145

Patrick laughed; he knew this one. "So I bought a steel whistle, but it steel wouldn't whistle."

"So I got a tin whistle—"

"And now I tin whistle." He was laughing so hard by the end his sides hurt. That old play on words had been one of the first complex things he'd understood while learning English from the monks. "I never thought you'd be corny." He fetched his mandolin, which vibrated in greeting as he picked it up, then returned to sit next to her. "Right. What's on the menu then, aside from corn?"

She lifted her chin and a tune slipped into his head unbidden. Huddled close, they began playing the opening of "The Plains of Kildare," at first holding the notes protectively to their chests. Then Caitlin straightened and Patrick followed her lead, releasing the sound into the room.

The notes became color.

For a moment, he forgot to strum. He could *see* the music now, soaring in the rigging—a rose-colored smoke wrapping around the beams and dipping back toward the stage, a constant stream emanating directly from their instruments. Rose shifted into creamy yellow, then stark white and wine red, then a gentle fade back into rose—all while curling around the room, parting around objects, then joining together again. A faint whiff of toasted orange peel blended into the mix, and tears pricked at the corners of his eyes—but after that first stumble Patrick never stopped playing. If he did, it would end. And he never wanted it to end, not after seeing this. Losing those sounds and smells and colors would be like having a hood clapped over his head.

The colors shifted hue again, becoming richer, bolder and more resonant. At some point, Mal joined them, unable to resist the siren call of a song. His piano complemented the whistle and mandy, buoying the music on a feather-light wave, and Patrick sneaked a glance at the piano. There was Mal, flinging his head around as though he still had hair, eyes closed. He made the piano cry and laugh and sigh and live—and now, Patrick understood he was in the Green Place.

Sheerie waved Ciaran toward the stage, delightedly flashing a mouth of feral white teeth. Patrick nodded, satisfied to have found at least one thing that would consistently separate the two of them. Ciaran jogged their way, guitar smacking against his back, and tried hopping up onstage with a mighty push. He slipped, staggering back, nearly crashing to his knees. Patrick left off playing and caught up his arm to give him a boost.

Jaysus, it's a broomstick, he thought. *Bone wrapped in cloth.*

Ciaran winced, getting up on his feet and plugging in the guitar. The electric notes overwhelmed the acoustic—and no color or scent flowed from the instrument. The notes were perfect, sweet and familiar—but that's all they were now. Notes.

When Patrick failed to pick up the tune again, Caitlin drifted off, then Mal—and the song collapsed. The room was a dull empty space again, pulsing gently.

"Well, that was something, wasn't it?" Patrick glanced between them all. Mal and Ciaran looked at each other and shrugged.

"Whistle's a nice addition," Mal allowed.

Of course: Only Patrick and Caitlin saw the colors. Smelled the fragrance. The discovery gave him a twinge of glee—for once he could do something with music even Mal could not—but behind that lurked sadness. There was no one he wanted to share all of this with more than the two of them, and a familiar separateness crept into him.

Swapping the mandy for the bass, Patrick leaned toward Ciaran. "All right?" They were standing inches from one another on the small stage, as close as he'd been to Ciaran in days—and he could tell that no, nothing was all right. Ciaran, their great bearish brute of a guitar player, was all angles and shadows and stark staring eyes. He wasn't himself.

"Mind your own," Ciaran growled. "I'm *fine*. Can we get the rest of this feckin' check done with?"

Patrick backed off, head aching dully. Mal shouted that he was ready to roll and called out the key and the tune.

Turning from his bandmates, Patrick faced the empty venue. The soundman tweaked his levels, the roadies carted away boxes. But they were like extras in a movie, mere background. What he really noticed was Sheerie at the back of the theater, burning white-hot with a brightness that left afterimages. Then she smiled, a slow intentional thing—not at Ciaran, not at Mal. At him.

Stunned, he barely felt Caitlin tug on his trouser leg. She pulled again, and he blinked a few times before glancing down.

"There's more to know, isn't there," he said quietly.

She was still vibrantly Technicolor, but her eyes had gone stormy. "Oh, yes," she said. "So much more."

The Imago

Ciaran hadn't planned to snap at Patrick. It wasn't Patch's fault that he felt like the undercarriage of a truck. But there'd been a *look* on his face as he'd helped Ciaran on the stage—shock, disgust, fear—that confirmed he was starting to look as terrible as he felt.

The last time Ciaran remembered feeling any shade of good was at Kennedy's, when they'd all been singing along to "Gloria." And before that, there'd been when they tore into his notebook of songs. Other than those moments, he felt like he was living in someone else's body. Respite came only when he sat down to transcribe the songs in his brain, or when he and Sheerie were tangled in the hotel bed sheets. The rest of his life he felt no fecking good for no fecking good reason. All he wanted these days was some unbroken sleep, and maybe his appetite back. Instead, the music had begun keeping him up all night. He wrote and wrote until his arm cramped and his bones felt like they were rubbing against one another.

He didn't have control anymore, that was part of it. Hauling off and slugging Jody had been impulsive and stupid, and he'd have given anything to go back a day and apologize to the poor sod. Like his life wasn't hard enough already, stuffing that shit up his nose, that he had to get punched by some great eejit while just trying to be friendly. Ciaran flexed his fist, which he'd stuck into ice the moment he got back to the hotel last night, but which was still swollen and red.

Sheerie made most things go away, and he wished he was holding her right now. At least then the tide would ebb for a time. They'd hidden out in the back of the bus for the short ride down from New York today and for at least those two hours, he'd had peace. But now the waves were licking at his feet again, threatening to pull him under. Thinking clearly wasn't easy to do without her around. He no longer considered sending her away.

On some level, Ciaran knew he needed a doctor. But there was no time and no money. What would a doctor say? *Get some rest, take it easy.* A doctor would not prescribe nightly shag sessions, daytime writing marathons, and two-hour-plus live shows each night. And they could not afford to miss any more dates. He had to suck it up and be a man.

Halfway through the Philadelphia soundcheck, though, things came to a head. Ciaran held up an arm and the song they'd been barreling through dragged to a halt. "Request," he told the others. "I'd like a bit o' solo time this evening."

Mal and Patrick exchanged a glance.

"Solo?" Mal asked.

"You get your *sean-nós.* I'd like one of me and the guitar only."

Demand your spotlight, Sheerie had said. *They'll never offer it to you. You have to take it. Malachi thinks he owns the stage, but we know best. We know of your hunger, do we not?*

"And what'll you play?" Patrick grinned. "Thin Lizzy covers?"

Ciaran's gut flared and he winced. "Got three notebooks of what to play. D'you?"

Mal made a high-noted tinkling sound on the keys and stood. "No harm, I suppose. Just—let us know when and we'll fit it into the list. Yes? Good."

Satisfied, Ciaran launched into the next bit of the soundcheck. They were perhaps a minute into the song when that needle in his stomach lanced through him again. This time, he wrenched to the side, mouth a surprised line of agony. Warm bile rose in the back of his mouth and he spat on the floor. After a few seconds he slid back into the song—but his heart was gone from it, his mind wandering, searching for relief.

For Sheerie.

He should say something to the others. He'd always relied on them having his back whenever trouble arose. But there was a distance between them lately, a distance precisely the length and breadth of that woman Caitlin. He'd never trusted her, the way she looked at him, the way she'd called him a fraud. And Mal and Patch were clearly on her side. He no longer knew if his old pals really were looking out for him anymore.

They envy your songs, Sheerie had whispered. *They can't understand what it's like to become the man you always knew you were.*

But it hurts.

Do you think the chrysalis in its case is untormented by transformation? Suffering is the wheel on which we are honed and shaped. And in the end, the imago emerges.

So I'm becoming a butterfly?

Oh, yes. She'd pressed against him, her warm, bare skin seeming to meld into his own.

Sheerie always knew how to cut through the clutter.

149

A Hair on a Flea on the Ear of a Horse

Patrick's room phone was ringing as he burst inside with a surprised laugh. Caitlin hung from his shoulders, over his back, and he let her drop to the bed with a soft whoofing sound. Carrying a whole other being—even one as light as a *sídhe*—did not lend to graceful entrances.

Just as he reached for it, the phone silenced. Shaking rain from his hair, he dropped the bag of Chinese food and righted himself with a dramatic groan.

"Good thing you make music." Her bell laugh chimed prettily through the room. "Your weightlifting skills are lacking."

The phone's message light blinked. "Can't help it if you're as dense as a dark star."

She threw a pillow at him.

Patrick ducked into the bathroom, securing towels, and tossed her one while mopping his face. Shortly after the show ended a deluge of rain had fallen on the city, coming down so hard and fast the gutters waterfalled with runoff. But he'd been starving, and there was a Chinese takeaway around the corner from the hotel—so they'd made a run for it, just him and Caitlin. While waiting for fried rice and soup, they'd created puddles on the restaurant floor, then had to dash back into the wet to get to the hotel. Caitlin had only agreed to the detour if he promised to give her a piggyback ride to the room.

Patrick couldn't deny her that.

The show still rang in his ears, his mind, his heart. Whatever Ciaran might look like lately, he was a cracking guitar player and had made the most of his four solo minutes. Mal had been livelier than ever behind the mic, whether bantering with the audience or lost in his own world while banging on the keys. It was their first show in about a week, and Patrick felt revitalized by finally getting to play in front of an appreciative crowd again.

But this night had something else. This was the first time he'd played live knowing who he was and—more importantly—believing it. As they played, he'd watched the band's songs transform into radiant, transparent colored ribbons that wrapped around the room with abandon. Complex scents emerged from every chord combination—each song had a vivid smell, from toasted bread with blueberry jam to new-mown grass or just-shampooed hair. As the colors drifted from the rigging and swooped over the sweating, singing crowd, they shifted into rich hues of aqua, mint, cocoa—as if they were no longer reflecting the music, but the listener. Or both.

Two hours into the show Patrick had been ready to go for a third, but Ciaran was clearly drained. Ciaran would never call it early, but everyone realized they were about to head into too much of a good thing—and Mal signaled to wrap things up. They kept the encore to just two songs. There had been the obligatory VIP after-party, but Patrick had convinced Robin to cut things short. Ciaran had appeared on the very edge of collapse, and Patrick still felt crispy from the night before. So Robin dashed around the roped-off area spreading rumors that the roads might be washed out from the onslaught of rain, and the room emptied quickly after that.

Now here he was, with Caitlin and a whole night to themselves. He didn't want her out of his sight, but he also wasn't sure how to begin. Questions, he still had so many of those. Or they could dip into the Green Place. Or they could open up the cooling Chinese food. Or—

Caitlin sat up on her knees, unwinding the towel from her head. Thick curls of red tumbled across her shoulders like a wild woman's, like the being who'd told him off back in Boston. Patrick's chest thudded and he kicked off his boots. Water dribbled into the carpeting.

She held out her hand, just as she had in Boston Common. A smile teased at her lips. "Now," she said.

Now—what? Oh.

He pulled her to him, and they tumbled against the duvet in a flurry of hands and mouths and skin. Soaked clothes peeled off and landed around the room, the smack of wet fabric on walls making them giggle, but the sounds were subdued and vanished in their yearning for one another. They spent a lot of time in explorations, and it was the only thing better than music.

At last, her skin lay flush with his and that tingle he always felt with her expanded tenfold, electricity flowing between them without barriers. Patrick moved over her lithe, wriggling form, finding great satisfaction in what was normal about her—flesh, blood, fingernails, eyelashes, just like him. As they joined, no swirling colors or random unexpected sensations overtook him beyond her flowery, earthy scent, and the only music they made came from shared gasps of pleasure. That satisfied Patrick immensely: For this act, having just one person, one sensation to concentrate on and give his entire focus to was more than sufficient. It was its own visit to another world.

Afterward they shared a shower, then settled among the tangled sheets, bundled loosely in hotel robes. Caitlin found an old movie on television, and they watched the black and white figures moving and shifting and murmuring.

That was my life before yesterday, he thought, glancing at the film. *Today, it's all about color.*

They pulled out the congealed Chinese food and picked through it, and he thought again about that night's show. "It's not me," he said. "The colors—the smells—when we play. I'm not *doing* it, am I?"

She shook her head. "That's how it always is, once you can see it right." She moved some vegetables around. "You three make a marvelous palette. Have done from the moment you met in that falling-down cottage."

He froze. "You—saw that?"

"I was told, later. But it was a signal. You'd been—taken from us sometime earlier and been almost, but not quite, forgotten about. Then you started making music, and it was like putting a candle in the window. We had to come."

"So that—"

"So that one day you could learn how to see and hear properly. It would have been cruel not to."

"What if I'd started serving drinks at a bar, or putting cans in bags at the shop?"

"You were a bit young for that." She grinned, but he didn't smile back. "Well. If you're not interesting to us, there's no reason to check up on you, is there?"

"Even knowing what I was."

She shrugged. "This is what happened. And here we are. Do you wish you *hadn't* found music?"

His life would have been simpler, no question. Quieter. Lonelier. A shade of normal. "Never."

Caitlin picked up the egg drop soup and drank it like ale, then made a face. She'd told him before that she could eat but rarely had the desire. Then she picked out each pea from the fried rice and popped them into her mouth like candy, missing more often than landing. Pretty soon she was surrounded in a halo of tiny green spheres. Patrick was so enrapt with watching her that he barely tasted anything.

"In a few more days, we're home," he said. "What happens then?"

"What would you like to happen?"

"I'd like you to stay."

She raised an eyebrow. "My job's done here, Padraig. You don't need me."

Caitlin had said something like that the night before. "Of course I do. And not just for—" He gestured around the room. "Being a road map. I need you *here.*" He tapped his chest, then caught up her head and gave her a firm kiss. "And here."

She was flushed and smiling. "I'll take it under consideration."

"I'd also like to know if someone from—your side of things—our side of things—" he blinked with comprehension, "isn't coming to annihilate me. That would be comforting."

Again, a shrug. "Can't say no one'll ever try, Padraig. But musicians are special. I don't suspect you'll have a thing to worry about." She paused. "You will want your name, though."

The only song worth singing.

"Da knows it, yes?"

"As does your *máthair.*"

"Herself?" But no. Herself was dead. And not of the Green Place, anyway. That's not who she meant. Ever since Caitlin had started to tell him his own story back in Boston, Patrick had done his best to leave the idea of a second *máthair* buried under a shadow in his heart. But there was no denying it anymore: He had a different *máthair* in the Green Place. A no-longer-mythical *sídhe.* Which meant—he pinched off the next logical step as a prickling heat ran across his scalp. He wasn't ready to think about that part of things. Not yet. Those on the other side of the worn-up places, who watched and evaluated and sent emissaries to spy—he hadn't wanted to think about whether they loved him, worried about him. Did fey have concerns? Did they even have children in the normal course of things? All of these questions lodged somewhere between his head and heart, and he turned away.

Caitlin looked disappointed.

"It's so much," he said. "I'm trying."

"I know." She leaned forward, kissing his forehead, his eyes, his mouth. "No hurry. I'll be around for now. And when I'm not—just take it easy with the rest. Go slow."

"Why?"

"Because that green field is a hair on a flea on the ear of a horse. There's so much you haven't seen. So much you can make happen. But don't try it all at once."

Don't pop yer fuse, Da had said.

"You have all the time you need to learn." Her voice became careful and slow. "All the time."

Someone knocked at the door.

Patrick ignored it, scanning her face, an inchoate fear gripping him again.

Another knock, followed by Mal's muffled voice. Patrick unwound himself from Caitlin with reluctance, tightened the belt on his robe, and opened the door.

"Rich phoned," Mal said without preliminary. "We're to ring him back, all three of us, straightaway."

"It's daybreak over there, Mal—what's he on about?"

"Feck if I know." But Mal sounded nervous. He waved at Caitlin. "You seem to be surrounded by peas."

Caitlin cleared space on the edge of the bed and gestured, but Mal remained standing, shifting back and forth. "I went to C's room first. Dead silent. Think they're—out?"

"Out cold, most like," said Patrick.

"Well, if he's asleep maybe we should let him to it. He needs more than a couple of winks."

Patrick felt raw from his conversation with Caitlin and didn't want to pussy-foot around. "He looks like he needs a doctor. I think he's ill."

Mal shook his head. "We're all worn through. Long tour." He blinked at Caitlin. "Things of an unusual nature occurin'. Be home in a couple of days."

"If you say so." Patrick was concerned about Ciaran, but also willing to be talked out of sorting things out in the middle of the night. He wanted a quiet evening in—even if he'd lost the *normal* part of it.

Mal sighed. "Well, I'll try the room again. Use my key if I have to. I've no shame here."

"Did you ever?"

Mal snatched a pillow from the floor and whacked him with it.

A Web of Shards

Ciaran lay flat on his bed naked, too tired to sleep. Not insomnia, but a distant cousin. He was like a deflated balloon, every ounce of his essence gone. Sheerie was half-wrapped around him, eyes closed but also not sleeping, and they were both catching their breath from their exertions.

If she thinks we can go again tonight, she's sore mistaken. Ciaran was done, for now at least. All he could think about now was that in three days they'd be going home, and Sheerie would be gone. Because of course she could not have a permanent residence in his life. He really *had* to be shut of her. Putting thousands of miles and an ocean between them was an excellent start. Yet the thought of not seeing her again made him nearly choke. It was as if he'd considered leaving a leg, or an arm in America.

He had to piss. They'd drunk a lot—well, he'd drunk a lot—after the show but it didn't take; he was as sober as if he'd been gulping water. The radio in his head was muted but starting to rise in volume again. He stirred and Sheerie was immediately alert.

"Be right back." He slid to the edge of the sheets, moving like an old man.

She straightened, quick and untired. "You want me to leave."

He sighed. The reading of his thoughts had gone from being cute to being downright scary. She didn't seem to know what he was thinking all the time—but if it had to do with her, she was plugged right in. "Not this minute."

The night before, he'd let one small comment fly: that they were returning home soon. He hadn't put anything on that, hadn't invited her back or suggested that they should wind down. But she'd known.

So you're saying we're through, she'd hissed.

No. Only said what's already planned.

I could be there, she'd volleyed in a cool voice. *I could be anywhere.*

I'm sure that's so.

Sheerie had pushed his chin up with a finger in a strong, controlled move. *So are you saying, Ciaran O'Conaill, that you're ready for everything to be over? That you want everything to be done?*

The tone had hit him more than the words. It wasn't that of an aggrieved lover; it was somehow … formal. As if she were reading from a rule book. It had been the way she'd spoken on their first night together, a strange ceremonial thing as they were ripping their clothes off and he was almost blind with need for her. She'd used his full name and he'd had to promise all manner of things he no longer remembered. With her comments last night, he'd felt a strange bookending happening—and almost had reached for it. Rip off the bandage and have done with it and deal with the fallout later.

But a small voice inside had shouted warning. The proffered apple was poisoned. His throat had tightened and his head swam. *What the hell is really going on here?*

No, he'd said finally. *Just that we should think on it.*

I am. She'd nodded. *I am thinking very seriously on it.*

Now, as he prepared to hoist himself from the bed, she returned to the topic. "But you do want us to end."

"Everything ends." He stood, wobbling in place. He had no idea why getting out of bed was so difficult, why he was moving through treacle just to get to the toilet. He glanced down the hallway at the door. There'd been some pounding on it a while back, but he'd been occupied at the time.

"Indeed it does," she said. "But when I go, we go together."

Ciaran wasn't hearing her. He was concentrating on taking steps to the toilet, staggering as if he had been off his feet for a long time. He turned and caught a glimpse in the full-length mirror hanging on the wall outside the bathroom, and stopped.

The scarecrow was back. Only this time, he got a full, unclothed picture—and didn't know what he was seeing. From top to toe his skin had taken on a dull luminosity, and despite the dimness of the foyer he could make out every blue vein poking straight up like welts. He'd touched a few ribs in Kennedy's the night before—now he could see more. It was as though his skeleton was so happy to be alive it was trying to leap out.

Leaning in, he squinted at the horror that was his face. He'd shaved … when? Back in New York? Before carrying his music down to Mal? He no longer remembered. But the fact was his face was as smooth as a baby's, as if he'd only just laid the razor down. What the beard no longer covered was an unfamiliar pallor, a combination of yellows and grays, above which his eyes flashed sharp, bright, aware. He'd come to this place in less than a month.

I'm wasting away into nothing, and nobody sees it but me.

Behind him, a key fitted into the lock and the door swung open. Mal took a step in, then froze. "Ciaran." His voice was a horrified whisper.

Ciaran staggered back from the mirror, a rage consuming him—and thrust his already-bruised fist into the image. The mirror dented into a web of shards, a few of which tumbled to the ground. One lodged deep between his knuckles and he roared as if it had split him in two.

Sheerie leaped up, standing on the bed, and made a broad waving gesture with her arms. The door smacked into Mal and knocked him against the wall before slamming shut. Mal bounced with a grunt, recovered, and briefly touched Ciaran's shoulder before ducking into the bathroom for a towel. He bounded back seconds later with a wetted one and sat next to where Ciaran had curled on the floor, looking him straight in the face, then down to the bloody hand—and yanked the shard from his fist.

Ciaran whimpered, gritting his teeth. He flung his head backward against the wall, leaving a dent. Mal wrapped the towel around the hand and held it fast even as it turned from white to dark rose.

Sheerie loomed over them both. "Get out." Her voice was rough, deep—different from any tone Ciaran had heard her use. It rattled in his bones.

"Fuck off," Mal growled.

Instantly, the door flew open again of its own accord. It crunched against the wall plaster, and Mal lifted into the air, flying backward into the hallway. He landed hard on the opposite side, tumbling to the ground. Ciaran met his eyes for a split second as they both gasped.

The door crashed shut between them—and latched.

Only moments elapsed between Mal leaving Patrick's room, promising to try his key on Ciaran's door—and Mal returning with a bloodied nose and wide, astounded eyes. He garbled something unintelligible, hands shaking. Patrick handed him minibar bottle after minibar bottle until the shaking subsided.

"Come—now." Mal gasped, and fled out the door again.

Patrick and Caitlin followed down the hallway.

"What? What?" Patrick kept asking.

"The mirror—his hand—all bones—" Mal wasn't making any sense.

Patrick pressed his ear against Ciaran's door and heard nothing. Slipping his key into the lock, he pushed and the door swung wide. He caught a glimpse of rumpled sheets, lights left on—but no presence in the room. All three of them ventured in to look around, but it was obvious that Sheerie and Ciaran had gone.

"What'd we miss?" Patrick asked.

Mal was focused on the mirror outside the bathroom, hovering his hand over the frame and glass. "I saw it." His voice was low and shaky. "This mirror—it was in a thousand pieces. He punched it. There was a piece in his *hand*."

Next to him, Patrick leaned closer. Of course the mirror was intact—or was it? The closer he looked the more he could focus … beneath it. As with the colors at soundcheck, he could see layers of mirror and plastic, as if a coating had been inexpertly layered over reality. Like … a glamour. Beneath the fakery the mirror was destroyed. He brought his fingers close to the glass and saw it ripple under his touch, a tiny disturbance that briefly laid bare what was hidden. When he pulled his hand away the glamour slid back in place.

He took short, rabbit breaths and thought of Sheerie, how bright she'd been. The mirror, covered in magic.

The more you believe, the more you will see.

Now he was seeing more than he'd ever wanted to. Patrick glanced at Caitlin, who held her palms aloft in offering. As if she were saying, *This is yours to share or not.*

Patrick calmed his nerves and waved a hand over the shimmer, focusing on it. The ripple widened, then dripped away and once again the mirror was ruined.

Mal gaped at it—then at him.

But Patrick had turned to Caitlin. "She's one of you, ain't she. Sheerie, I mean."

"She's not one of *me*," Caitlin flared.

"But she's a *sídhe*."

She hesitated. "A … special case. But—yes."

"Wait, what's this—" Mal gave Patrick a wide berth as he wheeled into the conversation. "She's—also—" He clutched at his head. "You knew and didn't tell us? Jaysus—"

Caitlin looked between them both, then put her fists on her hips. Her hair shivered in an invisible breeze. "Get over yourselves. You *knew*. You both knew. The minute he gave you those songs—you had to know. You just didn't want to *see*."

Patrick stood by the window, staring into the street below. How simple it was, to only see the surface and not the cracks beneath. "You came, and she came," he said in a measured voice. "And something else came for Mal."

"They all came for *you*," said Caitlin. "We were sent. I found you first, like I said. The others … well. Humans can be very distracting, particularly to mischief-makers." She raised an eyebrow at Mal. "We do like our shiny objects."

"We're not feckin' *objects*." Patrick whirled. "Jaysus, you can be so *thick*."

Caitlin flushed. "Of course, not just that. Never just that." She reached for his hand, but he stepped aside.

"They came … for us?" Mal, bewildered, glanced between the two of them. "Or they came just for—"

"Padraig," said Caitlin. "They came for him. We all did."

Mal tensed. "What makes him so damned special? All due respect, Patch."

"This doesn't help Ciaran," he told Mal. "He's the one we should be concentrating on."

Mal waved him aside. "I'm gonna wager he's being looked after just fine for now. Would you say that, Caitlin? Or whatever your name is? Fact is, I think this might just help in the long run. So. *Padraig*. You gonna explain why three … creatures none of us really believed existed until a week ago came after *you*? Or you want to just start with that little mirror magic you pulled?"

Mal always had been the smartest among them.

Patrick nodded at him and set his hand on Mal's shoulder. Then he twined Caitlin's fingers with his own. "Not here," he said. "Come with me."

He closed his eyes.

And took them to the Green Place.

A Hypothetical Sidhe Special Case

Mal spun around once, then twice, head ablaze and mouth agape. "Here," he whispered. "Here. We're … *here*. Again."

Caitlin had brought him last time to this world of his imagination. A place that existed between the notes of music. Once again he was beneath a vast sun-lit blue sky, standing on long, waving grasses. A wisp of vanilla tickled his nose, followed by something citrusy. Lemons?

Caitlin was watching him, head cocked, red locks dancing in the breeze. He turned to Patch, who was trying to be so serious—but a small smile dented the corners of his cheeks. Caitlin gestured at Patrick, as if presenting him onstage.

Patrick blushed. He clasped his hands behind his back and rocked on his heels.

Caitlin hadn't brought them here this time. Patch had.

"You," Mal said.

Patrick nodded.

"How can *you* do this?"

"Because … I've learned a few things recently." Patrick glanced at Caitlin. "About myself. About this place. About … where we connect. It's not just yer imagination. It's real. Call it whatever you want—the Green Place, beyond the Veil. It's the other side of the worn-up places."

He didn't say the other name, but Mal heard it in his head: *Tír na nÓg.*

"How long have you—"

"He's only just come to understand many things." Caitlin's voice was as soft as the wind. "But he's a fast learner."

The blush spread on Patrick's cheeks. Mal peered closer. Tried to see what had changed, what was different. But no—he was still just Patch: odd and quiet and all right, *otherly*. But surely not *this* otherly. "I can't believe I'm going to ask this, but you're not really—one of … the fey?"

Patrick let out a long breath. "I am. And I'm not. There's … story in here." He sat in the grasses and waited for the others to follow, then haltingly explained about his father. About what that meant for his parentage. How he was a liminal being. How while it explained so much, he wasn't sure how to take it all in. Then he ratcheted things up another notch: Understanding meant he now saw music in color and memory, and he could peer beneath the layers of the world. His voice trembled as he spoke, threatening to crack. But he wasn't only frightened by what he was telling Mal—he felt something akin to pride. Patrick had been different all his life. Now he knew why.

"How long have you known?" Mal asked when he finished.

"A day. Two."

Mal folded his arms. "And you waited to say something because …"

Patrick blinked. "What if it changed the way you saw me?"

Mal opened his mouth, but nothing came out. He wanted to slap Patch on the back and tell him that he was being ridiculous, that this was just some new incredible augmentation, like he had just learned to play the piano. But he couldn't. Patch was right. It changed everything. After all, if one of your oldest friends could be even part *sídhe*, then anything was up for grabs. Mal had always thought he wanted to believe in an elsewhere, an otherworldly kingdom of the imagination, but now that it had arrived he wasn't sure he was ready for it.

"I didn't ask for this," said Patrick. "It came looking for me. Minute we left home, these three … *sídhe* followed."

"Followed you."

"Followed all of you," said Caitlin.

"Because we're so feckin' fascinating," Mal snapped.

"Well," said Caitlin, her blue eyes like a mirror shard in his heart. "Yes."

The breeze kicked up, bending the grasses, and no one spoke for a long moment. Mal warred inside with what to do next. He had so many questions, but he had to keep focused. They were here right now not because he'd asked Patrick to show them a new trick, but because they had a parasite in their midst. Cool anger flickered inside. "So to sum up: We've banished one, I'm talkin' with one right now, and there's a third who's … malignant?"

Caitlin said nothing, but Patrick nodded.

"And ye didn't think to warn us?" Mal craned toward her.

Patrick pressed a hand on his chest. "She *can't*, Mal. She *couldn't*. There's … rules, apparently."

Mal glared at them both. "So break 'em. You tell us how we fix this—how we fix Ciaran."

Caitlin shook her head and he could have sworn she looked fainter, like she was preparing to vanish.

Mal stood, furious. "Then feck off." His voice was full of gravel. "Go back to where you came from, you useless thing."

Caitlin turned away, less solid than ever.

Patrick jumped up. "She is where she came from. We're on her turf now."

"*Your* turf, you mean. Both of you." A knot of fear and fury was forming in his gut. "Looks like you're cut from the same cloth."

Patrick shook his head. "Well, that didn't take long."

Everything was going wrong. The Green Place wasn't a dream; it was a nightmare. Around Mal, the skies darkened and the scents vanished from the breeze. Everything stilled. When Mal had woken up this morning, the last thing he thought he'd be doing was arguing with Patrick over his humanity. Or that he'd be trying to get a *sidhe* to help him save Ciaran.

"Caitlin." He swallowed hard, trying to remain calm. "Caitlin."

She gazed up from the grass, coiled and tense as a spring. Inches from leaving them alone in here.

"Can't you even give us the measure of what we're up against?" he pleaded. "Just … name the poison he's taken. We'll find the antidote."

Caitlin shook her head.

Patrick crossed his arms, thinking. He wandered in the grasses, head bent down. After a moment, he returned and said, "What if you don't speak about Sheerie at all. Just … tell us a story. Tell us about a *sidhe* like her. One that looked like her and walked and talked like her, but wasn't her."

The knot inside Mal stopped churning. His uncle had been a solicitor. "A hypothetical," he muttered.

"That!" Patrick pointed at him. "What then?"

A sly smile curled onto Caitlin's face, and her substance returned. She was here, with them, fully now. "Great stars, Padraig." She got to her feet and rested her hands on his forearm. "You are getting the measure of things. That should work, absolutely." She began strolling across the ground with purpose, and they trotted after. "The thing to know about a special case—not to name anyone, we're being a 100 percent hyper—"

"Hypothetical." Mal couldn't help it; he was being charmed by her all over again.

"Yes, our Hypothetical *Sidhe* Special Case—"

"HSSC, for short," Mal muttered.

"—is that … well, they're hybrids."

"Like me," said Patrick.

"Not exactly. Some hypothetical ones can be created. Invented. Called into being. This sort of," she turned to Mal, "HSSC is just that. A dark wish fueled by human fears about inspiration, lust, and hunger. One who flips the light switch of invention in a human, who inspires his imagination—but takes from the soul in exchange, one bite at a time."

All at once, he knew what they were talking about. Mal whirled around and walked backwards in front of her. "Jaysus, Cait—you're talkin' of the *leannán sí*. 'My Lagan Love.' 'La Belle Dame sans Merci.' The fairy mistress."

Caitlin applauded softly.

"*You're* well-informed," Patrick noted.

"Books, Patch, books. And—don't tell me, I know where I saw this—" He threw his hands in the air. "When you say she was created—you mean by the poets. Keats. Yeats. Campbell. They … conjured her?"

"Perhaps." Caitlin nodded. "Hypothetically."

Even Patrick seemed bewildered now.

"I'd kill 'em if they weren't already dead," said Mal. "But c'mon. These *poets* wrote somethin' down and it came to life?"

"It can happen. It has happened. They're not the only ones who've done such a thing."

Mal stopped walking. Then they all did. "You said it to me in Boston: You get a brilliant storyteller, and enough people believe in it … then it can happen. Everyone takes that bloody Yeats book like it's gospel, when it's mostly a fevered poet dream." He turned to Caitlin. "I'm dancin' nearby it, aren't I—hypothetically?"

She didn't contradict him. "Belief fuels our sort," she said. "Without belief we fade into nothing. Do you have *any* idea how many *leipreacháns* are loose in the world because of that? We're plagued by human clichés and stereotypes: too much faith, too little understanding. But—that aside, yes. Belief makes us stronger."

Patrick shook his head. "This is all somewhat cute and mad, but not helping. The point is—what do we *do* about an HSSC?"

"Ah," said Caitlin. "Well. An HSSC like the one we are discussing—she only truly becomes real when promised everything, to the very end. So your friend must have promised his soul, though he'll have no real memory of doing it. He's been giving her satisfying meals for weeks now as she nibbles through him. My guess—based on what you saw, Mal—is that she's preparing for the final course."

Mal's insides turned. "Try to remember that it's Ciaran we're talkin' about here. He's not a hypothetical."

"I'm sorry. An HSSC won't … relinquish easily. Especially not this late in the game. You'd have to offer her something more … intriguing."

"A trade-up." Patrick had folded his arms again, breath quickening. "She'd need to sign on with someone else first."

Caitlin studied him a long time. The teasing, knowing look she usually wore shifted into admiration. "Any hypothetical *leannán sí* can't handle more than one at a time. There are rules there, too. But since they're avaricious, they can be blind to all the angles. Present her with a more tantalizing option, and yes—I believe she'd go for something fresh. Something with more … time on it."

Mal frowned. "Solves nothing. Useless to save one person in exchange for another."

"But—" Patrick mused. "In any trade, someone can always say no. What if she tried to trade up and the new someone … turned her down?"

The breeze had returned and the sun was pouring down on them again. Mal caught sage this time, even a bit of cumin on the air. He recalled his convalescence in New York after the bed collapse, and the dream he'd had. Only he was sure it was no dream at all. Sheerie had come to him. That kiss had been transformational and damning; he'd wanted more even though he knew it would steal everything he already had. He ran his hands over the grass blades. "I reckon no one's ever turned that particular kind of HSSC down, though."

"No man I've known." There was a curious, encouraging lilt in Caitlin's voice.

Silence. When Mal looked up, she was holding both of Patrick's hands. For a moment, Mal recalled the little boy he met all those years ago, who he'd watched make music with Ciaran, then paid them out of his special collection with a small white stone. Padraig was still in there, and not buried so deep at all. Right now, it was Padraig the boy he saw in Patrick's eyes—wide, bright, afraid.

"Does she know … me?" he asked Caitlin. "What I am."

She nodded. "'Course. She came for you, same as me. Ciaran just got in the way."

"But she doesn't know what I've found out. She thinks I'm still in the dark. That's so?"

Mal started.

Caitlin was shaking her head. "Don't even think about it, Padraig. You can't know what the consequences are, to get in her way. In this, you're one of us. And it's not—done."

"If I don't do something, then Ciaran dies. Soon." He looked to Caitlin for confirmation, and she nodded. "She'll keep taking and taking until he's used up. We *know* that consequence."

Mal gaped at him. He was starting to understand and didn't like where this was heading. "No, Patch. We'll find another way."

"But we *won't*." His eyes flashed. "C doesn't have long left, based on what you saw today."

Mal nodded reluctantly.

"Right." Patrick took a long, ragged breath. "So—this is how we'll do this."

All Eyes on Me

Ciaran failed to return to his hotel room that night, and there was no sign of him in the morning. Caitlin kept watch as Mal and Patrick rested, or tried to. Both had collapsed on the double beds in Patrick's room, spending the remaining hours of the night tossing in the sheets, snatching brief naps as their heads whirled from all that had happened. But from time to time, when Mal was awake and Patrick lost to sleep, he'd peer at his friend's shape in the dark, trying to discover the physical manifestation of how things were different about him now.

Robin banged on Patrick's door early the next morning, offering two important pieces of information: the bus departure time, and Ciaran's status. "He called from the road," Robin said, looking underslept and anxious. "Said he'll be gettin' to the gig in Maryland under his own steam." He squinted. "Ain't this Patch's room?"

" 'Tis," said Mal, but didn't offer an explanation for why he was bunking there. "You doing all right, man?" For a moment, he wondered if Robin had also been set upon by one of the *sídhe*, discovering in that second just how much weirdness he'd bought into.

Robin shrugged and put on a tight grin. "Ready to get home already. An' next time you three need a roadie/road/manager/drummer, maybe look for *more* than one body. I'm gonna sleep for days once this's all over."

Mal empathized, but it wasn't until he closed the door that he started wondering just how Ciaran intended to get to the next city *on his own steam*. The

165

man had never been to Baltimore. He couldn't even drive. And he was as skint as the rest of them. Then there was the matter of a gashed-up hand—who knew if he could even pick up a guitar, much less play it—not to forget being in the company of a malignant supernatural being. A fecking *leannán sí*, actually.

The bus ride without him was an awkward, quiet trip.

Arriving in town, they scurried outside into air reeking of motor oil and fish entrails, then directly into the venue, a dilapidated brick-walled warehouse called Hammerjacks in an industrial end of nowhere.

Caitlin made herself scarce.

Twenty minutes after soundcheck was supposed to have started, the door opened and Sheerie strolled in, casual and appraising, like she was thinking of buying the place. Her black top fit every curve, while her short plaid skirt waved with every sashay, and seeing her made Mal freeze. He pictured himself running over and decking her, pummeling that self-satisfied face until it was nothing but pulp, then finding an incinerator to dump the rest of her body.

The image vanished and sweat rolled down his brow. *Jaysus*. He'd never hit a woman. Never even thought of it. But right now he wanted to throw every ounce of his fear and loathing at someone, and she was the ideal target. Why couldn't a person go after a *leannán sí*?

Then he remembered how she'd flung him from the hotel room without batting an eye. Gave him a nosebleed, too. Seething, he counted the seconds, waiting for Ciaran.

Nothing.

Mal swung around on his barstool, fingers clenched. His anger was cold and focused, comforting and unfamiliar. He knew the plan. He was going to *do* the plan. But he was not going to do anything *to her*. So he tried to relax, watching as she approached the stage where Patrick was replacing a string on his mandolin. It was roadie work, but he didn't seem to care. They all needed something mindless to be doing right now, so they wouldn't think too hard.

Sheerie leaned against the stage, observing Patrick at his work. His head hung over the instrument, disguised by dark curls. "Where is he?" he asked in a flat, affectless voice.

"Ciaran?" Her tone rang of circuses, of carillons. "He'll be along directly. When do you begin playing?"

Patrick turned to her for a brief moment, then shook his head.

"Well, *I'm* ready for music." She leaped onto the stage and grabbed Ciaran's guitar. "I'll play for him."

"You feckin' will not." Mal knew he was supposed to stand back, let Patrick do his … thing, but he couldn't help himself. He jumped from the stool and strode over. "Put that down." By the time he got to the stage, she'd slung the big electric over a shoulder. She was so tiny, it should have made her look like a child playing with a grown-up's toy—but instead it was as if she'd donned an essential part of herself. Mal had a brief flash of her as the wildest thing they could have had onstage with them.

Sheerie's gaze twinkled. "Care to stop me?"

"Leave it." Patrick brought the mandolin into tune with the single tweak of a knob. "No harm in it, if he's late. It's only a check."

Sheerie beamed at Patrick and their eyes connected.

Mal swallowed and thought he might be sick. Time to play his part, although he didn't have to act all that much. "I'm not doin' this." He wagged a finger at Patrick. "And you—you oughta know better."

"I do." Patrick lifted a hand to shield his eyes and ensure someone was at the soundboard, then called out, "We can roll."

"Sure?" Alex, their soundman, sounded dubious. "No one's at the piano."

"And no one will be," said Mal, stalking to the venue's exit in what he hoped was a believable diva huff. Behind him, the guitar and mandy kicked into gear—bright, exciting and somehow shiny new. Each note was like being smacked with broken glass.

They'd talked about this, in the green field. He knew his part in this little drama. It didn't make it feel right, though.

Outside the venue, the day was springlike, a warm breeze whistling in Mal's ears. He smacked the flat of his hand against the brick building, then paced the sidewalk.

There was so much to look forward to. His life was better than just a few days earlier, in large part thanks to Caitlin. His hair was coming back. He'd been cleared of whatever had plagued him. And now he knew that *sídhe* were not invulnerable, that they could be outwitted and fought. Dispelled.

But one other thing he'd learned about the fey from books was that they were not to be trusted. Sneaky, underhanded, outstandingly self-centered—the best a person could hope for was to never cross paths with them. These were not Grimm's or Disney's fairy-tales characters, where honor won out over cruelty and the clever outwitted the selfish. The random nature of *sídhe* made them feel more real—and more frightening. *Sídhe* lived outside civilization, or at least the human concept of civilization.

He'd begun thinking of the man inside Hammerjacks right now as Padraig again. Patrick had been someone they thought they'd known; Padraig was the strange little boy who came and stayed. The boy who'd blessed the dust, who emerged from the edges and, for a time, seemed to have gone back to them. The monks had tried civilizing him, too—but it had all been pretense. Leopards and spots, *sídhe* and anarchy. Couldn't change. Not deep down.

Because what kept needling Mal, who kept this cold, angry part of him stoked, was that it was Padraig's fault that these creatures had come. These—malignancies. Caitlin was all right in some ways, but she was as unknowable as the rest. She'd never have raised a finger to protect Ciaran without them begging. She was like them all, selfish and cruel, unwilling to help save a man's life. If this plan failed—and Mal held out little hope it could succeed—Ciaran would come home in a box, and Mal would lose the greatest friend he'd ever had.

Or rather, he'd lose two of them. Because if Ciaran died because of Padraig, he could never look him in the eye again.

Mal paced some more, trying to melt his anger. He didn't want to put it on Padraig but was finding it hard to dodge facts. All they'd wanted to do was make music. Getting paid for it meant you could make more music, play to more people—so money had to be involved. But really, it was all about the music. Bringing the cleaned-up and improved Patrick back into the fold had seemed like a good idea at the time—but it had led to where they were today. To where Mal, red-faced and huffing up and down a strange, empty street, had to worry about whether Ciaran had died yet.

The thought staggered him. He was sweating despite the breeze, eyes red and stinging. Mal took a deep breath and caught a glimpse of movement over by the bus, parked down the street from the venue.

Ciaran. Standing there, leaning against the door, watching him.

Mal raced over, wanting to embrace him but knowing it would raise more questions than he could answer.

"Was wondering when that train would pull into the station." Ciaran looked freshly cleaned and shaven, but he was so pallid and thin his wide smile was ghastly. "You were workin' that sidewalk pretty good."

"You." Mal didn't know whether to smack him on the back or give him a good shaking. "You're late."

"Well." He held up his hand, wrapped with so much gauze it resembled a mitten. "Don't worry so hard about me. Sheerie's been taking good care."

"Where the hells did you go?"

He chuckled like a man without care. "Funniest thing—Sheerie had this idea we'd drive down here. So we found a car and went for a ride."

"You *found* a car? Who drove? You haven't a license. And with what money?" Questions flew from him like darts.

Ciaran held up his hands in surrender. "I slept through most of it. But I called Robin—"

"Sure, he told us. But—your hand. Why go for a *ride* with your hand like that? Why not go to the hospital?"

"Eh, 'tis nothing. Burned it on some tea, so Sheerie put paste on it and bound it all up. Said it'll be right as rain for the check."

Mal couldn't understand what was happening. "You didn't burn yourself. You punched a mirror."

Ciaran laughed. "I'd remember that, pal." He reached around Mal's shoulders. "Let's get in there, warm up some instruments."

Mal gave in. There was no arguing with a cheerful madman. He was just so delighted to have him back and not—

dying.

Not yet, anyway.

They walked inside the silent club. Whatever impromptu soundcheck Sheerie and Patrick had concocted together had ended, and for that, Mal was grateful. If those first few chords had sent Mal into a sudden fury, he could only imagine how poorly Ciaran would have reacted.

Instead, they found them over by the bar. Patrick had a newspaper open, his fingers playing with a half-tumbler full of whiskey, the bottle nearby. He was reading aloud, and she was doing quarter turns on the rotating barstool next to him. She would listen eagerly for a moment, then do a partial turn with her arms aloft, laughing that chiming, funhouse laugh.

They glanced up and she reacted fastest, leaping from the stool and rushing to Ciaran, wrapping her arms around his waist and squeezing as if they'd been apart for weeks. Ciaran gasped softly, then embraced her back—though with less force. He patted her head with his thickly-gauzed hand.

Patrick said nothing, and Mal could sense a frost in the air.

"So!" Ciaran announced. "Anyone going to ask what I've been up to?"

"The hotel." Patrick's voice was flat and empty. This, too, was him following the plan. "You checked into the hotel and phoned Rich." He took a drink.

That dialed back some of Ciaran's enthusiasm. "Aw. Sheerie's been telling you things."

"Plenty."

"Well," said Ciaran. "Glad you two are finally getting along." He slid onto a barstool. "They're pouring here already?"

Patrick pushed the bottle his way. "Yer hand."

"Ah, only a flesh wound." Sheerie gave him a nod, and Ciaran held out his hand. She began unwrapping it. "You know how clumsy I am."

"Tea is apparently hazardous to his health," Mal told Patrick. "Least, that's what Sheerie says happened."

"Must be so," Patrick shot back. "Why'd you think she'd lie?"

Ciaran half-turned to Mal. "Yeah. Why say something like that?"

Mal took a step back. This was not a place he wanted to be in. He held his tongue as the last of the gauze unrolled.

Ciaran held up his hand, unblemished and whole. He flexed it a few times. "Perfect." He gave Sheerie a long, deep kiss. "My little miracle worker. So. What was I saying? Right. Had a jaw with Rich. He was complaining 'cause he said he called us all last night and left messages but no one returned."

The phone call. The one that had sent Mal to Ciaran's room—where he'd found him with a mirror stuck in his hand—that had started this whole new strange trip they were taking. Mal and Patrick had never called him back, not after the visit to the Green Place.

"I was busy." Patrick's tone was distracted. "We forgot." He left the stool and gestured at Ciaran's hand. "Let's see this tea burn."

"Gone." Ciaran wiggled his fingers. "Just like that." Patrick passed his hand over Ciaran's hand, then poked between the knuckles. "It's just a hand, Patch. Nothin' special about it."

Patrick backed off, shaking his head. Mal felt the same way. This wasn't like the mirror. There was no glamour there. The hand was healed, and that made Sheerie even more powerful than Mal had imagined. Still, he was oddly grateful to her: It was one less thing Ciaran had to suffer.

Ciaran eyed Patrick's bottle and made a dismissive sound. "Time for the good stuff," he said, slamming his palm on the bar. A barman emerged from the back room. "What's the best whiskey ya got?"

The barman pulled out a bottle of Johnnie Walker Blue Label and brought it over.

"Good enough," said Ciaran.

"There's plenty in the dressing room," said Mal. "No point wasting money on that shite. We're low enough as it is."

"Except—we are not." Ciaran filled glasses for them all, handed them around, then tossed back half a glass in one swallow. "Jaysus, that'll do." He was all but bouncing with excitement. "The money, boyos. It's back, says Rich. Bank error. Craziest feckin' thing. Like someone was playing a joke on us, then got bored."

Mal's legs buckled and he caught himself on the bar. He'd never connected their vanished money, the potential bankruptcy, and the expected lawsuits to the *fear dearg*.

"An' here's the other thing Rich had to share." Ciaran refilled the glasses. "President of the label saw us in New York. Wasn't even supposed to be in town, but we caught a lucky break on this one. He loved the shows. Already picked up our option for three more records, double the budget on each." He smiled at everyone, that horrible spreading of lips that seemed to swallow his entire head. "We are set up, fellas. For life."

Patrick had covered his face with his hands and his back shook.

Mal couldn't be sure if he was laughing.

Colors leapt from Patrick's bass that night: burnt umber, maroon, abyssal ocean blue—and swirled around the room, settling like rain on the audience. A rich scent of tobacco and hops surrounded him, and only some of that melange was from the actual smokers and drinkers. The rest came from his chords, his songs, his heightened sense of what the music could really be. It all folded together so naturally; it made sense in the way his fingers knew where to go and what string to pluck and how long to hold another down.

170

But he couldn't revel in it as he had back in Philadelphia. Patrick felt as if he were being held underwater, pulled further and further down, and no matter how much he struggled he couldn't surface. Everything around him was muffled and distant. The others were flinging themselves around their microphones as if nothing was amiss. Ciaran wouldn't stop grinning like a Samhain skull, and Mal—something had come over him since they'd last spoken in the green field. He wouldn't meet Patrick's eyes. Didn't address him directly, only gave short answers when spoken to. Was it all part of how he understood their plan? Patrick couldn't tell. All he knew was that his behavior reminded him of their days in New York, when Mal was trying out his little "experiment." Only this felt more genuine, more intentional.

Patrick didn't know what to believe anymore, and there was no one else he could turn to. Caitlin was absent, saying she had to be. Having her around would make it too easy for Sheerie to connect the dots, to guess that Patrick had been enlightened as to his heritage. It was better for their plan that she be away; Sheerie would think Patrick vulnerable and stupid, and that might make her sloppy. So Patrick had been left alone to flail, set on a course he was making up as he went along, yet could neither deviate from nor get wrong. He felt like a hollow man, abject and false. There was no way out except through, and he was afraid.

They were nearly done with the show when it came to him. A strange … pawing inside his mind. A softness. Then—vocalizations. A calling. A summoning. He peered through the scrim of color that painted the air inside Hammerjacks. In the far back, a number of fans had hoisted themselves on a raised ledge, legs dangling over the side, swaying. At the end of that line he discovered the source of the sound in his head—a single woman who moved to her own beat, tapping hands on her thighs, staring all the way across the distance directly at him. Before her, the colors parted like a curtain, creating a halo of clarity. He was a good ten yards away but he could make out every detail of Sheerie's fine, angled face and flowing, shining dark hair and moss-colored eyes. Heat rose in him.

Very good, the voice came in clearly now. *All eyes on me. Me and only me.*

Patrick broke away from that piercing stare, swallowing with difficulty. Tried to get back into the song, to pretend he hadn't seen her. But that wasn't the plan. He needed her attention, needed to hold it. The problem with summoning the siren, however, was in avoiding the temptations of the response. Even knowing everything she was and everything she was doing to Ciaran, it was not easy to close himself off. Part of him responded.

He took a swig of water, then swapped the bass for his mandy as they prepared to slide into the next tune. Mal was addressing the crowd, meandering through one of his long introductions that gave the rest of them a moment to catch their breath. Patrick approached the microphone, preparing the opening fingerings of the tune—and the voice came again.

171

Padraig. A pause. *Dear, sweet Padraig.* Another dramatic silence. *Can you love me like you love your friends?*

The sound cut off, as sure as a switch being flipped. Mal was still talking, unaware—but Ciaran stood rigid, his acoustic held in one hand as he stared into the audience. It was an odd, formal pose that he held for an awkward, extended moment. He only came out of the clench when Mal's piano intro began. Then he turned to Patrick—and he was not smiling. There was a dark intent in that hollow gaze. And it was more awful, more terrifying than any of his smiles had been.

The music began and Patrick was sure he heard distant, soft laughter.

Beautiful Melodic Bees

"*Taraigí anseo,*" beckoned Mal to the others after the show. As always, they huddled, faces hovering less than an inch from one another. The heat of their breaths made the small space thick and close—but there was a distance between them now, an absence of what had once been warm and easy.

Ciaran bent in because it was expected. To not do it was to say something to the others that might not be taken back. All night he'd felt he was on the precipice of the unforgivable, and it had only been through sheer willpower that he hadn't made the leap. If he was being honest, though, sheer willpower *and* a total lack of energy—but that was another matter.

Their eyes were on him, though he couldn't catch them staring. They were judging, evaluating. Seeing something on him that repulsed them. He'd always considered them like brothers; would have gone to the ends of the earth for them. No more. They were strangers he once knew, doing things around him, not with him.

The only person he trusted now was Sheerie.

Yet even she was making him wonder. During the shows, he'd come to enjoy hearing that silky, enticing voice in his mind, tugging and pushing and suggesting. Tonight, she'd been nearly silent. The absence had left a carved-out space that echoed. And then, just before the encore, she'd come in straight and clear.

What do you really know about your little friend Padraig?

What did *that* mean? He'd turned to Patrick and saw only fear and guilt on his face.

Now, Ciaran broke from the huddle with a jerk. The others stared at him, then shared a glance. Patrick threw on a shirt, packing up his small travel kit

173

for the bus—and before Ciaran knew it, he was out of the dressing room with a half-wave. That was it. No post-show discussion, no breakdown of the set.

"What's his feckin' hurry?" Ciaran asked.

Mal shrugged, pulling on his own dry shirt and picking up a comb before tossing it aside. "Sure and I don't know. Caitlin's out there, I imagine."

"I haven't seen her."

"She's lurking about." He tossed Ciaran a towel, eyes darting furtively. "So, C—a moment?"

Ciaran sopped the towel in the sink and ran it across his neck. He was still sweating and working to get air down; the high of the show wasn't so easy to dial back from, and he hadn't had anything to drink since soundcheck. Time to get started on that again: Heavy drinking made whatever was troubling him easier to cope with.

"What's up?" He wasn't much interested in what Mal had to say, though. Sheerie would call soon, and that would obliterate anything else, so he wasn't up for anything important.

Mal lowered himself into a battered plastic chair, pulling a second closer with his foot. "Have a sit."

Ciaran waved at him. "Look, I gotta go—"

"And find Sheerie."

He shrugged.

"How bad is it right now? The need to leave?"

He slipped the towel around his shoulders and took a seat. "What's that supposed to mean?"

"That sometimes you can't ignore her. Sometimes she's the only thing in your head. Am I right?"

Ciaran leaned forward. "What's this about? You never want to hear about Sheerie."

"I still don't. I'm talking about you." He breathed deeply. "I'm worried, C. You don't look right. You need a doctor, and I don't mean after we get home."

The words echoed in his head and for a moment things went foggy. He'd seen himself in a mirror not long ago. He'd been a bit … thin. "Jaysus, Mal, I just played for two hours. We've been on the road for weeks. We're all ragged on the edges."

Mal's voice was thick. "You look like you're dying, Ciaran. You look two days from breathing your last. I am not exaggerating. I need you to hear this."

Ciaran straightened. "Yer fuckin' with me."

Mal stared at him steadily.

"I'm fine." But it was a lie. That mirror, what had he seen in it? Why couldn't he remember?

"I need to tell you a few things." Mal's light blue eyes were intent and pained. "You've been … occupied these past few weeks and maybe you didn't notice but—there've been a lot of strange goings-on ever since Boston."

"Yer hair for one. And that feckin' bed. Sure."

"My hair and the bed—yes. But other things. Thing is, Ciaran, there's something … dangerous around us. Something we have to get rid of." Mal took a deep breath. "Or you'll die."

Come now

The soft entreaty made Ciaran jump from the chair. He reached for his shirt. "Shite. And it ain't funny."

"That was her, wasn't it? She called to you?"

Ciaran whirled, shirt half-on. "How the hells do you know about that?"

"She's not from this world, C." Mal stood up. "She's not … one of us."

Come now come now

It was like bees in his mind, replacing the music, beautiful melodic bees and he could think of little else. "You're making no sense at all," he said. "You're a good man, Mal, and you're my friend—but don't think of talkin' against Sheerie." He started to the door. On the other side a dance mix thudded, filtering through like a suppressed heartbeat.

Mal caught him in the chest. "Wait. Just— wait and talk to me."

"What the hell? I've got to go."

"You don't. You really don't."

"Fine. I want to. That better?"

Mal pressed harder but was losing ground as Ciaran advanced. "Don't you find it odd how if she calls you, you come? That she's in your *head*? C, it's wrong. That's not how it works." He paused and regrouped. "You make *her* come. That's how I always remembered it happening before."

Ciaran folded his arms. Part of him was tweaked by that; the other knew his source too well. He laughed. "Nice try there. I'm going because she's a great ride, and we've hardly any time left to be together. That good enough for you?"

"If you can stay, stay right here. Right now. Ten minutes. It'll make no difference. Then I won't stop you."

My love? I need you. Come now.

It was a high, hurting sound, and his gut clenched. Ciaran had never made her wait before, and on some level he knew it was not a wise idea. "I won't."

"You can't."

Ciaran exploded, thrusting his arms out, then grabbed the doorknob. The heartbeat outside was louder and faster than ever. "So what if I can't? What if I feckin' can't and there's nothing anybody can do about it?"

"Then don't you think that's a problem?"

The bees, the damned bees, they were so loud. Problem? Of course it was a problem, but if he admitted aloud that it was a problem then he'd have to admit so much more about himself than he was ready for. That maybe he wasn't going to be an imago, a butterfly. That maybe the man who'd played air guitar in Kenmore Square had always been fooling himself, would always have a nonexistent audience.

He turned. Nearly asked Mal for help.

And then the smallest of voices, shaped like a needle.

I guess Padraig can love me better than you.

That was all it took. A red fog came over his mind and he couldn't think. There was no reason to think. He had the door open, and the music blasted into the room like a physical force. Ciaran threw himself outside and scanned the club.

The usual gaggle of well-wishers fell on Patrick the moment he escaped the dressing room, but he passed through them without a glance. At some point in his trajectory he arrived in front of Sheerie and scooped up her hand. It was a cool, airless thing—more object than organic—but he laced his fingers around hers anyway and pulled her out of the venue.

The streets sparkled with wet, and he thought of the mist surrounding Boston the night the tinker had found them. The trees were still dripping. The air was clean and fresh.

"You found me first." Sheerie giggled as he paused on the sidewalk, scanning for the bus. For a moment he considered they just stroll to the hotel, but that would leave him open with her for too long. Too many opportunities for something to go awry. For her to get inside his head.

Think about nothing, he told himself. *Don't let her in there. She thinks you're weak and ignorant. She thinks she knows so much.*

He spun her to him in a quick movement; the shift was so fast she did a neat little twirl. He caught her up and stared into her face. Patrick wanted this to be Caitlin. Having Sheerie there in his arms was such a disappointment that his chest contracted. Still, she was lovely in the moonlight, her features sculpted like the work of a great artist, with wide green eyes that glinted and a ripe mouth shaped by surprise. Now his chest ached in a different way. He wanted her. That was a good thing—it meant she wanted him now, too. But this wasn't a seduction; it was an instinctive animal thing she was waking in him, and he had a moment of picturing her under him, screaming—

Patrick blinked. Released her from his arms. Hated himself a little.

All of this was wrong.

Then he pulled her down the street, to the bus.

Inside was dry and empty and dark; with the bus turned off, a small reserve of electricity lit some recessed lights or maybe the radio if they wanted. The refrigerator hummed. They were alone. Patrick brought her to the back of the bus, shutting the door behind them, and fell hard against the couch-shaped area that lined what they called the sitting room. Back here was a television, a stereo, windows with blinds covering one-way glass—everything a person might need, except space.

Sheerie remained standing, evaluating him. "You're so hard to read."

"I'm transparent." He squeezed her hand and pulled her to him. She settled on his leg and he hardly felt her there.

"This is quite an interesting scenario you've concocted," she said.

"I've been thinking about it for a long time."

Sheerie's eyes narrowed. "Funny that I haven't felt it from you before. Perhaps it's your … nature."

Patrick shook his head, all innocence. "Haven't a clue what you mean."

Don't let her in, Caitlin had warned. *This HSSC. She won't know for sure that you know who you are, not yet. You don't even know your name.*

"And here I thought Ciaran was important to you," she continued. "Why are you with me?"

"Am I with you?" When she didn't answer, he went on. "Ciaran isn't well. You need someone who is. Who can give you what you need. He's no good to you now. Besides, he'll just leave you behind when we get home." He drew her closer. "Won't happen with me."

"I go where I like," she said.

Jaysus, this is horrible, he thought. He wasn't like this with women; he was awkward and rarely spoke first. Envisioning how a Hollywood hero would have done it was making him seem like a B-movie actor *and* a piece of cardboard. "That's why you're here," he said. It was enough talking. He brought his mouth to hers and she resisted for just a second—but then they joined. It was a heated, living thing, this kiss. Her tongue and mouth were surprisingly sweet like syrup, with an undercurrent of the elemental—coal, metals. He pressed harder and brought a hand up to her breasts, kneading the fabric on them roughly. She arched her back to him and made soft yelping noises but didn't pull away. Sheerie straddled him on the couch, holding him down with a look of delight and triumph.

He tried to sit up—but she pushed harder and he fell back, head thumping on the back of the narrow couch. He realized in that moment that for all her submissiveness, if she wanted to put his head through the window she could—and he wouldn't even have time to react. All this girlishness was just a cover. Maybe some men she was with preferred the coquette, so that's what she gave them.

"You taste so strange," she said. "Like no one else I've been with."

"I'll take that as a compliment."

She set her hand between his legs and smiled. "I'll take that as *my* compliment."

"I'm sure you're used to it by now."

She hesitated. "What does that mean?"

Shite. He had to remind himself not to overplay his hand. He had to both hold himself back and give himself to her, and it wasn't an easy dance. Anyway, what he really wanted was to poke at her. To reveal her absurdity and maybe give some hurt back for all the pain she'd caused. But the longer he was with her, the easier it was to pretend this was how it was meant to be all along. That she really was supposed to be with him, and no other. That was her magic. Her power.

Patrick sat up and moved his hands to her. "Only that you must be used to having every head turn when you walk into the room."

She blushed and he wanted to cringe. "I suppose."

He kissed her again, holding her head, thinking of an egg. *I could do something horrible right now. Squeeze and squeeze until she popped—*

Again, he halted. What was it about being with her? Every ugly thing he'd ever seen or thought of bubbled to the surface, threatening to take him over. Things he'd never even conceived of were coming to mind. All at once he worried he might succeed in getting rid of her—but change the person he was in the process.

The truth was, he had no idea how this … change was supposed to take place. Caitlin had said Ciaran had made promises, so at some point he might be asked to do the same. When? As they kissed? When they were naked together? After fucking? He was flailing, unsure of course or destination.

Stop thinking so hard, he told himself. He reached up for the buttons that held her shirt together and twisted one free, then two. She wore nothing beneath, and that made him wonder about what lay—or didn't—beneath her skirt, what had been grinding against him. He slipped a hand into the shirt and moved around inside, rubbing and pinching again. She moaned and moved against him, reaching for his belt, tugging, and then stood up.

"Well." She smoothed down her skirt. "That is important information."

Jaysus, she knows. Wait. She can't know. "What is?"

She touched his nose. "I like you, Padraig. I *know* things about you that I can't wait to share. I mean, I wouldn't even be here if it wasn't for you. But Ciaran—he was too easy to pass up. I'm so delighted we'll have fun when I'm finished with him."

"Be finished with him now." Panic settled in him.

She tilted her head. "Do you even know what you're asking?"

"Just dump him. I'm here, right now. Where is he?"

"Oh." She tittered, covering her mouth. "He's on the way."

A Very Different Bucket O' Fish

Over the years, Ciaran had done battle over hurts large and small. But he'd never *begun* a fight. After a first tussle when he was six, over the fact that a neighborhood boy had refused to share his new bicycle, Ciaran's father sat him down and told him physical brawling was neither answer nor solution.

"That said," his father added more quietly so Ma couldn't hear, "self-defense is a very different bucket o' fish, you understand. I'm not for some pacifist liturgy that says turning the other cheek makes you the better man. I don't want to ever hear that my son started a fight. But if you're attacked first—you give back as good as you get, and a dram more. So they know not to mess with you again."

It was a good idea. It gave Ciaran a way to do as he liked and not get in trouble at home for it. He became a terrific provoker, a master of getting someone else to throw down the gauntlet. Also, then he'd know the swing was coming and could duck. Right after that, he'd turn his opponent into paste. And he could always say to both *athair* and *múinteoir* alike, "They started it."

Finding Sheerie was no trick at all. Her voice was an invisible thread he could track in the dark. He pushed out of the noisy club into the damp night, shoving past anyone trying to get into the venue. A few in the queue called his name, but all he could think about were the bees in his head and the music that never stopped, layered between the buzzing. Those sounds, those noises, were constant now—pausing only for the silky softness of her voice, pulling him on.

On some level he knew Patrick was with her. There was a deep, distant part of him that insisted—as it had done in the bar earlier, when he'd seen them sitting together—that there was no harm in it. This was Patch, after all. He

179

wouldn't mess with another man's business. Besides, Patrick had that other woman with him. Wasn't he occupied enough?

He's sweet.

Sheerie had said that back in Boston. It slipped through a funnel in his mind, echoed and faded. But she'd said other things this night that stilled his heart and sent up a volcanic rage he hadn't known was in him. In this moment all he could think of was that Sheerie and Patrick were alone together, and they were *not* just reading the newspaper, they were *not* just waiting for him to arrive and have a drink.

Sheerie was his. There was no sharing in this.

If he could think straight, he might be hurt. If he could think, he might wonder why. But since he was deprived of all but the most basic of instincts right now, Ciaran could only move forward. He'd been sorely provoked.

Patrick had started it.

He found the bus down the street, dark and quiet—but he knew they were inside. A rattle of the handle confirmed his expectations; the door was locked. He reared back, launching into a frenzy of kicking. How Patrick had already gained entrance he couldn't know, but leave it to that cunning little fucker to plan ahead and get the key from their driver. Still, as the seconds ticked by he couldn't think of anything better than to pound away. Right now, Ciaran was like a starving dog sensing meat on the other side of a fence, with no idea how to reach it.

Come now come now come now

Frustrated, he thought back to her: *Door's locked, missy.*

There was a click.

That cut through the madness. It said he hadn't been making up her voice, it said that she could both send and receive and what the feckin' hells did that mean—and also, that she could move things without touching them.

She's not from this world.

Mal's words were important. Ciaran knew he should have listened. Too late now. Too late to do anything more than act. Now, Ciaran couldn't care about such details. He yanked open the bus door and it slammed behind him.

Silence. Cold absence. He paused to scan the front, then with loping strides he passed the center bunks and arrived at the door that separated the sleeping area from the sitting room.

Now now now

The wash of red returned and, bracing his hands on the sides of the bunk walls, he lashed out with his foot. The door burst open, one hinge completely undone, the door dangling from the other like a loose tooth. Sheerie was cringing in the far corner, shirt undone, hair tousled. He caught a glimpse of an ivory breast. She looked terrified.

Patrick was not in the room.

Ciaran breathed heavily. "Where." His hands clenched and unclenched. The buzzing was lower now that he had found her, but his rage was still on full boil. He'd been right; the dirty urchin had gone after his girl.

Sheerie gestured with a finger, pointing behind him—then angled it to one side. The bunks.

Behind him, fabric shifted and he heard a muffled thump. Ciaran whirled, facing Patrick. "*Run*," he said in a strangled voice. "Run like you do."

Patrick didn't move. There was something in his eyes—a distance that reminded Ciaran of the way Caitlin had examined him after they'd played that strange, painful music in the hotel bar. Something faraway and alien, but familiar, too.

The moment passed. Ciaran surged forward, fingers catching on Patrick's jacket sleeve, which tore as he wrested away. They had nearly reached the front of the bus; once there, Patrick would have the advantage of space, but Ciaran didn't hesitate again. He made another lurching grab and found purchase in that head of thick curls. Closing his fingers, he made a fist and yanked backward, swinging Patrick's head like a hammer into the wall. Patrick bounced once and tumbled to the floor, then rolled toward the exit.

Ciaran made another swipe at him, but the urchin was slippery, and he all but fell down the steps and out the door, onto the sidewalk. Outside, Patrick stumbled and landed on his knees, giving Ciaran an extra second to jump after him. He had the sensation of many eyes on them as he stood over where Patrick had fallen awkwardly, inspecting him without emotion. A small trickle of blood ran down Patrick's scalp.

Stop came through, his first truly conscious thought in minutes. But behind that came a soft sob. Sheerie stood in the stairwell of the bus, hands over her mouth, stricken.

"You hurt?" Ciaran narrowed his eyes.

She nodded. *Go go go*, she thought at him. *More, please*.

Sheerie did love her blood sports. The red curtain fell again and heat filled his mind and all he could see on the ground was someone who'd tried to sneak between him and the only thing that made him feel good anymore. On the ground was a thief, a nothing, a nameless man who'd always been a stranger—it had just taken a long time to figure him out. Ciaran leaned over Patrick and shook him by his shirt. When that failed to rouse him, he drew his leg back and landed a kick in his side.

Patrick's eyes flew wide and he curled into the wounded place, breath whistling out.

"Hey!" someone called. Ciaran turned. A crowd of the curious had left the venue and formed nearby, some still holding their drinks. Like it was part of the show.

Ciaran glared at the gawkers, holding out his arms. "Somebody have something to say?" When no one moved, he took a step as if to rush them. The crowd flinched and he made an obscene gesture.

Something slammed him from behind, arms wrapped around his waist. He went down, tackled like a player in an American football game, falling hard against the curb and sidewalk. His hands scraped on gravel. With a roar Ciaran turned, flinging whatever his fingers could catch up at his assailant.

Patrick didn't see it coming. He clawed at his eyes when the gravel hit him.

That was all Ciaran needed. He cocked back and released a punch into Patrick's face so hard it spun him. Patch stumbled drunkenly against the bus, latching onto the side-view mirror to keep from falling. He tried standing up all the way, but his feet kept failing him. He stared at Ciaran, lip split and eyes almost sleepy, face contracted in pain and sorrow.

Ciaran put his fists up in a boxer's stance. "C'mon, y'pissant," he said. "Fight me like a man."

Patrick shook his head. "Won't," he slurred. "Do what y'will."

"Why the fuck not?"

"I'd kill you."

He wanted to laugh but couldn't. "Everybody thinks I'm half-past dead today," Ciaran barked. "I ain't going anywhere." He drove a fist into Patrick's gut and he bent in half like a soft toy, going down on his knees. Patrick held up shaking hands in defense.

Ciaran knelt next to him, grabbing at Patrick's face, which was starting to swell on one side. "Go near her again and I'll rip your feckin' lungs out. You understand me, *fear gan ainm?*"

Breathing hard, Patrick twisted away and spat something thick and wet into the street. At last, he stilled. "*Tá brón orm, a chara,*" he whispered. "*Ní féidir liom aon rud a ghealladh duit.*" He was sorry, but he could promise nothing.

"Ciaran O'Conaill!" Mal pushed his way through the crowd, a thunderous look clouding his face. "*Stad de sin anois.*" Stop this now.

"Keep out of it." Ciaran advanced on him. "This isn't about you."

"The fuck it's not." Mal squared off with him. Their eyes locked, and for a breath they were in a kind of dance. Ciaran spun around to return to Patrick ,and Mal grabbed his arm. He struggled, still wanting that piece of meat. Mal refused to let go—and Ciaran's strength finally ebbed. That had never happened before, but it was as if he'd used up everything in his reserve tank. He was empty. Yet he was still so furious he was growling.

With a mighty heave, Mal pulled him back and landed the flat of his hand on Ciaran's face, a smack that echoed.

A siren wailed in the distance.

The curtain was gone. Ciaran staggered, glancing at the crowd. Mal scanned his face a moment; satisfied, he ran over to help Patrick. "What in holy hells have you done?" he cried.

Ciaran was dazed, wondering how he'd gotten here. "He wouldn't ... fight." Words that made no sense. Who didn't want to fight? Why was everybody star-

182

ing at him? Why was Patch bent over? Why did his knuckles sting? He flexed his fingers. His palms were scraped up. He was exhausted.

A soft set of fingers slipped into his free hand and gave it a squeeze. Sheerie. He kissed the back of her hand, looking around. Everyone else was a stranger.

Everyone.

Do You Blame the Water?

Soft beeps. Faint light. Images and sounds sloshed around in Patrick's head like water in a bath—green grass, colors drifting down to the audience, Caitlin's face. A glare of nothingness like staring into the sun.

Returning to consciousness, Patrick discovered he was reclining on a gently sloped surface. A loose sheet had been draped over him. He cracked open his eyes slowly, flinching at the brightness. Over a shoulder hung an IV bag fat with fluid, the tube leading from it into his arm. Just beyond the tube stood a large square machine of signaling lights and noises.

He was enclosed by curtained walls. Turning slowly on the bed, he could make out muffled voices and the occasional shout from beyond the fabric. On the other side, the world was busy, moving. Within, all was still and quiet.

His tongue tasted like dirt and stones. When he reached up, his fingers brushed bandages twined around his head.

"That must have really hurt."

Caitlin perched on a chair in one corner, looking as if she'd just alit there. He nodded.

"You're all right," she said. "They stuck you into a big tube and ran magnets over your head. Nurse says no concussion. Mal's in the hall."

He was so grateful to see her he wanted to bolt from the bed and scoop her up—but in this moment all he could do was blink. Even a smile tired him out. He was thirsty.

Caitlin poked a straw through a Styrofoam cup lid, holding it to his mouth while he sipped the entire thing down in a go. He had a thirst for more than just water, but that would have to wait.

184

"Where've you been?" he croaked.

"Away. Looking into things about our … HSSC." She tossed the cup over a shoulder and leaped on the bed next to him, crossing her legs and leaning forward. "You did good."

"Good?" Patrick tried sitting up, but fell back immediately. "He nearly killed me." The fact of it was lodged in his chest like a rock; he could barely breathe from the weight of it.

"Of course he did. He'll try to do it properly next time."

He stared at her.

"Because that's what she wants."

"Sheerie wants me *dead*?"

Caitlin lay on her side and he shifted beneath the sheet to accommodate her. "Sheerie doesn't care, Padraig. She needs one of you dead so she can have the other. That's the choice you gave her. My opinion? She'd rather have you. You've given her a taste, and she's found you delicious. And you've got a lot more time left in you than he does."

"It doesn't … bother you? What happened on that bus?"

She propped her head on an elbow. "Should it?"

"Some women—"

"Ah. Not a woman." She tapped her chest. "I know, you're still learning. Those distinctions … aren't important for us, Padraig. Not when you have as many years as we do."

She kept hinting about vast amounts of time. "What does that mean? How much time do I have?"

Caitlin rubbed his leg. "Is this the conversation you want to have now? Let's just say … more than he does. Especially if he remains with her."

Patrick let that sit there, gazing at her as long as he could. She seemed exactly now as she had been on the Common, in that same denim jacket with the little buttons, hair askew, face clear, and those almost unseeable dots dancing across his nose. He ached in a way that had nothing to do with his injuries. Guilt washed through him. "I'm sorry."

"For?"

"She makes you want her. She makes me … cruel. I don't know who I am with her."

"Oh." She nodded. "Of course she does. It's useful that you see that."

"Why?"

"Because it means you don't need to beat yourself up more over it. It means she's got him by the short hairs anytime she takes it into her head. Hypothetically."

He didn't want to examine that too closely. But the more awake he became, the more the beating resonated. Patrick had never been afraid like that before. In formulating the plan in the Green Place, he'd been realistic about what might happen, and that had made him nervous and fearful. What he'd experienced in that bunk while hiding, hoping to avoid a confrontation—that was new. He'd been smacked around plenty as a boy; for Herself it had almost been a hobby. He could take a swat or a swing and it wasn't nothing but it wasn't the world's end, either. He'd been inured.

But having Ciaran come after him had been so much worse. Herself hadn't loved him. A beating was an obligation from her. He'd tolerated it because that's how life was. But—Ciaran was his friend. It had hurt so much worse, coming from him. And there was nothing Patrick could do about it; he'd mentioned this in the field, too. He couldn't hit back. In Ciaran's state, that might be all it would take to end things. Outside the bus Patrick had seen his chance when Ciaran had turned his back on him. He'd hoped to pin him on the tarmac until the madness subsided or Mal showed up to help—but Ciaran's blind rage had made him so much stronger than Patrick had anticipated.

"You told us he'd be fighting mad," he said now. "You said he wouldn't know who he was."

"Was I wrong?"

"He was out for murder. He was twice as strong as made sense for a man teetering the way he is."

"Well," she said after a moment. "We were talking in hypotheticals."

A flash of anger made him pull away. "It ain't right." He pointed a finger. "You not taking sides. You could stop all of this. You could've kept me from getting my head kicked in. You're almost making it worse, you know? We were confused before about what was up with him. Now we know—and it's worse 'cause we have to do this alone. *I'm* totally alone in this and you're just standing on the side like some damned referee, throwing flags."

Her face crumpled and she turned away. For a moment he swore she was fading—but then she came back, in full Technicolor. She sat up on the bed, back to him. "I know what you want me to do. You want me to give you the answers. I don't *know* them, Padraig. She's a special case invented by human need—and they didn't provide a solution. Only an end result." She paused. "Anyway, even if I did have the answers, it'd be exile for sure for me. I never did that before."

"I see."

"You don't. You can't."

"Maybe I can." His words came thick and slow. "I only have to picture life before I met you. Then I just think about how it'd all be again if it stopped tomorrow. It'd be like having my heart taken out."

"It … scares me," she said. "I've never been scared before."

"I know a lot about scared." He reached over, plucking at her sleeve. "Got a PhD. in that. Come here." He wanted to say he'd look after her, that he'd protect her—but as the night had proved, he wasn't in a position to protect anyone. He hugged her tightly and they lay there for a time, not speaking.

After a while, she slipped from his arms and helped him to sit up. Once the initial wooziness faded, she ran her fingers down the IV line; when they reached the bandage covering where the drip pierced flesh, she pressed down and eased out the needle. It swung away, dangling and dripping. Setting her hand over the punctured place, she leaned in and kissed him. Patrick combed his free hand through her hair, holding her as tightly as he could. His lip pricked at him where it had been split, but he didn't care; her tender touch made him feel cared for and alive again.

They parted, heads touching. "Should you even be here?" he asked.

"She's not aware," said Caitlin. "All of Sheerie's little antennae are focused on Ciaran right now, I promise."

"So—what happens next?"

She waited.

"I have to try again, don't I."

Still, nothing.

"I have to get her alone and try to—I don't know what."

"I believe you do."

"All right, I do—but I'd like to not have to," he growled. "She's disgusting. Death come in costume with a liar's tongue."

Caitlin ran a hand down his bandages. "Have a bit of pity, Padraig. She was created this way. It's what she does. A river drowns a man; do you blame the water?"

"Are you making excuses?"

"Just telling you what is. Ciaran's not blameless, either. He took from her. He's known from the first that he's taking, and he's made no real effort to push her aside. There's an empty place in him that she's found and is making bigger. That's something you should understand."

Patrick had known from the first that Caitlin was different. Then he'd learned how much of himself was like her. But this—he couldn't accept. He was not going to attempt empathy with a creature trying to kill his friend. That demanded too much.

"I hate her." It sounded childish but felt good to say aloud.

"Hate is easy. It makes you more like her and less like yourself."

He choked up. "And just who the hell is that, Caitlin? I've no idea anymore."

Caitlin lifted her hand from his arm. There was no puncture mark, no bruising, nothing. "I promise," she said. "One day, you will know."

A Trí

If singin' birds must sing, with no question of choice
Then living is our song, indeed our voice
Best agree you and me we're probably nightingales

—Paddy McAloon, "Nightingales"

Dance with the Thunder

As the first streaks of morning light appeared in the sky, Mal lifted his head from the hotel room pillow. Caitlin had turned a chair to face the window, awaiting the sun's slow rise. Her legs draped over an armrest and ember-colored light flowed lazily into the room, coating her in its warm glow. There were sparks in her hair. She had her eyes shut, but he sensed she wasn't asleep.

Once Patrick could stand on his own, he'd discharged himself from the emergency room by walking out, and all three of them had journeyed by taxi back to the hotel. Mal hadn't wanted to be alone, so he'd fallen into one of the double beds in Patrick's room and dozed restlessly, while Patrick had disappeared into a hard, instant sleep in the other.

Now, as Mal stirred, Caitlin beckoned him over. He slid from the sheets, dragging the room's other chair. They propped their feet on the windowsill. Outside, a dark jagged line of buildings came into greater definition with each moment. She'd opened the window a few inches, and early birdsong drifted into the room along with a tiny breeze that tickled Mal's feet.

"You were there for him last night," she said softly after a time. "He needed you to be."

Mal didn't think he'd done anything praiseworthy. In fact, he felt lousy about not having gotten there sooner. He'd known the moment Patrick left the dressing room where he was going, and after Ciaran bolted, he further knew the trains would collide. Yet he'd lingered, paralyzed, staring at his hands for far longer than he should have. A dark feeling was growing inside him, a need to blame someone for what was happening. Sheerie was out of his grasp. Patrick was not.

189

So he had waited, hands clenched, cold and hot at the same time—until he thought he heard a sound outside. Something crunching. Only then had he leapt into action.

"Never thought it'd come to that," he said. "We never—not to each other."

"They're not themselves. Neither of them." She leaned her head on a bent arm. "But they need you to bring them back. Padraig can't do it on his own. And—he'll never ask you himself. He thinks this is his fault."

"Isn't it, though?" He flicked a glance at Patrick, still sleeping. The bandage around his head was gone; in repose his face was marred by faint bruising. The lip was nearly healed. He stared hard, disbelieving. It was unnatural. "Without him, none of this ever would have happened."

"Yes." Her voice was firm and decisive. "Without him, none of this ever happened."

Mal raised an eyebrow.

"Without him, the two of you never make it off the streets back home."

He felt smacked. "Like hell."

Caitlin turned a sly look on him, but her words were quietly ferocious. "Without him, you teach piano. Young ones mostly. Some adults. Ciaran joins you on the streets in the afternoons, maybe weekends. But he's got this job in …" She glanced to one side, then back to him again. "Construction. Yes. House builder. Putting that brawn to use. And in a year or so, one of you gets your nice, local girl pregnant and—" She curled her fingers to her thumb and made a soft *pfft* as if completing a trick. "*Baile Átha Cliath*. Could spend your life in that town, never go anywhere. Not without some help."

"He thinks mighty well of himself if that's what he's been telling you." But an odd coolness had come over Mal. He lowered his feet to the floor, needing grounding. He had to remind himself that she wasn't just some sweet girl with lovely hair who hung around with them.

She made a dismissive noise. "He thinks the two of you hung the moon."

"You can't know that stuff." Mal's voice was oddly thick. "Bunch of gobshite."

"Best not to assume what our kind can and can't know." She paused. "Or what we can read from your own fears."

Mal leaned forward. "He barely had his fingering down when he came back from the monks. We watched him learn. He'd be up into the wee hours and arrive with bandages on every finger. Thought we didn't notice. He had to *work* at it."

She said nothing for a time. Then: "It's not about what he can play, Mal. It's about who he is. You can tell yourself whatever story you like, but we both know nothing was going for you and Ciaran until he popped back up. How long after he joined you did people really start noticing? How long before the wheels turned in your favor?"

"Not overnight," he parried.

"But it happened."

He stared at her. "How long have you been watching us?"

Caitlin glanced at Patrick. "Him? Nearly always. Not me. Another of us. But—if he'd stayed on our side of things, he'd've been dead before he turned a year. They don't let the mixed ones grow. Too—chancy. Too confusing. Too many go bad and sour, like milk left out. His Da saved him. We nearly let go then. He didn't know, might never have known. And then—you all started making music. We heard you. We discovered him again. Learned he might have real power. That saved him. The music, and the two of you—have saved him every day since."

She rested her hand on his arm. "In exchange, some of his light rubs off on you. And you were both born with so much light already. This way—you get to be … extraordinary. You get to not be a band in a local New York pub with a regular gig and a dissatisfaction in their gut about what might have been, if luck had broken their way. Kings of the pool table, and all that. By yourselves, you're individually quite good, in a slightly-above-average normal human way. But with Padraig—you get to be great. You can be the biggest band on the planet in a few years if you choose. But you are right. It never happens without him."

Mal felt as if he'd gone a few rounds with Ciaran's fists.

"Surely you've known for a long time there was something unusual about him."

"Sure, but." He paused. "I never thought—"

"Of course not. No one considers that anymore. Everything's so … civilized. We're something studied—badly, with poor texts—at university. Not something truly *believed* in. Except by the rare few. Through them, we survive. And we give back."

He'd never thought of any of it this way before.

"Try not to blame him," she said quietly. "It's not been all bad, this tour, has it?"

The sun was nearly risen and a small smile dawned on Mal as he revisited all those moments onstage. They were the whole reason anyone went through all the time-wasting and traveling and bad food and repetitive interviews and anonymous hotel rooms and attendant nonsense in the bizarre, ridiculous business they were in. It was for those hours with the spotlight on and the crowd in your ears and the music in every pore that anyone tolerated the rest. And yes, there had been transcendence on this tour—especially in this last part. He nodded.

"You can't dance with thunder if you fear getting wet," she said. "When all of this is done and you go home—do as you will. You can cut him out of your life if you choose. See how things go. That is a decision you get to make. But trust me—you will miss it. You'll miss him and miss what it means to be greater than ordinary. You will miss true, honest magic."

Robin's knock at the door woke Mal a short time later. He rose stiffly from the chair where he'd dozed off again. Caitlin was gone, Patrick still out cold. Robin's report: They were back on the road in a half hour. Ciaran would meet them at the next soundcheck, don't wait around. This time, Mal didn't even question it. Sheerie was in charge.

But not for much longer—one way or the other.

Mal closed the door on Robin and stood by Patrick's bed. A clamor of emotions rolled through him, but one was clearest. He rummaged around in his jeans pocket through the things he always carried. His hand closed around the small object, then leaned over.

"Wakey," he said.

Patrick rolled over, squinting into the daylight. He rubbed his face, which was nearly clear of injury now. He still wore the rumpled, creased clothing he'd worn when he took the beating, and a maroon splotch showed against the dark fabric of his jeans. His jacket was torn at the sleeve. His hair looked bigger, halo-like. Yet when he saw Mal, a smile came to his face as natural as the dawn.

"Well." His voice was like sandpaper. "Guess I lived."

"You look well for a man who got his lights kicked in," Mal marveled.

The night had been terrible, but in the light of day it could almost seem as if it had never happened. Calm came over Mal. He no longer knew what to make of Patrick—but that dark place inside him was gone. Healed, as sure as the man's wounds. He felt as if they'd emerged on the other side of something intact, and it gave him strength. *I'm ready to tango with whatever thunder—or hurricane—comes.*

"Time to go?"

"Nearly." Mal sat on the edge of his own bed and held out the object he'd taken from his pocket, the thing he'd carried for years. He offered it to Patrick: a small, perfectly smooth oblong whitish pebble, the kind only found near a beaten-down, abandoned cottage in a wild, strange part of town outside Dublin. It was a gift. It was a trade. It was both.

"Think maybe you ought to carry this for a while," said Mal.

Patrick turned it over in his palm, then closed his fingers around it. "You're jokin'."

"Not on my life."

"You—kept this?"

Mal shrugged. "Call me sentimental."

"What's it for?"

"For whatever you need," said Mal. "Now. Explain how I can help."

Robin met them on the sidewalk outside the hotel, sipping on a large cup of coffee. "Ah, good." He glanced at his watch. "Only a twenty-minute delay today. Thanks, fellas." They started to the door, but he held an arm up on the bus. "Bit of a surprise inside waiting for ya." Then he stood down. "I'll be in the follow van, let you all catch up a bit."

Mal jumped up the short staircase. Patrick hesitated, chest tight. He'd already decided he'd be the one with the roadies in the follow van. The idea of going back into the bus after what happened the night before made him queasy. But if Ciaran was on the bus—as Patrick now suspected—he'd have Sheerie with him. That was not a configuration he was ready to tolerate, even if the ride downstate was less than an hour. It would be like climbing into a war bunker with a hidden grenade whose pin might, or might not, have been pulled.

"Rich?" Mal's voice drifted through the open bus doors.

Patrick jumped in. And sure enough, there he was, the manager they hadn't seen since Boston—since before nearly everything changed.

Rich was gesturing at the broken divider door in the back of the bus, then at Mal's head. "What in all hells went on here? That's going to *cost* to fix, and—Jaysus, Mal, you look like somethin' out of a comic book, you do."

"Ah." Mal leaned up against the kitchenette. "Well, we've had a few … incidents."

"Rock 'n' roll," Patrick murmured.

The door shut and the driver called for them to brace. Patrick tossed his bag aside and sank into one of the booths at the front that served as a kitchen table. "When did you get in?" he asked.

"Came straight from the airport first thing this morning," Rich said, sliding in. "Thought I'd catch you boys unawares." He peered around. "But looks as if you've a few surprises for me."

"It's been a long couple of weeks." Mal eyed Patrick. "You heard about C not coming along."

"Yeah, he's met some bird and she's, what—driving them?"

"Driving right off the cliff," Patrick muttered.

Mal made a small gesture to tone it down. "So," he said. "We've an hour. Where'd you like to start?"

Patrick stared out the window as the remnants of Baltimore fell away and they rolled into another tunnel of trees and tarmac. He was pleased to see Rich, but their manager had missed so many things he could hardly be a confidant.

At least Mal was back to normal. Better than, even. Patrick had no idea what had made him go cold the day before or what had brought him back—but they seemed to be on the same page again. Whatever might happen, Mal would be at his side, and that took a load from Patrick's shoulders. He palmed the pebble in his jacket pocket, throat tightening. It was just a stone, but it was a piece of home. A powerful object. It pulsed against his skin as if it remembered him.

Stupid, stupid. He'd been a right eejit last night, to think what they were attempting could happen in an eye blink, like the removal of a bandage. He wanted things to go back to the way they'd been. Stable. Maybe not normal; Patrick understood he'd never lived *normal.* Some reasonable facsimile would be nice, though. But he'd forgotten that nothing would be as it once had been. He could see the world differently now, and it was like glancing into a mirror and not knowing who, or what, stared back. Knowledge in his head had not yet reached his heart.

So much newness brought incredible temptation. Last night, while hiding in the bunks and hoping to avoid Ciaran's fury, he'd thought about the Green Place. Not so hard that he'd disappeared into it—but the pull had been strong. If he'd wanted, he could vanish. He didn't even have to return. He could be there always, talking with Da or exploring the wide world. Make music night and day with Caitlin by his side. She'd turn up eventually and never judge. She'd never say he should have helped his friend if he could. All he'd had to do was *go*.

Instead, he'd shoved that desire to the side. Caitlin might never have judged him, but he'd have lived with it all his days. If he didn't do everything in his power to save Ciaran from his malignancy, he would have nothing. He'd escaped all his life when things got hard. Not anymore.

Patrick thought about what had happened with Sheerie in the back. He was reasonably certain that she'd caught on to what he knew about himself— and she'd never planned to go through with a swap. She played with him long enough to get Ciaran riled and divided them even further. She'd wanted a show; she was so confident in what she could do, there wasn't a drop of fear in her. He had to find a way to use that tonight. And with Mal's assistance, he believed they would rid themselves of her the way you'd burn a tick from your skin: without mercy, without pity. Patrick was harder than the night before and held on to that feeling as if it were armor. He only wished that he and Mal had more time to talk alone before it all began again. With Rich here, there was no chance.

He turned from the window and they broke off from speaking.

"With us again?" Rich asked. " 'Cause it's my turn to share a thing or two with you."

Patrick raised his eyebrows.

"Tonight's show. Bit of a change of plan."

The Main Event

College Park, Maryland

The tour bus rolled through a set of wide bay doors beneath the university's football stadium, then wheezed to a stop. Patrick was the first to disembark, jumping to the pavement with his travel sack over one shoulder. He caught a glimpse of the side-view mirror, where a smear of dried blood marred the reflection. He winced, seeing Ciaran's fist come at him again—and inched away from the bus. He had no intention of ever boarding that vehicle again.

The cool, cavernous storage area beneath the seats was vast enough to hold both vehicles and band equipment, and currently swarmed with all manner of people—security guards in black shirts and red vests, musicians toting instrument cases, and roadies doing the grunt work. Robin and the others had arrived in the follow van ahead of the bus and were practically finished unloading by the time Mal and Rich joined Patrick.

A young woman cradling a clipboard stepped up to them outside the bus, flashing a pearly smile. "I'm Rebecca." She held out a hand of long tapered fingers and manicured nails. "With the programming committee. I think they sent me to pick you up 'cause I've got red hair."

She reminded Patrick a bit of Caitlin for a moment, covered in jaunty freckles, and he managed a half-grin while Mal chuckled.

"You—one of you doesn't look like your photos." She rolled some pages on the clipboard back and forth.

"Manager." Rich tapped his chest. "Our third is—"

She nodded. "That explains things. I think I saw him earlier."

"C's here?" Mal glanced around.

"Tall, thin, dark hair, that's Ciaran, right?"

Patrick laughed. "I like her. She says names correctly."

"We don't have to resort to 'Ed,'" said Mal.

A familiar warmth spread through Patrick. It was possible, for a few seconds at a time, to forget how dire their circumstances were. He was thirsty for any drop of that.

Rebecca gestured for them to follow her. "We have you over in dressing room four." She pointed with a pencil at a prefab room with thin plasterboard walls and a makeshift door but no ceiling. It stood at the end of a short line of others exactly like it. "This'll do?"

Patrick and Mal exchanged glances. It certainly would not.

"'Course," said Rich. "You've got the rider. Just throw in some whiskey and there's no problem at all."

"Well—about that," she said. "We're a dry campus."

Patrick couldn't decide if that was a good thing or not. No matter how much Ciaran drank, it didn't seem to dull his reactions when Sheerie slipped into his brain. He'd put down half a bottle of the brown stuff yesterday before the show and still came out swinging.

"Now, I can't be responsible for what you all may smuggle in." Rebecca raised an eyebrow. "But we don't provide. Most of our students are under twenty-one. I believe we faxed that to your office a week or two ago."

"Yeees," Rich drawled. "I do seem to recall. Well. We'll make do."

"Terrific!" she chirped, reaching into a small bag slung around her shoulder. "These're your passes for the Art Attack—you'll need them to get in and out of the performance area and dressing rooms. Any questions, I'm on walkie-talkie. Check is at five; you're on at ten." She gave a sidelong glance to Rich. "Hope that particular memo made it through."

It had. On the bus, Rich had gone on at length: first, about the delights that awaited them with the label picking up their option and their schedule for the next five or six years. *Into the new millennium!* he'd crowed.

He praised them for the positive reviews the shows had gotten even in his absence, then revealed the surprise: Initially, the band had been set to play second on a bill with five acts total. It was part of the University of Maryland's two-day Art Attack concert for new or indie acts. But a few members of the programming committee had caught the band's New York shows, run home and done a little rejiggering of the lineup. Rich had just reached this part of his report when the bus had pulled into the parking garage, so he'd left off with a secretive smile. *More to come*, he'd said, drawing an X across his mouth with a finger.

Now, Rebecca's explanation of their set time sank in.

"Ten," Patrick repeated. "How many acts after us, then?"

"None," said Rich. "You're the main event tonight." He turned to Rebecca. "Sold out?"

She nodded. "Eight thousand strong, all on the field. Should really be something. I've never handled a show like this before. I mean, I'm only a junior." A gadget at her waist crackled and she pressed a button. "Got to run. I'll be at the front during the show but backstage after—in case you need anything." She waved. "Have fun!"

"Jaysus, she's cheerful," Patrick said, watching her go.

"*Main event*," Mal repeated.

"Well, you're famous now," said Rich. "Kind of a lucky break, eh?"

Mal sat down hard on a flimsy chair in their so-called dressing room and rested a hand on his head. "Where to start," he muttered, glancing around. Part of him wanted to bounce off the walls in excitement—eight thousand was three times more than they'd ever played to before; eight thousand in *America* was more than he could fathom.

Of course, if he'd tried bouncing off one of these walls, he'd catapult into the next dressing room—which, like their own, also had no private sink or toilet. A drummer in another band had explained everyone was supposed to share stalls off the staging area.

"What's the issue?" Rich looked around, catching the lack of ceiling. A person could gaze as much as thirty feet into the empty space and the under-seating area. "You go right back to the hotel afterward and can clean up there."

Patrick was shaking his head. This room wouldn't contain a determined kitten. There was no chance they could lock the door behind Ciaran after the show—which had been the plan they'd cooked up back in the Baltimore hotel room: Patrick would find Sheerie and do his thing, Mal would be Ciaran's bouncer. Rich's presence was a wild card, but Mal decided that two was better than one when it came to keeping Ciaran detained.

Mal took a deep breath. "Rich, I'm gonna say something here and I need you to go with me. This is absolutely not feckin' acceptable. They've put us in the lead slot. So—we deserve better. We demand a room with four solid walls *and* a roof."

"And a door that locks," Patrick added.

"Right." Mal and Patrick stared at Rich with straight faces.

His belly laugh rang skyward, then faded when they didn't join in. "Wait. Seriously?"

Mal held fast.

Rich's face reddened. "This's the biggest feckin' gig you three have ever had and you're going all diva on me? What's next, the brown M&Ms not acceptable to you?"

No one argued.

"And what'll you do when they tell you to go to hell?"

"We walk," said Patrick. "We don't play a note."

That did it: Rich went full scarlet. He was truly pissed off. "You are *not* doing this. This ain't you. What is going on?"

"Trust me," Mal said, still cool and unruffled. "That is what we want."

"I'll quit you if you don't go on," Rich blustered.

Patrick pinched the bridge of his nose. "We know how this plays out, Rich." There was an unyielding toughness Mal had never heard from him before. "We refuse, you terminate your contract, we get sued, we probably lose the label option. We're not *stupid*. Can you not just trust Mal when he says that we know all that and *we still need what we're asking for?*"

Rich lost some of his color and a respectful look came into his eye. "There's something going on here you're not telling me."

Mal nearly spoke, then reined it in. He wanted to explain. But they needed that room first.

Their manager yanked open the door and glared over his shoulder. He slammed it when he left, and the entire structure shimmied for a moment.

"Two with one blow," said Patrick.

Mal gave him an odd look.

"He's in the way."

"And what if he doesn't find a room?" Mal wondered. "What if this is it?"

Patrick sighed, shaking his head. They couldn't pull out on the gig for so many more reasons than could be counted, including what they had to make happen that night. They had to go on. But Rich didn't know that, so he hadn't called Patrick's bluff.

"Then—we improvise," he said.

And his face lit up.

Stars Like Souls Encircling My Heart

Ciaran nestled his head on a soft, cool pillow and stretched out his legs. All around him was green, green to the tips of his fingers and beyond. Sun coated him with warmth, and at least for this moment he could be still and contained, his thoughts his own.

The warmth entered him like medicine. He'd felt quite cold lately, and at night when he lay next to Sheerie there was never enough heat coming from her. He was left chattering in his clothes, a bone-deep chill coursing through every limb, every finger.

A hotel room might have made more sense right now. They could have cranked up the thermostat no matter how cold he was, but instead they'd spent the night in a car Sheerie had commandeered. She'd led him from Hammerjacks up the street and into another vehicle he'd never seen before, sat in the driver's seat next to him and with a small jolt from her finger into the dashboard the car was on. They glided down back roads and dirt paths at speeds he had not thought were possible. The world swam by and the hours ticked past as he curled into his seat, huddling inside his jacket. After a time, the gliding ended and they'd parked in a field of corn and all was quiet as she stroked his hair as she was doing now, and he caught a bit of sleep.

Now he was adrift, unable to surface. A scrim had come over everything he thought or saw. It was difficult to focus from one minute to the next—unless it was on Sheerie's voice. And she was speaking now, though whether it was aloud or in his mind he couldn't be sure.

My love, I know this is hard for you. This part is always ... difficult. Not for me, understand. For me this is the most delicate, delicious time, this moment just before departure. I will help you of course. I help all of you, when we come to this stage. My love is that strong.

Let me tell you a story. My story. You see, what you are experiencing now—it was ever so. My fathers fashioned me out of wishes and words and the purloined memories of those they barely knew, and left me to gestate in paper. They were young men full of fancy and romance and drama, and like all good parents, shaped me with their own desires. But I was not ready to be born for many years. By the time enough people believed in my existence, they were revered and loved and far older.

At last I was born, beneath the earth. I crawled through the dirt to the surface and took what I needed until I arrived on one of their doorsteps—the others were gone by then. I am here for you, *I said when this remaining father opened the door, and he was so beautiful in his confusion.* You have made me. *I smelled the need coming from him, intertwined with his vanity and raw talent.*

I told him who I was. He needed convincing. So I showed him who I was. Yes, darling, of course, don't be so shocked. Such is the way of things with my kind. I owed him my life; would you do less? I showed him again, and again until he believed—and his belief in me made me whole. Made me possible to go on, to become the inspiration to many others who burn bright, then gutter out like candles. I keep them all inside me, their souls like stars encircling my heart, and perhaps one day I will release them. It will be such a glorious spectacle: Birds will cry out, glass will crumble, the light will blind onlookers—and I will have accomplished my life.

My remaining father, you may ask? No, after I showed him who I was—I did not turn him into one of mine. I made him that promise. Instead, I lingered by his side, in the shadows, as he aged. Did my presence assist with his greatest triumphs, his grand awards, his late-found love? I believe so. Years passed and his legend grew. More read his works. And the more that read his offerings, the more came to believe in me. I grew stronger.

Then he journeyed with his family to France for the air and a change of scenery. At that time I was not yet able to travel far from my birthplace. London was mine. Glasgow was mine. Belfast and Galway and Kerry, all mine. But beyond Brittany, I began to fade. A journey such as this one, to this country, has been decades in the making.

I never saw him again. It is the great sadness of my life that I was unable to collect his soul as I have so many others. I remember him in my mind but my heart pines for the star that he was. Ever since then, I have searched for one like him, the one that will complete my collection.

Will you be the one, my love?

Will Mal? Will Padraig? Such a curious one, that Padraig. I have not yet figured him out.

Ciaran listened but had a hard time holding on to anything she said. Sheerie had fathers? She was made of stars? Even as she spoke, the words slipped over and around him like mercury, disappearing. He had holes in his recollections—last night, for example. He'd been in a dressing room with Mal talking about mirrors—and then he'd been holding Sheerie's hand and they were gliding, flying.

They'd arrived on this college campus a few hours ago and he'd been too worn through to do more than follow her. Walked where she walked. Stopped where she wanted. Sat on the big green field at the stadium's center and laid back on her legs, where she was still talking to him.

For a long time, his head had been full of music, sound, lyrics. The music was leaving him now. Once, he'd been so afraid to lose it; he had yearned to be the great songwriter, the very best guitarist, the music maker everyone revered. Now, he was tired. It was time. He wanted the music—and Sheerie—to go. When that happened it would be terrible, but he no longer cared. He just needed things to change.

A distant part of him thought he might die. A less distant part felt that was acceptable. And an even *less* distant part thought that if things did not change, he would find a way to end them. The bliss of being *nothing*, having been promised *everything*, had never been so appealing before, permanent rest like a promise he ached to keep.

He opened his eyes. Sheerie craned over him, fingers massaging his temples. Her smile was upside-down, her head blotting out the sun. "Yes, my love?"

"What happens next?"

She kissed his forehead. "Glance around you."

Ciaran lifted up on his elbows. They were on a gridiron field outlined in white, surrounded by rising rows of bleachers and folding chairs. At one end of the field a tall, wide stage had been set up with full rigging, klieg lights, backdrop. Roadies swarmed over it like worker ants. "For us?" he asked.

"For you." She smiled. "All for you."

"How?" His burst of energy faded and he lay in her lap again.

"Because you are extraordinary now. As I promised. And tonight, you become my butterfly."

"I'm not well, Sheerie. I can't be anyone's butterfly."

She chuckled gently. "When the time comes, you will be *spectacular*. I promise it."

Ciaran didn't think he had spectacular in him. But the distance between where he was now and a surface where he could breathe again was so enormous all he could do was believe in what she said. Believe in *her*. This was their last show. After that, things would change.

And if they didn't, he had options now. He was glad he'd worked that through in his head.

I was hungry once. I was hungry and you offered me food and I did eat.

"What is happening to me?" he asked in a small voice.

"Me, my love." Her smile was dark and eager. "I've been happening to you all this time."

That Terrible Skeletal Smile

About an hour after they sent Rich on his errand, the dressing room door opened, and once again the thin walls did their earthquake imitation.

"C'mon then." Rich's tone was irritated and parental. He stepped aside to reveal Rebecca, now less cheery by several degrees than she'd been at their arrival. She was gripping her clipboard in white-knuckled fingers.

Mal and Patrick jumped and slung their bags—including Ciaran's—over their shoulders, jogging out the door. Rebecca's boot heels echoed in the gigantic space, which was filling in with equipment and instrument containers on pallets as other bands loaded in. Musicians milled in and out of their prefab dressing rooms, shouting at one another in recognition; a few had gathered in different corners to jam.

A football sailed over Patrick's head. They paused to watch a skinny man in a leather jacket and shades snatch it from the air, hugging it to his chest. "Score!" he shouted, flipping the sunglasses into a thick Afro. Catching Patrick's eye, he cocked his arm back and sent the ball straight at him. Instinctively, Patrick lifted his hands in a cupping motion at his chest, catching it neatly—even with bags hanging off his shoulder.

"Nice," called Sunglasses. "Over here." He gestured far down the hall at a waving, shaggy-haired man.

Again without hesitation, Patrick hurled the ball in that general direction. It wobbled awkwardly, made an odd twist, corrected its course, and spiraled until it arrived exactly where it needed to be.

Mal raised an eyebrow, and Patrick shrugged.

Quite a bit of luck you're having lately.

Luck. What did that mean, anyway? Patrick had thought the felicitous streak he'd experienced since Caitlin's arrival had to do with her. But maybe it was time to start believing that he was making it for himself. *If half of me is—*he grimaced inwardly even to think of the word *magic—then what sort of … magic is it? Am I a prankster? A fortune-bringer? A … parasite?*

For now, he'd concentrate on luck. To make things go right tonight, they'd need all the good fortune they could get.

The ball went sailing again as they picked up the pace. Patrick wished that catching a ball was his major worry in life. Everything that lay before them weighed heavily on his shoulders, and he'd give almost anything to be free enough to play American footie for a few hours. Then—an idea that had occurred to him earlier began to bloom. The idea of improvisation. Leaning over to Mal, he asked, "Once we get settled—what's your plan until check?"

"Gonna find C. Want to get him away from her if I can."

"Right. I'll be in the new place. Going to try something out."

"Care to share?"

"Will do, if it works."

A moment later they arrived at the end of the long corridor, having traveled the length of the football field. Rebecca unlocked two oversized double doors and stood aside. "See you at five," she said, then turned briskly on a heel and strode away.

"Thanks!" Mal called after, but she gave no indication she'd heard.

It was a men's locker room, and perfect. Not only did it have a private toilet, it had fourteen. And open shower stalls. And a casual lounge area with a television on mute, beaming in everything happening onstage.

"Satisfied?" Rich hissed. "Had to nearly make that girl cry before she gave it to us."

"This'll do," said Mal, offloading his bag next to a sofa.

Patrick nodded. "It's grand."

"Well, it's not exactly on the level," Rich huffed. "She went on about the fire code. But when I told her you punks would pull out if you didn't get it, that got her scared. Tomorrow's gig ain't even half this full. They know who their bread and butter is tonight. You owe me, but I'll extract it from you eventually. For now—you owe her."

"We'll think of something," said Mal.

Rich folded his arms at Patrick, who was examining the doors. "Now what?"

"Another thing," he said.

A few minutes later, a deeply irritated Rich was racing away from them on his latest errand: a trip to the hardware store to locate a Kryptonite chain and lock.

"Is that necessary?" Mal wondered as they watched him steam off down the corridor.

"My face would appreciate knowing it's there," said Patrick.

Patrick burst onto the stage, huffing and puffing. The others were halfway through a wandering noodly introduction to the single, not quite starting the soundcheck without him—but appearing as if they might at any moment. Robin twirled his sticks behind the drums; they would need him on nearly every song tonight.

Patrick was late but not sorry. He'd been working. He shucked off his jacket, overheated from the run and the searing stage lights, and reached for his bass. It hummed in greeting, and he knew it was in tune without even touching it. So many strange things he could do and see and experience now. How quickly they were becoming second nature. He slung the strap over his damp T-shirt and nodded at Mal, ready.

Ciaran's hand clamped on his shoulder and Patrick tensed. *That was not a flinch. I am not flinching in front of him.* He ducked away from the hand and grabbed at a water bottle, taking a long swig before turning to face his attacker for the first time since the night before.

There was nothing unusual about him. Ciaran, no more, no less. A bit of color in his cheeks, even. A bounce in his step. That terrible skeletal smile, but genuine. He gave no indication that he remembered beating the hell out of Patrick the night before, as if the memory had faded with the bruises he'd inflicted. Ciaran nodded at Patrick, who dipped his chin in reply—and then they were into the song, shifting around its edges and basic form with the familiarity of a thousand plays.

Slowly, Patrick's heart resumed its normal pattern.

A second song and a third. Patrick could play these in his sleep, so he relaxed and gazed out over the largely-empty playing field, breathing in the scents of the songs as they mixed in the oncoming dusk—toasted almonds and cherry, lemongrass and eucalyptus. His thoughts wandered with the colors, their translucence floating high into the blue above, unrestrained by a roof or beams or rafters. They heartened him. They gave him some peace.

Ciaran dug into his solo lines, a perfect look of concentration on his heavy brow, and Patrick glanced offstage at a familiar figure watching in the wings. Sheerie stood with arms folded, an intense look on her lovely face.

Hey, Patrick thought at her, not expecting a reaction—but he got one. She stood straighter and he gave her a half-smile, a sly, conspiratorial thing. He wanted her to know they weren't finished with one another yet. It might make him sick to think about what had gone on last night, but he had to give her what she needed most: attention.

She mirrored his smile, then narrowed her eyes.

He returned to the music.

Songs Call to You

Back in the locker room after soundcheck, Patrick ducked into a shower, a gush of metallic-smelling water coating him. This was his first chance to scrub out the night before—the smoke and booze and gravel in his hair, blood in his nose. All washed away down the common drain in the middle of the room. He felt like a new man.

The shower gave him a chance to think about the check. Something was catching at him like a skip in a record. Sheerie had been watching Ciaran in a way he hadn't seen her do before, intent and focused, as if she were working hard to keep him   what, playing? Upright? Ciaran himself hadn't betrayed any sense of weakness or needing help—he'd run through the same songs as all of them, then come back to the locker room and crashed on the lounge sofa. Already he was sawing away in sleep.

Patrick shook his head under the water, letting the deluge pound his neck, fat drops cascading down his hair and back. The thing about Ciaran stuttered in his mind once more—and then he got it. That stage had been hot as hell for their fifteen-minute check—but Ciaran had never taken a sip of water, never removed his jacket or hat. He hadn't even been *sweating*. This, when everyone else had stripped to shirtsleeves.

Patrick thought of puppets and strings, of Sheerie and mind control. She'd watched him so closely.

He groaned.

"Patch?" Mal called from the other side of the wall. "I'm heading in there in about two minutes and I don't want to see anything I can't write home about."

The things not seen are as important as those under our noses, Patrick thought. "You just don't wanna know how massive a *sídhe's adharc* is," he called back, but it was a distracted parry.

Of course. Ciaran was in glamour; Sheerie had cloaked a whole person. No wonder she was focusing so hard, no wonder Ciaran had looked five, rather than two, steps from death. Every time Patrick thought he had her figured out, she one-upped him. She had so many tricks up her sleeve; it was as if she was made up of nothing but. As Caitlin had pointed out, she was born to this. Everything went her way, at all times.

Caitlin. His heart squeezed. He had to see her once more before the night was out. He understood why she was making herself scarce—but it didn't make things easier. He desperately wanted to be more sure about what came next, before he took irreversible steps.

Within a half hour they were all cleaned up except for Ciaran, who'd never ventured out of the lounge. Quiescent, they leaned back against the couches while wearing their clothes for the show. Patrick gave everyone a quick look. *Now*, he thought, picking up one of their spare acoustic guitars and fishing out a thin set of folded papers from his cast-aside jeans.

"Aw, Patch." Ciaran eyed him. "I'm beat. Didn't we already finish check?"

Patrick ignored him, smoothing open the pages and passing copies around. He slipped one to Robin and another to Rich, who'd been sulking silently in a corner all afternoon, reading his newspaper. Rich hadn't even given Ciaran's odd appearance a second glance—though if he had, Sheerie's glamour would have fooled him easily. Patrick was relieved; the less explaining they had to do right now, the better.

He waited while they scanned the pages—all crude mock-ups of sheet music. He'd been late to the stage that afternoon for a reason: He'd spent the hours between arrival and that moment with Ciaran's green notebooks of songs. Patrick had scanned every tune, read every line of the heartbreaking dangerous beauty, until he came upon one he could work with. Adapt. And by "adapt," he meant rearrange in a way that wouldn't make anyone's nose bleed. Or lose one of their senses.

At first, he hadn't known how to handle the music. He needed to keep the essence, yet make it something regular audiences could listen to. He thought about a drink to focus him—and then he put it together: He needed to distill the music like whiskey. No one drank straight-up mash if they knew what was good for them, but the base could be made palatable, even sensual.

He poked around with the tune until it ran clear in his head, then turned it this way and that way until he heard a *click* and he knew from there on how to filter the notes so they could be heard and played even on a dry campus—but sound like something entirely new. Something that might smell like the extract of sky, warm wool, autumn.

Why bother? He didn't know. Perhaps it was to prove something good might come from everything that had gone wrong between the three of them. Perhaps it was to rile Sheerie. Perhaps it was to rub in her face that they *could* handle what she was dishing out. He didn't know—but it was like an itch he needed to scratch. The version he showed everyone wasn't quite finished—the lyrics were more like ladder rungs Mal could grab and use as a guide—but he'd left it open-ended intentionally so they could improvise on it as long as they liked. The work had consumed his afternoon and every scrap of his attention, so that when he'd looked up, what had seemed like an hour of concentrated effort had been more like three. He'd raced to soundcheck and turned up breathless.

Now, Patrick thought of footballs launched in the air, caught with ease. "Thought we might run through this a couple of times. Maybe—take it to the stage tonight. Give it a tryout."

Ciaran shook his head at the music sheet—and now Patrick could see how his glamour was beginning to fade. Without Sheerie around to reinforce it, the magic was like makeup that wore through.

"You took this from my notebook," Ciaran said, but he didn't seem proprietary or angry.

Rich had set his newspaper aside and was frowning at the music.

Mal whooped. "Oh, yes." He sighed. "We must."

That was all they needed; the moment of respite ended as they retrieved whatever spare instruments were in the locker room. Robin laid down a beat on a bench with his sticks and in small increments they pulled the music together, weaving it here and there until at last they could travel straight through. They played it again and again, barely pausing between rounds. It was nourishment and they couldn't eat enough.

But it was more than that, something only Patrick could see: The colors of this music weren't faint misty shades—the moment they had the song together in one piece, those now-familiar hues turned explosive, shades like the colors only seen in dreams—brighter and more solid than ever before. There was a dimensionality to them, and he wondered if he might pluck them from the air or tug on the end of a strand like a hair ribbon. The visions seemed wearable, edible, touchable. The scent—that was harder to put into words, but it tickled at the back of his mind.

Eventually, they stopped. The ribbons dissolved as they fell to the ground.

"Brilliant. Well done, Patch." Ciaran was so genuine, so much like the person Patrick had always known, he didn't know how to respond. A crushing wave of despair passed over Patrick. What if they lost him? What if Ciaran didn't survive and all of this was for nothing?

A choked sob made them turn to the corner of the room. Rich had pushed his face deep into a bandanna he usually wore around his neck. "Don't look at me," he barked.

207

"That bad?" Mal tried.

He blew his nose in a loud honk, then wiped his face. "That was the best feckin' thing I ever heard, including me Mam's own lullabies. I know you're just getting started with it and that makes it even better. I'm proud of you boys. You found it. Whatever it was—you found it."

"Didn't we have it before?" Patrick asked.

Rich leaned forward. "You had *something*. Otherwise, we wouldn't be here. But that was *everything*. Where the hells did that come from?"

A long pause. "Don't look at me," said Robin, his voice faraway and soft. "I just work here."

Mal and Patrick turned to Ciaran, who had his eyes on the carpet.

"There's nothin' I ought to know, is there, boys?" Rich asked.

Patrick bit the inside of his mouth, avoiding Mal's face. He knew if he looked at him right now, the laughter he was suppressing would spiral into hysteria. Of course there were things Rich needed to know. Of course they would tell him nothing.

"Fine," Rich snapped after a long pause. He was pissed but also hurt. "Crafts table ought to be open by now. Rob, you hungry?"

"Er—sure," said Robin, unsure how to read the room. "Was gonna eat with the crew anyhow."

"Excellent." Rich stuffed the bandanna in a pocket, standing. "You three've been acting squirrely since I got back. You want privacy? You can have it. Do your little clubhouse handshake or wank each other off, for all I care." He snorted, striding to the door. Before opening it, he half-turned. "But know this: I ain't nobody's water-carrier. If this isn't a team effort anymore, I'm checkin' out. You get me?"

No one answered, so he yanked the door wide—and blinked in surprise. The entrance was jam-packed with onlookers, all members of the other bands. They stood several deep, peering into the room but respecting the threshold. Everyone wore a similar stunned, dreamy look—just like Rich had when they'd finished the song.

"You all lost?" Rich asked.

"Sorry, man," said the sunglasses-wearing football player from earlier, leaning in and ignoring him. "I'm Leon. We … heard something … unusual. Something really *good* and unusual. Coming from this room."

"We're in the back of beyond here," Rich argued. "You couldn't have."

Leon shrugged. "It's what happened. We heard, we came."

"*All* of you?" Mal stood.

"We felt … called over." A girl with a platinum bob wig swiped at her eyes. The group behind her made murmurs of assent. "What *was* that song?"

Patrick flushed and looked away.

"All right," said Rich. "We're getting into a weird area here. You want this door open or closed?"

"Open," said Mal. "We'll handle it."

"Fine. Make way." Rich plunged into the crowd, which parted to let him and Robin pass through.

Once they were gone, Leon spoke up again. There was a reverential tone in his voice. "You know how it is. Songs call to you, sometimes."

Patrick knew. They all knew, too well. He wanted to invite everyone in and start the music all over again—but there were other things more pressing they had to deal with.

"Ah, that's just some noodling around," said Mal, walking over. "Might try it on the stage later."

"Do," said a woman with sloe eyes and a French accent. "This should be shared. Not hidden away in the … back of the beyond."

Need radiated from them, a sensation so powerful Patrick felt it like the low rumble of an oncoming truck. He knew then that they were witnessing the future: This was what they might expect if they took Ciaran's songs—even distilled versions—before a crowd. They'd be playing on a frequency that would pull people out of their chairs for reasons they could never explain. And of course that frequency would be best and most clearly heard by those who lived and breathed music.

"We'll run it last," Patrick said. "Encore. Final song of the night."

The faces at the door lit up like children hearing Christmas was coming early.

"And then," he continued, "watch for a cue. If you want to, come up onstage and play with us."

"How many?" asked the blonde.

"Everyone," said Mal. "Right, C?"

Ciaran's smile was both shy and guilty.

"Everyone," echoed Patrick, and with that the low rumble of the truck faded—replaced by a bright, soothing warmth.

"Well," said Patrick, leaning against the closed doors. He could hear the musicians shuffling away on the other side, murmuring. "An interesting response to a song of yours, Ciaran."

Ciaran shrugged. Mal and Patrick watched him, waiting for more. "What?" he growled. "You two act like I'm gonna do a dance. Yeah, they were into it. Got Rich to cry. We already *know* it's good music."

Mal plopped down on the couch next to him. "Look, C. We're on your side. You can tell us anything. You know that."

"Nothin' to say," said Ciaran sullenly.

Patrick had to hold back. They couldn't get him riled. Sheerie fed on strong emotion, and they didn't want her in here. "Start with those songs. We know where they come from. And trust us—we know a lot more. Y'think ordinary music makes kids like those drop everything they're doing to listen on the other side of a door?"

"Kids." Mal shook his head. "They're our age. Ish."

"Seem half it," said Patrick. "I never felt so old." He stared at Ciaran. "You know that's feckin' strange, what just happened there. More than strange. So how about opening your gob and just tell us what's on your mind, C. We won't laugh. But—you gotta start trusting us again."

"Don't know what—"

"Stop it," said Mal. "You do know. Now you need to *say* it."

Ciaran opened his mouth, closed it—and then it spilled out in a rush. "Naemine."

It was so soft Patrick barely could make out the words. "Come again?"

"Not. Mine." Ciaran glared at him. "The songs. Never were."

"We know," said Mal.

Stunned, Ciaran took a breath. "Well—I also don't know where they came from—"

"There's a lie." Patrick's voice was sharp-edged. "You know exactly where they're from. She gives 'em to you, don't she. And they're not free."

"Patch," said Mal softly.

"Stop it," he hissed at Mal. "We've run out of time to play nice." He turned back to Ciaran. "Figured out yet what she's taking in exchange?"

Ciaran was breathing harder.

Mal set a restraining hand on Patrick's arm, but Patrick shrugged him off. Ciaran shivered, pulling the sides of his jacket around him, curling into the sofa. Patrick knelt on the floor. "*Breathnaigh orm.*" *Look at me.*

Time drew out—and finally, Ciaran did as asked. His shivering subsided.

"*Tar liom,*" said Patrick, beckoning. Ciaran made an effort to get up, but Patrick had to help. He was so light, as if there was nothing left in him. He led Ciaran over to the locker room changing area, where a ten-foot mirror hung lengthwise above the row of sinks. All three of them paused under harsh fluorescent lights—two healthy and one a bit under the weather, dull of eye, thin of body.

"Mirrors," said Ciaran. "I remember mirrors."

Mal backed up.

"*Tá brón orm, a chara,*" Patrick apologized, bringing up his hand to Ciaran's cheek. Just the slightest touch—and what was left of Sheerie's glamour was gone. A faint ripple spread across Ciaran's face, over his forehead and down his neck, revealing the yellowish-gray face of a walking corpse.

Ciaran recoiled, making a strangled sound in his throat. He stumbled over a bench and fell against a row of lockers. Mal arrested his fall, but he jerked away and returned to the image, leaning over the sinks. "I saw this … before," he whispered. "I saw this—I saw *him*—in Kennedy's. In Philadelphia. The mirror … broke." A long pause. "I broke it. My fist—all that blood."

Mal nodded, anguished.

Ciaran stared at his hands. "But—they're fine."

"Maybe." Patrick's tone was kinder. "Not much else is, though. Isn't that right?"

Ciaran sank onto a bench, bending his head between his knees. He took enormous gulps of air. "Jaysus jumpin' Christ. Can someone *please* tell me what the fuck is happening?"

Patrick took the seat next to him. "Let me."

Love, of a Kind

Eight thousand voices roaring in unison hit Patrick like a physical force, as if a hand reached through the bay doors and shook him. He was waiting with Mal and Ciaran for their cue as the roadies raced through the change of sets—pulling the piano onto its marks, leaving out water, setting up the guitars. It was past ten by now and full dark, all stars drowned out by the glare of stadium lights. Patrick stared skyward and felt upside-down, as if the stadium's open roof was a hole he could fall into and never touch bottom.

Padraig.

Startled, he bumped into Robin, then swerved around him to dart down the corridor. "Right back."

"Patch—it's nearly time!" Mal called after.

Ignoring him, Patrick kept going. Once she threw her voice into his head he knew he must go—there was no question as to where she was. But this time, it wasn't Sheerie. It was the one person he most acutely needed. At the first supporting girder he found Caitlin, still as fresh and windblown as he'd first seen her, weeks ago.

A life ago.

Without a word he wrapped his arms around her and their lips met. She buoyed him with that kiss. His mind cleared. "I needed that."

She tugged at a hank of his hair with a grin.

"Didn't know if I'd see you before the show," he said.

"Of course I'd be here. Of course."

"Any last words of advice—hypothetical advice, that is?"

She folded her arms. "You're not seeming very serious."

But he was. He'd never felt more serious in his life, even as his feet wouldn't still and he shifted from side to side, occasionally shaking his arms out. "This is just me. Before we go on. Always."

Caitlin made a small motion with her fingers and while they didn't *go* anywhere, it was as if they were encased in a bubble. All sound muffled.

"Our hypothetical. She finishes tonight," Caitlin said.

That stilled him. He'd expected it would be soon, but not this soon. "I don't know what to do. I'm only guessing. I thought—maybe I could just take C to the Green Place with me. He'd be safer there, maybe."

"He couldn't go, not now," said Caitlin. "Not while he's in thrall to her. She *owns* him, Padraig. Most of him, anyway. Soon, all of him. She just has to get him to … shed his body."

And then he got it. *Her dessert.* She wanted everything from him, every last drop. Including the man's soul. The task seemed insurmountable.

"I came to warn you," she said. "She suspects you, Padraig. She knows something isn't right."

"But how can she?"

"You're too fast a healer, for one thing."

The last thing Patrick had thought to do was examine himself in a mirror. He'd been too busy looking for Ciaran. But all day, no one had said anything about injuries so severe he'd landed in the hospital the night before. No one said, *I'd hate to see the other guy.* He ran his tongue over his lip, and it was whole, unsplit. "You didn't say that would happen."

"Am I now to be *múinteoir*?"

"Wasn't that the whole reason you showed up in the first place?"

Caitlin folded her arms, looking away. "I showed up because I was sent." Her voice was thick. "I stayed because you asked. Because … I wanted to." She took his hand and her eyes were moist. "But you have to believe in yourself now, *mo ghrá*. You have to follow your own tune. It's the only way you become yourself."

My love. She said it. He felt it. She was braver than he was.

"I've tried to explain this before," she went on. "You've only seen a thin wedge of what's possible, Padraig. Everything before now has been scribbling, not art."

"So the colors, the glamours, my instruments—"

She shook her head. "Not even the … opening act."

Was her world so vast? Had he been playing with toys all this time? "I still wonder," he said carefully, "that any of this has been real."

"After all that's happened, you say that?"

Patrick looked away.

Caitlin held his face, searching. "If you continue on this path with her, you will come to a place where belief is the only thing that will make it work. If you can't be open any further your fight is over. Deny the reality of who she is and what she can do—and your friend will be gone by morning."

213

That sank in like cold rain. "I am trying."

"Feel it here." She set a hand on his chest. "Your monk taught you about faith. So—this is another kind of faith. What feels right inside is the truth. That's what you must go with." She took a deep breath. "We could still leave right now. Come with me one last time, and don't look back." Her blue eyes reflected the lights, nearly glowing.

"Caitlin—why would I *do* that? You know—"

"Because if you do go all in, if you do believe in your heart and soul—and you try to interfere with her tonight, I don't know if you'll ever see the rest of what is possible, Padraig."

The floor dropped from beneath him. "How do you mean?"

"Because you're now bound by our rules. Yes, they're slippery. Yes, they have a lot of *maybes* in them. But—you have one foot in our world now. And you can't interfere without risking—consequences."

Exile. She'd told him about that before, how hard it was. *Most of us in exile don't survive; we're not made for this world over the long haul.* He would lose everything he'd gained, and things he'd never even known were gifts might be taken. He might lose Caitlin.

Patrick staggered against the girder and the bubble around them dissolved. Eight thousand voices roared back to him. He'd live. It wouldn't kill him. At least, not physically. But losing everything meant losing himself again. That hole in the sky, taking him in, never landing.

Footsteps sounded behind them. Caitlin leaned in, cheek against his. "You remember my name," she whispered.

"Of course," he said miserably.

"Say it to me."

So he sang-spoke it, that odd, complicated, musical phrase. The hairs on the back of his neck rose. He was surprised at how easily it came to his lips.

"What does it mean, to know my name?"

"Patch!" Rich was thundering toward them. "Come *on*, already!"

Patrick only had eyes for Caitlin.

"It's all right." She braced herself. "Go ahead. Beg your boon of me."

But he wouldn't. He wouldn't compel her to help them, even knowing what that might mean. If she were to help, it had to be her choice.

"I have to go."

Her face was stony.

"Will I—see you again?" His heart tore to even ask it.

Hesitating, she made a decision and grabbed the lapels of his jacket, tugging him close. He expected a kiss—and got her breath in his ear. "Remember this," she said—and spoke something else. Not merely breath or music but a prickly noise full of crackle and heat, like a forest fire about to surge out of control. It was music, the way an overweening guitar solo was musical—just on the point of pain.

She released him with a push and he stumbled back. Rich was there, just a foot away, waving his hands. Patrick touched his ear, the skin hot, his hearing dulled. His fingers came away spotted in blood. After a moment, sound returned. The ear cooled.

Caitlin wiped at her eyes.

In the distance he heard Mal's piano start up. They were on, with or without him—and the music was calling more loudly than anything else in the universe. Rich grabbed his arm and tugged—and Patrick stumbled after. He took one last glance over his shoulder—

But Caitlin was already gone.

The colors were the fiercest he'd ever known.

They attacked their instruments under the glaring stage lights, the crowd before them an undulating sea of arms, bodies, heads, lighters and rolling thunder, and Patrick drank in every bit of energy they gave him. But there was so much *more*: sea salt, honeysuckle, freshly-tilled soil, cardamom, peppermint all flooded at him as the songs blended from one into the next, and he wondered briefly whether the music created the scents or if it was some combination of the music and the *place* it was being played. Or even the people in the crowd. But it was a passing notion—almost from the moment he took the stage Patrick was lost, wrapped in the chaos of sensual connections, following blindly along. He existed only in the present tense as they moved from song to song.

Mal pounded behind the piano with every ounce of himself, so rousing that they almost negated the need for poor Robin, who sat half-obscured at the back of the stage on his low drum riser. But for all his enthusiasm, Mal was fully present tonight, not visiting his dreamy green space. Whenever Patrick caught his gaze those alert blue eyes flashed at him, and he knew all of Mal's concentration was for the show—and whatever Sheerie might have in mind.

For there was no way to know what Sheerie was planning. Patrick hadn't seen her since soundcheck, and as he scanned the audience all the way to the far back of the field where darkness engulfed the standing crowd, he saw nothing. He would have to find her after the show before she found Ciaran, and her absence was a small but persistent worry for him.

More concerning was what Ciaran would do. In the end, they'd had to be careful about what truths to share before the show. Whatever he knew it was possible Sheerie could discern, and they risked him laughing with disbelief if they told too much. So Patrick had just asked for Ciaran's trust and gave him three directives.

Fight her off. Resist her song with everything you've got. Next, listen just to me and Mal. No one else. And after the show—go with Mal to the locker room and stay until you get the all-clear.

215

Dazed, distracted, and unwell, Ciaran had sworn the oath of a man out of options. And then, fifteen minutes before they were due onstage, he'd transformed. Sitting up straight, color returned to his cheeks. Ciaran said nothing but his sudden jerky, alert movements were startling, as if he'd been plugged in. Only then did Patrick understand how far Sheerie had come in taking him over.

Whatever she had done—whatever she was still doing—Ciaran had come to the stage and was playing as enthusiastically as ever. A person would have to look hard to suspect anything was wrong.

So the songs blurred by, and by the second or third the band fully connected, locked in place like puzzle pieces. Patrick dropped the rest of his brooding and settled into the moment-by-moment experience of the show as it swept through him. He marveled at the colors, reaching like hands into that dark empty sky—the shocking reds and fiery oranges and misty blues vanishing into the heavens. He breathed deeply of the scented air, which had a new complexity tonight—not just simple fragrances but ones that evoked specific memories. He smelled a barn he'd played in once, the new-cut hay and damp clean smell of rain dripping through the slats. There'd been a girl, he'd nearly forgotten her, and she'd kissed him on the cheek before slipping out of his memory again—but she was in the music, too.

Song ten, twelve, fourteen. Now they were nearing the end. For their last pre-encore song, Mal kicked away his stool and leaped on the keys with such intensity the piano shook. Patrick took a step back, pawing at his mandy until his fingertips cried out, and gave Ciaran center stage to drive home the final, dramatic chords. Then Mal was nodding and they jumped once, twice, three times in the air, ending the song with a flourish. The colors burst into shards before settling over the audience and vanishing. The crowd noise enveloped the colors and the sound washed over the four of them onstage. It was sweetness incarnate. It was love, of a kind.

Breathing hard, they jogged off the stage, bouncing. Mal scampered to a nearby toilet. They had perhaps a minute before the encore, and Patrick felt a need for the bog as well—but someone had to keep an eye on Ciaran.

There was no sign of either Sheerie or Caitlin.

"That's about all I have in me." Ciaran bent over, hands on his knees.

Patrick offered him the sheet music from before. "Even for this?"

He tapped at his temple. "In here. Been there for weeks." He stood and blinked quickly. "It takes up so much space. And—your version isn't *so* different, you know." Even with the glamour, Patrick could see his eyes dulling again. "I'm so feckin' tired, Patch. I want it over. One way or the other."

Patrick's throat tightened. "It will be. We'll fix it."

Ciaran glanced over his shoulder, an antenna receiving a signal.

"C. Ciaran."

He shook himself all over like a dog wringing water from its coat. "I'm fine. I'm here."

"That's her, isn't it."

Ciaran sighed. "God help me, it is. She wants what she wants."

"Well, she can't have it." Patrick narrowed his eyes, feeling resolute. "Do you believe me?"

Ciaran gave a small nod.

"No, really. Tell me you believe that we can do this. You have to believe in us, not her. *Tell me*."

His friend's eyes widened and he *felt* it. A link being made, a connection forged. It had a taste as well as a feeling, like biting into a crisp apple. Ciaran did believe—at least, in this second he did. Patrick reached into his pocket and handed Ciaran the small pebble from the stream back home. "Take this," he said. "Keep it close."

"It's a rock, Patch."

"Maybe it's more."

Mal ran over just as the stage manager waved. "Right," he said. "Let's do this thing."

And they were back.

A Caught-Breath Moment of Wonder

Mal let out a small twinkling round of notes on the piano to kick off the encore, like a welcome introductory message. He leaned into his microphone and thanked the crowd—then did something he hadn't warned anyone about.

"This one's just something we're working on, so forgive if it stumbles a bit," he said. "But we wanted to use it to say thanks to the hardest-workin' woman here, who went out of her way to find us a home for the day. A safe place. So— this is for you, Rebecca of the red hair and cowboy boots, if you're still listening. And it's for anyone who ever needed a place of their own."

Patrick shook his head in delight. He'd rarely seen a more *Mal* moment.

Taking the lead, Mal let the piano build the new song gradually. This would be a second distillation now; Patrick knew the moment he handed over his version Mal would be rearranging it in his head, making it a thing created by the three of them. Stronger. More durable. Unbreakable.

Onstage, everyone turned to watch him reveal the shape he had chosen for the song, the rolling line of chords like waves landing on a beach. It breathed, stretching out a minute, two.

Then Patrick heard the absence.

There was no roar, no noise at all from the crowd. Hands were down, mouths clamped shut or slightly agape. All eight thousand of them were stilled and Patrick had to turn to make sure they hadn't been sucked into that dark hole of sky, raptured in a silent, surprised moment. But no, this was real. Thousands listened, all eyes on the stage. Only the music existed.

In the far distance of the playing field where the crowd wasn't so tightly packed together, something else was happening—additional entrances that led directly onto the field opened as people emerged. Two here, five or six there. People in their going-home jackets, venue workers holding walkie-talkies or clipboards or brooms. Security men in red vests and dark T-shirts and noise-canceling headphones. All came to the field, stopped, stared.

And then—the spell shifted. The audience began to hum, to vibrate. It was one massive collective *something*. Hands inched to the sky and the frozen state melted away as they began undulating, whistling.

Mal gave the signal and Patrick, Ciaran, and Robin crashed the song awake. Patrick dove in with his bass lines, Robin finding a fixed, steady beat—and the song had a spine. Ciaran wedged open a space for himself, with chords and harmonies, and then they were inside the song, making it live. The lyrics were improvisational, unimportant. Mal just kept making them up as he went, using them like handholds on a cliff face.

Three-dimensional color strands unfurled directly from their instruments, branching out into the audience, branching skyward, branching everywhere like fractals. Patrick's heart was in his ears as the layered colors rose and hovered, wrapping like clothing around each listener, shifting shade and hue and tone—at last twisting into the sky, vanishing.

Then the scent came to him: bigger and heartier and delicious—a scent he'd only breathed two or three times before. That of never-cut grass, of big unclouded skies, of trees like skyscrapers with fluttering leaves that made the sound of applause. The smell of eternal *nowness*, of unlimited promise. It was the smell of the Green Place and they'd brought it into the real world. They'd made this happen.

Patrick breathed deeply, tears blurring his eyes, joy taking him over.

Belief had been such a slippery thing. He didn't know how much he believed everything Caitlin had told him—but he believed in the music. Of that he was absolutely sure. A sound came from deep in his gut and he released it across the audience, a declaration of intent. He was going nowhere, that sound said. He would survive this night. It hurt his throat, but after making the noise Patrick felt more alive than he had in weeks.

Mal broke off from singing and grinned, then made his own primal roar. Ciaran picked it up from there and then the three of them were together, giving the song every bit they had left.

The audience roar was back, louder. More powerful. In the back, couples had broken away to dance in the open spaces, holding one another, being foolish and silly and not caring who saw. And in that moment, Patrick remembered his promise. He glanced into the wings, where a thick knot of musicians hovered impatiently. He gave them a quick wave and they flooded onstage, holding guitars, shaker instruments, pennywhistles. Someone had a banjo. They filed in behind Mal's piano and spread out like water, some sitting on the edge of the stage, some loosely grouped in the back, all finding places to fit into the song. They played with abandon. It all came together in a frenzied mix of the loveliest, most anarchic sounds Patrick had ever heard, smelled, tasted, or seen.

And as that happened, Patrick realized they were no longer playing the song. They were the song. Every one of them.

Patrick turned, openmouthed, to see how his friends were handling it. Ciaran had been surrounded by another five guitarists like acolytes. Mal was pounding away, oblivious to anyone else around him. And then—Patrick nearly stumbled in his playing. Someone else had come onstage with them, too. She stood upright on the piano, arms folded, face a tornado.

Sheerie stared right at him.

He ignored her. Tried to. Kept playing.

Stop now.

A piercing wail cut into Patrick's head and he lost a chord.

This is not for you, this music. Stop it now or I will stop it for you.

Patrick shrugged. Wondered what everyone else onstage saw. Didn't she stand out? The only one without an instrument, the only one not singing? The unmoving rock in the center of the rushing stream? But no, it seemed everyone else was so caught up in the music that she'd become unimportant, someone of no consequence. He wondered if that fact angered her further.

He hoped it did.

But then he heard her words again. Not for them? Hadn't Ciaran been buying this music with his life, inch by inch? Hadn't he been the one to write it down, hadn't Mal and Patrick been the ones to transform it into joy instead of pain? No. This was theirs. They'd refined it, distilled it, and shared it with the world. They owned it.

Sheerie could not take this music back, not even if she tried. No one could, whatever they called themselves.

Most of her kind use pseudonyms, don't they.

Patrick's ears burned and he thought of crackling, of fire. For a moment, he did stop playing.

The name by which you are known is the only song worth singing.

Caitlin. Jaysus, she *had* helped. He hadn't understood that until now. She'd done it voluntarily, the last thing she'd said to him. His heart soared with love.

Wrap it up, Sheerie insisted, and high above them one of the klieg lights sizzled and popped. *Listen to me.*

No, he thought back. *You listen to me.*

The mic was live. Patrick indicated he wanted it, so it was his turn to change the shape of the song. He turned to the no-longer-frail, no-longer-delicate woman still standing on Mal's piano. She was robust, healthy, glowing with every ounce of what she'd taken from Ciaran. A pink flush rose in her cheeks and a spark flashed in her horrible green eyes, and he thought of heat. Of forest fires. Of rage.

And then it was in his head, as loud and clear as the moment Caitlin had breathed it into his ear backstage. Patrick began to sing it, this song of crackle and heat, conflagrations that turn life into char, racing through a forest and consuming everything in their path. A voracious sound made of need and fury and fire—and behind him, Ciaran made his guitar shriek.

Patrick stumbled on the first syllable and then the second but after that false start he had it right. By the third try he was singing it correctly—though it was more a feeling than a knowing—and the noises began to sound beautiful in their own way, the pain was alien and human, it was a sound and a scent and a taste and it was a name.

Sheerie's name.

He knew he had it right when she reacted. Sheerie unfolded her arms and stared at him, astounded. Patrick's ears burned and his hearing dulled but he wouldn't let up. With every repetition of the name he saw her flinch and crawl into herself.

By the fifth or sixth, his voice doubled, trebled, exponentially more sure and strong. The others onstage picked up his odd chant and reframed it, so it now fit into the song. Mal had it, Ciaran had it, the other musicians followed suit. Even Robin came for the ride. It became part of the music, this odd guttural thing that wasn't English and wasn't Irish, but something far older. They chanted it again and again—and then the audience gathered it up and gave it back, and their roar was the sound of an inferno.

All Patrick had to do was stare at her as she wilted with each fresh lyric. They'd invoked her name, every one of them—and who knew what came next. He didn't care. This was the answer.

Everything plunged into darkness.

A hush fell over the stadium, a caught-breath moment of wonder. The last vestiges of ribboned, fractal color dissolved over the audience. The sky was soft and full of clouds, and the world was very dark.

Soft clicks like chattering teeth rose from the crowd as hundreds of pinpricks poked holes in the dark. Matches, lighters, flashlights—anything with a beam filled the stadium. Soon it was bright enough that Patrick could make out Mal's face on the far side of the stage, and they marveled at the carpet of tiny twinkling lights unfurling.

So that's where the stars went.

But this wasn't a moment of poetry. This was someone throwing a blanket up to cover her tracks. Sheerie was no longer on the piano. Whipping around, Patrick grabbed at Ciaran's arm to ensure he hadn't vanished. Instead, he clawed at air. Ciaran's Rickenbacker glowed softly from the ground, making twanging

221

noises like an abandoned pet. He met Sunglasses Leon's eyes, and the musician gestured with his flashlight down the corridor.

"Mal!" Patrick shouted, leaping down the stairs into the lightless backstage. He took off at a full run, into the dark.

Footsteps followed: Mal's.

Then more. Many more.

Be My Butterfly

*C*ome with me.

    The voice slipped into his head, hand in a glove, a perfect fit by now. When Ciaran heard that sweet call, pitched at precisely the frequency that lit up all his buttons, it felt so much like love that his body was responding before he even had a chance to wonder if he should go. He resisted. He'd promised he would fight back—and tried, but she was relentless. He lost feeling in his hands, then his arms, then his chest.

I'm waiting.

I can't breathe.

I have all the breath you require, my love.

Struggling, he unclipped his guitar. Tried to draw a breath but it was like being underwater. The world spun around and he wondered if he would faint. And then—the air came back. He gasped, starbursts in his eyes. He couldn't fight her anymore. It wasn't in him.

I'm coming. He stared at his guitar, as if it might have answers.

Leave it. You won't be needing that anymore.

Ciaran dropped the instrument on the stage and slipped away, heading to the locker room. That's where she was. And wasn't that where Mal wanted him anyway? Where Patrick had insisted he go after the show? He was just glad they'd all come to some agreement: Ciaran, in the locker room, with the *sídhe*. Done.

Days, weeks, years ago—he'd lost track—he recalled making a beeline for Sheerie, not unlike he was doing now. Back in the sound studios in Boston he'd had a lovely beer in one hand and a lovelier woman in his sights. When he'd stood before her, she was all eyes and hair and bewitchments. Since then, she'd burrowed under his skin, into his self. She'd never leave now.

In the end, the fucking had only been part of it. Not the biggest part, even. She'd *known* him, known what he most wanted and what he most needed and gave both to him day after day. *Love me*, she insisted, *and you will be everything you ever wanted.*

And he was, for a time. Smarter and more talented than Mal—so much music, pouring from *him* for once—and more enigmatic and handsome than Patrick. Sheerie was so easy to please. He only had to promise her every bit of him, every moment of his time, every ounce of his soul.

Which he suspected he'd long since lost claim to.

I need you, my love. Be my butterfly.

And despite everything he'd been warned against, despite what he knew was the wrong choice, Ciaran was weakened. *And weak, I've always been weak.* He capitulated to that familiar, lilting tone. Sapped and spent, he dragged himself forward, eyes unfocused. For now, he had one goal: the locker room.

After that, he didn't know.

As he ran, Patrick wondered where the hells the emergency generator was. There should be *something* that didn't strand thousands of people in the middle of a dark football field. The arena must be equipped for sudden outages. But, he reckoned, it was hard to prepare for a malevolent supernatural creature. Maybe there was a backup and she'd shorted that out, too.

Time ticked by without a sign of light, and he became aware of a crescendo-ing buzz, the silence on the field broken by hundreds, thousands of voices that were only now realizing that the band had left the stage, the show was over and they were stuck finding their own way out of a dark building. The buzzing grew into confused, frightened sounds just shy of panic that filtered even into the bowels of the stadium.

Patrick picked up speed. He had to get to the locker room before the audience began streaming in. Fortunately, the hallway was wide, and somehow he *felt* an oncoming obstacle before it blocked his path. He streamed and swerved around equipment cases and trash cans, not seeing them but hearing his footsteps echo off their shapes, and quickly came to trust that he would not run smack into a wall. *Echolocation*, he thought. *Sounds. Different music.* He had no time to unpack and examine this new marvel he'd discovered, though. He let it come and *believed.*

Things were easier once he did that.

The corridor ended and he skidded to a halt, taking deep breaths and trying to work up the courage to open the door. Mal arrived a few moments later and pushed his way in, shouting Ciaran's name. A flashlight darted between their faces, blinding them, then swung to one side to reveal a stony-faced Ciaran sitting on a changing bench with Rich, who held the torch.

Patrick gasped in relief.

"This venue is shit," said Rich in an unsteady voice.

"C?" Mal asked.

"She's calling." Ciaran's eyes were wet in the faint light. His jaw clenched and his hands gripped the edge of the bench.

"That's all he's been saying," Rich explained. "What the hells?"

Patrick groped around until he found the Kryptonite lock purchased earlier, but it hadn't even been removed from the packaging. Muttering swear words in multiple languages, he tore it free—just as high, thin screams began piercing the air and the walls. They seemed to come from the direction of the field. Patrick ran to the double doors, fumbling with the lock and key, prepared to lock them all in. Or himself out. He'd lost track of the plan. Then he froze: Once again, faces filled the locker room entrance.

"You gotta let us in," said Leon, no longer wearing his sunglasses.

It was like being followed by puppies; behind Leon stood the musicians who'd been onstage with them, faces stark with fear. Sweat dripped from Patrick's forehead and he struggled with what to do. Shutting himself in the room with Ciaran invited a replay of last night's beating, but pushing past the others and locking Ciaran in with Mal and Rich—the original plan—no longer seemed like such a great idea, either. A whole group of strangers was a factor he could never have anticipated.

And what was that shrieking?

"Hey." Mal spoke up behind him, opening both doors wide. The musicians crept in, whispering among themselves, dispersing.

Patrick couldn't bother worrying about them now. He fixated on a television monitor in the corner of the locker roomthat,, despite the electricity still being out, had sparked to life. It no longer focused on the vacated stage, but offered a wide angle shot of the field, stage and bleacher seats. Patrick shouldn't have been able to see anything on that screen with the lights out—but it was no longer dark. Someone had taken an enormous ring of light and described an oval that encircled the field, a shape that flickered and grew taller and wider even as they watched. Reflected glow revealed shifting shadows, moving bodies. The audience was trapped inside the oval light like cattle in a pen.

Not light, though. Fire.

The lock fell from Patrick's hands, thudding to the carpet.

Leon bounced behind Patrick. "Field lit up the minute y'all left the stage."

"Jaysus," Mal whispered. "This's her doing."

"Who the hell are all you people?" Rich barked at their guests. "Come on, everybody out the emergency exits. Shoo."

"Got an idea where those are?" Leon folded his arms. "None of us do. And something is telling me *this* room is the safest place to be right now."

Smart man, our Sunglasses, Patrick thought, dazed.

"That's not our concern—" Rich's gaze jumped to the monitor. "What the holy hells?"

Mal snatched Rich's flashlight, turning the beam on the bench behind him. It was empty. Patrick could only hear his own breathing, fast and heavy. He was waiting—and then it came.

Now. Little fear gan ainm. *I believe it is time you and I had a talk.*

Not Caitlin, not this time.

He knew where Ciaran had gone, or rather—he felt it. She pulled him along in the same direction, and he threaded his way through the others, striding past the lockers, the showers, a glassed-in head coach's office. He stopped at the high end of a ramp leading toward two more oversized doors.

More doors. Doors they'd never even expected were there. Doors, he guessed, that led directly onto the field. Patrick swore. How could they not have even thought to check? Why had none of them gone through this room and sussed out every window, every door, any and all manner of egress? Then again, how the hell were they supposed to know how American college football stadiums worked?

As he stood there, the doors opened wide, like gates inviting him in. They clicked into a locked position against respective walls. Through the opening, the bright orange night pulsed like a furnace.

Patrick stared at it, then stepped into the light.

Beg Your Boon

Leon had been right and wrong.

The field was on fire but not ablaze. As Patrick neared the wall of flame they'd seen on the monitor—it now reached about eight feet high—he could tell immediately it wasn't real. There was no scent of burning, and it seemed totally stable—neither searing the grass where it stood nor giving any sign of spreading. Or, for that matter, burning out. Every few moments it contracted a foot—then climbed higher again. A mix of mewling fear and outraged shouts from those captured inside mingled with the rustling of the flames.

Mal caught up behind him and they stared at the white-orange wall, then at each other. Behind them, Sunglasses Leon, Rich, and the others gathered in the doorway. Patrick glanced over his shoulder at them, their faces lit with shocking reds, dusky oranges and sickly yellows.

"Keep back," he called to Rich.

"No problem," their manager replied.

A soft, distant rumble crept across the sky.

Ciaran was inside there—Patrick knew it. So was Sheerie. There was only one choice to make, but Patrick still had no idea what to do once he'd made it. Caitlin wasn't here, and he couldn't rely on her to show up again. But at least Mal was.

"*Tá mé ag imeacht,*" he said. *I'm going.*

"*Ní gan mise,*" retorted Mal, but his voice shook. *Not without me.*

Patrick examined the flames, frowning. So much fire, but like a child's drawing of it. He was inches from the wall yet felt no real heat. His clothes should be smoldering by now. He lifted his hand toward the pulsing colors.

227

"Wait!" Mal shouted, but Patrick's hand flowed into the flame and out with ease. It felt neither hot nor cold—more like an empty, windless place. He waggled his fingers.

"For feck's sake," Mal's voice was still uneven. "Another *mirage*."

"And it's a good one." Patrick admired Sheerie's handiwork; this was better than her sloppy job with the mirror and Ciaran's face. She cared about this illusion and must be expending a great deal of energy to maintain it. He wondered what would happen if they stood back and did nothing—would she tire herself out and make her endgame with Ciaran impossible?

You're delaying, he thought.

"Right," he murmured, fanning his palm on the outside of the flame wall as if looking for a secret passage. Finding no weak spot, he took a breath—and shouldered his way through.

But did not immediately come out the other side. With a gasp, Patrick realized he'd fallen into a vacuum, like spinning in space without a suit, surrounded by a crushing sense of nothingness. This was a place of extremes, of overpowering sound and overwhelming smell and blinding light—like falling into a white noise machine. And it went on forever and ever—

Then he was falling in a different way and stumbled out onto the grass, landing awkwardly on his knees. Mal nearly bumped into him a second later, and they gasped, trying to remember how to breathe. There had been no burning—but passing through had been far from painless.

Ciaran stood stiffly where they'd entered, a soldier at his post. "Come on." His voice was as blank as his face. "She's asking for you."

Mal scrambled to his feet first and tugged on Ciaran's jacket sleeve. "Wait, C—no. You come with us."

Ciaran pulled free, walking into the dark, so they followed. Patrick glanced downfield. Over by the darkened stage he could make out crowd shapes, bunches of people milling around. Their fear transmitted to him like an aching chill in his bones, and he wondered why none of them had wandered to this end of the field.

And there was Sheerie. Ciaran halted next to her, wrapping his arms around his midsection as if trying to hold himself together. Every so often he shivered,but made no move to escape or sit. Patrick guessed where he was mentally right now—in that no-space, the vacuum between the flames. He ached just looking at him.

Sheerie strolled their way, sparks dancing in her eyes. "Welcome, welcome," she purred. "Padraig, you worked *so hard* to get my attention—I thought I should return the favor. Do I have it now?"

"You've nothing but," he said thinly.

"Grand. So—let's dispense with small things. You understand what is happening here now?"

"Yes, and no."

"The one you call Caitlin. She's a good guardian. Taught you quite a lot in a short time."

"I'm sure my education is far from complete."

"But she is a fast worker, that one. If I'd gotten to you first—we'd be having such a different discussion now."

Patrick held his tongue.

"You're thinking you wouldn't have fallen for me the way Ciaran did." She was still moving, encircling him, then Mal, tracing them all with her steps. "You believe you're more clever, more special, so this"—she poked Ciaran in the shoulder and he winced—"couldn't have happened to you. I assure you it could. I felt it from you on the bus. And after that first time, Padraig, leaving is a choice only I get to make."

"Why haven't you done it already?" Patrick asked. "Why all this—show?"

"Nothing wrong with a little drama." She grinned. "You all certainly know about the value of entertainment. Are you not entertained?"

Mal had been taking slow steps toward her, and she shot him a glance. He came to a hard halt, as if he'd hit a wall. "What do you want, then?" he asked flatly.

She grinned. Her teeth seemed whiter, shinier. Pointed. "Nothing with *you*, not now." She took Patrick's hand and pulled him to her. "My business is with this clever, clever man."

The moment she touched him, Patrick felt her trying to come inside. Her tendrils pierced his mind, looking for a place to anchor. It wasn't even something she controlled; she did this with everyone she met. He understood that now. If she found a soft place she would nest and make it her own. The way Mal took to the piano she took to people, playing them until their song ended. Ciaran's tune had been brief and bright, and now she wanted new music.

Patrick put everything out of his mind, the way he could onstage, and turned everything he had toward rebuffing her.

"Except," she went on, brushing her chest against his, "not entirely a man." She kissed him once, bright and hard. It was like pressing against a gemstone, and being with her on the bus rushed back to him with startling violence. She'd been so lush and desirable—yet he'd thought of hurting her, of making her suffer. The way she was doing with Ciaran now.

Pain laced through that memory and he tasted copper and salt in his mouth. She'd bitten directly on the spot where Ciaran had split his lip the night before. Stars exploded in his head and he tried shoving her aside, but it was like trying to move a cement block. "Interesting," she crooned. "Always wanted to see what an *arracht* tastes like."

Patrick's throat tightened and his gut twisted. Blood on the outside meant nothing. What he had to guard against was letting her cut his insides. Still, that word. Herself's word. Sheerie's aim was true. With a single word she reminded

229

him that the world he was falling in love with—the world Caitlin was so eager for him to know—would always think of him as a freak. Meanwhile, in this world he barely seemed to have a place on his best days. A ball of anger in his gut grew until it nearly filled him.

He dropped her hand and ... *shoved*. A hard, pointed thought, aimed right at her.

Sheerie staggered back a few steps, spitting red into the grass. Her lips, stained by his blood, parted in a pink grin. "Excellent. It's true: You learn so quickly. Enjoy it while you're able."

His heart thudded. "How long have you known about me?"

"Not as long as I should have. You're clever, and you've had help. Naughty Caitlin. But you're not as clever as you need to be. Shame. We would have had such fun times together." Sheerie slid her eyes to Mal. "You, however—" She lifted his hand.

He yanked it back. "You can keep far away from me."

"Ah, you'll never see me coming." She winked.

Just like the fear dearg, Patrick thought.

Patrick stepped toward her, and she made a slight bowing motion. "Right, clever *arracht*, let's talk." She crooked a finger, leading him to Ciaran, who had not stirred. "The truth is, until this afternoon I wasn't sure what you'd been told. Not until you looked at me from the stage. And it's been so long since someone surprised me." She sighed. "I'd thought about releasing him as a gift, to you. And then you threw that *music* in my face. That lovely music changed, perverted."

"You weren't ever gonna release him," he said. "And you were going to take all those tunes back once you took the life from him, weren't you."

She grinned. "What if I agreed to leave the music behind but still take him. Is that a fair trade?"

"Of course not."

"Indeed. The music is worth *far* more than his life." She gestured at Ciaran. "Or yours." She turned to Mal. "Or yours." Her forest eyes landed on Patrick last. "Especially yours." She glanced downfield at the milling crowd. "And *theirs*."

She comes in disguise offering love and presents, but there's none of it in her, he thought. *She's smoke and mirrors and tricks, and that's all.* "Why do you hate us?"

"Hate?" She shook her head. "Of course not. I collect. I look for the most valuable thing inside of every living person, and I take it. Most of you humans aren't even using yours. That is what I was created to do, and I see no reason to stop."

Patrick narrowed his eyes. He thought about how she'd come to be, how Caitlin had called her a creation. The poets' dream. "You never got an ending," he said. "They gave you a beginning and a center, but no finale. There's no purpose in what you do—and there's no way for you to learn how to stop doing it.

230

You're an invented cul-de-sac."

Sheerie's face turned thunderous. "My origins are none of your business." She waved her hand. "But all of this is delay. I am taking what is mine, and I will have a special pleasure in knowing you are here to witness it. Especially since there's not a damned thing you can do to prevent it."

Patrick lashed out, snatching her face in his hand. It was like trying to hold on to quicksilver. What should have been flesh and bone slid between his fingers. "You're the *arracht* here. You need to crawl back where you came from. And if you take your noises with you when you go, I couldn't give a good tinker's damn. But you leave him alone. You leave *all* of us alone when you go."

A moment of perfect silence descended and he felt freer, lighter for having spoken. In that moment she stilled, the unnatural green of her eyes bleeding away until there was nothing but darkness within, empty as a pit. He had to tear his gaze away or risk falling in. At her side, Ciaran made a soft, wounded sound.

The thunder rolled closer, stronger.

"No mercy," she hissed, and began to glow, burning with a low white light that hurt to look at. "This ends now. And you can live with the consequences."

Once more, Patrick was a half-step behind. What did he not yet understand? What had he missed? He braced for whatever she planned on throwing them next and prayed for a way to block her.

"Since you already know how all of this works," her voice was low and crackling, "go ahead. Beg your boon of me."

Patrick's breath caught. So formal, like part of a ritual. *Beg your boon* … just as Caitlin had said when he had spoken her name.

Her *name*.

Mal tapped his elbow. "What's she on about?"

"The song." Patrick's mind whirled. He was afraid to lose this moment of understanding. "The words I sang. All of us—sang. It means I can make a claim on her."

Mal shook his head, glancing at Ciaran. "Can't be that easy."

"I know."

"Padraig." Sheerie's voice was deep and stentorian. The sky rumbled. "If you wait much longer there will be nothing left to ask for."

What does that mean? But before he could ask, he followed her gaze downfield. In the time they had been speaking the wall of flame had thickened and grown. The upper edges now arced inward, threatening to join over the stadium. The screaming had intensified and that cold fear Patrick felt earlier was like a weight now, holding him down.

"But it's a lie," he said. "It won't hurt them."

"A lie? Not so long as they believe it to be real." She grinned. "That's the beauty of it. Their belief makes it real. Their faith will be their undoing, as it is

231

for so many of your kind."

Mal dashed toward the center of the field. With a small flip of her hand, Sheerie knocked him to the ground and he skidded hard in the grass. Patrick winced.

"No, my dear," she called to him. "There will be no warnings. Just a choice." She returned to Patrick. "You see, I can offer choices from time to time."

Mal limped back to Patrick, face twisted.

"So what will you ask of me?"

It was a choice but no choice at all. The decision was out of his hands. His heart stuck in his throat. Every one of those people would die of smoke inhalation or burns from a fire that did not exist, and she would let it happen. All those lives meant nothing to her. Ciaran stared at Patrick with stark recognition.

"*Tá brón orm*," Patrick whispered, choked. All of this time, all of this effort and it was too late. "Let them go. Turn off your fire and let those people leave unharmed."

Mal grabbed his shoulder. "Wait—can't you ask—"

Patrick whirled on him. "You'd choose differently?"

Mal clapped a hand on his mouth.

"Done." Sheerie's smile was wide and pleased.

The fire collapsed.

Darkness filled the stadium again, pierced only by Sheerie's glow, which grew and expanded by the moment. A collective gasp downfield gave way to muttering and raised voices, flashlights and shouts. The stage lights rekindled and guitars, left behind, whined until the sound tech shut off the feed. Security guards stepped forward, ushering the crowds toward the exits. And somehow, not one person chose to look at where the real show was.

A sturdy breeze swept across the grassy lawn, and the sky groaned again. The small hairs on Patrick's arms stood on end. He was drained.

Sheerie ran a hand down his cheek. "Don't feel too terrible." She caressed the side of his face with a white-lit hand, eyes still full of darkness. "I've been doing this longer than you have."

He jerked away. "If you touch me again I'll break your neck."

"I should like to see you try someday." She gave him a light kiss on the cheek, so fast he had no time to react. It burned like a brand. She turned to Ciaran. "And now, *mo chroí*, my love. Are you ready for me?"

Ciaran sank to his knees, and she knelt down with him, touching her head to his and stroking his hair. A crackling electricity rose between them, jolting through the grass and tingling up Patrick's legs. Whatever Sheerie *did* to her quarry, she was going to do it now.

This was it, the last moment. Patrick had promised he would not summon Caitlin. He would do this on his own. But he had failed. He had nothing more to offer. Ciaran was going to die if he didn't.

Patrick prepared to sing her name.

The Center Cannot Hold

Time slowed to a crawl as Mal watched Sheerie bend forward, her now blindingly bright light stealing over Ciaran like a fog. Or a fungus. With every moment the sickly glow she gave off advanced and he had less and less substance to him.

Mal had been patient. All this time he was certain something would come to help them, some idea would break through and they would solve this unearthly puzzle. Patrick had tried luring her away, and failed. They'd sung her name, and she'd tricked them. But that couldn't be the end of it. There had to be *something* else. He couldn't stand here and let her take what was left of his oldest friend. He wouldn't allow it.

So Mal did the only thing he could think of: He rushed at the pair of them, slamming into that wall of light she emitted. He bounced off. He tried again. And again. Each time his bones folded together, and he winced with the shock. But with each hit he felt a bit of give, then a bit more. He couldn't break through, though. He pushed hard once again, then shouted over his shoulder: "Jaysus, Patch, if you can do something, for feck's sake *do* it already."

Patrick made a sweeping gesture with his hands, shoving against the air. Mal slammed into the bright light once more—and then he was through, and Jaysus jumpin' Christ it was boiling in here, the heat was ungodly, the skin on him had to be bubbling off—

He opened his eyes and was back inside the flames, in that no-world of white sound and white vision and white taste and it hurt as if he was being consumed by a thousand tiny mouths. His skin was not on fire, but it felt so. He lashed out with a hand and latched on to Ciaran's shoulder. Searing fire crawled into his fingers and he gasped; he was being incinerated by inches. Pulling himself forward he set his arm across Ciaran's bony back, gritting his teeth, eyes narrowed. Tears sprang to his eyes and evaporated in the heat.

When he could bear it, he looked at Ciaran. His friend was still there. No longer fading. Substantial, present. He looked up at Sheerie, all black eyes and white form, and she was straining. He was making her *work*.

Fear left him. The act of reaching out to Ciaran, of refusing to stand there and let Sheerie take him, was enough. Without fear in him he saw her for what she was, this ill-formed, unloved creature, a primitive thing of desire and emotion and hunger. She stole what she wanted, took the good pieces and left the shell behind. She'd seen kindness and music in Ciaran and stole it because she was hungry.

This was one meal Mal would not let her have. He locked eyes with Sheerie and held on.

Stalemate.

But that wasn't true. The pain was getting worse. It was under his skin now. Mal felt lightheaded. He wouldn't let go on purpose. But he might pass out. And then she would have what she wanted. Mal, on his own, was not going to be enough.

Ciaran had been tired for so long he barely remembered feeling any other way. When she gestured for him to kneel and reached for him, it was fitting. Her caress felt like the pale hand of deliverance. She offered the chance to stop being so tired and empty, to lay down the burden of breathing.

Her hand brushed under his chin and light filled the world. Bright, hot, soothing. All he had to do was surrender and it would be done. He hunched forward, stove his hands into his pockets—and waited. But his fingers brushed against something in one of those pockets: a round, solid object, like a stone. In fact, just like a stone. The stone Patrick had given them both, so many years ago. And it was the one thing that kept him from falling over in utter surrender. Holding it, he was partly back in that falling-down cottage making music in candlelight as the rain fell outside.

He held on a little longer.

And then—there was contact. A familiar scent, invading their sterile white space. An odd flutter of hope blossomed. Mal was there at his side, arm sliding across his back and holding him down as if against a great storm—or the beginning of a huddle after their show. Mal wasn't at peace here, though. Something was tormenting him, racking his body. He hadn't been invited. This wasn't a place for him. Would Sheerie take him, too? Or did it mean that Ciaran had to keep breathing just a little longer, for Mal?

He opened his eyes. Sheerie had grown larger, her features sharp and almost unrecognizable. That sheen of perfect black hair was wild and raging. But for a long span, nothing else changed. There was just Mal, the Sheerie-*arracht*, and himself, frozen in the moment.

"G'way," he made his fists into balls. Inside one, he held the stone. "Leave us."

Sheerie said nothing, face fixed in concentration.

And he realized she *had* left him. There was a clear space in Ciaran's head, in his heart, and in his gut—a gap the size of a pebble. The music was gone, her voice was gone, any feeling toward her—gone. He could be himself again. And what Ciaran wanted right in this moment was *not* to be on his knees. He wanted to stand. He wanted to breathe. Bracing himself, he tried to rise. Stumbled. Tried again. Each time he felt weaker.

Then a third presence came into the light, first an arm and then a person, completing the circle. Braced and uplifted, Ciaran met Patrick's eyes, and the man's face was clear, serious, intent. Whatever plagued Mal didn't seem to affect him. Ciaran look in a long, ragged breath and released it; with each gasp his strength grew again. Aware of his friends' arms across his shoulders and his across theirs, he gave them each a quick nod and—then—they were standing. His legs wobbled, but he didn't fall. The others kept him aloft. Ciaran raised his head, squinting at Sheerie. She was so bright and terrible, enormous, full of heat and fury. Her true self, the creature whose name they had sung. Despite all that, she was paler. Weaker. Something was holding her back.

Release him. Her deep, authoritative tone cut through the white noise surrounding them. *Now.*

Go … hell, muttered Mal, cracking his eyes open long enough to spit out the words.

We're not so fond of being told what to do. This was Patrick. *You want him, you come through us.*

My pleasure.

An ear-splitting howl rose up around them. Sheerie engulfed the trio with all of the ferocity she had left, whirling them in a hurricane. Small bits went flying, tearing into their exposed skin like a desert haboob. They leaned into the circle, heads touching, backs to the storm, swallowed in a heat that became flame that became molten fury. Inside their circle they could only close their eyes and hold fast. The storm would pass. Or, so they hoped.

Mal was shouting. In his rich, full baritone he cried over the roar of the wind and flame surrounding them.

An rud is annamh is iontach.

What is rare, is wonderful.

Ciaran picked up the phrase, shouting the Irish in full. Patrick followed. They chanted it over and over, the words rolling like music, like thunder, like truth.

Then everything ended.

The heat was gone.

The white light disappeared.

Still linked, they staggered on the grass, the echo of the storm ringing in their ears, an afterimage of the glow blinding them for a time. They came back in pieces, slowly unfolding from their huddle. Mal ran his hands over his skin, which was unmarked—though his clothes were singed and tattered.

Patrick turned to Sheerie with a glazed, determined stare. She was smaller now, diminished.

"You can't touch us," he told her in a low voice. "You can't get in."

"Give me time," she hissed. There was nothing of the playful, tricksy girl in her now. "You can't watch over him forever."

"Maybe not," said Mal in a strained, hoarse voice. He cleaned his eyes with a free hand and coughed. "But you won't be back. You'll be leaving now, and you won't bother us again."

"Oh, really?" She cocked a hip and set a hand on it.

"Aye. Because I just realized, you owe Ciaran a boon, too."

Sheerie's mouth opened and nothing came out.

"I had a bit of time to think inside your storm," he said, still coughing. "And I did a bit of maths."

A whisper of a smile tugged at Patrick's mouth, but he wouldn't let it grow yet.

Mal kept an arm on Ciaran so he could stand, radiating a fierce righteousness. "See, we all did it. We all sang your name." He gestured at the remaining people on the field. "Out there are around eight thousand requests pending for your attention, Sheerie. Should we ask them all back here, to beg their own boons? To ask the creature who nearly incinerated them for a *favor*? Should keep you pretty busy for decades to come."

Sheerie fixed a dark, furious gaze on him, then Patrick, then Ciaran.

"Good," coughed Mal. "'Cause we only need to ask one more thing." He nudged Ciaran. "G'wan. Do it. Tell her."

Ciaran squared his shoulders, then swallowed. "Feck off," he told Sheerie. "Go home and don't ever come 'round us again."

Sheerie said nothing for a long, empty moment. Lightning cracked above them, a sound like bone snapping, bathing the field in a flash of brightness. Sparks and jagged edges flew in the sky, and the ground itself buzzed with energy. The wind picked up. Another storm had arrived, one she had no hand in.

"That is your wish?" Sheerie shouted over the wind.

"More than anything in the world," Ciaran told her. "I wish to be finished with you."

Sheerie craned forward, lips peeling back in a hissing sneer—and transformed. Became a swirling, charged thing. Electricity rose from the field, surrounding her, a funnel of sparks lifting her from the ground. A long, anguished wail grew in depth and tenor, an impossibly strong music to emerge from such a small creature. The howl crescendoed and expanded until they could hear snaps and cracks ripple through the stadium—the sound of the world's edges coming undone.

Things fall apart; the center cannot hold, thought Patrick. *Shoulda stuck with poems, W. B., and left the* sídhe *alone.*

The skies opened up to release a torrent of rain. And in that moment, every piece of glass in the stadium shattered. As one, shards and water rained down, coating the ground with cold sparkling light. Improbably, Patrick swore he heard the cawing of birds—and then watched as hundreds swooped over the stadium, dark shining ravens like pieces of the night taking flight. They dove and swooped, a ballet amid the rain as Sheerie rose into the air. She lay flat on her back, rising like a magician's assistant in a levitation trick, arms outstretched. She lifted higher, bending backward, her body twisting.

Another crack of lightning fired up the night—and Sheerie split open. Her chest cracked in half and out poured light, small stars escaping from inside, dozens upon dozens taking to the air. The ravens swooped in once more and plucked them from their flight, carrying each small gem of perfect brightness out of the stadium—and in a matter of seconds both lights and birds had been spirited away, leaving just the rain behind.

Not stars, thought Patrick. *Not lights. Souls.*

Sheerie was gone.

A scent of ozone wafted toward them.

Patrick wiped soaked hair from his face. He met Mal's stunned gaze with his own and they shook their heads in wonder and confusion.

"Well," said Mal, at a loss. "She does know how to make an exit."

They remembered Ciaran. He hung from their arms, eyes shut, and he wasn't moving.

"Jaysus, no, shit, no," Mal cried. They lowered him to the grass, shouting through the downpour. He made no move, no sound. Limp, cadaverous—he was gone. Raindrops spattered his cheeks and slid into the grass. One of his hands fell open, and a small white pebble fell out.

Patrick picked it up. Just a pale river stone in the end.

A raven swooped in, fighting against the water and the wind, and circled their heads. Mal blinked into the raindrops, reaching up a hand to swat it away, but Patrick shook his head. The raven settled on Ciaran's chest, beak clamped around a glowing gem.

Patrick didn't need to be told what to do. He held out his hand, the stone nestled in the soft center of his palm. The raven *cawed* once, releasing the gem, which shot directly into Ciaran's chest, vanishing. It pecked the stone from Patrick's hand, spread its mighty wings—and took back off into the night.

Another bolt of lightning forked in the sky—and Ciaran shuddered. His eyes flickered open. He blinked into the rain and shook his head like a dog. His face was pale but his eyes were bright. In a soft, cheeky voice, he rasped, "It's rainin' out, ya eejits."

Mal barked a laugh.

237

"*Fáilte ar ais*," Patrick murmured. *Welcome back.*

"*Is maith a bheith ar ais, a dheartháireacha*," Ciaran returned in a soft, weary voice. *It's good to be back, brothers.*

A noise somewhere between a laugh and a sob escaped from Patrick. *Brothers.* He'd spent his entire life feeling alone, or separate. But he'd always had two brothers. He'd do anything to make sure it stayed like that forever. He stared at Ciaran a long moment, then grabbed his jacket, hugging him as tightly as he dared. A moment later Mal's arms wrapped around them both and they held each other until the rain began slackening.

The storm faded. So much noise and fury, and in the end, just a good show. Nothing to fear—only water. Patrick raised his gaze to the heavens as the clouds parted, revealing the wonders behind them in clear, sparkling patches. He released his brothers and raised an arm, pointing.

"Look," he said, and they turned to the skies as one. "Stars."

Music of His Heart

Howth, Ireland

Padraig stretched out in the tall, yellow-green field and leaned back on his hands. Early summer sun bathed him in clear light, the sea breeze ruffling his hair, billowing his shirt, bowing the grasses around him. He was home.

At least, the home he'd grown up in. He'd been back for just over a month now, but this was his first return to a particular hillside on the peninsula north of Dublin. There were paths criss-crossing the fields and hills surrounding the small town, and he'd often walked through them when needing to clear his head, think up new songs, or—on occasion—bring a woman he fancied out for a day of "nature."

This hill was a spot they were all familiar with—a kilometer or so from the train station and a bit of a climb, it was isolated enough not to attract attention but spacious enough that they could spread out and make all the music they wanted. Over the years, the three of them had noodled around with whatever instruments were portable enough to carry in, particularly back in the days when they couldn't afford studio time and the streets were overrun with buskers.

All things that had happened to another person, a person who had gone away to a foreign land and returned more whole than before. Padraig knew so much had changed about himself, but he was delighted the hillside had remained the same.

He'd told the others where to find him and expected them soon. He could wait. He was learning to be good at waiting.

First, there'd been the waiting for Ciaran to come home. Rich had extended Mal, and Padraig's work visas when they were stuck in New York City for the extra dates, but he hadn't been able to pull that trick twice—so they came home without Ciaran, anxious and guilty about leaving him behind in a Maryland hospital. He'd needed several days of stabilizing before doctors would allow him the long flight back to Dublin, but once they had him hydrated and pumped full of nutrition—he put on a half-stone in three days under their care—he was discharged and at the airport within hours.

It was just enough time for Mal and Padraig to overcome their jet lag and reacclimatize. It would take much longer to shake off the persistent sense that they needed to be somewhere other than where they were at a given moment—a consequence of being on a long, heavily-scheduled tour. Padraig took a long time to adjust to waking up in his own bed, his own flat.

Then there was more waiting once Ciaran was home. He had another stay in a local hospital and, on doctor's orders, reluctantly agreed to a fortnight of bed rest after that. Hiring a nurse to look after him in his own flat had been an option, but Ciaran chose to bunk at his parents' home. And hadn't that been a sight, seeing him propped up in his old boyhood single bed, too big for the mattress yet still fragile, catered to by his Ma with home-cooked teas and dinners. They'd teased him mercilessly—Padraig, Mal, and his other pals who stopped by of an evening, sneaking in bottles of beer to gulp while they watched telly.

When anyone asked about Ciaran's sudden illness, they said he'd contracted a parasite overseas. It wasn't exactly a lie, and no one contradicted them.

Meanwhile Ciaran's rucksack went untouched in the corner of his room where he'd tossed it once he returned home. After his other friends would slip away each night for more exciting locales, leaving Padraig and Mal behind with him, Padraig would think about suggesting they open it—but never brought it up. The time never felt right. And while the three of them did a lot of talking during those evening visits, none of it was about music, or America, or *sídhe*. There was a thin scrim of ice between them all over what had happened at the end of the tour, and Padraig wondered how thick it was to become before someone kicked it in. They might get by without ever talking about what had gone on during the tour, but at some point, somehow—they would have to talk music again.

Gradually, Ciaran began filling out his shirts. He took short walks around the old neighborhood, then down to the local for a real drink. That first evening he polished off a half-pint swiftly enough, but the second half took much longer to disappear. From then on, he never ordered more than a half-pint, as if he'd lost his taste for it. *One and done* became his new custom, which provided another occasion to poke fun at him. He took it all with tolerant, if grim humor. Ciaran the bear had been—if not tamed, then gentled by his experience. He didn't seem to let things bother him the way they once had.

Neither he nor Mal fussed about Padraig's return to his given name. His choice. It took some days to wean from Patrick or Patch back to Padraig, but now it was second nature. The choice hadn't been a big decision for Patrick. Somewhere over the Atlantic on his flight home, the idea settled in him, natural as dew. This was his name. It was the only one he knew. His Da had given it to him. Yes, there was yet another name out there that was his. Perhaps one day, he'd learn its tune. For now, the only song he had to sing was *Padraig*, and he held on to it with both hands.

At last, Ciaran put a boot through the ice growing between them.

They'd been gathered at the local, Ciaran nursing his one small drink and Mal and Padraig somewhere between their second and third, and they were talking about some story in the news—or maybe the football score?—when Ciaran reached into an inner jacket pocket to reveal a curled, spiral-bound notebook with a green front and softened, bent edges. He dropped it on the scratched wooden tabletop and it unfurled slowly.

"It was calling to me," he said. "No—not like before. Christ, that bag stank when I unzipped it, but the notebooks … guess I got to thinking about music and how it might all be gone."

Mal picked it up, fanning the lined white pages. Each was still covered with hand-drawn, hurriedly-made but still perfect staves, notes, phrasings, arrangements—even a few words. "'Course, they'll need adapting." Ciaran looked at Padraig.

"And rearranging." Padraig met Mal's eye. "And true lyrics."

The table fell quiet for a time. Padraig had felt what was coming and braced himself. Were they finally to talk about what they'd gone through? No one spoke, and the ice began to form again.

"The hill," Padraig said at last. "Tomorrow. I'll bring the mandy, you bring the notebook and guitar. Right?"

Not having to revisit what had happened in America, along with the anticipation of making music together again, was an enormous relief. They all relaxed, glanced at each other, and nodded. Yes, this was a place they could visit again. And from there they could go anywhere.

"Anything to get me outta that room," Ciaran said.

"Last I checked, you still had a flat of your own," Mal prodded. "Or did the mice eat it all by now?"

"Ma's a good cook," Ciaran growled.

"So I noticed."

"Did he just call me fat, Padraig?"

Padraig had chuckled. "Maybe just a bit of a pudge."

It was always so easy to be with them. Still was. But the fact that one of them had to nudge the others about making music together proved it was far past time to do so. After the music, there would be time for everything else. Things that needed to be broached and understood before the scars and memories became fixed. Ciaran was still in the dark about many things, though Padraig now wondered if there was a point in him knowing everything that he and Mal did.

What could it help now?

Padraig had done yet another kind of waiting this past month.

He hadn't noticed the change right away. Absence was harder to recognize than presence, sometimes. And in the bustle and confusion of returning home, he hadn't time to focus on his newly-acquired talents and skills. Two days after landing they'd been in Rich's office, paying tiresome but necessary attention to the fact that the band was, all else aside, a business. That meant meetings, signings, and other financial details that bored him senseless. The disbursement of funds from the tour that went into his bank account and the explanation of the new record deal were satisfying on a certain level—but after Mal and he were freed from the boardroom, they raced down the street as if something was chasing them.

Then Ciaran had arrived with all his ongoing drama, and they focused on seeing him well again and visiting nightly. For a time, green fields and music that made colors and even Caitlin shifted to one side.

Though not entirely. Especially with Caitlin. She'd been with him so briefly, yet he yearned for her each day, a missing so strong he had to force himself to get out of bed each morning. There was an ache in him to see her in his city, to know he hadn't just made her up. At long last he'd come to believe in so many impossible things, and now there was no one to share them with. She'd never shown her face to him after that awkward goodbye before the final show.

A week after returning, though, life had settled enough, and the maddening itch to pick up his instruments and wring something lovely from them was overwhelming. So one night, after drinking warm canned beer in Ciaran's old bedroom, he settled at the kitchen table in his small flat, pulled the mandolin from the case and began strumming.

It was out of tune, so he tweaked the strings as he'd done for years. Played again. And because it could be hard to see what wasn't there, it took a good ten minutes of playing to notice the absence rather than the presence. First off, the instrument presented as merely a block of wood and strings; it didn't call to him or hum. Then the tuning—for a brief time he'd known whether an instrument was in tune merely by looking at it, but now the mandy needed serious attention. He only found that out by making it sing. Still, his attention hadn't been truly piqued until he understood: It was just sound. Pretty, twinkly, sometimes melancholy, but sound and nothing more. No colors. No scents. The notes erupted, echoed and faded in the empty kitchen, and not a single color came with them. The only smell was that of his burned toast from afternoon tea. He played harder. Tried the bass. Tried the guitar. Tried recalling the song he helped rewrite for the encore and managed a third from memory—but nothing.

He was still able to play. Play very well, in fact. But he was unable to play like even half a *sidhe*.

After an hour of trying, Padraig's fingers began to ache, and he collapsed on his bed, arms outstretched, still holding the guitar by the neck. He closed his eyes, breathed deeply, and thought of the Green Place. He was able to re-member it in great detail—but it wasn't real. He didn't *go*. He remained stuck, trapped in a flat that was closing in on him. And when he opened his eyes again, staring at a water stain on the ceiling, that home was the loneliest, emptiest place on earth.

He wasn't sure how long he lay there before he started to weep.

Or how long, once he started, before he stopped.

But now, the waiting was done. He would play music as he'd always done, as an ordinary person and not cut from special cloth, and he would be happy with it. That was better than most had. He would embrace it. Even though it would break his heart every day.

And he could start all over again just as soon as the others arrived on the hillside, where he now sat with the gentle breeze, trying not to be pained that it reminded him of the Green Place. When he closed his eyes he could nearly pretend he was there again, but that was as far as it went. He had no way to slip out of this world and into that one, a loss of access that was like a physical tear. He'd never even had a chance to explore the world, to know what went beyond—as Caitlin had put it—the thin wedge of knowledge he'd been shown.

Even more acutely, he despaired of ever seeing Da again. Da, who now seemed to exist in only one world, waiting for his son to visit.

Was it worth it?

Ciaran lived. So, yes.

It had to be.

A light flutter settled on his shoulder, then glanced off. A bell-like voice asked, "Care for some company?"

Not Mal. Not Ciaran. Padraig would have heard their approach. Instead, a tingle coursed through his body, and he was afraid to move, afraid to be wrong. The sun slipped lazily from behind a cloud, filling the field with light.

"Or should we just play?" Caitlin settled next to him, tin whistle with its well-gnawed mouthpiece sticking out of a pocket.

A month. A month and more. The hardest of all losses—even more than the Green Place and his abilities—had been not seeing Caitlin. He'd assumed that she, like everything else, had been lost. Now he stared at her, assuring himself of her reality. He found that spray of freckles across her nose and those astounding blue eyes. He gripped at the earth to ground himself, and in that moment she took out the tin whistle and began crafting a melody.

Padraig held his tongue as Caitlin played solo for some minutes, a piping, sweet tune he didn't recognize. He imagined seeing the notes thread between the stalks of wild grass, then sweep over the cliffside before diving into the ocean—then sighed and let the image go. The colors had always been beyond imagination, and they were not truly there for him anymore.

Eventually, he picked up the mandolin and made it do things. Strummed this chord and that, pairing with her guiding melody before harmonizing, diverging from it, making a pretty thing beautiful. Soon enough he slipped into the song with a cautious wariness, enjoying the rolling comfort and pleasure of making music with someone again—and not just anybody.

He left off playing, dropped the mandolin by his side. Soon she trailed off, too, holding the whistle with that half-smile she'd had on under the stadium in Maryland. Then he was reaching for her and she reached back and they were in one another's embrace. Her grip was so much stronger than he'd ever felt as she buried her face against his neck, breathing deeply of his skin. There was an unfamiliar, quiet, desperate nature to her hold on him. They lay in the grass together and he set a hand on her face, trying to take her in all at once.

"You've discovered that things are different now," she said quietly.

He nodded.

"I assume you know why."

Interference. Caitlin had mentioned it more than once. *Sídhe* might not have many rules, but getting in one another's way was taboo. He'd rooted for the wrong team—his own friends. Never mind why he'd done it, only that it had been done. As Sheerie had warned him that last night, he'd have to live with consequences. Still, what infuriated him most was that there had been no judge or jury, no chance for him to defend himself. Just an open window—slammed shut.

"How can you tell?" he asked.

"It's in your playing. I hear what you're missing every time you touch the strings."

He tugged at some grass, playing with a loose green shoot. "I miss it something fierce."

"I'm sorry. I didn't know how it would all go."

"Wouldn't have done anything different." He twirled the grass at the sun. "It's just—harder once you've been there to know you can't get back. Better never to have gone."

"Truly?"

Rolling over on his stomach, he squinted at her. "Sometimes." He paused. "Wait. How all *what* would go?"

Sheerie had called Caitlin a guardian; that was the word that fit best in the languages they shared. Caitlin had sought him out, as had Sheerie and the others. Some found other interests—but Caitlin stayed true and helped him as much as she could. He'd been under her protective wing.

"I complicated things," she said. "I wasn't supposed to help you."

"You did your best not to. I didn't—call your name. I didn't want you to have problems. But … thank you for what you did."

She waved the words away. "We both interfered. We both had consequences."

"I spent my life not knowing about that place," he said. "Now I can't imagine how I lived without. Is exile—permanent?"

"Can be."

He heard a small tweak of hope in those words and didn't dare to entertain it. "Not always?"

"One-hundred solstices," she said. "They gave you a hundred solstices."

At two a year, the maths was easy. "Fifty years, then." His heart sank. "Fifty years of exile."

She nodded. "I warned you. We're not superheroes. And our notions of *good* might not align with yours."

Padraig stared into the grass.

"But we do like to bargain. To … make exchanges." Caitlin turned to him, eyes cool and clear, hair splayed in the grass. "I argued for you. The Seelie Court said the time could be halved if I accepted it. So: fifty solstices for you, fifty for me."

Twenty-five years, each. The bird in his chest, the one he always felt with her, began fluttering madly again. "Why would you *do* that?"

She touched his cheek, and the tingle suffused him again. "Couldn't say. I'll come up with a reason you'll understand eventually."

His voice was stuck somewhere in his throat, but he managed, "So that means you're—"

"Plain as paper." For the first time he heard a twinge of fear in those words. She was the stranger in a strange land now.

"Never," he argued.

"Well. Then … not extraordinary."

Padraig jumped up and paced the field, trying to take it all in. It didn't seem possible that someone would do something like this for him. Then again, Caitlin had never been just *someone*. He returned, dropping to his knees and kissing her lightly, then harder. He wanted her to feel that she didn't have to fear being alone, that he was here for her the way she'd been for him. When he pulled back, some of the worry had faded from her face, and he ran his thumb over those light brown speckles.

"Still extraordinary," he whispered. "No one's ever done something like that for me."

"Well," she said. "Give your Da some credit."

His eyes burned as he clasped her hands in his and held them tight against his thudding chest. "*Is ceol mo chroí thú*," he said, and meant it: She was the music of his heart. "If I didn't say that before, I will now. Every day."

The freckles faded beneath a soft pink in her cheeks. "That will be a song worth hearing."

She'd given him a gift; he understood that. Still, the echo of twenty-five years—almost as long as he'd been on the earth—was a loud drumbeat, almost louder than his heart. He'd be middle-aged by then. Going gray. Getting soft. It was like hearing the cake only had a little poison.

"It's still a lot of time." He sighed. "When you want it to be tomorrow. I'll be a different person by then. An old man."

A strange glow lit her entire face. "Oh, Padraig. You still don't understand. Even in exile—you are who you are. I am who I am. That doesn't change. And we are *very* long-lived. No one can say how long you've got, or even how long I've got. But you will *never* be an old man."

The world fell away. He stared at her, unable to comprehend.

She held up the flat of her hand, where a puff of dandelion danced. "To us, twenty-five years"—she blew the mote away—"is a drop in the ocean. A note in the song. We're not going *anywhere*."

"Gimme that." Ciaran's voice swept up the steep hill from the walking path, interrupting Padraig's attempt to digest everything Caitlin had just told him. "I ain't a pup, I can tote me own guitar."

A soft twanging sound, then a thud of wood and Ciaran's head crested the rise. Padraig and Caitlin stood, catching a glimpse of Mal a few feet behind Ciaran, shouldering a large rucksack.

Ciaran was almost back to his old self, his gently canted eyes as lively as ever, dark hair long past needing a cut. Mal was bright and golden as a penny, his head coated in a soft fuzz of incoming hair. Soon enough it would blow in the breeze once more. And for a moment Padraig saw them not as the adults they were now but the boys who had dazzled him that first day in the leaky cottage, who continued to shine in his mind. What Caitlin had just told him—he couldn't absorb it now, it was too enormous to consider. He would do it later. After other business had been attended to.

Mal gave Padraig a quick wave before recognizing Caitlin and, dropping his pack, running her way. He had her scooped up in his arms and gone around once before anyone could say a word. She landed with a stumble, breathless. "You never said *she'd* be here," he cried at Padraig. "That's *brilliant*."

"Was a surprise to me as well."

Ciaran kept a shy distance from their guest, tugging on his ear. He turned his mouth this way and that. "I'm told I owe you a debt."

"Perhaps I owe you an apology." Caitlin stepped forward. "And if we let those facts cancel each other out, nobody has to say things they don't want to."

Ciaran brayed a wide, echoing laugh, something Padraig hadn't heard him do since coming home. "Jaysus, girl, I might like you after all." He swung the guitar from his back and braced it over a shoulder like an axe. "Mal, mind fishing that book out of the pack?"

Mal settled in the grasses with his bodhran first, then revealed the notebook. Caitlin started, holding out her hand. "Show me."

She paged through with alarming speed, then gave it back. Tears were in her eyes, but she looked happy—if a bit homesick. "Oh, my," she said. "I thought they'd be gone. It will be my pleasure to hear you wake those tunes up."

"Well, I've done a bit of tweaking," said Mal. "We're not getting stinkers drunk just so we can try 'em out here. But they're there. Notebooks of them. Four, last I checked."

"Four," nodded Ciaran.

"More than enough," said Padraig.

"Any chance you'd join in with us?" Mal asked Caitlin. "For as long as you feel like staying this time, that is?"

"That might be longer than you think." She eyed Padraig. "But—yes. As long as you want me here, I'll stay."

"I want it." Padraig took her hand. "Stay."

Ciaran settled with the guitar in his lap. "So, men—and Cait. Should we get something started here already?"

They were there for a thousand reasons. But in the end, it was the music that was most important and necessary. It was their own currency, their definition, their meaning. The four of them formed a circle in the long, waving grasses, instruments in hand and waiting for some kind of cue. Just then, the sea breeze kicked up and Padraig stared out at the blue of the ocean, up at the blue of the sky, and into the deep blue of Caitlin's eyes.

Their knees were touching. She winked at him.

"*A haon, dó, trí,*" counted off Ciaran, then nodded at Caitlin. "*Ceathair.*"

Caitlin laughed. *Padraig*, she thought at him, and it came in clear. *Play with me. Always*, thought Padraig.

Glossary

Máthair (Mother)

Athair (Father)

Arracht (monster)

Go raibh maith agat. (Thank you.)

Sídhe (One of several spellings and words for fairy/supernatural folk. In Scots Gaelic, it's *sith*.)

Bunscoil (primary school)

Leanbh (baby)

A haon, dó, trí (a one, two, three)

Táim togha (I'm fine)

Múinteoir (teacher)

Ná bac leis. Imeoidh sé. (Ignore him. He'll go away.)

Geall dom nach bhfuil tú ag insint bréag? (Swear to me you're not lying?)

Geallaim duit nach bhfuil mé ag insint bréag. (I swear to you I'm not lying.)

Páiste (child)

Taraigí anseo (Come here) (plural)

An rud is annamh is iontach. (What's rare, is wonderful.)

Anamchara (soulmate)

Mise (My name is)

Scoil (school)

Seanchaí (storyteller)

Lofa (rotten)

fear gan ainm (nameless man)

Bíodh an diabhal agat (go to hell)

Cacamas (crap)

Tá mo bhuachaill marbh. (My boy is dead.)

Amadán (stupid, idiot)

an buachaill beag (a little boy)

Tá brón orm, a chara. Ní féidir liom aon rud a ghealladh duit. (I'm sorry, my friend. But I can't promise anything.)

Stad de sin anois. (Stop this now.)

Adharc (slang for "penis")

Breathnaigh orm. (Look at me.) (singular)

Tar liom. (Come with me.) (singular)

Tá mé ag imeacht. (I'm going.)

Ní gan mise. (Not without me.)

Fáilte ar ais. (Welcome back.)

Is maith a bheith ar ais, a dhearbháireacha. (It's good to be back, brothers.)

Coda and Acknowledgements

Never say never.

It's a cliché, but there's always some grain of truth buried in a cliché. *The Only Song Worth Singing* started out life as *Joyride*, with a first draft from around ... *checks notes* ... 1995.

Time doesn't just fly, it takes a jet plane.

I was living in Boston in 1995, figuring out what shape my life was going to take: I had a college degree and no full-time job. I temped. A lot of the initial draft-writing of this book (and as we all know, the first draft is you telling yourself the story) came during downtimes at those temp jobs. Then I'd go home, scarf down a quick dinner, and dive back into the story again. It wasn't the same thing as getting paid to write fiction—but it was darned close.

What has paid my bills over the ensuing decades is my work as an entertainment journalist. When this book was originally being written, I was deep into several years as a music journalist and completely enthralled in a creative world I did not know how to participate in. I can play a bit, but writing a song? Performing it in front of the world? That's real-life magic.

Over the years, I spoke to a whole lot of musicians for articles, including many off-the-record, fascinating, late-night/early-morning chats (which can be a story for another book). I was astounded to be included—I never thought I was cool enough. But I can see more clearly now: These small outfits of musicians were often away from their home country for the first time, plopped into the giant expanse of America. They drove themselves, or were driven if they were on a better-financed record label, from town to town to play gigs in front of strangers. They always commented on how big the US was. How it was both like and unlike the movies they'd grown up watching. This was a world before smartphones and, largely, the internet. Some of these young men (and it was mostly men) didn't even have *landline* phones back home.

So the road can be a lonely place. You might have band members with you who were friends, but living out of each other's pockets for weeks, having no one with you that you could trust or understand beyond them—that's hard. It's harder for a bunch of wet-behind-the-ears twentysomethings. They were up for something real, something to connect to, something that wasn't just feeding the machine.

I understand that experience much better now.

And in case I need to underscore: We're not talking about the Rolling Stones. Or Led Zeppelin. This was not the rock lifestyle movies and TV show, making every musician an asshole. It's not about booze, broads, and bombast—as Ciaran thinks in this book—it's about making a dream happen, one sticky-floored, 900-person venue at a time. It's brave and daring and stupid and hopeful.

I was a little in love with all of them.

Quick question.

What's the name of the band in *The Only Song Worth Singing*?

Exactly.

The story is about names, about calling people by their right names and the power that lends. It's about finding yourself in the musical collection of sounds that we call our own names. The only song worth singing is the True Name that rings in your heart.

I didn't start out making Ciaran, Mal, and Padraig's band nameless, a *fear gan ainm* of musicians. But as the drafts went on I saw less and less need for it. Naming their band would be to stick a pin in them, to affix them to a particular place or meaning or interpretation. Of course their band has a name. But no need to sing it right now. Maybe in the future.

I'm just wondering if anyone noticed. In all the readings I've had from editors to friends to critique groups, only one person has asked me what it is. Cat Rambo, the exquisite author and editor assigned by Caezik/Arc Manor to give my book one more read before we headed to press—she wins the prize.

What is the name you heard in your heart that they should be called?

All of which brings me to the place where I need to thank a bunch of folks. I'm going to miss a few—thirty years of credits would be … a *lot*, and many of them are lost to the mists of time. So along with all the musicians I ever met or spoke to, let me add a few more recent names.

Big thanks to Arc Manor for taking a chance on this story—Shahid Mahumd, my publisher, and Lezli Robyn as the first (modern) reader. You two are the opening notes in finally taking this story where it needs to go.

The Only Song was the story that won the hearts of incredible authors and friends of mine Ellen Kushner and Delia Sherman. It's also the book that landed me my amazing agent Bridget Smith at JABberwocky, who knows a few things herself about the power of music.

One of my earliest readers deserves a shout-out: Rebecca Hoffman, whom I've been friends with since ninth grade, gets a bit of a Tuckerization in the story as the redhead who helps the band in their final gig at the Art Attack, a real event at the University of Maryland lo these many years. I don't imagine that the concert I've set up here bears a lot of resemblance to the real-life Ritchie Coliseum, where the event is held (certainly the college football team, the mighty Terrapins, doesn't play there), but details, details. Fiction is not reality, and often not even a good simulacrum.

Big thanks to Fantastic Books' Ian Randal Strock, who initially said he'd publish *The Only Song* some years ago but felt that the book could "do better"—encouragement that made me go out and look beyond my own borders to get this book into print. Ian's good people, and if you're not buying Arc Manor books, look for his publications.

Thank you to the translators I've pestered and paid for over the years in an attempt to get my Irish right, most recently Ray O'Donovan and my Fiverr hire Ciardhubh. Any errors are mine.

Many thanks to Sam Cowan, who published my *other* Sheerie story, "Rough Beast Slouching," in *Dim Shores Presents* (Vol. 2/Spring 2020), Chris Ryan, who reprinted the tale in his premiere *Soul Scream Antholozine*, Vol. 1 (2023), and Ellen Datlow, who long-listed the novella in her best of horror list of 2022.

Books never happen in a vacuum, so thank you to all the convention organizers who've given me platforms to share parts of this story over the years, all of the friends and friend-fans who urged me to keep working on this book (Vikki Ciaffone, L.J. Cohen, Sally Weiner Grotta, Rona Gofstein, and everyone in Broad Universe). If you read this book at some point over the last three decades, *thank you*. And thanks to my occasional lawyer Nicholas Ranallo, who gave me excellent advice about contracts until that became part of Bridget's job.

Lots of love to my found family and to Mom. She's my greatest cheerleader—even if she doesn't always know what the book is about.

Going further back, a shout out to W. B. Yeats. I'm not a folklore scholar, but I first discovered his *Irish Fairy and Folk Tales* while I was still in college, and it fired my imagination in a way I hadn't felt before. I was studying folk stories from around the world as part of a class taught by Elie Wiesel and wrote my final paper about Irish folk stories after basically inhaling Yeats' book. While Yeats' efforts are considered problematic in some realms these days, without him this story wouldn't exist, and possibly neither would the *leannán sí*. No wonder I had such a hard time tracking down previous references while researching at the National Folklore Collection at University College Dublin back in the 1990s.

And one more time, an encore: A full-hearted thank you to all the musicians I've come across over the years, whether by interviewing you, being transformed in a concert, or just listening to your dreams, your songs, your names. I'm honored that the incredible Mike Scott (of The Waterboys) and Paddy McAloon (of Prefab Sprout) gave me permission to use their lyrics (of course, the owners of the publishing rights also had to get involved), and thanks to their reps Danny Goldberg (Scott) and Keith Armstrong (McAloon) for helping facilitate.

Music moves me. Has meaning. Has structured the outline of some of my life choices. I've never seriously tried to write a tune, because that is a magic I'm happy to see made for me, not by me. The music makers—the dreamers of dreams, as they say—always hold a special place in my heart and my soul. Thank you for teaching me the real meaning of the only song worth singing.

Be sure to let me know what you think! Find me at RandeeDawn.com, and I hope you'll sign up on my mailing list.